THE SARGO INCIDENT

CLASSIFIED: TRUE FICTION

THE CONTROVERSIAL NEW ACCOUNT FROM:
THE ANONYMOUS AUTHOR KANENAS

THE SARGO INCIDENT

Copyright © 2022 by The Anonymous Author Kanenas.

All rights reserved. Printed by Amazon Publishing LLP, Ingram Spark and other global partners. No part of this book may be used or reproduced in any manner whatsoever without written permission except in the case of brief quotations embodied in critical articles or reviews.

Every word from here out is a work of True Fiction. Names, characters, businesses, organizations, places, events and incidents either are the product of the author's imagination or are used fictitiously based on the premise of a true story. Any use of actual persons, living or dead, events, or locales is entirely on that basis and from the memory and imagination of the author. Only some of this is real…….

For information contact:
Anonymous Publishing House
L23 - 111 Eagle Street
Sydney (Australia)
NSW
2000

info@anonymouspublishinghouse.com
www.anonymouspublishinghouse.com

Book and Cover design by Anonymous Publishing House
ISBN: 9780645720839

Black Edition: January 26th - 2023
10 9 8 7 6 5 4 3 2 1

Anonymous Publishing House

About the Author.

In the middle of 2022, our Junior Editor was revising manuscripts from Authors when she came across something special. After some deeper reading it appeared we had a True story, exposing some secrets the US Navy has spent the last 40 years desperately trying to hide. Not only was it a true story but it was all based on mountains of well-kept diaries and documents from an informant with firsthand knowledge of the specific details of, The Sargo Incident.

The Author had overwhelming proof and a great story to back it up, but the US Government doesn't forget and Classified is Classified even after 40 years.

Having been a writer his whole life and having been lucky enough to report on the News at some great institutions, such as the Washington Post & NY Times. The Author understood the importance of protecting his sources, from his primary source through to the sailors he interviewed and met in the years and decades after the death of so many.

Previously published and now teaching at an East Coast University, the Anonymous Author Kanenas is a brave and courageous writer with a unique style and language learned from his many years working with the words as his weapon. The stories he brings to the Anonymous Publishing House are the ones he was never allowed to tell.

During his 11 years at the Washington Post and 9 at the Times there were countless stories his sources would unearth that would not be allowed to run in the partisan organisational structures. However, manilla folders have travelled with him and The Sargo Incident, is just the first of his True fiction series as through APH we will share them all with the world.

APH

THE SARGO INCIDENT

"A Navy is essentially and necessarily aristocratic." – **John Paul Jones**

"I don't stop when I'm tired, I stop when I'm done." – **David Goggins**

"It doesn't take a hero to order men into battle. It takes a hero to be one of those men who goes into battle." – **General Norman Schwarzkopf**

"I can imagine no more rewarding a career. And any man who may be asked in this century what he did to make his life worthwhile, I think can respond with a good deal of pride and satisfaction: 'I served in the United States Navy." – **John F. Kennedy**

"Those who dare to fail miserably can achieve greatly." – **John F. Kennedy**

"They shall grow not old, as we that are left grow old.

Age shall not weary them, nor the years condemn.

At the going down of the sun and in the morning,

We will remember them." – **Laurence Binyan**

AAK

THE SARGO INCIDENT

Introduction

The Atom is the fundamental building block of every chemical element. The Atom is made up of the Electrons which have a negative charge and the Nucleus, or Core, of the Atom. Inside the Nucleus there are two principal types of particles: Protons which have a positive charge equivalent to that of the Electrons and Neutrons.

All Atoms of a particular chemical element have the same number of Protons, but the number of Neutrons present can vary.

All Atoms of Uranium, for example, have 92 protons, but they can have anywhere from 140 to 147 Neutrons. Atoms of the same chemical element whose nuclei contain different numbers of Neutrons, are known as Isotopes. Isotopes are denoted by the total number of Protons and Neutrons. U-235 is thus a Uranium Atom with 92 protons and 143 neutrons, while U-238 is a Uranium Atom with 92 Protons and 146 Neutrons.

These Isotopes of Uranium are split into Atoms of lighter elements when bombarded by Neutrons. Accompanying this splitting of the nucleus, which is called Fission, is the release of a tremendous amount of energy and the emission of two or more new Neutrons. In order for a Fission reaction to be self-sustaining, it is necessary for at least one of the new Neutrons emitted when the nucleus splits, to strike another nucleus.

The Nuclear Reactor is based on this principle of chain reaction. This rate of Fission is carefully controlled. In order to sustain a chain reaction in a reactor, a critical mass of fissile material must be present. The exact mass is dependent upon a number of factors, including the particular Fissile Isotope present, its concentration and the geometrical arrangement of the material.

Because a sphere has the highest volume-to-surface ratio of any solid shape and the least number of escaping Neutrons per unit of material, it is the shape for which the critical mass is smallest. For a sphere of U-235 the critical mass is approximately 50 kg, for U-233 about 12 kg. If the material is surrounded by a substance capable of reflecting some of the Neutrons which would otherwise escape, or if it is compressed to increase its density, a lower critical mass can be obtained.

The rate of Fission in a Nuclear Reactor is carefully controlled at a constant speed over a long period of time. In contrast, a Fission Bomb is designed to release a large amount of energy in a very short time.

The simplest Fission weapons generally involve use of either a gun or an implosion device. For a gun device, two pieces of fissile material, usually U-235, each at subcritical mass, are suddenly forced together in a gun-like assembly by the detonation of a conventional explosive. The resulting supercritical mass produces an explosion. This was the kind of Fission Bomb dropped in Hiroshima, Japan.

The implosion device relies upon an increase in the fissile material's density, rather than its size, in order to achieve a supercritical condition. It involves a fissile material below critical mass formed in the shape of a sphere and surrounded by a conventional explosive. When detonated, the conventional explosive creates an ongoing shockwave or implosion which compresses the sphere into a supercritical mass by increasing its density by a factor of two or more. This was the principle used with Plutonium PU-239 in the first U.S. nuclear test and the bomb dropped in Nagasaki, Japan.

A nuclear power reactor is a heat-generating device fuelled by fissionable material. It differs from a non-nuclear power plant in that it uses a nuclear "Core" to produce steam, which drives a condensing steam turbine, which is connected to a generator, which produces electricity; rather than a boiler to burn fossil fuel to produce steam.

Glossary of Terms:

CORE: The central portion of the reactor which contains the nuclear fuel. It is in this region that the Fission reactions occur.

FUEL: Material containing fissile nuclei. The fuel of a power reactor may consist of natural Uranium (containing 0.7 per cent fissile U-235 and 99.3 per cent non fissile U-238), enriched Uranium in which the percentage of the isotope U-235 has been artificially increased, U-233 produced by conversion of Th-232 and PU-239 produced by conversion of U-238, or a combination of all these materials.

MODERATOR: Usually ordinary water that slows neutrons, thereby increasing their chance of being absorbed by a fissile nucleus.

COOLANT: Water which is circulated through the reactor core for the dual purpose of removing the nuclear-generated heat and transferring it for use outside the core. Water serves as both the coolant and the moderator.

CONTROL ELEMENTS: These regulate the rate of fission. These are usually rods containing neutron-absorbing material which can prevent the neutrons from causing further Fission.

REFLECTOR: The material that surrounds the reactor core and directs back into the core some of the neutrons which might otherwise escape.

REACTOR VESSEL: Contains the Nuclear Core and isolates radioactive parts of the reactor system.

THE SARGO INCIDENT

Chapter 1

Person of Interest

The black Saab EMS Turbo tires hissed taking a curve on this foggy drizzly Monday morning on the wet pavement of the Duval - Woodinville Highway Northeast of Seattle, Washington. The NPR station announced the temperature in Seattle at 38 degrees Fahrenheit on this December morning and worst in the East Coast and the Mid-West. Michael shivered involuntarily, smiling when the announcer ended up with Honolulu, Hawaii 85 degrees and clear.

Michael was in his late twenties. Born in Hydra, Greece. Influenced by European education. Five eight, one hundred eighty pounds. Dark hair. Muscular built. His hair was very thick, cut short, parted to the left. His skin was olive and tanned easily. He played golf and had a single digit handicap. He enjoyed sailing. He was attractive. Very masculine looking. Bedroom eyes. He got looks from women, but he was oblivious to the fact that he caused that kind of attraction. He would not make the first move in relations with the opposite sex. Inadvertently, he ended up encouraging other women with his mannerisms.

He was smart, well read and quick on his feet when it came to arguing. In College he played varsity soccer and he was in the University Boxing Team. This had led him to the USA Golden Gloves in the Welterweight Division. He was meticulous. Organized. A person who planed ahead, allowing, however, for change in plans when taking into account all contingencies. He did not shoot from the hip.

In business relationships he was sure of himself, very aggressive and he took a dominant role. Socially, he was a wall flower. He masked his shyness behind a wall of aloofness verging on snobbery. He elicited a reaction, however. People either loved him and would go through fire for him or they hated him with a passion. Regardless of the lovers or haters however, everyone admired him, was afraid of him and would kill to be on his team. Because, invariably would always, without fail he would end up on top and make money.

Michael felt lucky living only less than a 5-mile commute from the office; both located in Woodinville, 14 miles from Seattle, on the

Northeast shore of lake Washington. He was approaching his thirtieth birthday this coming April and his career progress so far has been nothing short of meteoric.

A few short years after graduating from Washington State University in Chemical Engineering and already at the top of his profession, Project Manager, for two years now. He still remembers the day two years ago, still a Project Engineer at the time, when the President of the company, another Cougar Alum and his tennis playing partner, called him in his office with a proposition and a challenge.

"We need a Project Manager for the Power Plant at the Trident Submarine Base at Bangor, Washington." A short ferry ride on Puget Sound across from Seattle; "The job is yours. If you accept it, your salary will be quadrupled immediately and you will have your own office on the second floor of the building. If you succeed; i.e., end up with a profitable and working project, you will be given stock in the company, you will become a partner and you will be part of the Board of Directors. If you fail, either in the profit or the function of the plant, you will be fired. If you don't accept the challenge, you will stay where you are."

"I am in!" Michael replied without the slightest hesitation.

"GO COUGS! I knew you would undertake the challenge." The President replied with a big smile on his face. "Now for the important stuff. You know this afternoon we have the doubles final at the Washington Athletic Club. I depend on your net play. Are you ready?"

"Packed bag and two rackets in my car." Was Michael's reply.

Michael smiled reminiscing. During the summer of 1967, while attending Washington State University, he worked at the Washington Athletic Club in the kitchen and room service. The chef told him that he envisioned him coming back, a few years down the road, as a Club member for lunch and leaving a five-dollar tip. For two years now he left the house every day hauling his gym bag and two tennis rackets on his way to work. His net play was partly the deciding factor in getting the job initially. The question of his ability to play tennis competitively was asked during the interview process.

Being a red shirt tennis player during his 1966 Summer School attendance at the U Dub, the name for short of the University of Washington in Seattle, squad was a plus. He remembered when his daughter was in kindergarten and was asked together with the rest of the students in class during the first day of school what their father was doing for a living; when her turn came, she replied: "He plays tennis and goes out to lunch".

That challenge now seemed a lifetime ago. The Power Plant at the Trident Submarine Base ended up being the most profitable Project in the history of the fifty-year-old company and it worked like a Swiss clock after a bumpy start-up which necessitated the introduction of some innovative instrumentation changes at the Power Plant Combustion Control Panel. The project became the stepping stone for Michael to solidify his new position. Become a partner and start a separate Division specializing in Government work to which he became its Charter Director. A new Company within the Company doing a little over seventeen million dollars' worth of work a year, mostly for the Department of Defence.

Michael pulled into the company parking lot and eased into the space with his name initials and title stencilled on the curb. There were less than a dozen cars parked already in a parking lot with sixty parking spaces. He looked at his watch. An Omega Speed

Master Professional, the first watch worn on the moon as the inscription said at the back. It was only 7:28 AM; still early he thought for the 8:00 AM office work start. He grabbed his briefcase and made his way into the building using his key; up the stairs to the second floor, where the executive offices were located, down the corridor to his corner office, with a detour on the way to the Board of Directors Conference Room for a cup of tea; Twinning Earl Grey. He never got over the beauty of the Conference Room, from the intricate pattern on the hardwood floor, the leather club chairs, recessed ceiling lighting, granite stone fireplace and the African Rosewood panelling on all the walls. He turned on the corridor lighting and headed for his office.

He used this quiet time every morning, before the others arrived and the phone started ringing, to drink his tea and read the Daily Journal of Commerce already delivered today and siting open on his desk, which meant that his secretary, Grace McDonald was already there.

At 8:00 o'clock sharp Grace, his fifty something secretary, appeared at the door of Michael's office with an armful of documents.

Grace is 5 feet four inches tall, around 140 pounds. She was a Scottish - Mexican mix, gray hair, blue eyes, very good olive skin, well-groomed and conservatively dressed. She was the poster child of the ideal secretary. Organized with a highly developed insight on her Boss; anticipating his every need. She may be having, in her fantasy, a love affair with him. She believes she would have, if he was older, or better yet if she was twenty years younger.

"Good morning. How was your weekend?" She greets Michael who lifts his head shoving the newspaper on the side to make room for the pile of documents deposited in front of him by his secretary.

"How was yours?" He answered with a question; force of habit ingrained in his subconscious over time.

"Boring." Grace replied. "The weather you know. Angus and I, were going to play golf, but I bailed out. He went. You know he is a Scotts man; he is used to the rain. I went shopping instead. You?"

"Between gigs. Bird hunting season is over. Too sloppy to go skiing. Too rainy to start cutting wood for next winter. Too early in the year to start watching the horseback riding shows my daughter participates. Way too early to start working on my sail boat. I just spent the weekend reading and smoking cigars."

"It's what you like best anyway. I know you. The rest is just an excuse, so you can bail out and do what you like best, reading novels and smoking cigars."

"What do you like to do?" Michael looked her in the eyes. "And don't tell me golf. I know better. You only have taken it up to please your husband."

"I am a sun and beach bum at heart." She replied wistfully. "I never forgot my roots. Puerto Penasco, born and raised."

"Where is Puerto Penasco?" Michael asked.

"It's a sleepy little fishing town at the end of the Sea of Cortes in Mexico. The climate is tropical like Hawaii. It's like Honolulu was, a hundred years ago."

"I didn't know you were from Mexico." Michael looked at her differently for the first time; "What are you doing in Seattle? The people here don't tan, they just rust."

"Life." Grace whispered. "You will find out. You are still a kid. People plan and God is laughing... Speaking of sun," she said changing the subject, "you better read the Daily Construction Report from the Pearl Harbor project. Something is rotten in Hawaii". With this Delphic Oracle she left Michael's office.

It's been a week since the project started. Granted its performance duration and Date of Completion was two and a half years down the road; but still, in the meantime, some progress had to be made. The report still claimed 'Mobilization'. Bill Scott was the superintendent.

He was in his fifties, born in a small town in Idaho. Very dark skin with Native American characteristics. Not very smart, Michael had heard. However, he made up for it in loyalty and dependability. He lived the life of a vagabond that took him all over the world. He went where the work took him. He drank big, he partied big, he lived for today. This changed somewhat, the word was out, ever since he got married to a younger woman a year ago. Bill Scott does exactly what Michael tells him to do and as result he sleeps easy. No responsibility and no accountability.

Michael did not know him very well, personally. He never worked an entire project with him directly. He selected him because he liked Bill's paperwork ethic. He put everything in writing. That's what the Hawaii Project required. It was subcontracted out one hundred percent to local subcontractors, necessitating a good clerk type superintendent, rather than one in the conventional sense. The Construction Schedule Michael prepared, which was accepted by every subcontractor, dictated the progress and tied everyone to a time of performance, of a little over two years. 'Mobilization' meant moving the office trailer in place, getting phone service, dropping off the dumpster and the portable chemical toilets. This should have been done in a couple of days, a week at the most and the job should have been 'shovel ready' by now.

Maybe he should re-do the Construction Schedule with actual dates rather than the generic week one, week two...he was forced to produce for submittal to the Navy, when he did not have the Notice to Proceed date yet. They still did not receive the official NTP letter from the Navy. So, the Final Schedule with the actual dates was on hold for the moment. Speaking of submittals, they should already had been sent to the Navy. What was the status of the returned submittals? Were they approved? With that last thought in mind, he reached for the intercom to call the Chief Engineer, Dan McCoy.

Dan was in his early forties. Five eight. 190 pounds. Irish born and raised in Belfast, Ireland. Michael's good friend and integral part of the Project Team. Dan tended to view things black or white. He paid attention to the details and got things done. He was the nuts and the bolts man of the operation. He had an Irish temper and like Michael he believed in the superiority of the European Education.

Dan was a bit abrasive at dealing with others, particularly if he thought the individual was at a lower social or educational level from himself. His behaviour was influenced to a great extent by the Class structure he had been brought up with. He demanded obedience by his subordinates and offered respect in exchange to his perceived betters.

"Danny boy. Mike here. Could you come to my office for a sec and bring the submittal log for the Pearl Harbor Project?"

"Michael me boy." Dan McCoy replied with an exaggerated Irish brogue. "Long time, no see since your promotion. You don't visit anymore, us grunts sweating our life away in the dungeon; doing all the work to make you look good up there in your Ivory Tower."

Michael, under other circumstances, liked nothing better than engage Dan McCoy in a duel of witticisms. Now, however, was not the time. He had a single-track mind. Like a bulldog, once he got his teeth onto something he did not let go. He did not get easily side tracked. Right now, he wanted to get to the bottom of a potential job progress obstruction and getting an update from Dan would ordinarily appear preliminary information, but in this case, vital and prerequisite to moving forward. He had to make eye witness sure that contractually, they were squeaky clean. The submittals were due to the Navy within thirty days after the Contract award date.

"Dan I would like nothing better than coming down and engaging in a duel of wits with you, however, it is not sporting to duel with an unarmed man." Michael replied succinctly. "Plus, I am short of time at this very moment. I am trying to drain a swamp and I am up to my ass in alligators. Accordingly, get your butt up here pronto." And with that he set the phone down gently on its receiver.

Dan Mc Coy was the Chief Engineer. Ten years older than Michael. Born and raised in Belfast, Ireland and a rare protestant, which put him in the minority there. A graduate from Trinity, brought in Seattle by Boeing during the mid-sixties when they had run out of engineering talent in the United States. By the late sixties combined with the loss of the Super Sonic Transport program via federal legislation prohibiting civilian flights of same; Boeing started massive layoffs which by the start of the seventies reached one hundred sixty thousand. Seattle, being basically a one employer town, led the Nation with an unemployment rate of almost thirty percent. Dan, an early casualty of the layoffs, found a home at National Energy Production Corporation which was building power plants all over the country.

He started out as a Mechanical Engineer and worked his way up by attrition and keeping his nose to the grind stone to be the Chief Engineer of the Company. Michael was hired as a Project Engineer working under Dan for two years and then one day Dan finds himself working for Michael. They were friends, but the unfairness of it, in Dan's eyes still stung. He was priming Michael to become the Assistant Chief Engineer only to see Michael abandoning Engineering altogether for Management; and succeeding. Money talks and bull shit walks as they say and Dan was smart enough to see that Michael was going places due to his ability to make money. He no longer felt jealous and instead attached himself to the coat tails of Michael's success by making sure he was involved in every project of the Government Division.

"What do you want to know?" Dan exclaimed walking into Michael's office, not knocking out of courtesy and carrying a thick folder.

Michael looked up from what he was reading towards the chubby Irishman with the pale blue yes. "Have we finished the submittal process? Have we gotten a response from the Navy?"

In order to exercise control over the quality of the Project, Michael insisted upon placing his own orders on all the major equipment for the Project and subcontracting the rest. This way the fixed costs were initially identified and locked in; while the labour which was the main variable and potential exposure for the Project was left to local subcontractors on fixed price subcontracts. That way the Project was guaranteed to work at the end and the costs were already known and secured before the onsite activities even started. The costs of the onsite, such as supervision, a Superintendent and a Quality Control representative, were also a known quantity; tied into the Project Time of Performance in the field, which they were going to beat, provided they followed the Schedule.

"Here we go." Dan said taking the chair on the right, in front of Michael's desk and unfurling an accordion style document that was titled Submittal Log. Michael noted that it included the list of all the equipment with the date it was mailed to the Navy. The oldest was thirty days ago and the most recent a little over a week.

"Doesn't the Contract stipulate a two week turn around?" Michael asked rhetorically demonstrating his knowledge of the Contract, not expecting an answer to his question. "However, I don't see in your chart the response from the Navy and the date that it came."

"That's because there have been no responses to date," Dan acknowledged. "I am not surprised though," he continued. "The specifications were vague. You ordered top of the line equipment which precluded any possibility of rejection by the Navy; though I don't blame you for it. If you had enough in your estimate that's what I would have done in your place in order to guarantee that the final product will work and for a long time afterwards, without warranty hassles. Let's face it, the Drawings are cartoons. I could not build the project from them. Whoever drew them must have been an Architect. They are merely renditions of what the final product was going to look like at the end, not how to go about putting the whole thing together. They just copied catalogue cuts and slapped the equipment together on the Drawings."

"What about shop Drawings? Are they not a Contract requirement?" Michael countered.

"They would be if you had a Drawing upon which to base them on. Unfortunately, in this case you don't. How did you order the equipment by the way? Don't take this the wrong way. I am not questioning you. I did some checking myself and you are dead on. I mean how did you select them? How did you size them? Are you clairvoyant?" Dan added with mischief on his face.

"I did some calculations." Michael responded, reaching out and pulling a thick three ring binder from the book case behind him and setting it in front of Dan.

"Boy!" Dan whistled leafing through the folder; "You Engineered the whole Project. We were not supposed to do that. This was supposed to be a pre-engineered job. You have turned it into a Design Build project."

"I know it. When the time comes, I will let the Navy know. I believe Dan that you should put a team of Draftsmen together and start on a new set of As Build Drawings for the Project. I believe if you put three men on the project you will be done in thirty days. Time is of the essence."

"Who is going to pay for that?" Dan asked with a mocking laugh.

"I don't know at the moment." Michael replied cautiously. "I have not as yet met the powers to be on the Navy side. I believe, however, that whoever they are they will see the logic and pay. At any rate we are talking peanuts here; under $25,000.00. The time element on the other hand, if we do not proceed, will certainly kill us. I will tell you something else and it stays right here: at this point we are making over $800,000.00 profit on the project. That's over ten percent. I believe doing the Engineering and coming up with the As Build Drawings that could be used in the field is the right thing to do."

Michael looked at his watch, basically calling an end to the meeting. Dan started putting the chart back in his folder, getting the message. It was a little after ten and with the three-hour time difference, it was seven in Hawaii. The start of a new work day.

Michael punched the quick dial for the number of the field office in Hawaii already programmed in his telephone.

"National Energy, may I help you?"

The voice was female deep, breathy, throaty reminiscent of the voice announcing the fifties television drama 'It's Burke's Law'. Michael wondered for a moment whether he dialled the wrong number, then he remembered he used auto dial.

"May I speak to Bill Scott." Michael uttered hesitantly.

"Sure." The voice replied, with a distinct Boston reply and accent. "Who shall I say is calling?

"Michael Matrozos."

"What's up Boss?" Bill came on the line instantly. Michael wanted to reply 'Don't get personal now' which under the circumstances wouldn't be far off the mark, considering his present state. He put away his prurient thoughts for the moment and asked instead.

"Who was that on the line?"

"Oh, that was Roxanne, the new secretary."

"Who hired her? Since when can we afford a secretary on the job site?" Michael responded aggressively putting all other thoughts aside.

"Now, now don't get your shorts in a knot, Boss. Hear me out. The job is spread out over ten acres. I have to be in the field to answer questions and solve field problems, unless of course you want me to sit in the office all day long. If I am in the field, who is going to answer the phone? Who is going to check on the equipment and material deliveries? I cannot be in two places at the same time. I thought we would need a secretary, which incidentally will double as an Assistant Contract Quality Control, CQC, representative. It is a Contract requirement; I am the Superintendent. I am not allowed to be both. However, as you know, in the Contract, the CQC requirement, it's a joke. That's where Roxanne comes in. She is smart. She has an associate degree from a Community College back East someplace. She is local. The Navy accepted her as Assistant CQC. I know that you appointed Steve Crane as CQC. But the CQC has to review all the submittals from the subcontractors. Collect and submit all the Davis-Bacon forms from the subcontractors every week and submit them to the Navy. It's a two-man job to keep the records the way you want them. I took the liberty to hire Roxanne because that way we are coming way ahead in the field supervision budget you specified."

Michael remained silent. What Bill was saying made sense. He may have resented that he had not thought of it himself to begin with; but he was smart enough not to be going around tilting at wind mills on a lose-lose scenario. All of a sudden, he remembered when he had first met Bill Scott and where. It was on the U.S. Plywood job in Bonner, Montana. He visited the job on a fact-finding mission regarding a specialty 'stop non return valve' that was presumably never delivered, according to the job superintendent. That was two years ago. The field office there had a wall phone already pre-installed. He opened the door and saw a four foot something man standing on a wooden crate talking on the phone.

The missing valve was inside the crate he was standing to reach the phone. It turned out that it was delivered the first day on the job, same time as the office trailer and the superintendent had been using it ever since as a booster step to dial the phone.

"I hope it does not turn out to be another case of the missing stop non return valve." Michael finally spoke, laughing.

"You still remember, eh?" Bill replied joining in the laughter. "On a more serious thought Boss, when are you coming over? The Navy wants to meet you. We are done with all the mobilization stuff and we are ready to start. The Navy is anxious to have a pre-construction meeting and issue the Notice to Proceed."

"I was under the impression that this was behind us. We had a meeting in San Francisco at the Naval Facilities Engineering Command (NAVFAC) in San Bruno.

"We signed the Contract. We gave them the Payment and Performance Bond. A Construction Schedule showing the time of performance, which was less than the one required by Contract. They accepted it. What's left to discuss? You already started working on site. No one has stopped you, that I know of."

"The two concrete duct banks underneath where the Demineralizing Tanks and Chemical System are supposed to be located, according to the Bid Drawings is stopping us. As for the pre-construction meeting, the local folks were not there. They want their own meeting. Government... Boss, need I say more."

"I will be there tomorrow." Michael said impulsively. "Set the meeting with the Navy for Wednesday and while I am there, I will investigate the Differing Site Conditions you mentioned. I will leave Friday from Honolulu to be back in Seattle for the weekend."

"Have you lost your mind Boss? You don't want to spend the weekend in Hawaii? Man, this is as close to Paradise as I have been."

"Not without my family." Michael replied succinctly.

"Why don't you bring them along." Bill replied with enthusiasm. "If you don't, you would only wish you had, once you get here. Believe me it is an experience you don't want to deny them."

"Bill, let me tell you something. Because the job is in Hawaii, it changes nothing as far as I am concerned. Hawaii; Bonner, Montana; Berlin, New Hampshire ....they are all the same as far as I am concerned. A job is a job. Regardless of the location."

Michael recalled another meeting with Bill when he was a superintendent of the absorbent paper mill for James River Corporation in Berlin New Hampshire. Bill's thought of the local women as 'sleeping pills' and holding hostage the whole New England by the asshole for the summer during a prolonged start-up resulting in a toilet paper shortage, buzzed through his head.

"I will think about it and see you tomorrow." Were the last words before Michael set the phone down without waiting for Bill's reply.

He dialled the intercom asking Grace to buy an airplane ticket for him to Honolulu, Hawaii for tomorrow, Tuesday, with return flight to Seattle on Friday; hotel reservations for the nights of Tuesday, Wednesday and Thursday together with a rental car from the Honolulu Airport for these same days.

He then buzzed Dan McCoy and asked him if he was ready for lunch. He felt he needed to spend some time alone out of the office with Dan to smooth any ruffled feathers.

An hour later Michael was back in his office. Grace made her way to meet him and hand him his itinerary. He was flying Braniff Airline out of Seattle at 10:00 AM. His ticket would be waiting for him at the ticket counter. He was staying at the Hilton Hawaiian Village in Waikiki. The rental was from Avis. His return flight from Honolulu was at 2:00 PM Friday. With the three-hour time difference between the West coast and Honolulu, this meant that he would be arriving back to Seattle sometime after 10:00 PM. He called Grace back telling her to extend his stay to include the weekend and reschedule the departure for Sunday night.

He then called the travel agency the Company was using and added tickets for his wife and two children. He used his accumulated millage to pay for the tickets and upgrade all to First Class. He had been traveling on the average over 250,000 miles per year.

He spent the rest of the afternoon getting ready for his trip including copies of the Contract, Specifications and Drawings, such as they were, which triggered another thought. This time he went downstairs to Dan McCoy's cubicle.

"Thanks for lunch." Dan said as soon as he spotted Michael at the entrance to his cubicle.

"Don't mention it." Michael replied expansively. "I just stopped by for a couple of copies of the Construction Schedule and a copy of the Submittal Log."

"When are you going to take me along with you to Hawaii?" Dan asked wishfully as he summoned a draftsman with instructions to fulfill Michael's request.

"Do you remember the Power Plant Project at Mare Island Naval Shipyard, in San Francisco, California? I took you there with your wife for a week..."

"How could I forget. MaryAnn still talks about it. But that was then. This is now."

"It's a long project Dan. One of these days. Who knows? Should it be required, you will be the first one I will ask." Michael replied diplomatically. "As a matter of fact, you may start laying the foundation for the trip already." Michael remembered the idea he had in his office before coming downstairs. "You told me that the Drawings and the Specifications are screwed up, right?" Dan nodded in consent.

"Well, why don't you start another Log calling it Errors and Inconsistencies in the Contract Documents. This will go hand in hand with the new set of 'Shop', rather As Build Drawings we talked about earlier. If there is going to be a battle to convince the Navy that the Contract Documents issued at the time of the bid were deficient, so they will authorize payment for the 'Shop' Drawings, I sure as hell would like you sitting on my side of the table".

There was a change in Dan's demeanour. He immediately took up the task. If there were any reservations before undertaking the effort to draw the Project as Build Drawings, they were instantly gone away.

Michael went upstairs as soon as he got copies of the Construction Schedule and Submittal Log leaving Dan in a newly formed huddle with three draftsmen the topic of which he could only guess.

He opened his Diary before packing it in his briefcase and as was his habit, took out his Mont Blank fountain pen and made some notes to himself, summarizing the aim and desired results to come out of his trip to the Power Plant and Demineralized Water Facility Project at Pearl Harbor Naval Shipyard.

He loved his Mont Blanc, which was part of his business uniform, in his shirt pocket next to two full flavour cigars. Punch Signature Series was his current favourite. The pen was a gift from his father when he was nine years old and graduated from writing in pencil to writing in ink. The school desk was equipped with an inkwell and the teacher handed a pen to the select students who in her opinion mastered the art of writing in pencil and were now ready to do so in ink. The school issued pen was nothing more than a stick with a place at one end to fit a nib. An extra nib was issued in case the one mounted broke; which was a common occurrence since the pen was often used for target practice.

The school issued inkwell for the other side of the desk was spill proof and virtually indestructible. Some of the well to do students were given fountain pens by their parents which they proudly wore in their shirt pocket. It was considered a status symbol in Grade School. The choices then were Pelican, Parker or at the top of the heap Mont Blanc, which boasted Life Time Warranty. Michael's father gave him a Mont Blanc as a present in 1957. The Mont Blanc fountain pen was king. The ball point pen was a couple of years away from getting invented. Now, over twenty years later, Michael still carried the Mont Blanc everywhere and used that same fountain pen, his father had given him when he was nine years old, still functioning in perfect order. It was his affectation and trade mark. The resilience of a Mont Blanc.

Chapter 2

Unhinged

Michael decided to leave work early. He throws a harried goodbye to the receptionist, Laura L. Lambert, otherwise known as triple L. Just out of High School. Local girl from a blue-collar family. This was her first real job. Long hair. Brown eyes. Good figure. She wanted a boyfriend, but the only people interested were the guys in the fabrication shop. Blue Collar workers. She wouldn't mind someone like a younger version of Michael with an equivalent job. Come to think about it, for that matter, Michael himself.

Michael is excited to break the news to his wife and his two children. Todd, ten years old and Elli, seven that they were all coming to Hawaii with him. The only problem would be, once they got there, trying to get them to leave. They had to fly back on Sunday night to make sure he was back to the office on Monday. He was, among other job descriptions, the acknowledged captain of the SWATT team for the company. He was sent on site of what-ever job exhibited signs of heading 'South'. He was able, so far, to turn the project around in record time and return back home. Usually, he was gone on Monday and back home by Friday.

If it was necessary to stay longer, over the weekend, he had always taken his family along. He believed that taking the kids out of school was worth the experience they gained by visiting various parts of the United States. They were both straight 'A' students; proof that his unorthodox way of adding to their education was working. He logged over quarter of a million miles a year flying and this status with the airlines together with the accumulated millage availed him to fly First Class when he took his family along. His wife loved this lifestyle. She went skiing with her girlfriends right after she took the kids to the school bus stop and let the housekeeping slide. Every Friday she made the effort to clean the house and put everything in its place, before daddy came home.

Michael in turn, would enjoy the weekend at home and play rather than be strapped down adjudicating the day in, day out trivia, meting justice, in other words playing the role of the Lord of Discipline, which he hated. This arrangement worked out for all concerned. Why change it? He was on record saying to the Superintendents that the venue did not matter. Going to Hawaii in February was the same as going to New England. Right. Trading 10 degrees below zero Fahrenheit or 42 degrees charcoal sky and constant drizzle in Seattle with 85-degree sunny weather, azure skies and welcoming beaches was no big thing. He had to admit, however, that in spite of what he was saying to the Superintendents, he was excited and was looking forward to the trip.

Before he realized it, the left turn came up from the paved Woodinville - Duval Road to the gravel entrance of Raquanna. A Fifty or so custom build home development; each home on a five-acre lot. The development was a total of three hundred eighty-five wooded acres and trails. Michael originally bought the five-acre parcel five years ago as a place for his son to ride his motorcycle. Todd's godfather and Michael's college roommate, had bought as an appropriate present for a five-year old's birthday, a 50 cc Honda off road motorcycle. Michael's wife of course had a fit; but Michael saved the day by buying a five-acre lot in a heavily wooded private development for his son to ride his motorcycle without fear of other cars around.

Theirs was the first built house in the development a year later contracted by them. A four thousand square foot two story colonial that resembled more a bed and breakfast building than a private home. The long meandering gravel driveway was guarded at the entrance on either side by two brick clad reinforced concrete four-foot columns with twin lions on top. A heavy chain stretched across, that was rated to stop a pickup truck going fifty-five miles per hour. The four hundred foot long 'S' shaped circular driveway, over the pond, ended at a clearing in front of the two-car garage. Cedar, Hemlock and Alder trees lined the driveway and the whole property was heavily wooded. All left to nature, except for the house, the two-horse barn and the arena. Christina and Elli opting for the real thing shortly after Todd acquired his motorized horse. Two quarter horses. Christina's Philly Bar Dia and Elli's gelding Macho Poco Bar, grazing in the pasture next to the garage, whiny a greeting, as Michael parked and got out of the car.

"Home early today." His wife, Christina, pecks Michael on the cheek as soon as he enters the family room by way of the garage; "What's the occasion?"

Christina was in her early thirties, 10 months older than Michael. Born in Seattle, Washington. She met Michael on a blind date at Washington State University. They were married shortly after graduation. Five one, 110 pounds, light hair, green eyes, slender but shapely built. Her hair is long. Her skin is light but tans well, making her whole complexion, including hair, the colour of ripe wheat.

She loves horses and she rides year around. In the winter she also skies. She does not care for the actual sailing who her husband lives for. However, she enjoys the Nautical Life. Tying next to strangers in different ports and socializing with them.

Christina is very social and outgoing. She likes her role as a wife and mother. She does not want to compete with her husband in the business world. She controls their economics and social life. She is deeply religious. Religion controls many aspects of hers and that of her family's life. This causes a little friction with her husband who is more of a person who believes that attending church every Christmas and Easter, only, is the way to go.

Christina gives the impression of a very proper, well behaved, aristocratic lady. She exercises self-control, in public. She is well groomed and she smells of Poison. Her favourite perfume.

"Need to pack for a week's worth. Have to go out of town tomorrow." Michael says.

"Where?"

"The job site at Pearl Harbor."

"Hawaii!" The exclamation is joined by the two kids who were overhearing the adult's discussion.

"That's right." Michael acknowledges, which follows crestfallen looks by the rest of the family. "However, since I will be gone over the weekend, I made arrangements so you can all come with me; provided your mother could work out the logistics. It's basically up to her".

"Mom! Please! Please! Can we go?" The kids chorus reverberates as they were jumping up and down.

Todd the oldest, a boy, was born with a silver spoon in his mouth. He believes he is entitled to everything he wants, by birthright. Everything has come easy for him. His good looks; he looks like an Armani model in the making. Good looks, combined with intelligence.

Elli, the daughter, is daddy's girl. Dark, long, curly hair, brown eyes, voluptuous body for which she will have to diet when she gets older. She feels fortunate and thankful for what she's got. Sometimes she feels guilty at the lack of toys and family misfortune of others.

"You know me." Christina interrupted. "My middle name is 'GO'. I will work it out. In the mean time you kids go upstairs and pick clothes from your closet for summer, because that's what it would be like in Hawaii."

Christina and Michael graduated in 1969 and 1970 respectively from Washington State University where they met in 1966 and got married in 1969. Christina claimed she went to college to get her MRS degree along with her Bachelors of Arts in English and Foreign Languages, Spanish and Russian. She did not like to work. She saw her role as mother and wife and she was content She liked to travel and she viewed her husband's frequent flier status as one of her personal fringe benefits to supplement her career as homemaker.

She quickly made a couple of calls which took care of the logistics. The neighbour behind would take care of the horses for the privilege of riding them. She would drop the two dogs with the neighbour across the street. All she had to do was drop a twenty-pound bag of dog food along with them. They will be well cared for; since the neighbours across the street had a whole kennel with dog runs already in place. The cat will stay out of the house and sleep in the barn to fend for itself as it was already doing. Between the mice in the barn and the birds throughout the property Zorro, the cat, was set. As for water, the creek in the property was year around and fed the pond with fresh water, many times to overflowing.

They pack immediately and have a virtually sleepless night with the kids knocking on their door every hour on the hour asking whether: "Is it morning yet?" Reminiscent of Christmas Eve, only this time inquiring not about missing their presents but whether they may miss their flight to Hawaii.

They load Christina's Bronco at 8:00 o'clock in the morning, as it had more room for all the luggage than the SAAB, the company car, and set off for the airport, at the tail end of the rush hour traffic. Christina is driving on this cold drizzly, rainy, typical Seattle, Winter's Day. Michael is snoozing in the passenger seat. Secretly glad to get away for a break from this miserable weather, but he is careful not to show how relieved he is to get away. The kids are restless in the back seat. The windshield wipers, are sweeping the windshield intermittently. Christina turned on the car's fog lights. There is a slight fog. Low to the ground fog.

"It should not affect take off." Michael reassures her.

The morning commuter traffic on I-405 is heavy. After a slight back up for the floating bridge that connected the East side, Bellevue and Kirkland, to Seattle, they found themselves in the Sea - Tac Airport exit loop. They proceeded to the Sea-Tac Airport long term circular parking structure and parked the Bronco a little before 9:00 AM. They loaded their suitcases onto an airport cart and headed for the Braniff ticket counter. Their first-class tickets were waiting there. They checked the suitcases and received their boarding passes. The flight was leaving from Gate S12 in the South Satellite Terminal. Michael kept his briefcase, as carry on, with all the project paperwork to review during the four-and-a-half-hour flight. The flight is scheduled to take off at 11:00 o'clock. Plenty of time for breakfast.

They go through security and take the automatic subway that connects all Terminals. They get off it, two stops later at the South Terminal Gates. They head towards the Braniff gate terminal to locate their gate first. They then stop at the nearest restaurant. After breakfast they go back to the gate waiting area which is full of Seattle tourists anxious to leave the drizzle, for Hawaii. The gate Board reads 'SEATTLE - HONOLULU 11:00 AM ON TIME'.

First Class is called to board first. They take the airport telescopic causeway towards the airplane gate. The airplane is a Boeing 747. Michael is leading the way and subconsciously notices the airplane gate resting on the bottom of the causeway frame. The notion to say something to the stewardess welcoming them leaves his mind as he is busy herding his family towards First Class. Their seats are wide made of brown leather. The stewardess tells them that the 747 airplane is equipped with a loft accessible from First Class by the circular stairway in front of them behind the cockpit.

"As soon as the airplane reaches altitude and the seat belt sign goes off, you are free to move around and explore." This remark is addressed mainly for the children. "In the meantime, would you like something to drink?"

They place their order and immediately their drinks appear. First Class is more than half empty. Behind the curtain they notice the hordes of people in economy class jostling to find their seats. 'The airplane is going to be a full flight', it is announced through the loud speaker. After half the passengers boarded, the boarding was suspended. Then the Captain ordered all the passengers that have already boarded to deplane. The two stewardesses in First Class told the passengers to deplane also but to leave their belongings on board if they wished.

"What's the matter?" Michael asked.

"I don't know. It usually is some mechanical malfunction…"

"I bet it's the door!" Michael exclaimed. "As soon as the passengers started boarding, the airplane suspension settled and seared the door off its hinges."

This was confirmed as soon as they passed the door which was laying on its side with its hinges seared off.

After a forty-five-minute wait Braniff Airline announces through the loud speaker that they had bad news and good news. The bad news was that there was no other airplane available. The good news was that since the airplane was a Boeing 747, the company was contacted and they were on their way with a replacement door. The Boeing parts factory in Kent being only a few minutes away from the Airport.

The economy class passengers were given a sandwich, a bag of potato chips and a can of soda, while they waited. The first-class passengers were given a voucher, good at any restaurant in the airport.

Christina went to the counter to collect their four meal vouchers leaving Michael to watch the kids, deep in thought. Was the trip necessary? Could he had managed to handle the matter by telephone or a letter? Would he be on the plane if the destination was Missoula, Montana instead of Honolulu, Hawaii? Is Roxanne subconsciously influencing his decision to go to the job site? Is the little head doing the thinking of the big head? Is Bill Scott's call for help motivated by past adventures and good times?

Michael remembers one of those. A boiler feed water pump seized at the James River Paper Mill in Berlin, New Hampshire. Bill Scott was the job superintendent at the time. He shipped the damaged pump to the Ingersoll-Rand factory in Norwich, Connecticut. The Company had sent Michael at the factory to witness the opening of the pump, safeguarding the Company's interests. The pump ended up being repaired at the manufacturer's expense. Michael drove from Norwich, Connecticut to Berlin, New Hampshire to supervise the installation of the rebuilt pump.

He arrived at the Gorham Inn at five in the afternoon, exhausted, having driven all day in heavy traffic in the middle of the New England Winter. He didn't have a chance to open his suitcase and the phone rang. Bill Scott was on the line. He was downstairs in the lobby. He wanted to take Michael to the bar's happy hour and get to know each other. Michael was tired. He could not sleep yet, but he did not want to go out either. Bill would not take 'No' for an answer.

"Maybe what you need Boss is a sleeping pill. I am coming right up to drop you one."

A few minutes later, a knock on the door. Michael opens the door to find Bill with two young women in tow. Michael found out that Bill called all women sleeping pills; Michael smiled reminiscing.

It actually turned out to be a fun evening, trying to find their way back to Gorham from the Lobster Trap in Conway, New Hampshire; lost in the fog crossing the White Mountains. They ended up back at the Hotel. The girls were more than willing. Michael was a good sport, up to a point. Refusing to cross that fine line that would bring him past the point of no return. Michael had more fun playing with fire. Testing, teasing and exercising his self-control. Roxanne will be no different, he thought.

Michael walks to the Airline counter after his wife returns with their meal vouchers. He is a frequent milage flyer. He is going to Honolulu on business. He will be missing a day due to the Airline mishap. He demands that day back, at Braniff Airline's expense. He gets it together with a Braniff Airline credit card.

"What was all that about?" His wife inquires when he gets back.

"Nothing." He mumbles keeping the extra day at the Airline's expense a secret for the time being. "Let's go have some lunch. I am in favour of Ivar's Clam Chowder."

They leisurely return to their Gate 12 as they hear the loudspeaker announcing that boarding has started for Flight 82 Seattle to Honolulu on Gate S12. The door repair must have been completed early. They arrive at the Gate in the midst of boarding. Mad scramble by the Airline to accommodate them. The kids are all excited with the fuss and commotion. First Class is the only way to travel. Michael solves the halfway point problem solution and passes it on to the kids who they submit it to the stewardess for the competition. They both win. The stewardess comes to their seat with champagne and flowers. Finds out that the winners are children. Gives the champagne and flowers to Christina and returns with two boogie boards, a red for Elli and a green for Todd. The kids are having the time of their life. Michael and Christina, seasoned travellers, enjoy the trip and the First-Class accommodations through the eyes of their children.

They arrive in Honolulu late at night. As soon as they step foot on the ground, they get assaulted by the heat and humidity, together with Plumeria, Coconut and Pineapple smells. They are given leis by the Airline. Michael rents a convertible and puts the top down. The night is balmy. Honolulu City lights sparkle up ahead. Waikiki is crowded, although it's past midnight. They check in at the Hilton Hawaiian Village. Valet parking. They have a corner two room suite on the top floor, right below the penthouse, overlooking Diamond Head and the beach. The water below is lit up and inviting. They put their bathing suits on and go out for a midnight dip. They are a little hungry when they come back. Michael orders a late-night snack from room service. They finally go to bed in the wee hours. Michael and Christina have the sleep of the just.

Chapter 3

The CIA Area Rules

Michael gets up early, before anyone else. He gets ready without noise, leaves a note and goes downstairs in the lobby. He has the rental car brought around front. On a gorgeous morning like that, he puts the top down. He lights an

Arturo Fuente, Hemingway signature series cigar and rolls over from the Hotel's circular drive into Kalakaua Boulevard. He follows Ala Moana Boulevard into Nimitz Highway.

Nearing the overpass into H-1, he hits heavy traffic. Stop and go, gawking the building of the viaduct. Michael finds himself involuntarily joining the looky looks. Not much to see. One guy working and five others watching him. He wonders if this was the real reason their own project was not moving forward. His first glimpse of construction work, Hawaiian style.

Finally, onto H-1 freeway. Pearl Harbor / Hickam AFB exit up ahead. At Pearl Harbor Nimitz gate, he stops at the pass office. Window No. 4 for a week-long vehicle and driver's Permit Pass. Michael tapes the car pass on the front driver's side lower corner. The Marine guard waves him into the Base. He turns right after the Gate on his way to see the Resident Officer in Charge of Construction. Up ahead, one hundred yards or so, the traffic is stopped, both ways. He pulls up behind the stopped car in his lane. All the car drivers are out of their cars standing at attention. Michael follows suit not knowing any better as to what was happening. Soon music started playing followed by the National Anthem. When it ended. Silence. The people remained standing next to their cars. Then the taps and everyone got into their cars to resume their trip.

"We are lucky." A voice next to Michael whispered. "There are no foreign ships at Pearl Harbor at the moment."

"What if there were?" Michael asked curiously.

"In that case we would be standing at attention until all the National Anthems played out. I've been standing at attention for close to half an hour once."

Michael shook his head and got back in his car. He continues driving and arrives at his destination, the ROICC Office. He meets Commander Dave Walsh, the ROICC. Six foot, 200 pounds, All American in football, Fraternity Boy looks; although now a little heavy set with age. The ROICC does as he is told and does not make waves. He may disagree sometimes with the orders he has received, but he rationalizes them and depending on his final belief of right and wrong, he applies the commensurate degree of effort behind a given order.

He instantly likes Michael. He has heard a lot about him before he even met him and the resentment of others, because Michael got the better of them, is nothing more than added admiration on his part for a cleverly executed move on Michael's part which left the Navy flatfooted. He vowed never to place himself on Michael's wrong side and everything would turn out peachy. He will find, many times, torn between an order he has received from above and doing the right thing. He tends to delegate all work. After all the Navy employees more people than needed. He sees his tour of duty in Hawaii as reward for having to put up with the 'shit hole' of places he had been assigned by the Navy throughout his career.

Commander Walsh takes Michael across the street and introduces him to Captain Henry "Hank" Reinhardt, the OICC, Officer in Charge of Construction. They exchange pleasantries.

The captain is over six feet tall. A non-rescript individual. Brown hair, balding, slight frame. He wants to make Admiral before he retires, in a couple of years. He wants to be able to retire in Hawaii. He sees Michael, by reputation, as an obstacle to his plans. He would not hesitate to lie, cheat and even kill to achieve his objective, as long as the order originated from someone else, or if he, himself, had issued the order, there was someone else carrying it out. Someone else to blame if things went wrong. He is ruthless, but deep down a coward.

Captain Reinhardt explains the importance of the Project for the Navy. The Power Plant and the Demineralizing Water Facility. The Pearl Harbor Naval Shipyard wants to expand and service more nuclear submarines. The new Demineralizing Water Facility, will produce all the distilled quality water required to clean the submarine reactor's cooling systems and the nuclear submarine's bilges.

Michael brings up the problem concerning the communication lines encased in concrete discovered, occupying the same real estate as the Demineralizing Water Equipment Apparatus, as shown on the Contract Drawings. Both Navy officers profess ignorance. Michael explains that it is his understanding the interference was brought up to the attention of the government by the CQC and the job superintendent on the Project via the Daily Report hand delivered to the Navy Inspector a few days ago.

Michael tells them that he had decided to visit the job site himself to verify the Differing Site Conditions as a result of the government's inaction towards resolving the matter. Captain Reinhardt becomes defensive. He had not reviewed the CQC Report and he was ignorant of the issues surrounding the alleged interference. It is apparent that neither had Michael, because so far, has brought forth second hand facts given to him by others.

Michael is taken aback at this sudden hostility by the OICC. Commander Walsh steps in to calm the tense atmosphere by launching on how happy the Navy was that National Energy Production Corporation, NEPCO, has viewed the situation serious enough to send their top man to eyewitness the facts and try to resolve the matter. He suggests a follow up meeting as soon as Michael had the chance to examine the situation first hand. The meeting breaks up with pleasantries on the surface, while rip tides and undercurrents rage below. On the government's side denials and disclaimers. On the contractor's side realization that the Navy is resolved not to part with their money without a struggle.

Michael and Commander Walsh leave the OICC Building together. Commander Walsh, who is about the same age as Michael, goes out of his way in being nice. He asks Michael where he was staying in Honolulu and expands after he is told, on the night life in Waikiki Beach. He extends an invitation to Michael to have lunch with him at the Officer's Club. Michael explains that he needs to get together with his onsite staff. Thanks, the ROICC and promises that he will take him up on his offer another day.

Commander Walsh explains to Michael that the job site is in a sensitive area on the Base; so, in order for him to gain access into the CIA Area, he must obtain a second picture I.D. type badge. He escorts Michael to the CIA Pass Office and introduces him to the Lieutenant on duty as a VIP.

Michael is handed a four-page questionnaire to complete. The document states that his answers will be checked and verified by the FBI under threat of perjury. He then is taken into a theatre to see a video concerning pollutants on Base. Mercury is not allowed in any device in the CIA Area. What to do when a transformer with PCB's explodes or leaks. How to handle Lead Paint or Asbestos. Finally, what to do if you encounter a yellow rectangle with a magenta sign painted on it. Michael copies the phone numbers to notify, shown on the screen. It is unlikely that he will ever encounter radioactive substances, but you never know. The Lieutenant may be checking on his way out whether he had the emergency contact numbers. Finally, he is fingerprinted, his picture taken and he is issued with a picture I. D. with his signature and thump print. He gets a map of the CIA Area from the rack and goes out in the blinding light.

By now it is past ten thirty in the morning. He consults the map and establishes the shortest route to Building 155 prior to getting inside the rental car, which by now must be like an oven. He takes the top down and starts toward the CIA Area gate. As soon as he passes the harbor control and observation tower, he sees Building 155 up ahead to the right. From the chain link fenced yard that is serving as a construction lay down and storage area, clouds of smoke are billowing. It is not a fire, like his original inclination told him; but something like a bar-b-cue, it came to him as the flaming charcoal assaulted his nostrils. What is that all about he wonders as he makes his way, under the 15 MPH posted speed limit, towards the Bayshore Drive; a road running along the wharf to the left and the job site entrance to the right.

He stops hesitantly at the 20-foot-wide gate, barely missing the pickup truck with his company's insignia on the doors that was coming down the Bayshore Drive from the opposite direction, cutting a mean left turn, almost on two wheels, into the gate in front of him. A surf board bouncing in the bed of the truck providing a split-second view and a coconut, from the pile of coconuts, rolled out of the bed of the truck as it rounded the corner, bounced on the pavement and wedged itself between the front bumper of his rental car and the road.

Shaking slightly, adrenaline flowing, Michael kicks the coconut aside and turns right, into the job site. He has a set Agenda: Who was the driver of the truck? What was the origin of the smoke? The Differing Site Conditions Change Order. Oh yea! Let's not forget the load of coconuts.

One of his questions is answered as soon as he sees half a dozen workers tending the fires of an equal number of hibachi type charcoal bar-b-cues. The pickup truck is nowhere in sight. It's tire marks visible in the gravel parking space adjacent to the far-right entrance to the trailer in front of the A. C. Unit and the power hook up to the office trailer. He parks by the door on the opposite side and turns off the ignition.

Bill Scott comes down the steps. Handshakes, slaps on the back, small talk about the flight. Michael turns and looks questioningly at the hibachis. Bill Scott explains the virtues of the Hawaiian plate lunch. Today's menu is Houli-Houli chicken. It's simply that the workers will not bring sandwiches, like in the mainland, but insist upon cooking on site.

"At any rate it is not our company's concern, since they are subcontractors' employees. They are on someone else's dime. The pickup truck issue, it must have been that darn Steve Crane, coming back from the mail run; by way of catching the early morning swells."

Steve Crane in his mid-twenties. Five six, skin and bones, a little runt. All his life, everyone has been picking on him. He has finally found a home and self-respect working for Michael. He uses Michael's name and influence to get things done. He is loyal. He is trustworthy, up to a point when there was a buck to be made for Steve, without hurting anybody. Rules were made to be bent, rather than obeyed.

As on cue, the truck appears around the trailer from the opposite corner they were standing, backing with considerable tire spin action, into the same rut infested parking space. Michael and Bill head that way as Steve Crane hops down carrying the mail bag. Michael looks in the truck bed. No surf board. No coconuts. He knows better than to ask. Who knows what deal Steve has been cooking on the side.

He remembers when he arrived at the job site at Mare Island Naval Shipyard last year to find that it was converted into a giant parking lot by Steve Crane for the Base personnel, because parking on Base was at a premium. At five bucks a car for all day parking, Steve was an enterprising dude alright. Michael did not mind Steve's indiscretions as long as they did not affect the company's bottom line or the job performance. Steve was his man; devoted and ready for the 'salto mortale', the jump of death, if need be, at Michael's command.

Steve Crane, however, had his limitations; which Michael recognized. He could photographically report what he was looking at. However, he could neither spot nor understand the concept of Differing Site Conditions, so he was useless as far as Michael was concerned to argue the Merit of the communication lines duct bank interference with the location, as shown on the Contract Drawings, of the Demineralizing Water Facility.

Michael's attention wanders. His eyes set upon an ankle belonging to a thoroughbred philly pushing the office door open and then at eye level revealing an exquisite leg that took his breath away before the hem of the skirt appears two hands above revealing a shapely knee. He could not quite make the face, blocked by the outgoing box of mail she was carrying. She could have rested the entire box on that exploding set of lungs. She lifts her arms above her head stretching the fabric of her dress to its design limits as she studies the distance between the threshold and the first step; hesitating to bring the other foot forward. The trio of men stays like statues watching the progress in religious silence.

Roxanne, in her mid to late twenties, born in Boston, Massachusetts. Michael was told later that she had lost her mother at a young age and had run away from home at sixteen, to get away from an abusive relationship. 42-26-36. Five two, 125 pounds. Double 'D' of earth-shaking sexuality. Strawberry blond, blue eyes, tans well. She looks and behaves like she just got out of bed and she wants to get right back to it with whomever she was talking along with her. She seduces every male she encounters with her eyes and mannerisms.

She firmly believes that the way to the man's heart is through his crotch. She is cunning. Poorly educated in the social graces. She is not very well educated, period. On the other hand, she is very sexual. She does things on the spirit of the moment without giving a thought to the consequences. Her attitude is that of a flower child of the sixties. If it feels good, do it. Immediate gratification. She cannot see past the end of her nose.

Her highs are very high and her lows are very low. She is an extrovert who is used to getting her own way socially. Michael represents for her what she always aspired for: Looks, culture, sophistication, wealth, stability and knowledge; combined with intelligence and a sense of humour to keep her entertained. All the things that were denied to her all her life. She is the girl who was born on the wrong side on the tracks and Michael represents her ticket out of there.

"Isn't any of you gentlemen going to help a lady in destress?" The sound of her throaty voice brings goosebumps at the back of Michael's neck.

The trio galvanizes into simultaneous motion. Steve Crane winning the race up the steps to hold the door open.

"This is Roxanne." Bill Scott introduces her to Michael, as soon as she makes her way down the portable office trailer steps.

The sound of open heel wooden sandals clicking down the metal steps like a hammer striking the hot anvil, sending shivers down Michael's spine. She passes the outgoing mail to Steve Crane and extends her hand. Michael comes in contact with a pliant warm hand that disappears in his. He looks down at her feet and notices that she is standing in drying mud at the edge of the ruts.

"Bill. You must do something about repairing this parking space. It is the low point in the parking lot and will flood after a rain storm, which I understand in Hawaii they occur almost daily. And Steve, please henceforth, slow down." Michael says with authority.

"The night sprinklers soften up the ground." Bill replies. "It's not entirely Steve's fault. By noon the ground is dry anyway. All the overnight collected water evaporates. At any rate it is not something that needs to be done right now. There are more important things to discuss. One of these days I will tell a sub to throw a couple of shovelfuls of gravel and the puddle will disappear."

Michael consults his watch. It's past 11:30 AM.

"Do you know of a good place to have lunch? The Company is paying and everyone is invited." Michael announces.

"In that case we will go to the Pearl City Tavern." Bill Scott decides for everyone. He makes reservations from the office phone for four at noon.

Steve Crane is going to drop off the mail at the Airport Post Office for faster service with the mainland and check the Company Post Office box for late deliveries. He will meet them at the restaurant. He takes off in the company pickup truck. This time though backing carefully and avoiding jack rabbit starts.

The rest might as well take one car only. They pile up in the convertible. Bill Scott in the back seat. Michael opens the passenger door for Roxanne. She backs into the seat, swinging her legs afterwards, rewarding Michael with a generous glimpse of thigh and pink panties.

Chapter 4

Differing Site Conditions

Michael, Bill and Roxanne are the first to arrive at the Pearl City Tavern. They go, passed the giant lobster at the entrance and turn left into the monkey bar. Twelve feet high and the length of the bar, there is a glass wall panel behind the bar. It separates the bar from the jungle terrarium with four dozen monkeys frolicking in the manmade habitat. It has every conceivable tropical plant. A little lake. Vines hanging from manmade the trees for the monkeys to swing. The bar is almost full with the regulars. Watching the monkeys and sucking them up. From the condition of many, probably clear to the happy hour.

Bill finds a table by the rail leading to the main restaurant lounge. The table must have been for two, because it is tiny. Michael looks around and discovers that all the tables are similar, postage stamp size. They squeeze four chairs around the table. Michael bumps his knee at something under the table trying to sit down. He takes a look under the table and discovers that he bumped his knee on the bamboo bars of a cage fitted underneath the table. Bill informs him that the cages were left over from the olden days.

Bill lifts the lamp from the middle of the table and uncovers a four-inch diameter hole through the table top.

"The customers used to select a monkey from the bar's tropical tableau. The monkey was brought at their table screaming and kicking. It was locked into the cage under the table. Only its head sticking four-inch above the table through the hole, at eye level. The waiter would come to the table and take the top of the monkey's head off with a swift swing of his machete. The customers then would pick the monkey's brains from the skull with chopsticks, while the monkey was still alive and dip them into various sauces before eating them. It was considered the specialty of the Tavern. Now only the decor remains." Bill added sadly. "The statehood in 1959 changed a lot of the old traditions and habits."

"That's one tradition and habit I am glad it got changed!" Roxanne says, breaking into a shiver. "Bill you are disgusting. What a story to tell before lunch of all times. What is Michael going to think his first day on the island?" She added, smiling demurely squeezing Michael's forearm in the process; her touch lingering but just short of the limits of propriety.

A waiter comes to their table.

"Is everything OK Bra?" He says to Michael who was rather obviously staring at the waiter's hands, as he was approaching their table.

"He is looking for your machete Kimo." Bill said good naturally. "Next time bring your prop along for maximum effect. I just explained the purpose of the bamboo cage underneath the table."

Kimo ignores Bill and asks for their drink order.

Michael informs him that a fourth party will be joining them shortly, at which time they will adjourn to an available table in the dining room.

The waiter leaves their table with their drink order and heads for the bar.

Michael is anxious to get the conversation around the Demineralizing Water Facility interference with the existing communication lines embedded in concrete.

"The demolition has been completed outside the existing building." Bill launched. "The demolition crews moved inside the building, while a new crew started excavation for the Demineralizing Water Tanks and Chemical Tanks foundations in the location shown on the Contract Drawings. The area was tested by sounding equipment, prior to the excavation. No underground utilities showed up on the screen. None were shown on the Contract Drawings. The backhoe uncovered two concrete communication ducts occupying the same real estate as the

Demineralizing and the Chemical Tanks. The foundation crew stopped work and the ROICC was that same day verbally notified by me, and in writing via the Daily CQC Report handed the following morning to the Navy Inspector by Steve Crane. Roxanne has a copy of it in the office at the job site."

The waiter comes with their drinks. Michael opens his writing pad and starts writing a draft letter to the Navy. He briefly describes the deficiency and the sequence of events. He puts the government on notice that it constitutes a Constructive Change under the terms of the Contract. He offers an alternate solution and quotes a figure of not to exceed five thousand dollars to implement the Change, provided they receive an immediate Notice to Proceed. If he does not receive direction by the close of business today, he informs the Navy that it will mean a 'de facto' Suspension of Work, with the costs escalating accordingly. He tears the page from his pad and hands it to Roxanne to type when they get back. She puts it in her purse.

Steve Crane shows up. He goes to the bar and orders a drink. The hostess calls over a dining room waitress who carries the drinks to their table. She hands them menus. Michael orders a salad and shrimp tempura. Roxanne orders the same. Bill Scott orders a steak. Steve Crane orders a lobster. Bill Scott changes his order to lobster also. The waitress departs with their orders.

"I haven't slipped a good piece of tail since our foggy outing in Conway, New Hampshire." Bill winks at Michael.

Roxanne gets real excited and wants to know the nefarious details.

"It's not what you are thinking." Michael assures her. "We actually went to eat lobsters one evening in Conway, New

Hampshire at a restaurant called the Lobster Trap. The term 'slipping tail' is a New England expression and it means to separate the lobster tail from its shell, intact. By breaking off the end piece of the tail, someone can actually slide the lobster tail intact from its shell."

Bill and Steve start laughing, while Roxanne looks disappointed.

Steve Crane brings up that it is customary in Hawaii to have the Project blessed on site by a Kahuna, followed by a feast for all the workers and invited guests, a Luau.

The wine steward approaches their table with the wine catalogue and hands it to Michael. Michael tells him, without opening it, that since everyone ordered sea food, whether they had a good Mersault. The wine steward, at $64.00 a bottle figure dancing in his head, sucks up to Michael and complements him on the excellent selection and his knowledge of good wine.

Bill Scott asks Michael what kind of wine was that. Michael tells him it's a French white wine, very light, very clear, dry but not astringent. It compliments lobster quite well.

"Where do you find the time to know so much about wine?" Roxanne asks Michael.

"Through the Company lawyer and personal mentor for eight years now, Don Davidson. Once a month we go for a three-hour lunch at an exquisite restaurant, bistro or even someone's private cellar. We eat a gourmet meal prepared by executive chefs and sample a variety of wines that the proprietor wishes to find out our opinion. During the meal we discuss all sorts of issues and problems."

Don Davidson is in his late fifties, struck with polio while attending Law School at Dartmouth. He moves around on crutches.

He sees his handicap as an asset and utilizes it in Court by gaining the jury's sympathy, struggling along. When he speaks, he concentrates on the substance rather than the form. He is disorganized. This should have worked to his disadvantage during Trial.

However, the Law Firm of Fergusson and Burdell has always assigned to him a newly hired lawyer who had just passed the Bar Exam, to work for Don Davidson for a couple of years, in training, to keep his paperwork straight and provide him with the document he needed during Trial at the exact moment he needed it.

He is a connoisseur of fine food and wine. He has adopted Michael, like a son he never had, back in 1973 and has served as his lawyer and mentor ever since. He thinks Michael is the smartest person he has met in his life. He uses Michael's mind many times during their lunches together to feed him the information he knows on his own Court Cases and see to his amazement, every time, Michael trail blazing an opinion that is both innovative, logical and legally correct; because Michael not knowing the concept of 'Precedent' has just come up with a new innovative solution to his problem.

As Michael's knowledge of the Law expands, Don Davidson sees their professional relationship sooner or later coming to an end. He tries to make up for it, by stimulating and educating Michael in food and wine. He loves to discuss literature with Michael, who is better read than Don, and is always amazed at Michael's analytical mind.

"Don Davidson, who is twenty years my senior, poses various legal problems and tests my ability to solve them without knowledge of a Precedent, rather based on my ability to get to the heart of the matter and provide a solution based strictly on logic. I believe he uses me to look at his legal issues with a new perspective."

"I have heard that Michael has a wine cellar at his mansion and has frequent wine tasting parties." Bill Scott said to Roxanne. "I was never invited of course." He added with regret and envy.

Michael gets red in the face and uneasy. Almost everyone thinks that this is a result of Bill's comment. In actuality, it is more because of the bare toes that are stroking his shin under the table. He steals a glance at Roxanne's direction. She is licentiously passing her tongue over her lips and the tip of a bread stick.

Steve Crane wants to know what was Michael's decision on the job site blessing. Michael is suspecting that Steve is running some kind of a scam; probably with one of the cousins of the Big Kahuna. He cannot concentrate on the conversation. The toes on his shin make him feel dizzy. His head is throbbing, but he does not have a headache. Steve keeps talking about another contractor at the Aloha Stadium job that did not believe in blessing the Project. After the third accident on the job, he stopped everything and called the Big Kahuna.

"Fine!" Michael says, more to get rid of him than anything else. "Set it up."

Steve assures Michael that he will get right to it so that Michael and Christina can attend the ceremony while they were here on the island, because the ceremony was quite colourful. At the sound of his wife's name, Michael brings his feet under the chair, breaking contact with Roxanne and slowly returning to coherence.

The waitress comes with their food on a push cart trolley. Michael turns the discussion for the rest of the meal around his staff and their leisure activities on the island of Oahu.

They finish their lunch and return to the job site. Roxanne types the Request for Change letter Michael had drafted at the restaurant. Michael visits the location of the Differing Site Conditions and draws a new alternate equipment General Arrangement. Michael likes the new equipment General Arrangement. They will save money because in the new equipment location the pipe runs will be shorter. Michael signs the typed letter and takes the original together with the new general arrangement sketches he made to the ROICC office with Bill Scott.

At the ROICC office, Bill and Michael meet with Commander Walsh. Michael hands the ROICC the letter with the attached sketches and explains the Differing Site Conditions together with the impact they are having on the Project Time of Performance.

Commander Walsh will study the alternate locations and will be on site first thing tomorrow morning to verify the new locations and hopefully give them a Notice to Proceed on the Change with the costs not to exceed $5,000.00.

Michael and Bill leave the ROICC office and walk back to the job site.

Michael tells Bill Scott that his wife will be using the rental car to take the kids around the island. Roxanne offers her company car and asks Michael for a ride home. Michael considers it, but asks Bill Scott instead to pick him up in the morning from the hotel, on his way to work. Then they will stop someplace and Michael will buy him breakfast.

Steve Crane announces that it's 3:30 PM. Half hour before quitting time. But Surf's up. Quitting time as far as Steve Crane is concerned.

Everyone starts securing the place and locking up the office trailer.

Michael gets into the rental car and drives away.

Chapter 5

Sargo and Swordfish

Michael gets up early because the kids wake him up from the next room, excited to get going on their adventures for the day. Michael goes out to their Lanai and watches the sunrise over Diamond Head. Christina calls up room service and orders breakfast for herself and the kids. She covers the mouthpiece and asks her husband what he would like for breakfast.

"I will have breakfast with Bill Scott, who will be calling any minute from the hotel lobby." Michael responds.

Michael is absent minded this morning. He is worried about the government's indecision concerning the Differing Site Conditions Change. He wonders, if no decision is forthcoming, whether to shut the job down all together. He is concerned over the Navy's stalling tactics. He is worried about the pace of work in Hawaii and is thankful of his decision to subcontract everything at a fixed price. He makes a mental note of the items he wishes to discuss with Bill Scott over breakfast.

He looks at his wife getting out of bed, putting her matching robe over the silk night gown. He compares his wife's body with Roxanne's using his imagination. He is unhappy at the results of his findings. Feeling guilty, he chases the impure thoughts away. Roxanne has bewitched him. He must be careful or his marriage may be heading for the shoals; the reef is not much further. It's easy, with Roxanne's care free attitude and reckless abandon, to find himself immersed in an affair. That's a step he has not taken yet, since he got married; thinking back on all the opportunities.

Darn it! He is taking control of his feelings. It's so easy here in Hawaii to local out and passively let the events sweep him into a tropical fling. Scenes from Bali High and South Pacific flood his brain...The phone rings. Christina answers. It's Bill Scott downstairs.

Michael grabs his briefcase. Second day on the job and he has already traded his suit for chinos, aloha shirt and Sargol deck shoes without shocks. He kisses Christina and the kid's goodbye. Wishes them a fun day at Hanauma Bay. He will be working late on the job site. There are some problems to solve. They should go out to dinner by themselves. Not to wait up for him. He leaves their suite, pangs of quilt already gnawing at his insides.

Michael gets out of the Hilton Rainbow Towers elevator. Bill Scott is sitting in the lobby reading the Honolulu Advertiser, the morning paper. They get in Bill's pickup truck with the company decals on the door panels, parked up front by the entrance circular drive. They drive from the Hilton Hawaiian Village, up Kalakaua Avenue and merge onto the H-1 freeway with the morning traffic.

They reminisce about their time together at the Berlin, New Hampshire job. It must be eight below there now, this time of the year and three feet of snow with the winds howling down from the White Mountains. Speaking of winds, Michael reminds Bill of the monument at the start of Tuckerman's Ravine in the White Mountains memorializing the strongest wind, ever, recorded on earth at 257 MPH, at that exact spot.

Downtown is now behind them and Michael reminds Bill of his offer yesterday to buy them breakfast. Bill has not forgotten. He wants to take Michael to a real local place. Away from Waikiki, with no tourists in sight. He signals for Houghtailing Exit and turns left heading Makai, towards the water, into the Dillingham Plaza. They park in front a hole in the wall, bearing the dubious sign 'The Original Pancake House'. The place inside is immense in comparison with its frontage. Packed with working class Hawaiians who momentarily stop eating at the sight of the two 'Haulis', white people, at the entrance by the ancient cash register.

An affable host, who introduces himself as a retired Navy man, hands them two menus and tells them to seat themselves wherever they wished. A table for four becomes vacant to their right and they seat themselves before it is even cleaned up. An old Philippine bus boy comes over pushing a trolley with tubs of dirty cups and dishes. He cleans their table as a waitress of Samoan ancestry and proportions brings two new settings and water.

Michael stares open mouthed at their waitress. She is wearing an old-fashioned muumuu. Not much more than five feet tall and equally wide. She was well over two hundred eighty pounds of chocolate pudding, giggling and shaking all over while she was setting the table with amazing economy of motion. She was young and quite pretty. If beauty was measured by the pound, Leilani, Michael thought, reading her name tag, would be their queen.

Michael looks up from his menu and asks for her recommendation. She informs him that their home-made Portuguese sausage 'Broke da Mout'. Michael will have Portuguese sausage and scrambled eggs. Bill Scott opts for an omelette. They both will try the macadamia nut pancakes, on the side hash browns, toast and a large fresh squeezed orange juice. Another waitress, the twin of Leilani approaches their table with two steaming cups of Kona coffee.

Michael comments that if they keep eating breakfast every day at 'The Original Pancake House', they will soon look like their waitresses. They exchange conspiratorial looks on what it would be like to make it with a woman of Leilani's proportions.

"Speaking of making it with another woman," Bill Scott asks Michael, "what do you think of Roxanne?"

He tells Michael that she has not stopped talking about him and asking Bill confidentially all sorts of questions about Michael's life, his tastes, his habits. Bill seems to think that she was falling for Michael or at the very least she was ready for the taking. Michael listens feigning indifference while deep down burns with curiosity. Their breakfast arrives and it takes their entire four-person table to accommodate all the plates.

"What do you think of shutting the job down until the Navy provides direction on how to proceed on the Change?" Michael asks Bill as soon as their waitress moved out of ear shot.

"Are you trying to ruin my breakfast?" Bill asks in reply. "I cannot answer that, because I have a vested interest. My job! You are the Boss and a Company man. I am sure you will do whatever you will do to maximize the profit for the Company. Why are you asking me? Or is this a rhetorical question?"

They eat in silence avoiding looking at each other.

"Is it really that bad?" Bill dares after a while.

"I don't know." Michael responds. "The Navy avoids the issue. I don't know which way to jump. We need a catalyst. Some event that will force their hand one way or another. We cannot afford the overhead on our dime."

"What do you mean?" Bill asks not knowing whether he should be insulted.

"People may lie Bill, but numbers don't. When we Bid the job, we estimated to complete a certain portion of work each month, which translates into rolling over a given amount of the Contract price. This was sufficient to cover the field and office overhead. The moment we reduce the roll over amount, we must reduce the overhead by a commensurate amount. If we are guaranteed Return on our Investment at some future date, with interest, we will bite the bullet and front the money. Otherwise, our options are limited."

"I understand." Bill acknowledges. "What do you want me to do?"

"Find some way to force the Navy to acknowledge the Change in writing and provide us with written direction on what to do."

They finish their breakfast in silence. Michael pays with a Company credit card and they leave, each absorbed in his own thoughts. They take the Airport Exit off H-1 and then the Pearl Harbor/ Hickam Air Force Base ramp to Nimitz Gate. Bill Scott turns left at the second opportunity, passed the Stop sign in front of the OICC Building and right into the CIA Control Gate.

They show their badges to the Marines guarding the Gate. Bill Scott looks at his watch.

"Do you want to make a bet?" He asks Michael.

"Bet about what?" Michael answers the question with a question. He looks at his watch also. It is almost 7:50 AM.

Bill Scott puts the car in drive and accelerates up ahead with purpose, throwing Michael backwards onto the headrest and breaking the 15 MPH speed limit.

"What gotten into you?" Michael asks as the truck lurches to a stop short of the Pearl Harbor Bayshore Drive.

"Shit! I thought I could make it into the job site before taps." Bill replies.

He turns the car ignition off and opens the driver's side door. Michael could hear marching type music coming from the loudspeakers in every telephone pole on Base. He gets out of the truck from the passenger side and slams the door shut. He sees that all the cars behind them have also stopped and their passengers staying at attention outside their vehicles.

"The Navy is playing the National Anthem of every visiting ship's country of origin." Bill volunteers. "Sometimes it's fast, sometimes it may take 20 minutes or more. Depends. When you hear the U.S. National Anthem, we are at the end of the rendition."

Well, Michael is thinking, you couldn't ask for a more premier spot to stop, as the Canadian National Anthem started. Michael stared at the blue expanse up ahead, with Ford Island to the right and the entrance to Pearl Harbor Naval Shipyard on the left. The water was starting at spitting distance from where he was standing. The job site chain link fence was within touching distance to his right. They were parked sixty yards away from the Project entrance after turning right into the Bayshore Drive from the Stop sign. The shipyard dry docks were stretching to the right into forever with all manner of ships tied to them, all hands-on deck saluting the colours. The wharf along the Bayshore Drive was crowded also with the exception of the length of three football fields directly in front of Building 155 where the Project job site area was located.

Everything was at a standstill. From the corner of his left eye, Michael detected movement. A low-profile shape was slowly making its way from the mouth of the entrance of Pearl Harbor Naval Shipyard on a bee line to their truck. It was making progress deceptively, without the tell-tale sign of a wake. However, it was coming, coming closer, because it was getting bigger, and still kept coming in defiance the French National Anthem that was starting at that moment in the loudspeakers. The submarine turned on a dime in front of their truck and was side slipping full length into the wharf space, ever so slowly, making progress forward at the same time. It was the nuclear submarine 'SWORDFISH', Michael could clearly read its name some fifty feet away. As the submarine stopped side slipping towards the wharf, the main hatch opened and about twenty sailors climbed out and stood on its sleek deck at attention.

Michael turned left to look at Bill; whether he was enjoying the show as much as he was, when he noticed a second dark shape, duplicate of the first one making its way into the harbor on the wake of 'SWORDFISH'.

"Can you make out the name of the second nuclear submarine?" Michael whispers to Bill.

"It must be its sister sub "SARGO'." Bill replies. "I've seen them before. They are on the return leg of their patrol Guam to Pearl Harbor."

Why aren't they saluting the colours? Michael wondered, like 'SWORDFISH'. 'SARGO' instead was making progress slowly, hatches buttoned down, bilge water streaming from both sides, overboard, as the first notes of Stars and Stripes sounded through the Pearl Harbor Naval Shipyard loudspeaker system.

Chapter 6

The Sargo Incident

Aboard the Polaris-class nuclear attack submarine 'SARGO'. Captain Bill Rudich was having problems. For the past two days, the secondary circuit circulating water pumps have been cavitating. Which means that a portion of the water was turning into steam pitting the pump impeller. As a result, the pump capacity has been progressively diminishing. The feed water pumps were unable to keep up with the submarine's Nuclear Core cooling demand. Consequently, the steam production has being reduced drastically. The turbines with inadequate steam supply could not maintain the submarine's cruising speed.

The secondary circuit circulating water was deriving its heat from the primary water loop through a heat exchanger in which the heat was passed from one circuit to the other until equilibrium was reached. Since the secondary circuit water was in short supply, the coolant which was circulating through the reactor core, was not removing the nuclear generated heat because it had no place to transfer it outside the Core.

The Annunciator Alarm of LOW COOLING WATER FLOW had been going off every few minutes annoying everybody. It had since been disconnected, the red flashing light remaining the only Alarm indicator, requiring vigilance by the Control Panel operators on duty. The only water available on board was the drainage water collected in the submarine bilges and pumped out occasionally when the water level reached the overflow point.

This water was now being used as make-up water to supplement the secondary circuit, with any excess pumped back to the bilges through the sea cocks. Ordinarily, this arrangement could work temporarily. The crew having to be both alert and knowledgeable because several automated procedures were now being performed manually.

The downward spiral of the domino principle could be staved off until the submarine was able to limp to Pearl Harbor Naval Shipyard for repairs. Why then was the SARGO coming in assisted on the last legs of its electric battery, having previously exhausted all the diesel fuel for the back-up engine?

SARGO and its sister ship Polaris-type nuclear attack submarine SWORDFISH were built in 1967. Their primary propulsion system was a nuclear Pressurized Water Reactor (PWR); developed by the U.S. Navy under the direction of Admiral Hyman Rickover. From the beginning both ships have been experiencing the presence of excess oxygen in the secondary circuit circulating water that had been attacking all the wetted surfaces causing excessive corrosion that was cutting down the life of its equipment. Particularly in the tube sheets of the heat exchanger. They both had a major overhaul in Guam, Micronesia. They were heading for the Pearl Harbor Naval Shipyard for inspection of the repairs and to enter into the Shipyard maintenance schedule.

SARGO Commander, Captain Bill Rudich together with Lieutenant Jake Patterson, both ambitious and hungry for promotion, the latter for his own command, got together with the Shipyard engineers in Guam and equipped the submarine cooling system with Oxygen scavenging devices which utilized chemicals. One of the chemicals had a Sulphite root which was hungry to reach a state of equilibrium as Sulphate by absorbing Oxygen from the water and becoming an acid in the process. Then by adding Caustic, Calcium Hydroxide a base, to neutralize the acid and gain a neutral pH of 7.

These chemicals were introduced into the secondary cooling water circulating pump suction. The water in that loop, heated by the primary loop in a heat exchanger, was kept pressurized to prevent it from boiling and turning into steam. A delicate balance was maintained between the water, the water pressure and temperature as it entered the circulating pump suction.

The circulating pumps had a Required, designed by the pump manufacturer, NPSH, Net Positive Suction Head, in FT. The piping configuration and the height between the water level in the condensate receiving tank and the centreline of the pump suction determined the NPSH Available. The NPSH Available, less the friction losses in the interconnecting piping, must always be greater than the NPSH required, otherwise, the pressurized hot water will flash into steam and the feed water pump will start cavitating, losing portions of its impeller in the process.

In Nuclear Reactors built and operating on land, there is always adequate space in the plant so that the NPSH Available could comfortably surpass the NPSH Required by the pump. The nuclear submarine, however, was limited in that regard by the overall body design, specifically its height. The NPSH Available in the stream lined, low profile body style of the Polaris-type attack submarine was closely tracking the NPSH Required.

The medium temperature and pressure were, within limits, kept constant. The water temperature in the secondary circuit circulating pumps was, however, increased without a corresponding increase in the pressure to maintain equilibrium, resulting in the water flashing into steam, cavitating the pump impeller, progressively diminishing the pump's pumping capacity.

The water in the pumps being hot to begin with, reached the flashing point because of the reaction between the acid and the base is an exothermic reaction, meaning it produces and releases heat, causing at that point the NPSH Required to exceed the NPSH Available, causing the exploding steam bubbles to disintegrate the pump impeller.

If the problem was analysed and caught at its inception, the situation presently aboard SARGO could have been averted; by simply introducing the oxygen scavenging chemicals at the circulating water pump discharge in lieu of the suction. This way the exothermic chemical reaction would not interfere with the pump internals. The Control Panel Annunciator was not equipped with a secondary loop High Temperature Alarm.

The circulating water pumps did not have a pressure gauge at both inlet and outlet, so that the operator may be able to see a pressure differential change. The sole gauge was at the pump discharge indicating the TDH, Total Developed Head, which dropped ever so slowly that it was not noticed by the operators, until two days ago when the secondary loop water capacity became inadequate to properly cool the water in the primary loop, resulting in the overheating of the Reactor Core. The Central Control Panel Annunciator picked the diminished cooling water flow signal and sounded the Alarm.

At that instant, the Reactor Room Chief, no other than Lieutenant Jake Patterson, should have initiated emergency Reactor shut down procedures. Although the cooling of the Reactor would have taken several days, the submarine was equipped with a diesel engine as a secondary propulsion system and a back-up electric battery. Granted that under diesel power, SARGO would be forced to periodically raise a snorkel devise to draw in fresh air for the diesel engine combustion and crew to be able to breath and to carry away exhaust gasses. The back-up battery could operate an electric motor that could propel the submarine twelve knots maximum for ten hours.

The Lieutenant realized immediately that the cause for the Reactor overheating was inadequate water quantity in the secondary circuit. Accordingly, instead of shutting down the Reactor, he activated the stand-by water circulating pump.

The submarine had two water circulating pumps. One on line at all times and the second one as an emergency stand-by. In order to ensure readiness of the stand-by pump, it was put on line interchangeably, rendering the active pump and the stand-by to switch. Hence in this case both pumps sustained cavitation, unable to provide the required water volume capacity on demand.

By the time Lieutenant Patterson realized the fact that the stand-by pump was in no better shape than the primary one, the reactor temperature had moved into the red sector indicating imminent meltdown. The Annunciator Horn had long been disconnected, so the grave situation of the engine room was not widely known but for Lieutenant Patterson and three other crew members assigned to the engine room.

By the time Lieutenant Patterson decided to shut down the Reactor, it was too late. Only the ingenuity of Ensign Bob Pizzano in the engine room, prevented a complete melt down. He switched to the diesel-powered propulsion system and jury rigged the bilge pumps to pump water into the secondary cooling system, bringing the temperature indicator into the Orange Sector.

Lieutenant Jake Patterson informed Captain Bill Rudich that he was forced to shut down the Reactor because the secondary cooling water circuit pumps had lost their ability to pump water due to the loss of their impeller as a result of cavitation.

"No, it was not excess oxygen. It was a rise in the water temperature that turned the water into steam, eroding the pump impeller."

"No, I do not know the cause of the temperature rise."

Lieutenant Patterson of course omitted in his Report to the Captain to mention that the Reactor remained for a considerable amount of time with its Core temperature indicator in the Red Sector.

All is well that ends well.

In the case of SARGO though it was not to be.

The wall between the primary and secondary loop cracked. The secondary water circuit was thus contaminated with radiation. Since it was circulated by the bilge pumps, they were now contaminated together with the bilge walls themselves. Since the cooling of the reactor was now on manual, occasionally there was overflow of secondary cooling water in designated spill areas. These areas now hot and radioactive were cleaned and moped by crew members.

For the past two days the sick bay was experiencing an unusually large number of cases reporting inability to fulfill their duties. The Captain was informed. Further testing revealed that the ailing crew members were suffering from radiation sickness.

The Captain was given a progress report just before entering Pearl Harbor Naval Shipyard. He in turn dispatched a May Day distress signal to the Shipyard Nuclear Containment Office. He was ordered to dock in his designated spot and remain there with all the hatches closed, until a portable hospital unit and other emergency vehicles could be dispatched at his location.

Captain Rudich, while waiting for the Shipyard portable hospital to arrive, in an effort to reduce radiation exposure to the SARGO crew, he orders his men to manually pump the bilges overboard, dumping contaminated water into the Pearl Harbor Naval Shipyard Bay. *

THE SARGO INCIDENT

*The author was made aware of the information, as relayed in Chapter 6, 17 years after the incident, by a sole survivor of the submarine SARGO serving at the time of the incident in the SARGO submarine engine room.

Chapter 7

Emergency Safety Exercise

The last notes of the U.S. National Anthem sound off. Michael and Bill go back to the truck, facing the water. The first nuclear submarine, the SWORDFISH is tied up at the wharf in front of the job site. The second nuclear submarine, the SARGO, twin of the first one, approaches with its hatches buttoned down. Not a soul on deck; while several sailors walk the deck of SWORDFISH.

Bill Scott starts the pick-up engine. Suddenly there is a mad scramble on board the SWORDFISH. Sailors are getting back inside while others untie it from the wharf. The SARGO is approaching unaffected by the activity aboard the SWORDFISH, which is frantically trying to get free, speeding out of the path of the oncoming SARGO towards the dry docks to the right.

SARGO takes the space previously occupied by SWORDFISH in front of the job site. The SWORDFISH is no longer visible from the truck where Michael and Bill are sitting watching the activities taking place in front of their windshield. Bill and Michael look at each other unable to come up with an explanation. Bill shakes his head and turns right. They pass in front of the docked submarine SARGO. Michael cranes his head studying the submarine's name and serial number in white letters, emblazoned on the turret and bow against a gun metal black background. Still the hatches remain closed and there is no activity on deck. It's like the ghost ship, the Flying Dutchman, coming to port with no crew on board.

The pick-up truck turns right, through the twenty-foot entrance gate to the job site and parks in front of the office trailer. Michael gets out the passenger side and notices that yesterday's tire ruts, to the right, had turned overnight into a rain water puddle at the foot of the portable office stairway leading to the secretarial office and looks at Bill making shovelling motions. Bill waves at him good naturally, 'Manana', as the trailer door opens and there on top of the stairway stands Roxanne.

A girl of noble proportions, her legs visible up to her hips. She is wearing a mini skirt which looks as though it had shrunk in the wash. Her breasts are like swimming puppy dogs, eager to keep their nostrils above the water line. Michael looks up and finds himself facing the sexiest pair of powder blue lace panties. He has a silly smile on his face, frozen in place; his mind elsewhere lured by Roxanne's dazzling smile, push up bra and the faint vision of a vertical smile staring at him behind the see-through powder blue lace.

The sound of sirens brings him out of his reverie. Marine guards appear out of nowhere and block the streets surrounding the job site to all traffic. They even stretch a chain across the entrance to the job site. A Navy safety crew with green crosses on their back hang yellow square signs on the street barricades and the job site entrance chain, with magenta insignia of nuclear danger. Steve Crane comes out of the other side trailer door to see what the commotion was all about. Bill Scott approaches the chain on the twenty-foot-wide entrance and remaining on the job site side of the chain is shouting, trying to attract the attention of the safety officers and SP's, Shore Patrol, to find out the reason for all that activity. When he comes back and joins the others, he relays to them that it is some sort of Emergency Response Training Exercise. Evidently the Navy was implementing and testing their rescue procedures by conducting safety and emergency procedure readiness.

Another siren is heard in the background. The Marine guards remove the barricades to the Bayshore Drive in order to admit a portable hospital unit followed by a gaggle of emergency vehicles and two fire engines. The Bayshore Drive in front of the job site is crowded with personnel in 'space suits' that come out of the portable hospital. They attach plastic hoses the size of tunnels to the submarine hatches and connect them to the portable hospital access doors. The SARGO is now isolated, covered in plastic. The work crews and staff at the job site are all gawking at the spectacle to which they possess grand stand seats. The scene is reminiscent of the movie ET.

The Navy safety personnel unlock and enter the submarine hatches and start removing stretchers with body bags out of the submarine, disappearing with them into the portable hospital. The exercise looks very realistic, the only thing missing is blood and gore to add to the authenticity. One by one the submarine crew is carried in stretchers either to the portable hospital or are huddled in one of the waiting ambulances which leave periodically sirens and lights ablaze. There is frantic activity, where a little while ago was just the sleek dark shape of the submarine, pissing water into the harbor.

Michael goes inside the trailer to call the ROICC office. He wants to know what time the exercise will be over and the streets will open back to traffic. He further wants to find out whether Commander Walsh intends to walk over to Building 155, the job site, from his office to give them the go ahead on the Change Order or alternatively provide some type of direction. He gets through to the ROICC after several tries and of being put on hold indefinitely. Commander Walsh sounds cautious over the phone.

"I don't know when I will be able to visit the job site." He exclaims. "I am very busy this morning."

"We need immediate direction." Michael counters. "With all this activity taking place this morning, I am getting ready shut down the job…"

"What activity?" Commander Walsh exclaims. "I have not heard or seen any unusual activity by the wharf."

"Look out of your office window." Michael raises his voice. "You cannot miss seeing the portable hospital, emergency vehicles, sirens and flashing lights crowding the street in front of the job site. It looks like they are filming the sequel to ET."

Commander Walsh laughs and tells Michael that he will try to sneak passed the barricades on foot.

"When I get there, I will decide on the Change Order and find out for myself what the commotion is all about. I will check first though and find out if I will be allowed through and call you right back."

A few minutes later, instead, the OICC, Captain Reinhardt calls Michael and tells him that what is taking place in front of the job site is nothing more than an exercise in Disaster Containment.

"You are directed to advise your employees to stay on your side of the chain at the entrance to the job site and abstain from interfering in any way with the Navy's testing of their Emergency Procedures." The OICC announces.

"How long will these Testing Procedures take?" Michael wants to know.

"I don't know how long the exercise may last. For all I can guess it could be all day. In the meantime, no one could come in or out of the barricaded areas."

"We need direction on the Change Order. The interior demolition will be completed today. Absent further direction we would be out of work and the job site will 'de facto' be shut down." Michael cautions the OICC.

"Concerning the Constructive Change Order, The OICC is referring the matter to MIDPAC Contracts for their determination and direction." The OICC counters.

"What are we supposed to be doing while all this is taking place?" Michael asks.

"The government is acknowledging that the Differing Site Conditions constituted a Change under the Terms of the Contract. A letter is being typed issuing a Suspension of Work, while maintaining the General Contractor's on-site staff on the payroll."

"Under the circumstances we will be forced to Demobilize all our subcontractors and return all the excavation equipment back to the rental suppliers." Michael reminds the OICC. "The Demobilization and Remobilization costs would be added to the direct costs of the Change Order."

"What is all that in dollars and cents?" The OICC inquires.

"That means that the five thousand dollars in direct costs for the Change previously quoted, provided we implement the Change immediately, will escalate to thirty-five thousand dollars in direct costs assuming we are provided with direction within a month and the Scope of Work for the Change remains the same as shown in the sketches provided to the ROICC."

The OICC recognizes and accepts the added costs and blames the Contract Terms and Conditions as the cause.

Bill Scott comes in the trailer to find out what is taking Michael so long and hears the tail end of the telephone conversation. Michael hangs up the phone. It appears that he will not be forced to lay off Bill, Roxanne and Steve. The Navy just picked up their salary during the shutdown. Michael recounts to Bill his entire conversation with the OICC. He tells Bill to hand out a copy of the Suspension of Work by the Navy to each of the subcontractors. He warns him that for the next month not much will be happening on the job site.

Michael calls the Hilton Hawaiian Village and leaves a message to his room voice mail that the Navy was running some sort of Emergency Safety Exercise. They have closed, as a result, access from and to the job site. Michael did not know when the exercise will be completed and the barricades removed so that traffic may resume. He warns Christina that he may be late coming back to the hotel.

Commander Walsh calls back.

"The MPS, the Marine guards have orders not to let anyone in or out through the road blocks except for a medical emergency."

Michael relays to him his conversation with the OICC. It appears that the ROICC visit to the job site is not necessary.

"Due to the exercise, lunch today is on the government." The ROICC informs Michael. "A lunch wagon will be parked along the fence on the 'Mauka', inland, away from the water, towards the mountains, side of Building 155."

Michael and Bill Scott go outside where Bill informs all the others of the free lunch.

Plate lunch 'al fresco' while watching the submarine evacuation exercises. 'Paenem und Circenses', Bread and Circuses, as the Romans used to reward their citizens in the Coliseum to keep them calm and obedient.

Demolition is slowly progressing as people get back to work after lunch.

At the end of the day no work available is left. 'De facto' suspension of all new work.

Michael needs a car to get back to the hotel. He would like to use a company vehicle to allow Christina and the kids full use of the rental car. Roxanne volunteers her company car. She already has an extra car of her own. She only asks that she may be dropped off at home. It is on his way, so Michael volunteers.

Michael finds a quiet corner and makes some notes on today's events that he would later incorporate into his Diary.

The SP's, Shore Patrol, lower the chain at 4:00 PM. Everyone charges the gate like the start of the 24 hours car race at Le Mans.

* * * * *

Roxanne locks up the office trailer. An OICC messenger arrives with the Suspension of Work Order and acknowledgment of the Constructive Change due to Differing Site Conditions. Michael reads them briefly. He doesn't want to unlock the office trailer again to put them inside. Instead, contrary to his policy against taking originals home, he puts the OICC documents in his briefcase.

Roxanne hands him the keys to the FORD Ranger pick-up truck. They climb on board. They are the last car remaining on site. The pick-up truck stops as soon as it clears the chain link fence gate. Michael gets out of the truck. He closes the gate making sure that he uses their own, Company, lock so they can open in the morning. He gets back in the pick-up.

The nuclear submarine looks abandoned after the morning's activities. He would like to take a look inside, but the hatches are closed. The area remains in deafening silence after the earlier clamouring. The yellow rectangles with the magenta nuclear insignia, left over on the job site chain link fencing and the barricades, now moved to the side, remnants and silent sentinels, reminders of this day's earlier Emergency Safety Drill.

Chapter 8

Playing With Fire

Michael and Roxanne in the company pick-up truck are leaving the CIA area on their way to the Shipyard Nimitz Main Gate. Roxanne is very excited. She recounts the day's events blow by blow and the staged rescue exercise by the Navy.

"Victims and rescuers are probably having a few by now." She concludes.

Michael shares in her enthusiasm but for different reasons. He has snatched victory from the jaws of defeat. In his briefcase he has the proof. The Navy letters are in effect a blank signed check.

He stops at the Nimitz Gate and stares at the Marine on duty who waves him to proceed out. Evidently, they only check the incoming traffic, giving a per functioning look at the outgoing. Someone could leave the Base with a missile or a torpedo and none would be the wiser.

Quarter of a mile from the Base Gate they hit the anticipated commuter traffic jam. Michael reaches over and turns on the radio at 88.1 FM, the Honolulu Public Radio Station. The first bars of Beethoven's Fifth reverberate as he reaches in his shirt pocket and unwraps a Romeo y Julieta Churchill style cigar.

"Will the cigar smoke bother you?" He asks Roxanne. "I will leave my window wide open."

"No. In fact, I love the smoke from a good cigar." Roxanne replies.

Michael is trying to drive with a stick shift, clutch, in a traffic jam and at the same time cut the end of his cigar with a cigar cutter he got out of his pocket. Roxanne volunteers her assistance. She moves from the far side of the seat, tight next to Michael. She pulls up her skirt, lifts her left leg and straddles the gear shift, which is mounted on the floor.

Michael hands her the cigar and the cigar cutter. He looks down. Her dress is hiked past mid-thigh. The gear shift knob sticks up between her legs in such a precarious position that Michael is afraid and tingling at the same time with anticipation when they hit the freeway and he has to shift into the fourth gear. He can almost sense the back of his hand brushing against the see-through powder blue panties.

Michael picks up the cigar from Roxanne who had already struck a wooden match with her thumb nail, lighting Michael's cigar by keeping the flame an inch below the cigar end. Michael puffs on the cigar drawing the flame, rotating at the same time the cigar to insure uniform draw. He inspects the lit end of his cigar as Roxanne extinguishes the match flame with a breathy sigh.

The pickup truck signals to turn right into the freeway entrance marked H-1 East which would take them to Honolulu.

"Keep going straight." Roxanne announces the last minute. "Take the H-1 West instead."

Michael does as Roxanne had asked and gives her a questioning look.

"I lied. I don't live on the East Side of Oahu where your hotel is. I live on the West Side a little South of Makaha."

'Half hour to forty-five minutes out of my way', Michael is thinking. 'Good thing I had called and left a message warning Christina that I would be late coming back to the hotel'.

Roxanne is sensing that Michael is not happy with the latest disclosure.

"You must be getting hungry. I will cook for you the best steak you've ever tasted as soon as we get home."

Michael remains silent, but is starting to have second thoughts about this new development. Roxanne takes Michael's silence as quiet acquiescence and moves closer snuggling up to him. She is behaving in a provocative manner. She leans forward offering an unobstructed view of 'double D' cleavage all the way to her navel.

Michael is passive and keeps on driving in silence. He tolerates and does not discourage her mannerisms. He realizes that he is playing with fire, but he is confident that he can handle it. He is doing nothing wrong, himself. Roxanne is just an employee. She decided to try to be his friend. She has gone a little overboard in her efforts to become his friend. As a result, he feels a little intoxicated with desire, but he will do nothing about it. No one will accuse him of doing something wrong. A passing infatuation. He is just flattered by the attentions of this sensuous woman. He can't help it, if he is lusting in his heart. What can he do? He is a healthy, almost thirty-year-old, man. It's only natural.

Roxanne lives in a beach house rental between Waianae and Makaha, in the West, leeward, side of the island of Oahu. The sun is starting to set in a spectacular sunset by the time the pick-up pulls into the carport next to a weather-beaten Volvo with salt air-initiated body decay and rust spots spreading like measles. Roxanne opens the passenger door and steps off closing the door behind her.

Michael pauses for a moment with the engine running. Should he back the truck right out and head East without too much loss of face. He realizes that he is no longer in the talking and flirting stage. He is standing at the gateway, possibly, of the point of no return. 'Do I turn off the ignition or do I put the car in reverse'? He is thinking.

Roxanne forces the decision by reaching over the passenger side open window and taking Michael's briefcase and unlocking the front door of the house. No problem. He can handle it. It's just dinner with a friend.

Michael shuts the truck engine. Puts the keys in his pocket and follows Roxanne into the house.

A small foyer. A utilitarian kitchen with a bar counter, opening to a modest dining room with a rattan style glass top table and four comfortable looking chairs of the same ilk. An open spacious sitting room furnished with more rattan furniture, leading through two sliding doors outside to a lanai. A door to the left and two to the right; probably bathroom, bedroom and storage.

Roxanne places Michael's briefcase on the coffee table and opens the sliding doors outside to the Lanai. The afternoon trades suck the stale pot residue smell that was immediately noticeable mixed with incense. Michael picks up his briefcase and heads outside in the patio inhaling the sea breeze and puffing on the remnants of his cigar. He sits down in one of the two deck chairs. Twenty feet of an ill maintained lawn and the Makaha beach stretching for miles in each direction. The sun, ten to twelve feet up from the horizon, is sinking ever so slowly, in a dazzle of reflections.

Michael opens his briefcase and starts transferring the notes of the events of the day into his Diary. Roxanne comes out with two glasses of white wine. Michael takes a sip and sets his down on the Lanai table, trying not to make a face.

"You should type the diary notes of today's events and together with a copy of the Navy's letters," which he folds and places in the diary, "you should mail the whole package to the home office in

Seattle, so they may be appraised of the situation at the job site in Honolulu." He explains to Roxanne.

Roxanne announces that she will start dinner. She brings out a bag of charcoal briquettes and starting fire fluid.

Michael, ever the Boy Scout, finds the remnants of last Sunday's newspaper and starts the barbecue without the use of the lighter fluid. The coals will need a while to burn down.

"Let's go for a dip in the ocean." Roxanne suggests.

"I don't have a bathing suit with me." Michael protests.

Roxanne looks up and down the beach. No one in the water. No one on the beach.

"The sun is setting. Pretty soon we will be invisible." Roxanne pronounces.

She starts unbuttoning Michael's Aloha shirt. She starts loosening his belt. Michael grabs her hand in a half-hearted effort to stop her.

Roxanne backs up, she unzips the back of her dress and in one fluid motion she shimmies shoulders, waist and hips, and the dress ends up neatly at her ankles. The pale blue lace underpants and matching bra step out of the circle of dress. She kicks the high heel sandals and starts backing on the beach towards the water, sinking with each retreating step deeper into the bright orange circle of dimming light. She suddenly reverses direction and approaches Michael.

Foreign feeling hands hastily peel off Michael's clothing. In his silk boxer shorts he finds himself retracing the footsteps of the siren towards the ocean, the giver of life and the sinking sun, the fiery inferno.

Roxanne waits for Michael at the water's edge. She takes his hand and pulls him towards her. She embraces him, turns him around and suddenly puts her full weight on his body forcing him into a back flop on the shallows with her on top hungrily seeking his lips.

The rest of the swim is spent in frolicking abandon. Michael feels the years being shed from his back. Back to his childhood and the carefree life. Roxanne has become Madelene, Maria, Anna, Lynn and all the other girlfriends of his childhood and early teens. They are swimming, splashing, wrestling, hugging, kissing, groping. The sun is setting. They wait for the green flash when the sun deeps below the horizon as their signal to come out of the water.

Roxanne gives Michael a towel and she disappears to change. Michael dries himself and changes quickly out in the lanai. He takes off his boxer shorts and lays them on a shrub to dry. He puts his pants back on, commando, without underwear.

Roxanne comes out to the lanai wearing cut-off jeans over dance leotards and carrying the steaks. She will make a green salad while the steaks are cooking. Michael is the designated steak cook. The potatoes have been in the oven before their swim and are about done.

Michael sets the steaks on the grill. Roxanne comes with a surprising good Cabernet Sauvignon by Chateau St. Michelle and a cork screw opener. She starts setting the table out in the lanai. She takes Michael's Diary and puts it on top of a chair. She places his brief case on top of it.

Michael compliments her on her choice of the wine.

"It is perfect for steak and the winery is within a mile of my home in Woodinville, Washington." He says.

They eat chatting animatedly about the day's events. Michael feels like he has been in Hawaii for a week with everything that has taken place.

Roxanne tells Michael about her childhood and her life. They sit after dinner and talk like old friends. Michael takes out a cigar. Roxanne reaches over and takes it. Clips it and lights it herself, the same way she observed Michael doing it in the car on their way to her house. They continue talking. The conversation becomes progressively personal.

"I am attracted to you." Roxanne admits. "I think I am falling in love with you."

Michael remains silent.

"How about you. What are your feelings?" Roxanne insists, asking.

"Ordinarily, I put a glass wall around me. People come near but cannot penetrate that transparent barrier. You have somehow broken through. My defences are down and I feel extremely vulnerable. At the same time, you bring the irresponsible child in me of years gone by. An explosively dangerous combination. Please don't take advantage of me in the state I am presently."

Michael's feelings are in an uproar and confusion.

Roxanne goes inside the house.

"I will be right back." She yells from inside the house.

Michael gets up. After a momentary hesitation, he doesn't even go through the house. He grabs his briefcase and leaves by way of the Lanai, opening the back fence gate. He streaks to the carport, gets into the truck, starts the engine and backs out quickly before the little head starts doing the thinking of the big head.

His confusion and emotional upheaval is such that he is unaware that he forgot his Diary on the Lanai chair back at Roxanne's home; or for that matter that his boxer shorts have remained; trophy of tonight's encounter blowing in the Makaha wind keeping company to his Diary with the Navy original letters folded inside.

Chapter 9

The NIS Enters

Michael gets up real early the next morning. Christina and the kids were sound asleep when he came in late last night, after all the sun and fresh air at Hanauma Bay. A good thing too, because when he took his clothes off, he discovered he was minus his boxer shorts. He was no good at making up stories. Not to his wife, anyway.

He orders a large breakfast for everyone from room service. He gets ready and goes to the adjacent room to wake up the kids. They are excited about all the fish they saw yesterday and fed them frozen peas out of their hand at Hanauma Bay. Michael tells them that he was leaving the rental car with them again. He describes possible outings. The Polynesian Cultural Centre on the North Shore. The Castle Park Wet World where you go with your bathing suit and hop on all the rides. The Pearl Harbor tour and the Arizona Memorial. Horseback riding at the Dole pineapple plantation. Sandy Beach. Makapuu. Sunset Beach. Waimea Bay…The talk becomes very animated. It wakes up Christina.

Room service knocks on the door. Breakfast at the Lanai overlooking Diamond Head and Waikiki Beach. Michael recounts during breakfast the Navy emergency rescue exercise that closed all access to and from the job site for the entire day. The reason that he arrived late last night was that the Navy took him to dinner at the Officer's Club at Pearl Harbor Naval Shipyard as a consolation for all the hardship caused by the emergency rescue exercise. He feels guilty for the alternate version of the events.

"How about a date?" He asks Christina.

"What brought this all of a sudden?" Christina looks him in the eyes. "Not that I am complaining. What do you have in mind?"

"Something romantic…like Michael's Colony Surf."

"I will make reservations for 7:30 PM tonight and order a hotel sitter. Kids you stay in the room. Order dinner from room service and watch videos."

Michael leaves for work. He arrives at Pearl Harbor Naval Shipyard Nimitz Gate well before the National Anthem. From the CIA Gate he notices activity on the wharf in front of the job site. As he approaches, he sees a Navy work crew with platforms tied up on SARGO in bosun's chairs painting. On closer inspection he sees that they are painting over the name SARGO and the numbers identifying the submarine. He stops and watches. An SP, Shore Patrol, sailor with a sidearm, swinging a club by its lease approaches the pick-up truck. He asks for Michael's I.D. and after a close examination tells him to move.

The chain across the twenty-foot gate to the job site with the yellow and magenta nuclear signs is on the ground. One end still attached to the gate post. He drives into the job site and parks in front of the office trailer. The puddle from the morning showers is overflowing and forces him to jump from the cab to avoid getting his shoes wet. He climbs the office trailer steps two at a time and goes to the secretary's office. Roxanne is not there.

He takes a blank page from her desk pad and writes the SARGO, now the ghost submarine's name and registration number. He is searching in vain for his Diary. He takes apart his briefcase. It's not there. Where did he leave it? He must have left it at the hotel, he concludes.

Bill Scott comes in the office and tells Michael that Roxanne called earlier. She was having car trouble. Her car had been sitting for so long in the carport, it wouldn't start. Steve Crane will give her a ride to work on his way back from the Airport picking the mail. Michael leaves the truck keys on her desk so that she would have the means to get back home. He asks Bill Scott to give him a ride back to the hotel at the end of the day.

Michael and Bill have a discussion over the latest developments. From the office trailer window, they can see the painting crew finishing up. Why was the Navy concealing the identity of the submarine if it was merely involved in a training exercise? The Navy work detail packs-up and leaves. The Marines arrive and barricade Bayshore Drive in both directions to all through traffic and post guards at each station. Only the vehicles of the workers are allowed through.

Bill Scott asks Michael for the original Navy letters pertaining to the Change Order and the Suspension of Work. It's no good for only the originals floating around. He wants to make several copies in the office copier, Michael remembers putting them in his briefcase, last thing on the job site yesterday. He opens his briefcase and looks. He cannot find them. First his Diary, now the OICC letters. He has become sloppy and lackadaisical; like the people he came over to correct.

He leaves the office trailer to go to the ROICC Office to ask for a copy of the letters. While he is there, he will try to find out why did the Navy erase, earlier that morning, all the identifying information of the submarine. He takes his briefcase with him so the 'mennehoonies', gremlins in Hawaiian, won't come during his absence and remove any more documents from it.

Commander Walsh is very friendly meeting with Michael. He provides him with two copies of the Navy letters. One for the Change Order and the other for Suspension of Work effective yesterday.

"The Change Order Request together with the sketches you made has gone all the way to NAVFAC, Naval Facilities Engineering Command, in San Bruno, California for their determination. I bet they copy your sketches and revise the Contract Drawings accordingly, to show the new location of the Demineralizing Plant."

Michael draws in red on Commander Walsh's set of Plans the new Demineralizing Plant location.

"I will make a copy of this and mail it to the NAVFAC. I bet I will have back the revised plans in less than thirty calendar days."

"This thirty-day delay will end up costing the taxpayers a minimum of an extra thirty-five thousand dollars." Michael warns him.

"I understand, but my hands are tied up." Commander Walsh responds. "The OICC decided to go by the book on this matter. I take my orders from him. The OICC wants to administer the Contract in accordance with the Terms and Conditions spelled out in the FAR, Federal Acquisition Regulations."

Michael changes the subject and mentions the scene he encountered this morning with the Navy work detail painting over the SARGO name and number.

"They were probably painting the hull of the submarine in spots that the paint was pealing in order to protect the structure from the alkaline environment."

Michael looks Commander Walsh in the eyes.

"The Navy painters I saw this morning were not removing rust. They were painting over the name and registration number of the submarine." Michael replies.

Commander Walsh gets all red in the face. He is stumbling and fumbling to come up with a plausible explanation.

"Why has the Bayshore Drive Street been barricaded, as of this morning, closed to all through traffic?" Michael asks, and before Commander Walsh has recovered from the barrage of questions, he continues.

"This barricade action on the part of the government constitutes a Constructive Change Order under the heading of Denial of Job Site Access."

"But...But...The Marines were told to let all the workers through so the job site would remain open." Commander Walsh responds in a knee jerk fashion.

"Why is only the contractor and his subcontractors allowed access in the immediate area?" Michael inquires. "How come there isn't a government employee to be seen in the area? Where have they gone? Is there something wrong with the area around the submarine SARGO that would render it unsuitable for the health and welfare of the people?"

Commander Walsh keeps mumbling unintelligibly and shuffles papers on his desk.

Michael becomes progressively suspicious.

"Is really something wrong? Something happened during the exercise yesterday and now all that is happening today is nothing more than an attempt by the government to cover it up?"

Michael requests an emergency meeting on the job site and a member of the Navy Safety Division to be present.

"None is available." Commander Walsh says in a whisper.

Michael is really getting pissed off now. The Navy Rules and Regulations require the presence of a Navy Safety inspector on any construction site. They had one on site every day since yesterday. Commander Walsh was obviously lying.

"Since the yellow rectangles with the nuclear magenta sign were brought on site by the Navy, and still are present as of this minute, I want a Geiger Counter brought on site to measure the levels of radiation coming out of the barricaded area around the submarine." Michael insists.

Commander Walsh is really acting guilty now.

"The Contract requires that all communications between the General Contractor and the Navy be put in writing. The government will not respond on a verbal request."

Michael opens up his briefcase. He takes out a blank Speed-Letter Form with an attached carbon copy. He writes a letter describing what he has seen to date and requesting radiation testing of the job site. He dates it, signs it, hands the original to Commander Walsh and keeps the yellow copy.

"If the Geiger Counter is not on the job site by the close of business today, I am calling the media with the name and registration number of the submarine, together with a detailed description of what transpired and eye witnessed by yours truly. I have written a very detailed account in my Diary with names and statements of various government witnesses." Michael pronounces with finality getting ready to leave.

Commander Walsh tries to pacify Michael downplaying the security measures as government paranoia, spurned on as an aftermath of the hostage situation in Iran which has heightened the alert status of the Defence Department.

Michael points out, with all due respect, that the Commander got his locales mixed up. They are siting and talking in Honolulu, Hawaii and the Commander is bringing Teheran, Iran into the conversation. Michael was not aware that there were that many Muslim fundamentalists employed at Pearl Harbor Naval Shipyard.

Commander Walsh keeps talking about unrest in the Middle-East...

Michael cuts him off asking what all that got to do with the Navy Emergency Procedure Testing at Pearl Harbor Naval Shipyard?

"I am not convinced that I am getting the straight story from you, Commander Walsh." Michael concludes.

"I will admit to you, in confidence, that I am not told everything by the powers to be either. I am kept in the dark to the same extent you are." Commander Walsh admits.

Michael puts the yellow copy of the Speed-Letter in his briefcase. Closes it. Picks it up and without saying another word, leaves the ROICC Office.

* * * * *

Immediately after Michael leaves, Commander Walsh, the ROICC, calls his superior, the OICC, Captain Henry 'Hank' Reinhardt and tells him that Michael is threatening to go to the media unless the Navy provides him with a Geiger Counter to test the job site and the area around the submarine, by the close of business today.

He adds that he is convinced that Michael was not bluffing. He intends to go through with his threat. He was kicking himself requesting of Michael to put it in writing. The Navy now had the original of the request and Michael the only copy.

The OICC admonished the ROICC for creating a paper trail. This is the last thing the Navy wanted.

The ROICC warns the OICC that Michael has a Diary in his briefcase on which he has made a detailed accounting of yesterday's happenings with supporting evidence and statements by unknown others; quite possibly the list may include government personnel who may inadvertently made statements that they shouldn't. Michael has a detailed list of names and titles in his Diary.

"The little I know of Michael; he is not bluffing." Commander Walsh ended his tale.

Captain Reinaert is quite disturbed by these developments.

"As soon as I hang up, I will call my superior Rear Admiral Alexander Riffey to appraise him and I will recommend that we involve the NIS, Naval Intelligence Service, to assess the damage and initiate damage control."

* * * * *

Michael returns to the job site. He meets Bill Scott and gives him a summary of what transpired at the ROICC Office. Bill Scott tells Michael that Steve Crane has left to pick up the mail and give Roxanne a ride to the job site on his way back. Michael hands Bill a copy of the two letters from the OICC.

"Make several copies and forward them to the all the subcontractors on the project so that they may be appraised of the status of the Contract."

"All the subs?" Bill Scott protests. "Even the ones that are not involved with the Demineralizing Plant and the Chemical Yard excavation?"

"The Change Order will extend the Contract Completion Date. This action by the Navy has both Direct and Indirect Costs associated with the Change. It will affect all the subcontractors. As to the Suspension of Work letter, it is 'ipso facto'."

"As always, you know best." Bill Scott says with admiration.

"The Indirect Costs invariably involve time of performance. The extension of the Contract Completion Date, as a result of the Suspension of Work, certainly will adversely affect all the subcontractors. However, let the subcontractor's figure that for themselves. I don't want the Navy coming back to us accusing us of trying to run up the costs of the Change Order." Michael cautioned Bill.

"What's the bottom line on the Incident with SARGO?" Bill Scott changed subject.

"I don't really know." Michael admitted. "I suspect something happened during the exercise that was not supposed to take place and the Navy is trying to cover it up, by treating us like mushrooms. Keeping us in the dark and feeding us a lot of shit."

Bill Scott exploded laughing.

"I needed my fly-fishing wadders a little while ago to go through all the bull I was thrown at during my meeting with the ROICC." Michael continues.

Bill Scott in an effort to lighten up the talk, tells Michael that the blessing of the job site was scheduled for the day after tomorrow.

"What is it going to cost to appease the Spirits?" Michael is asking.

"Steve Crane is working on it." Bill Scott replies.

"I need to know the bottom line," Michael reiterates, "before I give you guys my approval."

There is a knock on the office trailer door. Two civilian dressed guys enter. They identify themselves as NIS Agents. They ask who is Michael.

Michael requests to see their I.D. cards. He makes a point of writing down their names and I. D. numbers.

They request that Michael follow them.

"The 'Man' wants to see you." One of them blurbs.

"Who is the 'Man'?" Bill Scott inquired.

"Admiral Riffey!" They both reply.

Michael wants to take Bill Scott with him as a witness.

The NIS Agents refuse.

Michael jests with them that they act as if he was under arrest.

"That can be very easily arranged." One of the NIS Agents replies.

"When am I going to be back? It is almost lunch time." Michael protests.

The NIS Agents merely look at each other and smile.

"How late did Admiral Riffey intend to keep me at CINPACFLT?" Michael wants to know. "I have a dinner engagement."

The NIS Agents are not helpful. They probably don't know what's happening. They were told to pick up Michael and deliver him somewhere. As to why? This was above their pay grade. They sure though are anxious to leave the job site.

At the same time, Michael senses that they don't want to physically force him to follow them. This arrest idle threat was a bunch of 'cock and bull'. This was not Russia or China or some third world Banana Republic. These NIS Agents were behaving like members of some sort of 'Death Squad'.

Michael decides to follow the NIS Agents voluntarily. Curious more than anything to meet Admiral Riffey and find out from the horse's mouth, so to speak, what was happening.

"I will wait for you right here." Were Bill Scott's parting words. "If you are not back by quitting time, I will call your wife and the press." He said the last for the NIS Agents benefit.

"When is quitting time?" One of the NIS Agents inquired in passing.

"Four o'clock on the dot." Was Bill Scott's reply. "I need to give Michael a ride back at his Hotel in Waikiki."

Chapter 10

A Guest of NIS

The NIS Agents had parked their unmarked white Dodge four door 'K' type car on the Bayshore Drive, just outside the construction gate. The 'ghost submarine', originally named SARGO, was tied up at the wharf twenty-five yards away. The NIS Agents walked to their car. One got in the driver's seat. The other opened the back door for Michael to get in. He shuts it and gets himself up front in the passenger seat. Michael notices that the back door window cranks and latches have been removed. The only way out is for someone to open the back doors from the outside. The windows are tinted to such extreme, so someone on the outside cannot identify the person in the back seat. He realizes that more or less he has become a prisoner.

The NIS car starts up and they commence driving all over the Pearl Harbor Naval Shipyard Base. They get on the main Base drag going the opposite direction from the Makalapa Gate where they have to exit to get to the CINPACFLT Building. He asks the NIS Agents where they are going. They remain silent refusing to even acknowledge that he even exists in the back seat. They drive onwards the far East Base Gate where it joins with Hickam Air Force Base.

Michael starts complaining. He demands to be taken back to the job site. He wants to call a lawyer. No response from the NIS Agents. They stop in front of a windowless building next to the Base Brig. The NIS Agents get out of the car and lock the front doors. Michael realizes that he is now locked up inside the car. They go around the car and one of them unlocks and opens the back car door closest to the sidewalk. He signals for Michael to get out of the car. They escort him inside the mystery building's main entrance. Inside, he finds himself in a Spartan lobby totally enclosed with a bulletproof window counter up ahead and a steel door to the right.

The NIS Agents step in front of the steel door. One of the NIS Agents walks up to a speaker phone on the door and talks to someone inside. Michael strains to hear because they talk in whispers. The steel door does not have a handle. Only a box on the wall with numbered buttons 0 to 9. The NIS Agent enters a five-digit code in the cypher lock box. The steel door opens inward with an audible click. Michael is pointed to enter first followed by the two NIS Agents. The door closes behind them by itself and locks with the same click as when it was opened.

They start down the long CMU constructed hallway with precast concrete for a ceiling. The corridor turns right, then left and branches off in three different directions. They signal Michael to take the right branch. Halfway down this new hallway, they stop in front of another steel door with a cypher lock instead of hardware. Michael feels as if he had walked straight into the pages of Franz Kafka's novel 'The Trial'.

One of the NIS Agents enters a five-digit code number into the cypher lock. Same click and the metal door opens inward a few inches. The other NIS Agent pushes the door halfway and signals Michael to enter the room. It is dark inside the room and Michael hesitates. He feels a palm at the small of his back prodding him forward. He enters the room. The door shuts behind him with the same click.

Michael stops in his tracks. He is in total darkness, such as he has never experienced in his life. He is afraid to move in any direction, for fear that he will bump into furniture. He stretches out his hand like a blind man feeling his way around. He cannot see the end of his hand. His outstretched fingers send no signal to his brain by touch. There is nothing out there. He backs up slowly a couple of steps until his progress is stopped by the back of his head and shoulders coming in contact with the five-digit steel door. He turns around and feels a flange all around the door which prevents even the slightest ray of light from the corridor outside. He feels for a switch on the side of the door. Nothing, just some canvas feeling material filled with a spongy substance. He turns his back to the door again.

A flash of white light forces his eyes shut. He blinks several times to adjust his eyes to the sudden light that was coming from a single light bulb, mounted on the ten-foot-high ceiling surrounded by a steel metal cage. He finds himself in a ten-by-ten feet windowless room with padded walls. There is no furniture in the room except for a three-foot-long metal bench in the centre of the far wall facing the metal door. Metal pipes for legs are embedded in the concrete floor.

He sits down on the bench, facing the steel door, which is the only wall surface in the room that is devoid of padding. He leans his back against the wall. Padding floor to ceiling stopping at the flange around the steel door. Concrete floor and ceiling with the sole metal cage protrusion that is surrounding the light bulb. 'What has he gotten himself into?' He is thinking, 'What has he done to get himself locked up like that?'

Hunger pains and a growling stomach remind him that it is past lunch time. He consults his watch, confirming the fact that it was now one o'clock. He studies the room. It must have air duct openings behind the padding, otherwise he would have run out of air. That and the fact that the room was cold, while outside it must be at least 85 degrees Fahrenheit.

His eyes lock on the door, because of the click he heard followed by the steel door springing open inwards a few inches. A short slight man in civilian clothes comes in with a briefcase, holding a folding chair with a writing arm rest, reminiscent of the student lecture chairs in College. The door clicks shut again. The man unfolds the chair and sets it down halfway between the steel door and the bench where Michael is sitting. He approaches Michael.

"My name is Dave Brown. I am the NIS Agent in charge of the case." He announces.

Five six, horned rimmed glasses. 125 pounds, curly light brown hair. Nervous fascial tics and busy hands playing with a rubber band. He reminds Michael of the actor in a similar position in the movie 'Absence of Malice'. Dave Brown wants to move up in the NIS. He sees himself as a District Director. He sees nailing Michael as his ticket and final step towards that goal.

Early thirties. Not married. He is the zealot of his outfit. The cloak and dagger stuff consumes him. He is a workaholic and expects all others working for the NIS to emulate his example. He lies and distorts reality to suit his purpose. He considers it as part of his job.

He flips open a billfold which contains a picture I.D. on one side and the NIS shield in the other. He puts his credentials away and sits down on the folding student chair, moves his brief case between his legs. He opens it and takes out a blank tablet. He pulls out a folded page from his briefcase and hands it to Michael. It is a standard Form concerning the National Secrecy Act with a place at the bottom for Michael to sign. In addition, it Certified that the present interview was being conducted on a volunteer basis and Michael was a Cooperating Witness.

Dave Brown follows Michael's eyes reading the form. He assures Michael after he had finished reading the Form that their interview will remain and be stamped Confidential. He tells Michael that he is the NIS Agent charged by MIDPAC to conduct civilian psychological tests of the subjects who have viewed the realistic re-enactment of a Nuclear Rescue Operation. He fishes a ballpoint pen out of his breast pocket and extends it to Michael.

Michael ignores him. He pulls out his Mont Blanc fountain pen, 18 K gold with platinum nib, out of his shirt pocket and starts writing at the bottom of the disclaimer Form that he was taken by NIS Agents so and so from the job site under threat of arrest. He was currently held against his will and he is being deceitfully asked by a Dave Brown, identifying himself as the NIS Agent in 'Charge of the Case', to sign and endorse this document under Duress.

Michael screws the cap back on his pen, puts it back in his shirt pocket and hands the document back to Agent Brown. NIS Agent Dave Brown reads what has been written on the form by Michael.

"The 'Man' will be unhappy at your refusal to cooperate with the government."

"Based on my firsthand experience of the 'Rescue' and conversations with government employees, I believe that a Nuclear Accident took place yesterday and the government has been trying to cover it up."

Michael's gambit had its immediate results. The NIS Agent Dave Brown stiffens immediately and says in a measured tone of voice.

"This is a dangerous information to possess. You are not in Seattle. Your support organization is 3,500 miles away. Accidents have been known to happen to people away from home."

Now it is Michael's turn to stiffen at the veiled threat on his life, but he keeps his composure behind a poker face and tells NIS Agent Dave Brown in equally measured voice.

"I have mailed to our main office and a copy to our Company lawyer last night a detailed copy from my Diary of the sequence of events associated with the Rescue Mission on the submarine

SARGO with its registration number; accompanied with affidavits from eye witnesses and others knowledgeable of the facts, who explain the SARGO Incident as a nuclear accident and its aftermath. If something happens to me, I have instructed the recipients to immediately start an investigation pursuant to the Freedom of Information Act who has recently passed by Congress. Are you familiar with the Freedom of Information Act, Agent Brown?"

Agent Brown went pale. His lips quivering with impotent rage.

'I got them on the run'. Michael took heart. 'Why not go for the 'coup de grace'? He is thinking.

"I have sent a second copy of a letter to the Company in Seattle and the Company attorney over my concerns over the welfare and safety of the employees working on the Power Plant and The Demineralizing Facility a mere 40 yards away from the submarine SARGO; directing them in case of an accident to submit my Report to the GAO, General Accounting Office, together with a Complaint concerning John Doe, Taxpayer, and the way his money was being squandered by the Navy."

NIS Agent Dave Brown literally jumps from his seat, bumping his knee on the writing arm of his chair. He throws the blank tablet and defaced Secrecy Acts Form in his briefcase and kicks it shut. The door click is heard almost simultaneously with the bang of the shutting briefcase. Agent Brown abruptly exits the room, deserting his folding student chair. Michael pulls it closer to the stationary bench. He slouches comfortably against the padded wall and puts his feet up with a smug look on his face. He has put his head inside the lion's mouth and lived to talk about it.

*****

Meeting at NIS Agent Dave Brown's office. Present are the ROICC Commander Walsh, the OICC Captain Reinhardt and the

Admiral Alexander Riffey sitting comfortably in the wingback arm chair of honour, smoking a cigar. A television in front of them shows Michael in his cell with his feet up and a smug grin on his face.

Admiral Rifey is a one-star Admiral, called in the Navy Rear Admiral. Five ten. 160 pounds. He is sporting the wet hair look about him, a few years out of fashion. Dark hair, very pale skin, almost transparent. All his life he has been doing the dirty work of others. It paid off. He was promoted to Rear Admiral. He is now the 'hatchet man' of the Navy, and he's got others to do the dirty work for him. Typical government employee. Follows Orders. Gives Orders. Have always someone else to blame, if things go wrong.

Dave Brown opens the door and comes in. He is very agitated as he sets his briefcase down on the credenza of his desk, knocking over some family pictures in the process. After a period of silence, the Admiral speaks first, knocking the lengthening ash of his cigar into a standing ashtray by his wing back chair.

"I wish the SOB was on our side, working for us. I can't call it. The bastard has brass 'cojones', at any rate."

Captain Reinhardt wants to call an ambulance to take Michael with an induced heart attack which will not survive on his way to Tripler Military Hospital.

"Michael never bluffs. That has been my experience talking to him extensively." Commander Walsh puts in his two cents worth.

Everyone is looking at Dave Brown. He is an experienced investigator. What is he thinking?

"Michael got the Reports and his Diary with all the affidavits, out. I am thoroughly convinced of that by the way he was talking. It had the ring of 'fate accompli'. I wouldn't second guess him."

Commander Walsh agrees with Dave Brown.

Captain Reinhardt insists that Michael was bluffing and they ought to stop him by taking him out right there and then.

"Like the Change Order?" Commander Walsh lets it slip out.

"What Change Order?" Inquires Admiral Riffey.

Commander Walsh explains the issue of the Differing Site Conditions associated with the Demineralizing Facility. He brought it up to the OICC and was told by Captain Reinhardt to stonewall the matter.

"Michael got the best of us and now," Commander Walsh admits, "a $5,000.00 Change Order will end up North of $35,000.00. Because as I said before Michael does not bluff. He is like a bulldog. He never quits. Once he got a hold of something he will run it to the ground. That's who he is..."

Admiral Riffey interrupts Commander Walsh and issues the Final Decision: "We cannot take the risk at this time. The NIS should put Michael and everyone he comes in contact with under surveillance and see what develops. When the fact of whether he sent the documents out is verified and found that he did not, he should be taken out immediately, with no further discussion."

* * * * *

The two NIS Agents who escorted Michael in, enter the cell. They escort Michael out of the building the same way they had come in. When the steel building door closes behind him, Michael feels like Jonah, the moment he exited the whale. However, he keeps a poker face knowing full well that the surveillance cameras were all around him observing his every move and fascial expression.

The NIS car drops Michael off at the entrance to the construction site still open. He looks at his watch. Five o'clock in the afternoon. One hour past quitting time and Bill Scott is patiently waiting for him.

He is very circumspect with details of his ordeal. His life has been threatened. He is no longer certain whom he could trust and to what extent. There is only Bill Scott's car in the parking lot. Roxanne must have taken her truck home. They get into Bill's truck and leave the job site after locking the entrance. Unbeknown to them an unmarked NIS car is shadowing them discretely.

Chapter 11

Not Your Run of The Mill B&E

Bill Scott is driving Michael to the Hilton Hawaiian Village Hotel. The going is slow because they are caught in the tail end of the commuter rush hour traffic.

"Am I taking you out of your way, home?" Michael inquires concerned.

"My wife and I live in a condo along the Ala Wai canal in Waikiki." Bill responds.

Good Michael is thinking, just a couple of blocks from where Bill would be dropping me off.

"I didn't know you were married?" Michael says. Because a couple of years ago when their paths crossed in Berlin, New Hampshire, Michael would swear Bill Scott was single. At least he was behaving as if he was single.

"I got married, almost a year ago, to a young gal, in Lima, Peru." Bill provides the explanation relieving Michael of his extrapolations.

"I sure am glad you waited for me!" Michael exclaimed. "Did you call my wife?"

"I was getting ready to; but then you showed up in the nick of time. They kept you for six hours. What did they want?"

Michael tells Bill some parts of his interview. He leaves out the veiled threats on his life. Bill brings up that knowing the government, he wouldn't be surprised if the Navy turns loose a 'Death Squad' to sever all ties and witnesses to the SARGO Incident.

"I have not verbalized this uneasy feeling I have to anyone before this moment. I have developed this extra sense, which kept me alive in Viet Nam. I am sensing danger now. I feel the eyes of the jungle are watching us." Bill admits.

Michael gets goosebumps listening to Bill.

The conversation drifts back to their wives.

"I was hoping we will get a chance to go out together with our wives while you are here. However, now that you were made V-P in the company, this seems unlikely." Bill Scott complains.

Michael is shamed into inviting Bill and his wife for dinner that same night.

"7:30 PM at Michael's. It's located at the Colony Surf. It's a little after the Aquarium on the same beach road with all the iron wood trees. If you pass the Outrigger Canoe Club, you've gone too far. In that case keep going until you reach the fountain and go around it, backtracking." Michael says.

Bill Scott drops Michael off at the Hilton Hawaiian Village circular drive.

The NIS car goes across the street at the Hale Koa Hotel parking lot and waits.

Michael takes one of the elevators of the Rainbow Towers. Their rooms are on the top floor, right below the penthouse. Their suite has a breath-taking view of Diamond Head and Waikiki Beach in the East, all the way to the Waikiki Yacht Club and Ala Wai Yacht Harbor to the West. He uses his key card to enter their room. His wife is in the shower. The kids are watching a movie on TV. He is tempted to surprise his wife, Christina in the shower. Instead, he calls Michael's the restaurant and ups their reservation from two to four. He feels restless. He calls the Hotel lobby and checks on the baby-sitter situation. Everything was in order. She should be knocking on their suite door any minute now.

He goes in the kids' room through the interconnecting door with the Hotel menu. They've been to Castle Park all day and are sunburned and wore out. He is wondering in what condition, Christina was. He orders the same for both. This way there would be less fighting. For each a steak sandwich, french fries, fruit salad and ice cream. He tells them to get their drinks from the room bar.

A knock on the door. The baby-sitter has arrived. She looks like someone's grandma. Michael introduces her to the kids.

"They are supposed to stay in their room." He tells the baby-sitter. "I will lock the interconnecting door to our room."

He tells his son to tell the room service person, after he or she delivered their food, to go next door so Michael could sign the chit.

He closes and locks the interconnecting door behind him. Christina comes out of the shower.

"How was your day. You don't look sunburned."

"I sat all day reading a book under the umbrella and let the kids loose to run amok. The place was safe. Lifeguards and security all over the place. They had a ball."

Michael could tell that Christina was rearing to go. Michael tells her of the last-minute change of plans. The Scotts' would be dinning with them. Christina does not mind.

"However, keep in mind that I have designs on you after dinner." She adds.

Michael walks in the bathroom to take a shower. Christina on his heels.

"How was your day? Any more drills? What happened to SARGO? Still sitting tied up at the wharf?"

Michael answers laconically. He does not want the conversation to drift towards SARGO. He might slip and tell her about today's events and worry her needlessly. Christina goes next door to check on the kids and the sitter. Michael hears conversation in the hallway, it must be the room service, he is thinking. He puts on a clean Aloha shirt, tan slacks and deck shoes. He reminds himself next time he comes to Hawaii to bring a carry on and lose the suitcase, as he is looking at a closet full of suits he brought and will not wear.

Christina comes back in the room munching on French fries with one hand and holding a spear of pineapple with the other.

"The kids are fine watching TV." She announces. "They will probably go to bed early tonight. Too much fresh air and sun during the day."

Christina tells Michael that she informed the baby-sitter that they will back before midnight. They take the elevator to the lobby. The convertible is brought to them by the valet service. Michael tells Christina that he will be using the car from now on.

"Anyway, it's only for tomorrow. The next day you and the kids are welcome to come with me to the job site for the blessing by the Big Kahuna and the Luau afterwards. The next day after the blessing, we are leaving on the red eye flight to Seattle."

Christina is sad about leaving Hawaii, but excited about the blessing and the feast afterwards. New experiences.

They take the sightseeing route through Kalakaua Avenue to the heart of Waikiki. They cut through Kapiolani Park along the iron wood tree lined drive. Diamond Head is looming up ahead. A full moon is peaking around the corner by the lighthouse. The Honolulu City lights sparkle behind them. They arrive at the Colony Surf parking lot. They get out of their car and make their way towards Michael's. They are shown to their table. They are the first to arrive.

The place is elegant. French food with a Continental ambiance. Christina orders Absolute on the rocks with a twist. Michael a Beck's beer. They are both hungry, so Michael orders the blackened Ahi as an appetizer. It is sheared yellow fin tuna cooked on the outside only and basted with Cajun spices to about a quarter inch depth and raw in the middle. The pieces are thinly sliced and stacked in rows for easy picking with chopsticks. Framed and surrealistically decorated with a mixture of mustard sauces. They devour it in no time.

Bill Scott appears at the end of the restaurant following the Maître D with a little girl in tow. She did not look over sixteen years old. 'She couldn't be his wife', Michael and Christina are whispering. 'She does not look old enough to drink.'

Bill introduces his wife, Maria.

Up close, she looks no more than eighteen years old, five two, vivacious, curly black hair, voluptuous with fire in her eyes. Very animated when she tries to introduce herself to Michael and his wife. She uses her hands to make a point and has a tendency to touch people to drive her point home. 'She looks hot in bed'. Michael is thinking.

"She is twenty-one years old." Bill Scott says looking at Michael. "I met her in Lima, Peru. I was there, a year ago, building a paper mill for Georgia Pacific, getting over a divorce. The job site was out of town on the shores of the Amazon River. Maria, barely eighteen, she was paddling her uncle's canoe every day and was selling food and drinks to the laborers. She as basically operating a lunch wagon on the water. I was buying my lunch every day from her and the romance blossomed. Within a few months we got married in Lima, although she was eighteen and I was fifty at the time. When the job was over, I brought her back to the United States. She is attending the University of Hawaii School of Nursing. She will be a Registered Nurse in another year."

Maria proves to be bubbly and delightful person. She tells them of her adventures on the Amazon River, fighting crocodiles and some other human reptiles who were trying to take advantage of a single eighteen-year-old girl.

Bill and Michael can't help but laugh at the jokes and adventures of Maria. Christina, however, really gets into them. She asks questions and monopolizes the evening with Maria. She catches Michael and Bill exchange conspiratorial looks. She is sensing a cloud hanging over them.

The waiter comes over and they order. Michael orders a Chateaunef Du Pape by La Fiolle which will go very well with the French Onion soup.

Maria continues with stories from Peru. Comparing the poverty there with the splendour of the restaurant they were presently sitting. Christina catches Michael and Bill communicating in some kind of Code and abruptly changes the subject.

"What's the latest with SARGO?" She asks Bill Scott.

Bill is silent looking at Michael.

Christina using the Socratic approach elicits from Bill what happened today. She is horrified that the government can behave in such a way. If it was anyone else it would be tantamount to kidnapping. Kidnapping her husband, holding him incommunicado for close to six hours.

"I wouldn't be surprised if these NIS characters were spying on us this very minute in the restaurant." Christina says.

"I doubt it." Says Michael. "Not because of any decency on their part, merely because they could not afford the prices of this restaurant. They would have a heck of a time justifying the price of the meal in their expense account. After all, living well is the best revenge."

Michael changes the topic of the conversation to that of the upcoming blessing of the job site by the Big Kahuna. Maria finds that Christina is coming and she wants to come also. She will cut school that day. Bill relents and agrees to bring her along.

The rest of the evening moves along. Good food. Good drink. Good friends. They finally, sated, leave the restaurant. In the car Christina is pressing Michael about details of the NIS interrogation. Michael is evasive. In the hotel they knock on the kid's door. The baby-sitter opens. The kids are asleep. They were no trouble at all. Michael pays the babysitter. She leaves. They quietly close the kids room door on their way out. They go next door to their room.

Michael unlocks the door. It opens three inches and stops. The chain is across from the inside of the room. How could that be? They got out of their room; not the kid's room. Someone put the chain from the inside of their room after they left. Michael goes pale. He looks up and down the hallway. All is quiet. Not a sound from inside their room.

They go back to the kid's room. Michael calls the front desk. Security men are running down the hallway in no time. A big Samoan crashes the door of their room breaking the chain. The room is in shambles. Even the stuffing is sliced out of the chairs. The bed mattress is sliced. All the drawers are pulled out and the contents dumped on the floor. The sliding door to the ocean front Lanai is open. Michael remembers closing and locking it. He goes out to the Lanai. Their room is forty-two stories up. How could someone climb up or down without being seen? With the room chained from the inside it is obviously he or she or they got in and out through the Lanai.

Michael looks up. The Penthouse and the roof. He can see the faint rope chafing on the stucco wall. They must have gotten onto the roof and rappelled down to the Lanai.

"We must be dealing with the Hawaii version of the Spiderman." He tells the head of Hilton security standing with him on the Lanai.

"It certainly is not your run of the mill B & E." The head of Hilton security says drawing a deep breath. "Your room was targeted."

"I bet they left the same way they got in. With the Lanai door open and the entrance to the room blocked from the inside, whoever was in the room had plenty of warning and time to get out in a hurry if need be and be assured of a clean getaway if the outside surveillance failed to warn them." Michael concluded.

"It sounds like you know who the perpetrator may be." The head of security said thoughtfully.

"I don't know for sure. I am guessing." Michael admitted. "The government Agencies have certainly learned from the Watergate fiasco." Michael added coming back to the room.

The chief of security for the Hilton Hawaiian Village hotel complex is very disturbed at the daring and skill of the perpetrators.

"Can you tell what's missing?" He asked Michael

"My briefcase and all the loose papers and documents I had left lying around the room."

The Honolulu Police Department had been called and finally arrive on the scene.

"This is not a burglary." They conclude after they went over the scene. "This is a professional hit."

They proceed to interview Michael. Who he is and what is he doing in Hawaii. As soon as they learn and hear NIS, they call the Navy Intelligence at Pearl Harbor Naval Shipyard and Report the incident.

Within minutes of the HPD call two new NIS Agents show up. Michael takes them aside.

"Get a message to Agent Dave Brown that unless my briefcase and all the documents are not returned to me before breakfast at 7:00 AM, I am calling a Press Conference."

"We don't know of a Dave Brown. Not with the NIS anyway." The two NIS Agents protest in unison.

Christina overhears their conversation. As soon as everyone leaves the room, she grills Michael. He tells her everything, leaving Roxanne out.

The hotel changes their suite for one a floor below. An army of hotel employees transfer their belongings to the new suite of rooms. The sleeping kids are transported on roll away beds and deposited in their new room permanent beds.

Michael and Christina go to bed apprehensive of what the future holds. They love Hawaii but they are definitely afraid of their government. Their romantic evening had turned into a disaster.

Chapter 12

A Signed Blank Cheque

Michael wakes up because of a persistent knock on the door. He is still sleepy. The HPD didn't leave their room until three in the morning. He opens the door. A HPD Police Officer, a mere patrolman, is standing outside the door in full regalia holding a sealed banker's box.

"I was directed to deliver this box to you sir before seven o'clock this morning." He says snapping at attention.

"What's in the box?" Michael asks before attempting to touch the banker's box which by the way the Police Officer was handling, did not appear to be very heavy.

"I don't know sir. The box was given to me by one of my superiors with no explanation other than where, to whom and at what time to hand deliver it."

Michael gets the box and closes the door to his room. He had a good idea as to what was inside the box. A present from the non-existent NIS Agent Dave Brown.

He cuts the tape and opens the box. Inside he finds his briefcase and all the loose papers. Everything appears to be in order. Everything is there...except the Diary with the affidavits and Navy letters folded inside it. Michael is worried. If the NIS got their hands on his Diary, he better be prepared to convince them once again that he made copies of the pertinent pages when he said he did and has mailed them to his Home Office and his lawyer in the mainland.

He picks the shirt he wore yesterday from the floor. There are two pieces of paper folded in the breast pocket. One of them was the notes he made of the name and registration number of the submarine before they were painted over. The other was the copy of the speed letter he handed Commander Walsh. He puts them both in his briefcase.

Christina has decided that she and the kids will definitely be staying at the hotel. Go swimming in the lagoon and ocean. Eat hamburgers at the poolside snack bar. Come to the room after lunch for a nap. Michael promises that he will call her from work.

Michael has the rental car brought around by the valet service. He gets in and starts down Ala Moana Boulevard heading for Pearl Harbor Naval Shipyard. An NIS unmarked car is following him. Michael is unaware that he is under surveillance. He drives leisurely checking the bouncing tits of the morning joggers at the Ala Moana Park. He breaks hard to admire a particular enticing set of natural boobs. The NIS car right behind him just about rear ends Michael's car. The agents make a note of Michael's interest in the hard bodies.

Michael arrives on site after nine o'clock. Roxanne is back. Michael is tense and jumpy. Roxanne senses Michael's apprehension. She flirts with him shamelessly. She finds a moment alone with him and corners him pressing her tits on him. Michael backs into a wall looking over her shoulder, scarred that someone will step in her office and find them in a compromising position. She stuffs her hand in the front of his pants. Michael misunderstands her gesture. After she removes her hand, he realizes that she stuffed in his pants his silk boxer shorts, he left at her house the other day. His pants are now are bulging at the crotch.

Roxanne asks him playfully, staring at his crotch, if he is glad to see her. She turns around and picks her purse. From the inside she retrieves Michaels Diary stuffed with affidavits, the original Navy letters and hands it to him.

"I've taken care of sending copies to the Home Office in Seattle, yesterday, as you requested."

A big weight is lifted form Michael's shoulders. Michael is feeling compelled to hug and kiss Roxanne. A good thing he did not follow through to his impulse because Bill Scott enters Roxanne's office. Michael asks him whether the Navy delivered the Geiger Counter.

"They did not." Was Bill's response "However, you and I are invited to attend a meeting with the OICC Captain; starting in about ten minutes." Bill says consulting his watch. "I was coming to get you."

Roxanne right then remembers that she had a message for Michael.

"The OICC had called." Roxanne hands the message to Michael.

Michael looks at her. She knows she made a mistake not letting him know right away. Michael is thinking that he broke one of his rules. Getting overly familiar with the hired help. His mother drummed into him since childhood that 'familiarity breeds contempt'. He is packing his briefcase for the meeting placing his Diary in its compartment, while quietly considering what to do with Roxanne.

* * * * *

A meeting is taking place at the OICC Office between Captain Reinhardt, Commander Walsh, Michael and Bill Scott. Michael opens up aggressively demanding to know why the Geiger Counter was not on site.

Captain Reinhardt tells him that it is not coming because it is not necessary.

"You are not going to force the Navy, ultimately the taxpayers, into added expense running unnecessary tests. The SARGO Incident was no more than a scheduled Navy exercise to test their emergency procedures in case of a nuclear accident. If you feel differently, go ahead and contact the newspapers. The government has nothing to hide. However, if you insist and implement your threat, the government will take the position that you are making False Statements. In that case you will be indicted and criminally prosecuted to the full extent of the law, together with your staff as co-conspirators."

Bill Scott is visibly shaken over the last statement.

Michael knows that Captain Reinhardt is bluffing. He adopted Napoleon's strategy. A good defence, is a good offense. However, he has no proof or even evidence to call him on his bluff. He is staring at Captain Reinhardt. He looks at Commander Walsh. He cannot make up his mind who is shaken more at the moment, Commander Walsh or Bill Scott. He stares again at Captain Reinhardt, eye ball to eye ball. Time will tell or time will cure all, Michael is thinking.

Captain Reinhardt senses that he has gained some sort of intangible tactical advantage and presses on, changing the subject at the same time.

"The Navy feels that the Change Order in the amount of $35,000.00 is exorbitant." Captain Reinhardt pronounces.

Michael points out the direct costs associated with the Demobilization and Re-Mobilization together with the field staff salaries and expenses, come close to $35,000.00.

"There are also indirect costs associated with the thirty-day Suspension of Work which will require commensurate Contract Completion Day extension." Michael adds.

Michael goes on to explain how time translates into money utilizing the Eichleay formula.

The two Navy officers don't know what Michael is talking about.

Michael launches into the legal explanation of the theory of Unabsorbed Overhead as was argued in the early sixties in front of the ASBCA, Armed Services Board of Contract Appeals, by the

Eichleay Corporation of Pittsburgh, Pennsylvania vs. The United States.

Michael easily demonstrates that he has superior knowledge and that he is no match for the two Navy officials.

Captain Reinhardt senses that the tables have now turned. The Navy is now at a disadvantage. He wants the meeting to end.

"Thank you for the clarification." He addresses Michael. "The Navy will review the aspects of the Change when direction from the NAVFAC arrives and will get back to the Contractor."

Michael and Bill Scott leave the meeting.

* * * * *

The Captain and the Commander have a wrap up meeting to review how they stood.

"Is Michael an attorney?" Captain Reinhardt asks.

"I don't know.", Commander Walsh responds. "The FBI background Report indicates," the Commander reads from the Report in his hands, "that he is a naturalized U.S. citizen since 1973. Born in Hydra, Greece. Graduated from Washington State University in 1970, in Chemical Engineering and he got his Professional Chemical Engineering License in 1973. He is registered in the State of Washington. Married in 1969 and still is with the same woman. Two children. He signed and keeps signing every year all the paperwork required, because he belongs to the Studies and Observations Group, for life since 1970. This means that he was considered at that time one of the smartest people in the Country, back in 1970. That's all. Nothing about being a lawyer."

"Well, he talks like one." Captain Reinhardt adds. "As for being smart, I'd vouch for that. I would advise caution. You may be thinking you are dealing with an Engineer, when in fact a ringer has slipped against us in the line-up. I feel however, comfortable that I hosed fear on Michael in sufficient quantity that the fear the Navy had that he would be going to the press, has been averted. At least for the time being. This does not mean that we are safe. Michael is a time bomb ready to go off. The NIS were unable to find his Diary with the affidavits. So, it looks like he was not bluffing. You were right Commander. However, I am afraid that's not the last of it. As you said he will keep on digging and one of these days, the time bomb will go off on our faces. The Navy has to get the upper hand…or else. I assigned Dave Brown and the NIS the task to keep digging to find something to hold over Michael's head."

Commander Walsh was just listening with no input to his superior's monologue.

"Look what he did with the Change Order." Captain Reinhardt continued. "The bastard has taken the government's own Rules and Regulations and somehow, he turned them around against us. Time now is working against the government."

"We need some kind of leverage." Commander Walsh said. "Something to bring Michael into the negotiating table, when the time comes, in a temperate mood to actually be reasonable. Each time I have faced him so far, I felt gaged and hogtied, while Michael walked in with an Uzi, set at full automatic…"

"I know what you mean." Captain Reinhardt agrees. "I know exactly what we need and the man to carry out the dirty deed."

Captain Reinhardt picks up the phone and says something to his secretary. A few minutes later a distinguished looking, in a British sort of way, handlebar moustache and all, gentleman, walks in. The

Captain introduces him to the Commander, as John Muchmore. A Civilian Engineer from MIDPAC assigned to the OICC Command for special projects.

"Have we got a project for you John!" The Captain exclaimed.

Captain Reinhardt goes briefly into the Change Order that has necessitated the issue of the Suspension of Work letter.

"The contractor is unreasonable..." Captain Reinhardt announces.

"The Navy cannot have an unruly contractor on their hands." John Muchmore pronounces. "How much of a negotiating leverage would you like?" He addresses the Captain.

The Captain is delighted that Muchmore has caught on immediately. He appreciates an Iago type character with his lips firmly planted on his superior's asshole, whoever that may be. It was the Navy way. Muchmore will prove himself to be 'a Rear Admiral' in the truest sense of the word.

"Notify the Consulting Engineering firm who prepared the Drawings and the Specifications," Muchmore addresses both Navy officers, "to go over, with a fine-tooth comb, all the contractor's submittals on the proposed equipment. Compare them with the Specifications and the Drawings and find ways and reasons to reject them for noncompliance with the Contract. Keep doing that way indefinitely with each new submittal, until this Michael fellow sees the error of his ways and comes to the negotiating table."

"I will have the bastard on his knees begging to do the Change Order at No Cost to the government!" Captain Reinhardt exclaims.

He turns to Commander Walsh and tells him to spread the word to the Navy inspector and CME on the project to be 'fussy' on the quality of the finished product and tough on safety.

Commander Walsh puts a half-hearted moral argument as to the legality for the Navy treating a contractor differently from the others. Captain Reinhardt gives him a steely stare, stopping the Commander in mid-sentence. The mood in the room is silent acquiescence. After all the government signs their pay checks. Michael, in a way, represents a threat to their pay checks and careers.

Commander Walsh and John Muchmore leave the Captain's office.

Captain Reinhardt gets on the phone to Rear Admiral Riffey at CINCPACFLT.

"The dam leak has been temporarily plugged." He announces cryptically. "I don't know whether the patch will hold or for how long. In the meantime, the NIS will keep up surveillance on the subject and inform. As soon as the subject becomes a target, it will be eliminated..."

"I don't want to know details!" Admiral Riffey cuts Captain Reinhardt off, with emphasis. "You are authorized to use your own judgement and make the call. I will be busy for the next few days. Admiral Hyman Rickover is on his way from Washington DC to Honolulu to investigate the SARGO Incident. Admiral Rickover has a lot riding on this because he was the one who originally made the decision to adopt the pressurized water-cooling system utilized in all the Polaris - Class nuclear submarines. I'd advise you to work in close contact with Dave Brown of the NIS and stop the leak, at first opportunity, permanently and with prejudice. However, exercise at the same time all due caution. Do not act hastily, because the Navy could not afford a battle at this point on yet another front."

* * * * *

Michael and Bill are walking back to the job site from their meeting at the OICC. Bill seems to think that the meeting went very well.

"The Navy just handed you a signed blank check." Bill Scott announces.

"The Navy will tighten inspections and job safety requirements as a result." Michael warns Bill. "They will raise the subjective standards of good workmanship. You should make the subcontractors aware of this."

"The Navy will lose interest after a while." Is Bill's response, "Particularly if they find out that their moves have been anticipated. The government rarely acts without the element of surprise on their side."

"I decided to go to the 'mattresses' against the Navy over the Change Order. I am determined to collect all the money due under the Terms of the Contract. The way the government behaves, I bet you it will end up in excess of the $35,000.00 currently on the table. Every day the Navy delays in providing direction, the Quantum of the Change will be that much more. The Merit of the Change is no longer an issue, since the Navy issued a Change Order."

"We will prevail." Bill speaks prophetically. "I have never known you to be wrong in the past. Plus, you have perseverance and tenacity, which the Navy lacks, in the long run. What do you think on the SARGO Incident?"

"I am not sure any more." Michael admits. "Maybe it was an exercise. I'll let it play out. I am not going to take the gamble and go public for the time being. Just watch what happens from this point on and let me know with periodic Reports. I believe the government is their own worst enemy. Let them have enough rope and they will hang themselves."

The SARGO is where they left it. The SP's have barricaded the through access on the Bayshore Drive. Two NIS Agents are sitting outside the construction site, parked in an unmarked white, four door American made sedan with all four windows open. Michael and Bill wave at them as they walk by towards the gate.

They walk into the office trailer and Michael calls a meeting with Steve Crane, Roxanne Malone and Bill Scott. He summarizes the salient points of their meeting at the OICC Office. He warns them that the construction site is under surveillance by the NIS. Steve tells Michael that he is having problems negotiating with the Big Kahuna's representative.

"He refuses to be tied down to a specific sum of money." Steve Crane admits.

"I'll tell you what." Michael informs Steve. "I am willing to part with $2,000.00 for the blessing. $500.00 for the Big Kahuna and $1,500.00 for the Luau. Make the whole thing a package deal. I am certain that since the blessing is followed by a Luau, the Big Kahuna's family must have gone into the catering business by now. At any rate, two "G's" is the price of superstition."

"There is no work being conducted due to the Navy Suspension of Work letter." Steve admits. "We will wait for your next trip here to negotiate the Change with the Navy. As for the blessing, I think the postponement will work to our advantage to convince the Big Kahuna to be reasonable. I will tell his representative that $2,000.00

was the limit or we will start exploring other options and approach his competitors. I am sure the Big Kahuna will take our offer."

Roxanne hands Michael a typed Report straight out of his Diary on the SARGO Incident. She has made several copies. Michael puts one of the copies in his briefcase. He tells her to mail one copy to a Law Firm in Seattle for which he provides her with an address, and directs her to mark on the outside of the envelope, PERSONAL TO THE ATTENTION OF DON DAVIDSON.

He hands Roxanne his original Diary and tells her to drive over to the Hilton Hawaiian Village.

"It is now 11:15 AM. At 12:00 noon, go to the poolside bar and grill. My wife Christina will be there with my kids. A boy ten and a girl seven. Identify yourself, have lunch with them and hand my wife the Diary with all the documents inside it. After you leave them mail the Report, I just gave you and then go home. We will all leave here from the job site at the same time." Michael says pointing to Bill and Roxanne. "Steve, you stay to lock up. The NIS will be at a quandary with three cars involved, whom to follow. I bet they follow mine."

Roxanne puts the Diary in her purse and goes to her car. Michael and Bill Scott go out also. Two pickup trucks and a convertible make their way out the job site gate going in opposite directions. The NIS car follows Bill's truck and Michael's convertible which both turned left at the job site gate. Roxanne's truck has turned right. No one has followed her. Roxanne, with no surveillance behind is going to Honolulu by the Makalapa Gate, getting on 78 passing the Aloha Stadium.

Chapter 13

The Weak Link

Michael and Bill are aware that they have drawn the NIS tail. They set off at a brisk pace towards the Ward Centre parking structure. They park on the 4th floor and go to lunch at Ryan's. The NIS car parks on the first floor watching both entrance and exit. Michael carries in his breast pocket an envelope with the typed Diary pages folded inside. Bill and Michael go in the restaurant. Michael gives his name at the reservation desk. Lunch for two at 12 and goes to the phone bank at the restaurant lounge. He calls Hilton Hawaiian Village and asks to be connected to the pool side bar and grill. When he is connected, he asks for Christina to be paged. She comes to the phone a few minutes later.

"What's all this 'cloak and dagger' shit?" She inquires as soon as she finds out that her husband is on the other end.

"The NIS has me under surveillance. I found my Diary. It was in the field office trailer. The field office secretary will be there in 15 minutes to deliver it to you. Keep it someplace safe and out of the passers-by sight. Her name is Roxanne. Treat her to lunch."

He then goes and describes Roxanne and what she will be wearing.

* * * * *

Roxanne takes the King Street exit from the H-1 freeway and backtracks along Kuhio Avenue all the way to the Hilton Hawaiian Village. She pulls up at the main entrance circular drive and leaves the pickup truck engine running for the valet service. No one is following her. She makes her way to the pool side snack bar. She zeroes in on Christina sitting alone with children's clothes, towels and toys on adjacent chairs. The kids are swimming in the pool.

Roxanne approaches Christina's table in the crowded Bar. Christina raises her head from the book she was reading and looks her over. Roxanne has that slutty look about her that Michael finds attractive in women. He seems to think it makes them look sensuous. Christina is the opposite. She has that lady look. She is not into role playing. Instinctively, she does not like the look behind Roxanne's smile that says: 'I know something you do not'.

They introduce themselves. Christina makes Roxanne aware that Michael had called her and told her that he was sending over a messenger to deliver an article of his; she extends her hand to receive Michael's Diary. Christina's tone of voice takes the air out of Roxanne's sails, as she obediently hands over the Diary from her purse. Christina lets it drop inside her open beach bag by her feet.

Christina invites Roxanne to sit down and have lunch with her and the kids. Roxanne sits down. Christina looks her over at eye level. An uneasy feeling is hovering over her. Roxanne still has that: 'I am going to steal your husband'; look about her. Christina flags down a waiter and orders three hamburgers with potato chips, a Hilton Hawaiian Village specialty. Roxanne orders the same together with a bloody Mary from the bar.

Christina and Roxanne find that it is easy to talk to each other. Their conversation always returns back to Michael. Roxanne tells Christina anecdotes from work, while Christina relays some of the lighter moments of their personal life. Their food and drinks arrive. Christina calls the kids from the pool. They come running drying themselves in their towels. They sit down and attack their burgers and potato chips.

Roxanne and Christina pace themselves eating and stealing glances at each other. They find they like each other, but sense that Michael will remain the apple of the 'Eris' between them, which will prevent them from ever becoming friends. Christina wants to keep exclusively what she has. Roxanne wants what Christina has and is not trying to hide it. The kids wolf down their lunch and are off to the swimming pool. Christina is not a believer of the old wives tale dictating to wait a couple of hours after you eat before resuming physical activities.

Roxanne and Christina attract looks from neighbouring tables of sales conventioneers drinking their lunch. They start flirting with both of them. The kids come back from the pool thirsty and dripping; clumsily wrapping themselves with the towels trying to get a drink of soda, breaking up the convention of the 'Sancho's' at its inception.

* * * *

Michael calls Seattle from Ryan's, long distance using his telephone credit card. He asks for Don Davidson, his friend, mentor and partner of the prestigious law firm of Fergusson and Burdell on Union Square Building in Seattle. After the pleasantries of being in Paradise, Michael gets into the heart of the matter concerning the purpose of his phone call, the SARGO Incident. Don Davidson realizes the seriousness of the situation. Michael's life may be in danger.

"Where are you calling me from?" Don Davidson inquires.

"Public telephone bank at a restaurant. I am mailing you copies of my Diary describing the Incident I've witnessed, affidavits from other witnesses as the event was happening, the Navy's formal responses and Minutes of subsequent meetings. I have been under surveillance; being followed at all times by an NIS car."

"You are under surveillance for the time being. That's the good news. You have not become a target yet. Otherwise, there would be a small army of cars following you around. The government subscribes to the overkill notion."

"I will fly back to Seattle in a couple of days. How about lunch on Monday? You should have my documents I marked PERSONAL."

"Fine, but if you need legal advice and/or intervention while you are still there, we have reciprocal privileges with Howard Hodick's Office in Honolulu. Their address is downtown on Bishop Street."

"That is not very far from where I am calling you. Ward Street."

"I will call Howard as soon as I hang up with you and give him a heads up."

"It's almost lunch time in Honolulu. Howard may have plans. I will give him a couple of hours and then go there."

"If you have duplicates of the documents you sent me, give a set to Howard. Howard will treat the documents confidentially. I will talk to him."

Michael thanks Don and hangs up. He hears his name being paged that their table is ready. He sends Bill Scott over to be seated. He will be right behind him. He just needs to make another call. He tells Bill to order a Weisteiner on Draft for him. He calls Hilton Hawaiian Village and tells the operator to page Roxanne Malone in the Rainbow Tower pool side snack bar.

* * * *

Roxanne is playing with Michael's children. Children are her Achilles heel. She does not have any yet, after an unsuccessful marriage. The time clock is ticking and she is not getting any younger with each stroke. Michael's kids are adorable. They could or rather should have been hers if she had gone to WSU, the same College as Michael. She would then be sitting where this woman with the lady like bitchiness written all over her face and her condescending manners.

Christina is not making things easier for Roxanne, with a content look on her face shouting out in silence: 'Look what I have created with Michael. They are adorable and they are mine'. The kids, particularly the boy, are showing off for Roxanne. Roxanne hears her name paged. She goes to the bar phone. Michael is on the other end. He tells her that he is with Bill Scott at Ryan's in Ward Centre about to have lunch. He asks her to come over in an hour and a half to Ryan's to give him a ride downtown. The NIS is parked on the first floor. Michael was going to send Bill Scott first in the hope that NIS will follow his truck. He needs her because downtown is very busy. Virtually no parking available at that hour. He needs to deliver some documents. She will drop him off on her run-down Bishop Street; circle the block and pick him up 10 to 15 minutes later from the same spot she had dropped him off.

Roxanne goes back to the table. She explains to Christina that the phone call was from Michael. He needed her for something confidential. She plays with her tone of voice and on the fact that Michael had chosen her in his hour of need. Christina about had it with the late work, the weird hours, the break-ins, boxes mysteriously delivered overnight with the proceeds of the robbery, NIS, SARGO and now this Roxanne who's been seeing lately of Michael more than herself and looks like Michael's wet dream poster girl, going to do with her husband who knows what.

Roxanne excuses herself and goes to the nearby boutique. She comes out wearing the sexiest Brazilian bikini imaginable. She comes to the table, drops her clothes on a chair with her purse and tells Christina to watch them for her. She goes over by the pool and does a spectacular dive. Todd, the boy, is in love with her. Roxanne is hugging and kissing the kids. Roughhouses with them in the swimming pool, wrestling and splashing. Christina is seething but maintains the lady like facade.

* * * * *

Bill Scott and Michael are sitting in the main dining room of Ryan's at a window table overlooking the Kewalo Basin where all the Charter fishing boats in Honolulu come back to tie-up and show off the day's catch of Marlin and Yellow Fin Tuna for picture taking with the lucky fisherman and advertisement for future charters.

They have plenty of time, so they eat their lunch slowly enjoying every morsel of Ono for Michael and Papio for Bill. Bill realizes that in a little while, he will act as a decoy. He is alright with this. Michael was the 'rain man', the money maker for the company. Bill would like to work for him exclusively. When it's said and done money talks, bull shit walks. Michael is a bottom-line kind of guy. His bottom line translates into big bonuses for the people working for him. The sooner the Navy settles with him on that Change Order, the better they all will be. He'd seen it before. If the Navy choses to play games, six months from now, they would wish they had the time back to start all over. Live and learn.

* * * * *

Bill Scott is driving the pick-up truck out of the Ward Centre parking structure. The NIS car starts. Moves a few feet forward starting to follow the pick-up truck. They stop abruptly, because one of the Agents sees out of the corner of his eye, Roxanne coming into the parking structure, driving another company pick-up truck. The NIS surveillance car makes a 'U' turn, comes back and hides among the other parked cars on the first floor, waiting. Bill Scott's pick-up truck is long gone, unescorted.

* * * * *

Roxanne enters the restaurant. Waves off the hostess and makes a bee line for Michael's table by the window. Before Michael could react, she plants a passionate kiss on his lips right there in public, asserting the rights of a wife dropping in on her husband. Heads of nearby patrons turn, witnessing the scene. Michael is too absorbed addressing an envelope to notice. Roxanne has taken the role of the wife trying to convince her workaholic husband to take the afternoon off for a 'nooner'. Michael is oblivious to the audience that are about to cheer: 'Go for it'. Instead, he methodically explains to Roxanne the sequence of events for a successful operation.

Roxanne is there in body only. In her mind she is in bed somewhere with Michael. She strokes his hair. Her fascial expression betrays her thoughts. One of the NIS Agents surreptitiously made it inside the restaurant and is hiding behind the fern grotto by the entrance. He sees Michael and Roxanne all alone at the table. The way Roxanne is trying to virtually make love to Michael in public. 'Lucky prick', he is thinking. 'I bet a pay check, he is porking her'.

The waiter comes to their table with the credit card and the bill imprint. Michael signs and takes the credit card and the yellow copy of the credit card transaction. They are getting up. Roxanne puts her arm in Michael's like an adoring wife. The NIS Agent makes a note of all this. He breaks surveillance to join his partner in the waiting car.

Michael and Roxanne go to the company pick-up truck. Roxanne is driving. The NIS surveillance car is following them at a distance with several other cars in between. The pick-up truck turns left on Ward Street and then immediately right on Ala Moana Boulevard at the stop light. They stay on Ala Moana Boulevard for a while until they pass the new Federal Building. They turn right on Alakea Street and then 'Makai' on Bishop Street. Bishop Street is one way down to Ala Moana Boulevard. The NIS car veers off several lanes to the right hiding in the traffic.

The pick-up truck pulls to the left curb just before Queen Street. Michael gets out of the truck. The NIS car stays put, watching. Roxanne moves on turning left on Queen Street to go around the block. She turns left at first opportunity to go back up, 'Mauka', on Alakea Street.

Michael walks into the Dillingham Building. One of the NIS Agents gets out of the car and follows him in. Michael catches the elevator with two secretaries loaded with legal documents. The elevator stops on the 24th floor. The NIS Agent is waiting in the building lobby, his eyes glued on the elevator status indicator. The elevator starts coming down. The NIS Agent goes to the Building Directory and sees that the entire twenty fourth floor is occupied by the Law Offices of Howard Hoddick. He makes a note of this on his pad and goes out of the building, back to the waiting NIS car.

* * * * *

Michael comes out of the elevator. He opens and holds the door to the Law Offices open for the secretaries. Howard Hoddick is standing in the Law Offices lobby in front to the reception counter, in person. He introduces himself to Michael. Michael takes the envelope out of his breast pocket and hands it to Howard Hoddick.

Howard Hoddick is in his sixties. Five foot six. Compact. 200 pounds. White hair. Well groomed. Aloha shirt, tasteful, not what the tourists wear. He exuded presence and power. Michael would want him for an ally. He would have spelled trouble for the enemy. Red nose and cheeks. He liked his afternoon Martini's; Michael was thinking.

Howard invites Michael back to his office. He opens the envelope and extracts the typed Diary pages and the affidavits. He asks Michael to number them and sign at bottom of each one in his presence. Howard witnesses Michael's signature. He then calls a secretary in. He puts all the documents in a pre-addressed envelope with Don Davidson's name and address and places the whole works in a Federal Express envelope and seals it. He tells Michael, giving the envelope to his secretary, that Fed Ex will be in the office within the hour for their daily pick-up. Don Davidson will have the documents overnight. He gives Michael a couple of his business cards and Michael gives him one of his with a one-dollar bill attached.

"You are now officially my client, while you are in Hawaii; by reciprocity to Fergusson and Burdell to which you are already a client. I will be one phone call way for immediate action." Howard Hoddick assures Michael.

Michael thanks him for all his help and takes the elevator down to the building lobby. He goes out of the Dillingham Building and stands on the sidewalk of Bishop Street. Roxanne comes down Bishop Street. She stops the pick-up at the curb. Michael gets in. Roxanne has been a nervous wreck all this time that Michael was away. She saw an NIS Agent following him inside the building. She was afraid Michael would end up down an elevator shaft. Her worry turns into relief and exuberance now that Michael is back safe and sound.

They turn left on Ala Moana Boulevard to get back to Ward Centre parking structure and Michael's rental car on the fourth floor. At Roxanne's initiative, every stop for a red light, becomes a hot bed of desire as they both behave like sex starved teenagers. The NIS surveillance cars following them making careful notes of their behaviour. They were probably wishing they had a video camera with them. Michael and Roxanne receive honks of approval by early commuter cars. Finally, they arrive where Michael had parked his car.

* * * * *

The NIS Agents report to Dave Brown. They conclude that Michael has succeeded in getting the story out. Agent Brown realizes that the SOB bluffed them out of their shorts the other day. They now have to be very careful with him, because there are two sets of lawyers involved. One local and the other in the mainland.

The only bright spot for the government is Roxanne, the secretary. Dave Brown and the two NIS Agents conducting the surveillance suspect that Michael is having an affair with her. Dave Brown orders the two NIS Agents that henceforth to concentrate on Roxanne.

"The other woman is always the weak link." He concludes. "If you catch her with Michael in 'fragrante dillecto' our problem will be solved. We will have something on Michael. If he gives us trouble, he will be discredited."

He orders the two Agents to pretend to arrest Roxanne and bring her in, at the earliest opportunity, terrify her and see what shakes out of the tree.

Chapter 14

The Confidential Informant

Michael leaves the Ward Centre parking structure. He suspects that the NIS surveillance has been terminated. He is worried that he needs to mend a lot of fences as far as Christina was concerned. He stops at Ala Moana Shopping

Centre. He buys a two-pound box of Godiva dark chocolate truffles from the Liberty House. On his way down the escalator he spots at a Jewellery store, a pink coral ring on display surrounded by pearls. He buys it on the spot.

Michael comes in their room. He finds Christina crying quietly. The kids are taking a nap in their room with the interconnecting door closed. Michael closes their room door softly. He takes Christina in his arms hugging her tightly and assures her that he had not gone to bed with Roxanne. He admits that he is infatuated with Roxanne, but he will never leave his wife. Christina is the one he loves. She is the one and only.

They lock the kids room door and make love tenderly. Christina feels a lot better. Michael surprises her with the box of Godiva chocolates, which he knows are her favourite and the pearl with pink coral ring. It fits her perfectly. Christina behaves like a little kid at Christmas with her presents. The noise wakes up the children. They start pounding on the room interconnecting door until Michael unlocks it. The immediately spot the box of chocolate truffles and charge on it. Christina hordes the truffles. It's her present. Michael tells the kids that it is too close to dinner and eating chocolates before dinner will spoil their appetite.

They get dressed and walk over to the Bon Appetite restaurant. It is almost across the street, on Ala Moana Boulevard, from the Hilton Hawaiian Village Hotel. It is a French restaurant Michael explains on the way.

"As long as they don't serve guts and stuff." Todd protests.

"Don't order sweetbreads then..." Michael advises.

"What's sweetbreads?" Elli inquires. "It sounds delicious."

"It is an acquired taste. In actuality it is the animal's pancreas." Michael explains, competing with the gagging sounds of the rest of his family.

"This reminds me of our first trip to Greece." Christina cuts in. "Do you remember? The dinner with all your family? The appetizer your uncle ordered? And you made me taste it?"

"Vaguely." Michael responds.

"What was it mom?" Both children inquire simultaneously.

"It was like someone set a football in the middle of a platter. It was made of the same material. The stomach of the animal…"

"Stop it mom! I am going to throw up!" Todd exclaimed.

"That was nothing." Christina continued. "The waiter used a sharp knife and split the stomach on the platter. It was filled inside by every conceivable organ you can imagine. Pieces of heart, lungs, kidneys, pancreas etc. etc. You get the idea. I wanted to go to the bathroom and throw up. Instead your father, so he won't lose face in front of his family, insisted that at least I taste it. I did and spit it in my napkin. It was the foulest thing I had tasted in my life."

"As I said before. It's an acquired taste." Michael said as he opens the door to the Bon Appetite restaurant.

They were immediately assaulted by the smell of garlic, onion, tarragon, oregano, broiled beef and a subtle smell of wine.

"I told you." Michael started. "This does not smell so bad…"

"Don't judge a book by its cover." Christina was quick to pronounce judgment of her own.

They were seated in a plush booth. Michael imagined himself being with his mentor, Don Davidson, and started ordering for everyone in French. After the entire family devoured the first appetizer, escargot, they started raving and asking Michael what they had just eaten.

"If you liked it, don't ask and I will not tell." Was Michael's standard response for the evening.

For the main course Michael ordered a chauteubriant for four with all the trimmings sliced into thin slices at their table. By the end of the evening the entire family had become Francophiles and they pronounced the French food far superior to everything they had tasted in their life.

* * * * *

Roxanne gets in the company pick-up truck and leaves the job site. The NIS surveillance car follows close behind. She picks a pack of cigarettes out of her purse. The pack is empty. She stops at the Commissary on the way to the Nimitz Gate to buy a pack. The NIS Agents park outside the commissary. On her way out the NIS Agents accost her. They identify themselves and take her away in their car. They drive her to the NIS Building and they put her in the same cell they held Michael, after they confiscate everything she has on her. Dave Brown visits her cell after she spends 15 minutes in isolation.

Dave Brown introduces himself as the NIS Agent in charge and starts interrogating her. Roxanne is scared and intimidates easy. She tells the NIS Agent, all that transpired today, in detail. Brown has now Roxanne's testimony on tape, which corroborates the Report of his two Agents.

In effect Michael was bluffing the other day and they all swallowed the hook, including line and sinker. The other confirming point is that the information regarding the SARGO Incident was now in the hands of two Law Firms with powerful political connections. The lawyers were next to impossible to be gotten to. Dave Brown needs to consult with the others. He leaves Roxanne sobbing in the cell; terrified and uncertain of her future.

* * * * *

There is a conference taking place in Agent Brown's office. The ROICC, OICC, the Admiral and now Dave Brown joins. They study Roxanne on the TV screen, exhibiting the same interest as they would watching a primate at the zoo.

The participants are informed by Rear Admiral Riffey that the Grand Old Navy Man, the father of the Navy Nuclear Submarine program, Four Star Admiral Rickover was in Honolulu staying at the Hale Koa Hotel penthouse next to the Hilton Hawaiian Village where Michael was staying.

"The Admiral could look into Michael's suite and vice versa." He chuckles. "Of course Admiral Rickover was not told that Michael and his family were staying at the Hilton Hawaiian Village next door. He was bound to of course, go there himself in the middle of the night and plug Michael with his navy revolver and instead of solving one problem, we would have now created another."

The Navy officers have a good laugh at the unlikely scenario. Captain Reinhardt tosses his drink in a single gulp and bangs his glass on the table.

"I should have insisted we take Michael out when we had the chance two days ago. Now the fucker is bullet proof." The OICC announces.

"Michael is a time bomb," Admiral Rifey exclaims, "and the Navy cannot rely on his discretion. His knowledge limits the government's options of resolving the SARGO Incident. Michael certainly can no longer be met with an unfortunate accident, however, every effort should be made so that he can be discredited. His credibility eroded to the point that no one pays attention to what he is saying."

"Are we talking here about a possible Felony Conviction?" Captain Reinhardt's eyes light up.

"All in good time." Admiral Rifey replies. "We have to be patient and persistent. Chip away at the foundation, the building won't be far behind, collapsing."

The Admiral continues listing Michael's strengths and apparent weaknesses.

"He doesn't do drugs. He doesn't drink, to speak of. He smokes a pipe and cigars. He seems to be sleeping around. Not proven, however. This is to be verified and exploited to its fullest potential. His honesty has not been tested. It appears that Roxanne is the weak link. Work on her. Now that a joint has been found in her purse, on government property, the necessary lever to pull, has suddenly materialized."

* * * * *

Two NIS Agents, heavies, enter Roxanne's cell. They accuse her of having in her purse a marihuana cigarette.

"On government property of all places!" One of the NIS Agents screams.

"This is a Federal Offense punishable by a mandatory five-year sentence in a Federal Prison!" The other NIS Agent screams on her other side.

Roxanne starts crying again. She makes pathetic attempts at seducing the two NIS Agents. She offers them anything and everything.

Dave Brown at that point enters the cell with a prepared confession on the marihuana possession. Roxanne signs it as she is told to do. The heavies leave the cell with the signed confession. Dave Brown tells Roxanne that she is now working for the NIS.

"You are in effect a CW, Confidential Witness. If at any time, you do not do as you are told, I will pull out your confession, date it and send it to the U.S. Attorney's Office for prosecution. If you cooperate, I will tear the confession up and the matter never happened."

He informs her that the NIS has started an investigation. The target of the investigation is her Boss, Michael. She cannot disclose any of this to Michael or any other person nor their present conversation.

"You have become a CW, Confidential Witness, for the government. Your identity will remain secret and will be monetarily rewarded by the NIS."

He gives her a blank envelope containing ten one-hundred-dollar bills and asks her to sign a receipt.

Roxanne stops crying and her eyes light up. She never had so much cash in her life. What does Mr. Brown want her to do? She is willing to fuck every NIS Agent in place, if that is what he wishes.

Love, romance and loyalty to Michael go out the window. Agent Brown reads her thoughts and tells her that there is a lot more where this came from. He is assured of her cooperation.

"You are to take no action for the time being. You will be contacted by me or another NIS Agent when an opportunity avails itself. For the present, maintain sexual relations with Michael and try to make him experiment with drugs."

Roxanne admits red faced that she had not slept with Michael. She also doubts whether he will ever do drugs.

Dave Brown is crestfallen. He does not allow the disappointment to show on his face. He does not want to see Roxanne discouraged. After all she remains their best hope.

The two NIS Agents who picked her up materialize with her property, minus the joint. They drive and deposit her back at the commissary by the Nimitz Gate where she finds the company pick-up truck waiting for her where she left it.

* * * * *

Michael and Christina hand in hand stroll on Kalakaua Avenue. Michael is enjoying an after-dinner cigar. They wander in Duke's Lane and the Rainbow Bazar. The kids up ahead try to strike bargains with the vendors on 'beads and trinkets' with the money Michael has given them.

Christina is very happy. She won her husband back. He is a decent person. Even in the midst of a potential whirlwind love affair he behaved like a gentleman. He never crossed the point of no return.

"This is our last evening in Honolulu." Michael reminds his wife. "The blessing and the Luau have to remain on hold until our return in the near future. Tomorrow we are catching the 2:00 PM flight back to Seattle. I will go to the job site early in the morning, but will stay there briefly. I will be back at the hotel before 11:00 AM. You and the kids are supposed to be packed and ready to go. We will check out of the hotel and have a leisurely lunch before the flight."

They stay out late, strolling and talking. They return back to the hotel by the beach. They take their shoes off and wade in the surf. The kids get all wet in the balmy night splashing and playing with other kids on the beach in front of the hotel. NIS and SARGO are a million miles away. 'Maybe the Navy was right', Michael is thinking. 'It was an emergency testing procedure after all'.

* * * * *

On the penthouse of the Hale Koa, the VIP Hotel owned by the Department of Defence, Admiral Hyman Rickover cannot sleep. He is on the lanai smoking a cigar and breathing the fresh salt air. 'How many more of the Polaris submarines will be lost before they can correct the problem?', he is thinking. 'The Navy is going about it all wrong.' He read Michael's FBI Report on their background investigation. 'He is definitely smart. One of the two thousand smartest people in the country back in 1970. Otherwise, he wouldn't be in the Studies and Observation Group. 'The Navy should be using that smart Engineer, Michael, to solve the cooling problem, instead of gunning for him', he is thinking. 'If he could meet him and explain the problem, face to face...maybe he should make his point across to the others tomorrow'. His mind is drifting away following the smoke of his cigar.

Children's laughter brings him back. He looks below. A little boy and girl are splashing on the surf. Their parents hold each other watching over them. They seem so happy, so carefree. The Admiral feels like an intruder to their moment of happiness and silently retreats inside his suite.

Chapter 15

Evidence to The Contrary

Michael gets up early. He gets ready quietly so he would not wake Christina up. He packs everything in his suitcase and drapes his overcoat over it for when they get to the Sea-Tac Airport.

He takes the elevator to the lobby. He leaves a wake-up call for 8:00 AM for his family and orders a Continental breakfast for three, pastries, croissants and a fruit basket. Guava juice for three, two milks and a pot of coffee.

He grabs a scone on the run from the Patisserie across the street and by the time he recrosses the street, the convertible is brought around.

He decides to turn left at the Waikiki Yacht Club. By the time he reaches the Ala Moana Park the scone has settled in his stomach like concrete, coating his throat in the process. He takes the scenic route through the Park and pulls in front of the concession stand on the beach. He parks and gets out of his car. He orders a large soda to get his voice back and unwraps a Monte Christo No. 2 torpedo cigar.

He cuts the pointy end of his cigar and tests the draw watching several teams of senior citizens playing croquet in the infield of the park on the right, while vixens have already staked out, on the beach to the left, the location of their temple of worship to their God, the Sun.

He picks up his soda and places it in the cup holder of the car. He gets in. Takes several gulps from the soda and puts it back in the cup holder. He lights his cigar and admires the hard bodies. He would have a problem making it to work every day if he lived permanently on the island of Oahu, he is thinking with all the distractions around him. He puffs on the Monte Christo and starts the car.

The beachfront loop joins the Ala Moana Boulevard and Michael finds himself smack in the middle of the morning commuter traffic, without the distraction, thank God for that, of the hard bodies on the beach. Their place however, has been taken by the morning joggers in Brazilian bikini's running with or against the morning traffic on the Ala Moana Park paths.

He goes through the Nimitz Gate of the Pearl Harbor Naval Shipyard Base still daydreaming of the bouncing T & A. He sobers up through the drive in the Base and makes it through the CIA Area in a breeze. He arrives at the job site with no delays.

The staff is waiting for him outside the office trailer. They seem restless. Michael is looking from Roxanne to Bill to Steve and back to Roxanne…trying to guess the origin of their excitement. Their attention seems diverted towards the bay.

"I give up!" Michael exclaims. "What's up?"

"Don't you see anything different?" Bill Scott gives Michael a clue.

'Of course I made good time.' Michael is thinking. 'No SP's to stop me. No barricades to be removed to let my car through. How come? What happened to the nuclear submarine SARGO? The wharf where it was tied up till yesterday is empty today. He got used to the dark shape to his left as he approached the job site gate as part of the environment. He did not notice that it was missing this morning; although he passed the spot that was tied in, no more than twenty yards away.'

"Anyone knows where it went?" Michael asks the staff.

He follows their gaze. There in the middle of Pearl Harbor, the SARGO is sitting all by itself. The Harbor traffic giving it a wide berth, as they traverse its location.

'From where I am standing,' Michael is thinking, 'with my driver I can bounce golf balls on its deck. This means a 265-yard carry.'

"Why are all the ships avoiding it?" Michael is wondering. The SARGO is stationary surrounded by buoys; a yellow rope 265-yard stretched between the floats. Bright yellow rectangles bearing the magenta nuclear sign are hanging from the yellow rope at five-foot intervals, like greeting cards warning buoys; the Harbor traffic off.

"When did it get there?" He is thinking out loud. "Must have been last night." He answers his own question. "How did it get there? Probably towed. "Why is it parked in the middle of the Bay? How is it anchored?"

All these unanswered questions. All these theories. Nothing concrete. Anyway, it will be an interesting topic of speculation for a while, until the black ghost becomes a fixture in its new environment and then invisible.

Michael is startled and jumps, causing the entire staff to spook. He looks down because something touched his leg. He sees a gray cat coming around for a second pass, rubbing his leg, purring audibly and sounding like snoring.

Bill Scott makes a comment to the effect that all pussies are after poor Michael; which starts Roxanne giggling. She has been very quiet and reserved all morning, which is inconsistent with her behaviour yesterday afternoon during their drive back, after the clandestine operation of dropping off documents to the local attorney's office.

PMS, Michael is thinking and dismisses it. He actually prefers this side of Roxanne, better. Aggressive women exhaust him, being constantly on stage, playacting some role, requiring constant reassurance and applause.

Michael stoops down and rubs the cat's ears.

"Has she always been so fat?" He asks. "There must be a lot of left-over lunches."

"She is fat alright." Bill Scott says. "But the lunch scraps are not entirely to blame. She is pregnant. She is the job site cat. We adopted her. She is a working cat. She keeps down the rat population."

"Well, pregnant or fat or both, it sure is a big cat." Michael comments as he gently pushes her aside with the outside of his foot.

He reviews the work accomplished to date. He makes comments to Bill and Steve who take Michaels comments down on their pads. Although progress is curtailed, Michael is not worried, because it's all on account of the Change Order which caused the Suspension of Work and will ultimately be charged to the Navy.

"I will return," Michael promises to the staff, "as soon as the Navy provides us with revised Drawings and I have submitted the direct costs in Change Order Cost Estimate Proposal. I bet I will be back in a couple of months to sign the Change Order."

It's a little after ten in the morning and Michael wants to get a head start on the noon traffic. He says goodbye to Bill Scott and Steve Crane. He is told that Roxanne is on the phone inside the office. Michael walks to the far side of the trailer. He jumps around the shrinking puddle of water to get to the first step of the stairway to the trailer door.

He looks at Bill Scott pointing to the water puddle.

"I will have it filled by the time you get back." Bill Scott responds.

Michael climbs the steps to say a quick goodbye to Roxanne, so she would not have to disrupt her telephone conversation. He opens the trailer door. Roxanne is not on the phone. She grabs him and is all over him.

Michael is at a loss of a plan of action after the initial shock. He is not encouraging her, but neither is discouraging her. Although in a state of passive resistance, he feels himself getting hard.

Roxanne drops to her knees and is trying to unzip him. That is going to be crossing the line and Michael backs off.

"We shouldn't. Someone may just come to the office." He offers as an excuse.

Roxanne understands. She does not want to do anything to compromise Michael's position.

"I just lose my mind every time I see you. I am very much attracted to you."

She proposes that she follow him out the Base, meet somewhere close and check into a hotel.

Michael says that he got to return to his hotel to pick up his wife and kids by 11:00 AM, if he is to make the flight back to Seattle today.

Roxanne gives him a lingering passionate kiss to which Michael does not respond, but neither pulls away.

She tells him that when he comes back next time, to come alone. Michael just smiles and backs out the door.

Although driving on the freeway with the top down to aerate his clothes, Michael arrives at the hotel with a faint, residual smell of Chloe. Roxanne's perfume.

Christina smells it immediately and puts Michael through the third degree.

"Roxanne just hugged me goodbye. What can I do if she drenches herself in perfume?"

Christina appears convinced, but Michael still remains a sexual suspect, never to be left alone out of her sight. If he had plans to ever come to Hawaii alone, it's best to revise them. Christina was coming with him every time, no matter what. She needs to protect her investment.

A Hotel porter comes to their suite and picks up their luggage. Christina makes a last-minute inspection of the rooms, in case they left something behind. She finds the odd slipper and part of a bathing suit under the kid's beds. She puts them in their carry-ons. By the time they reach the lobby, their car is loaded up.

They go for lunch to 'It's Greek to me', restaurant at the Prince Kuhio Shopping Centre in the heart of Waikiki. Michael picked the place on purpose as the last eating stop on Oahu, Hawaii, so that their kid's last taste of the islands will be the distinct taste in their mouths of homemade 'gyro' cooked to a crisp on a charcoal rotisserie.

Weeks later, in Seattle, they will all come down with the Hawaii blues and have their taste buds recall the tastes of Hawaii, resulting in a 'It's Greek to me' gyro attack.

They make it to the Airport. Go through the Agricultural Check Station and with the sticker on their luggage they check into the Braniff Airline ticket counter.

Sadness for leaving Paradise settles on all of them, not even the appointments and service of First Class can cure.

They land in Seattle on a cold and drizzly night. After Hawaii, they really feel the gloom and cold of the Northwest weather.

They are the picture of health at the Terminal. Their tan sticking out among the pale faces who had just arrived from back East.

They pick up their luggage and go out to the parking structure via the Skybridge on the 4th Floor.

Christina is having to go through the entire hellhole of a purse in order to find the piece of paper she wrote the parking level and space number of their car.

405 Freeway all the way. Windshield wipers on and off. Forty-five minutes later and a windshield water bottle down, they arrive at home, sweet home.

"Why don't we move to Hawaii?" The kids inquire as they step into a cold damp house.

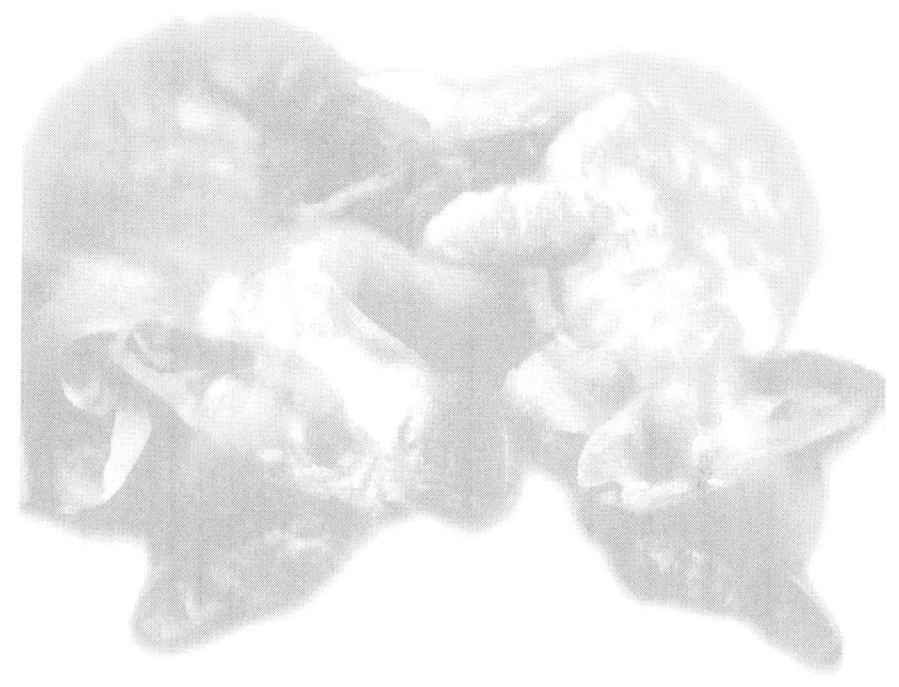

Chapter 16

The Misdirect

Michael shows up at the office the next day, sporting an Aloha shirt under his blue blazer, open collar and a pukka shell necklace. He sticks out among the pale face three-piece suits and ties crowd; the same way he stuck out in Hawaii the first day in a coat and tie.

He goes to the African Rosewood panelled executive conference room, stone fireplace blazing, plush leather chairs and a wet bar. It resembled a private men's club rather than a Company conference room. Something to do with all fourteen partners being male, although the female employees in the company outnumbered the men more than two to one.

Michael is basking in the fireplace flame glow, being the centre of attention, having recently returned from a trip to a tropical paradise. Danny McCoy, the Chief Engineer, nursing a crippling attack of a case of premature arteritis, hobbles into the conference room, precariously balancing a steaming coffee cup on top of an armload of documents.

"You must have gotten the better of them on a Change Order." Dan McCoy says addressing Michael.

"How do you know?" Michael inquires, surprised.

"Not only that," Dan continues, "But you must have put the screws on the Navy's thumbs." He concludes, pushing the pile of documents he had been carrying towards Michael's direction.

Michael leafs through them. He scans the comments made in red pencil. It appeared on cursory review that all the submittals have been returned by the Navy's Consulting Engineers on the project, marked 'Rejected' with at least ten comments explaining the reason, why.

"What do you have to say about this?" Dan exclaimed after he sensed Michael was done reading the Consulting Engineer's comments.

"One would conclude that the Engineering Department in the future should pay close attention to ensure that they have provided all the information necessary to prove to the Navy Consultant that the equipment submitted for approval are in compliance with the Contract Requirements."

"But we are!" Dan protested.

"Then the submittals fail to show…"

"They do!" Dan McCoy interrupted.

"Are you telling me that the Navy's Consultant is fabricating comments on fictitious Contract Requirements?"

"That's exactly what I am saying."

"I refuse to believe that the Navy would sabotage their own project." Michael concluded. "Go ahead and answer their comments and provide the additional information…"

"Even if the Specifications do not require it?"

"Well, let's do it anyway. Let's put faith on the government that they are doing the right thing. It will make us a better Contractor for it."

Grumpily, Dan McCoy takes the 'Rejected' submittals back downstairs.

* * * * *

By the end of the day, Dan McCoy informs Michael that all comments have been answered and the additional information, not required by Contract, has been provided.

"Who is going to pay for all this additional administration time?" Dan McCoy inquires.

"If the Navy is causing us to incur addition costs due to over inspection," Michael comments, "we will collect the incurred costs with interest."

Dan McCoy is sceptical about this whole government contracting business, with all the Rules and Regulations that are totally unnecessary. They cost the Company money. Now Michael promises that the expense will boomerang and come out of the government's pocket. He knows that Michael has a reputation for managing the government Contracts and bringing them in at the end with the highest Margin of all the company Contracts. In this case however, he believes this go around will not be the end of it.

* * * * *

A month later the above scene repeats itself. Michael tells Dan that this time he wants to see the revised submittals before they go out.

"If they pass my inspection, they will pass the Navy's." Michael assures Dan.

"They made ten different comments, this time, none of which are a Contract requirement." Dan McCoy protests. "This way, if they keep that up, we will have the submittal process extended to perpetuity."

"Who is signing the submittals on behalf of the Navy?" Michael inquires.

"Some new guy in the OICC by the name of John Muchmore."

Michael admits that he has not met him. He was not introduced to him by the OICC. He must be a young kid he concludes, newly hired who tries to make a name for himself by how tough he is on the contractors. In this case however, he just rubber stamps the Navy A/E Consultant's comments.

"Give this John Muchmore a call." He instructs Bill. "Introduce yourself and find out what the Navy wants. Tell him that the information requested by these submittals is beyond the Scope of the Contract. See what he says. If he argues that the information requested by the marked-up submittals is within the Scope of the Contract; don't argue. Prepare the new submittals, let me review them, so we are done with them. Everyone loses when you play tennis with the submittals."

Michael goes to his office and calls the Pearl Harbor job site. Roxanne answers the phone and wants to tell Michael a joke she heard. Michael is not in the mood for socializing. He asks for Bill Scott.

"It's been a month since I was at the job site. Has the Navy issued the revised Contract Drawings showing the new Demineralizing equipment location?" Michael gets to the heart of the matter without preamble.

"They have not." Bill replies. "They already know where they should go. Same place as you drew with red on the Contract Drawings last time you were here. They also know the price associated with the Change: $35 G's in Direct Costs, and they don't like it."

"What are they waiting for? They must know by now that time is money accrued against them."

"They do, that's why the Navy inspector told me yesterday that if you agreed on fifty cents to the dollar, the submittals would be immediately approved."

It's hard to believe, but Michael is now considering whether there is indeed a conspiracy on the part of the government to use the submittal process as a negotiating leverage to force him to accept less on the Change Order. Now, if the government approached him directly on it with an above the board trade, that would be a different story all together. They could trade half of the Change Order cost with a gentlemen's agreement to add it on a future Change Order. He has done similar 'horse trade' agreements in the past, with all the Defence Department Branches. Nothing however, like the method the Hawaii Navy is proposing. Trade the submittal expense and give the Navy a break. In this case the Navy wants their cake and eat it too. They are willing to penalize a contractor who goes by the book and does the right thing. So in response they raise the standard of performance on him. The government is their own worst enemy. Give them enough rope and they will hang themselves. If indeed that was what they were doing with the submittals, they will keep doing it with progressive impunity, until they were caught.

"Michael, the cat..." Bill starts in a low voice bringing his mouth close to the receiver.

"What cat?" Michael responds mechanically; in his mind still playing chess with the Navy.

"The job site cat..." Bill says quietly.

"Oh, yeah! That cat. The one you thought was pregnant."

"That's the one." Bill confirms.

"Well, what happened? Did it give birth? How many kittens?"

"That's the thing. It gave birth, but all the kittens died."

"Gee, that's too bad. How is Roxanne taking it?"

"No Michael. You don't understand. The kittens were killed. We found them dead in the morning. They were poisoned together with the cat."

"What makes you think that Bill?"

"Because they were monsters. One had three legs. Some had no eyes. Fur was growing and skin covered the holes where the eyes ought to have been. Two were joined together at the shoulder. Michael I am telling you, they looked like the by-products of an experiment gone awry."

"What do you think caused those birth defects Bill?"

"What else. Exposure to radiation. The cat was pregnant when the SARGO Incident occurred."

"What's happening with the SARGO?" Michael asks.

"Still tied up in the middle of the Harbor. Hardly anyone pays attention to it anymore. But I tell you one thing. I don't believe the Navy anymore that it was a scheduled exercise. Something happened. Before, during or after. Look what happened to the cat!"

"OK. This is serious. Let's think about this carefully, Bill. Does the cat go anywhere else than our job site?"

"Who knows?"

"Well, it could have wondered in some Dry Dock where the Navy was changing the core of a nuclear submarine and she got a dose of radiation. Being pregnant and all, that's all it takes."

"You are right. We cannot be sure it was the SARGO that did it."

"That's right Bill. You need proof…"

"What about someone killing them all?"

"Now you tell me that the Navy has out there on Oahu, Hawaii, Death Squads? What do they call them? 'Pussy no More'?"

"Hey that's a good one!" Bill says above his laughter.

"Tell it to Roxanne." Michael tells Bill. "When we get off the phone."

Michael tells Bill that he is a bit too close to the trees and he may not be seeing the forest.

At that moment, Grace, Michael's secretary, walks into his office bringing him the mail. On top of the pile is a Certified Letter from the Navy OICC Office. Michael tells Bill not to go away and puts Bill on hold. He opens the Certified Letter and reads it.

"You are definitely not seeing the forest." He tells Bill. "Guess what I just got in the mail. A letter from the Navy complaining that the equipment delivery is being delayed because of lack of approved submittals. Look at those bastards. They refuse to acknowledge the 'de facto' Suspension of Work Letter they have issued over a month ago due to Differing Site Conditions that has stopped all work. They grasp at straws over the manufactured delay on the submittals which the Navy is causing themselves unnecessarily."

"I told you so…" Bill starts.

"It's time to have lunch with Don Davidson." Michael interrupts him. He covers the mouth piece and tells Grace to set up lunch with Don Davidson. "The sooner the better. Preferably today."

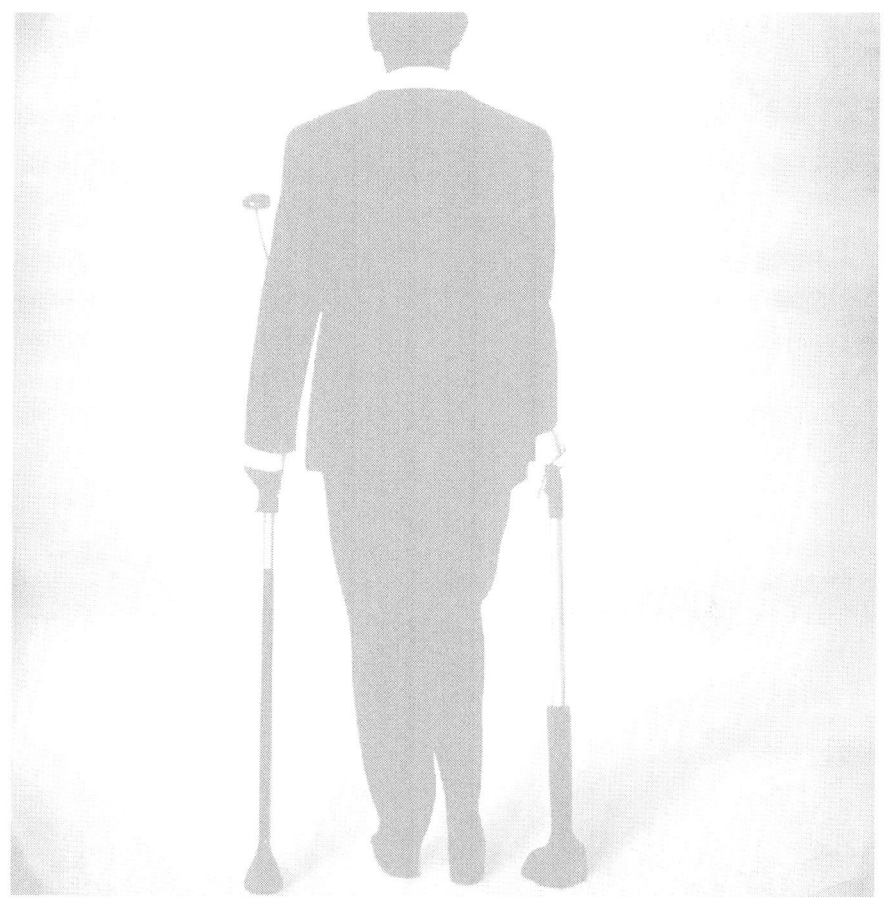

Chapter 17

The Way The Big Boys Play

Michael is driving on Interstate 405 going South. He takes the floating bridge over Lake Washington. He exits the bridge on the Seattle side of the lake and takes 520 into Interstate 5 Freeway going South. He takes the Union Street Exit, the heart of downtown Seattle. He pulls into the One Union Plaza

Tower and parks his Saab EMS Turbo in a visitor's stall. He takes the elevator down to the lobby and switches to the elevator bank that would take him to the 37th Floor of the building. The entire floor is the Law Offices of Fergusson and Burdell.

Nora, Don's private secretary, ushers him in as soon as Michael reports to the main desk that he has arrived. Don Davidson is sitting behind his desk, his chair turned to his right, playing with some mechanical contraption on the floor. The desk and floor are littered with tools. The unsuspecting visitor may confuse the law office for a garage.

"Do you know what this was?" Were Don's first words. Before Michael had a chance to speak, Don volunteers. "It was the braking system of the first elevator installed in Seattle at the turn of the Century."

He demonstrated how it worked, based on the moment of inertia principle. As soon as the unit was put on free fall and the acceleration exceeded the set point, the brakes would spring outwards and arrest the free fall.

Michael smiles and looks around the huge office and the collection of antique mechanical devices. At $250.00 per hour, Don could indulge in his hobby. Nature was unkind to Don. He was struck with polio in High School, ending prematurely a budding basketball career.

Don attended Dartmouth and stayed there until he got his Law Degree. He returned home to Seattle, Washington where he passed the Bar, on his first try and joined the Law Firm of Fergusson and Burdell. He bought a lakeshore home on the NE end of Lake Washington, overlooking the Seattle City Lights. He hands dug a basement to his house which he converted into a wine cellar, capable of holding 5,000 bottles of wine. His wine tasting parties, many to which Michael and his wife were invited and attended became legendary.

His handicap became his secret weapon in the Court Room. What jury would not be sympathetic to a cripple old man struggling and dropping documents and crutches. Assisted, many times, by the other side legal team. He was the darling of the Judges and he returned the vote of confidence by his brilliance of reasoning.

His Achilles heel was his preparation and neatness. Accordingly, over the years, the Law Firm assigned him one or two young attorneys at a time to practice and learn under his tutelage, in exchange of doing all his leg work and keeping his paperwork straight.

Don Davidson goes to his private bathroom to wash his hands and exchanges, on his return, the socket wrench for a yellow legal pad and Parker fountain pen. Michael hands him a copy of the Certified Navy letter he had just received to gather with a copy of the letters dated almost two months ago he received on site at Pearl Harbor Naval Shipyard, suspending all work due to Differing Site Conditions and the Change Order letter itself.

Don puts on his reading glasses and is absorbed in the two letters. Michael admires the view. The building is actually straddling the I-5 freeway and Michael is looking South from where he is sitting smack into the oncoming traffic heading North. Mount Rainier is looming at the end of the Northbound lanes, the top two thirds of it covered with snow.

Don looks up. Michael explains to him how the Change to the Contract came about. How he believes he solved the matter by red lining the Contact Drawings with the new location of the Demineralizing equipment. How the Navy submitted the revised

Drawings to MIDPAC and how they in turn forwarded them to NAVFAC for approval. He explained that the method the Navy implemented caused a $5,000.00 Change Order to escalate to $35,000.00 in Direct Costs alone and delay the project because of the Navy issued Suspension of Work letter.

"The Indirect Costs are currently unknown until the Navy lifts the Suspension of Work. They refuse to do so and instead are trying to use as leverage to bring me to the negotiating table by requiring a higher standard of performance in their submittal review. The Navy through Over Inspection are requiring the submittals to surpass the level of performance required by Contract and when they comply with the Navy demands, the Navy comes up with a list of more requirements which exceeded the Specification requirements. In effect the Navy has manufactured the delay associated with the submittals to offset the delay and incurring costs associated with the Suspension of Work letter due to Differing Site Conditions. They offered to our job Superintendent on site immediate approval of the submittals if I was 'reasonable', which meant to accept 50 cents to the dollar, with the Direct Costs of the Change. However, we could not proceed with the Contract, even if we received approval on all the equipment overnight, until the Navy issued revised Contract Drawings. Which they refuse to do. The Contract Drawings in their present condition are 'cartoons'. The Architect put them together by copying the catalogue cuts of equipment. There is no way to build the Power Plant and the Demineralizing Facility unless new Drawings are made. The Navy Consultant realizes this, but he is unwilling or unable to produce new Drawings. I don't believe the Navy is aware if this, yet."

"What you are telling me is that the Contract Documents constitute an Impossibility of Construction." Don Davidson concluded.

"That's correct. But I don't think the Navy has realized it yet. Though they should have had an inkling by now. Let me explain. We submitted the Intermittent and the Continuous Blowdown Tanks. There are shown nowhere in the Contract Drawings nor called out in the Specifications. We submitted them because they are required in the design. They came back marked 'Rejected'. The same holds true for the boiler Chemical System. It is required to keep the boiler tubes clean, but not shown on the Drawings or called out in the Specifications. We submitted Sulphite to scavenge the oxygen from the boiler feed water. Caustic to neutralize the produced Sulphate acid and Amines to kill the organic growth in the boiler tubes. It came back stamped 'Rejected'. OK. This equipment does not even appear anywhere in the Contract Documents. If the Navy and their Consultant does not like our choices, then revise the Drawings and disclose what they want instead. We are certain that the plant will not operate as shown on the Contract Drawings and Specifications. This is why I have directed our Engineering Department to prepare new Drawings for the entire project. Sometime in the future I am hoping to get paid for them."

"I have heard enough!" Don picks up the phone and calls Nora, his secretary. He tells her to get the Secretary of State on the phone in Washington D.C.

Don winks at Michael. "He was my roommate for a year at Dartmouth." He says conspiratorially.

Michael is frozen in place waiting with baited breath the results of this Power Play.

Nora comes to the office announcing that the Secretary of State was on the Senate floor to drum up the vote on a critical issue for the President of the United States. However, the undersecretary was on hold, very familiar with the relationship between Don and the Secretary and waiting to assist him. His name is Jack.

"Hello Jack." Don Davidson started without preamble. "I got here in my office a young contractor who is treated, in my opinion. unfairly by you boys in our government. Specifically, the Navy in Hawaii. They are threatening him when they are in the wrong and they try to make their argument stick by ignoring the issues and making up rules to suit them."

* * * * *

"Yeah! A call to NAVFAC is the ticket."

Don passes a note to Nora to get on the phone the Solicitor General at the General Accounting Office, the feared GAO, the watchdog of Congress and the guardian of the taxpayer's money.

After some pleasantries with the Undersecretary of State Don concludes the call because Nora tells him that the Solicitor General was on hold on the blinking line.

Don picks up the phone and tells the Solicitor General, another College friend, that he wants to report a government Abuse of Power under Colour of Law. The case is going to cost the taxpayers a huge amount of money. That amount was getting bigger by the day since the Navy was refusing to issue revised Contract Drawings, he felt it was his duty to report this matter to the proper authorities.

Don demands that a meeting be called immediately by the Navy at Pearl Harbor Naval Shipyard. However, the contractor has not been treated fairly by the Contracting Officer, the OICC, and he has no confidence in his impartiality.

"Accordingly, I request that the GAO send two independent investigators and audit the style of Contract Administration implemented by the Navy there and treat their budget accordingly next time."

* * * * *

"Be up front about the whole thing. Call NAVFAC in Washington D.C. and notify them of my formal Complaint. It is my understanding that the GAO is looking for a negotiating leverage to hold over the head of the Navy when they come for their annual budget talks. Your representatives in the meeting in Hawaii will provide you with such a Report. This case, in my opinion, is a prime example of government abuse and waste of taxpayers' money."

"Let's go to lunch." Don tells Michael as soon as he hangs up. "I believe the Navy will be burning the telephone lines trying to extend an invitation to you for a meeting, like yesterday."

Michael is the designated driver. He puts the top down, so Don Davidson may have more room to manoeuvre. Don throws his crutches in the back seat of the Saab and he buckles up. Michael puts the top back up and starts the engine. They head for the parking exit and Michael produces the parking stub and is waiting for the tally. The attendant looks inside the car and notices Don Davidson in the passenger seat. He crumbles the parking stub and waves Michael through.

Don keeps giving Michael directions as soon as they clear the building parking structure. They end up at the main warehouse of JLG, Jean Lois Gagnier, Wine Importers and Distributors. Michael is led by a sexy French lady employee with Don Davidson bringing the rear onto a freight elevator down to the basement of the warehouse and into the private dining room of the owner.

There is a sole table for two, set by a sexy French waitress in a black shinning silk super mini uniform; white ruffled lace underpants are decorating an adorable behind peeking under the mini skirt. Black net stockings. Short, lace trimmed, white apron.

The menu and beverages are pre-set. Coqui Saint Jaques and escargot for appetizer, with a bottle of Puilly Fusse. Followed with a three cheese french onion soup with slices of truffles, accompanied with a bottle of Chatenauf Du Pape by La Fiolle. The bottles of this particular brand are hand blown glass. Each one distinctly different. No two bottles are alike. Their bottle, the neck is slightly bent, off centre. Michael tells the waitress that he would like to take the bottle with him when they leave.

The main course is Tournedos Rossini. Slices of chateaubriand with mushrooms and onions in a Madeira sauce poured on top, with a hint of Roquefort, topped off with a slice of Fuad Graf. The wine, a St. Emillion to start and a Margaux to finish.

A mixed wild greens salad at the end of the meal in a vinaigrette sauce to cleanse the palate for the desert tray of pastries of every conceivable kind.

Michael takes an almond torte and a chocolate decadence wishing he had not eaten so much of the meal and had room for yet more desert.

Over Grand Marnier and cigars Don and Michael discuss the upcoming trip to Hawaii and lay out a plan of attack. Michael will need to brush up on all the submittals, comments by the Navy, answers by the contractor and the Contract requirements.

Don will not be available for consultation, because he will be taking off for a wine tasting tour in France and participating there on the famous Michelin tour. An Epicurean extravaganza of eating at all the three-star restaurants, all over Europe.

Their talk returns to the SARGO Incident.

"What do you make of it?" Michael asks.

"Something unusual happened there; otherwise the Navy would not be acting that way." Don responds.

Michael tells Don the latest involving the pregnant job site cat and its demise including the deformed kittens.

"You should be very careful." Don Davidson advises Michael. "If you find out too much, the government has no other alternative but to silence you; either permanently or by discrediting you, so your credibility becomes an issue should you decide, ever, to tell. At any rate it's too soon to make an issue of it. You have documented the Incident and my copy is safe in the Law Offices vault; and our Law Offices carry political clout."

"When will the time come that I will be forced to do something about it?" Michael asks.

"Before a Complaint is brought against the Navy, the injured party must have sustained an injury or a loss; otherwise, the Court will find that no damages exist and will throw the case out."

Michael looks at his watch. It is a little after two o'clock in the afternoon. It's always the same. They come in with the early comers at eleven o'clock to beat the twelve o'clock lunch crowd and end up leaving with the last of the late comers.

Ordinarily, they would stay a lot longer talking in the executive dining room of JLG, because they were not preventing other customers waiting to eat. However, Michael needed to get back to his office to face an annoyed Navy.

Chapter 18

The Spider & The Fly

Michael realizes, as soon as he opens the entrance to the Company Building, that "an annoyed Navy" may have been the understatement of the year. From the moment he winked past 'triple L', Laura Linda Lambert, the receptionist he realized that he has walked into a hornet's nest. Laura hands him a stack of pink messages from the Office of the Secretary of State,

GAO, Pentagon, NAVFAC, MIDPAC, OICC Pearl Harbor Naval Shipyard and lesser Naval tributaries in between.

"Have fun!" Laura says sardonically looking his way as Michael takes the steps up to his office two at the time.

He finds the pink slip from the OICC Pearl harbor and dials for Captain Reinhardt. The Captain's secretary answers the telephone and as soon as she is told who is on the other line, she puts the call immediately through. Captain Hank Reinhardt comes on the line.

"What in heavens did you do to get everyone up at arms from Washington D.C. to Honolulu and everyplace in between?" Are the Captain's first words. "Has anyone from the government talked to you?"

"No." Michael replies, speaking the truth.

"How could it be?" Captain Reinhardt says incredulously. "My telephone has not stopped ringing as of a couple of hours ago."

"I wouldn't know and I cannot help explain, as you are the one and only Navy person I have talked and currently speaking." Michael replies, humbly. "By the way I am in receipt of a Certified Navy Letter and would like to know what was that all about?"

"The letter is a misunderstanding." Captain Reinhardt is backpedalling. "Why don't you come to Hawaii and we will sit down and discuss the matter, just the two of us, straighten everything out and give me back the letter. This would straighten out everything, as far as I am concerned."

"When does the Navy want me in Hawaii?" Michael asks.

"How about the day after tomorrow at o'eight hundred, at the OICC Office Main Conference Room."

"I will be there." Michael ends the telephone call to the OICC, on that note.

He calls Christina at home and tells her that he needs to go to Hawaii tomorrow.

"I have been invited by the OICC to attend a meeting at eight o'clock in the morning the day after tomorrow. I will catch an early morning flight tomorrow morning."

"You are going nowhere without me!" Christina announces. "Especially Hawaii!"

Michael realizes that he is a sexual suspect on an indefinite probation period.

"In that case, you better find a babysitter for the kids, horses, dogs and cat." Michael tells his wife and hangs up.

He dials Grace McDonald, his secretary, in the intercom.

"I need two First Class Tickets to Honolulu, Hawaii, leaving first thing in the morning tomorrow with an open return. Use my accumulated air milage for the upgrade to First class. One of the tickets in my name, the other in my wife's. Make a reservation for four nights at the Hilton Hawaiian Village and a car rental from the Airport."

While Grace is getting the details of his trip to Honolulu taken care of, Michael goes downstairs in the Engineering Department and into Dan McCoy's, the Chief Engineer's, office.

"Round up all the submittals for the Pearl Harbor job. The navy's comments and our response each time they rejected the submittals. I also want the Submittal Log with the dates each submittal was sent and the date it was received back rejected. I want to have the paper trail and particularly the dates of the original submittals, the date they were returned and each subsequent transaction. Box all these documents with a clean set of Contract Drawings and Specifications. I will take the box with me at the end of the day because I am not coming in the office tomorrow morning."

"Where are you heading? If I may ask." Dan McCoy says with a sly smile.

"I am going to leave home tomorrow morning for the Airport. The Navy has just invited me for a meeting at the OICC Office, day after tomorrow."

"Can I come along?" Dan McCoy asks hopefully.

"How are the Drawings you are preparing for the project coming along?" Michael asks, stalling.

"They were completed, checked and corrected as of noon today." Dan says with pride in his eyes.

"Make three copies of them today. We will take them with us."

"You said with us! Does that mean that I am coming along?" Dan asks with baited breath.

Instead, Michael picks up the telephone from Danny McCoy's desk and dials Grace via intercom.

"Grace, please get two more tickets, for Dan McCoy and his wife, Coach, with open return. Reservations to the Hilton Hawaiian Village. We will use my rental car."

"No kids." Michael says to Dan McCoy with finality, leaving to go upstairs to his own office while Bill is dialling his home number. At the same time, he is yelling at a draftsman to make three copies of the in-house Drawings for the Pearl Harbor job.

Michael goes back up to his office and selects from the files the correspondence he will take with him together with a copy of the Navy Certified letter and puts all the documents in his briefcase next to his Diary, updated after his telephone conversation with Bill Scott, the job superintendent.

At 4:30 PM Grace comes into Michael's office with the Airline ticket vouchers and the rental car and hotel reservations. Michael thanks her and puts them in his briefcase. Grace gives Michael Dan McCoy's tickets and his hotel reservation.

Michael goes downstairs to the Engineering Department and finds Dan McCoy. He hands him his ticket vouchers and hotel reservation. The box Michael requested is ready. Addressed with the job site address, taped and with a nice touch he had not asked for: A detachable wooden handle so that he can carry it. He tells Bill that the three sets of the in-house Drawings will be his burden to carry to the Airport and subsequently to the meeting. They will use one car to go to the Airport tomorrow morning. Michael believes his wife's Ford Bronco will be adequate to carry the four of them and all their luggage.

He carries the box and his briefcase to his car and puts them in the trunk. He starts the Saab and heads home.

At home, he finds his mother-in-law in the house, so he does not need to ask his wife, Christina, how the babysitting issue was cared for.

Michael packs light this time. A good thing with the cardboard box as added luggage.

They get up early next day. They load the Bronco and with Christina driving they head towards the McCoy's home which happens to be in the same development two driveways down the hill. Dan and MaryAnn are waiting for them outside their garage all packed and ready to go. He sees that Dan had engineered a similar contraption to carry the three rolls of Drawings. Dan and MaryAnn load their belongings in the back of the Bronco and take the seats behind Michael and Christina.

Michael explains to Dan that the company had bought for him and his wife Coach Class Airline tickets, but since Michael was a frequent flier with over 250,000 Miles a Year, he used his millage to upgrade his and his wife's tickets to First Class. If Dan paid the difference out of his pocket, he could upgrade theirs as well.

Dan, a notorious cheapskate, informs Michael that they will use the Coach Class tickets. They arrive at the Sea-Tac Airport uneventfully. Michael explains to Dan what happened with their flight last time.

"I think Braniff Airlines have learned their lesson." Michael comments.

He notices seating in First Class is ready to Board. He waits for Dan and his wife boarding to be called so they may all board together. While boarding, Dan is stopping, leaning down and inspecting the clearance of the Airplane door with the floor of the telescopic jetway.

As soon as the Seat Belt sign is off, Michael asks his wife to go back in coach for a few minutes and sit with MaryAnn and tell Dan to come on up to First Class. He wants to discuss with him the SARGO Incident of which Dan McCoy has no clue.

Dan comes on over pleased as punch and immediately orders a Drambuie on the rocks from the First-Class Stewardess with some nuts. Michael explains to him what he had witnessed while on the job site last time. He consults his diary occasionally for accuracy.

"Did you witness a Nuclear Accident?" Dan McCoy inquires between swallows.

"The Navy has responded formally, that it was an emergency exercise following a staged accident. The darn thing looked so real though. Do you remember E.T. and the portable hospital scene? I thought they were filming a sequel."

"What about the submarine being isolated in the middle of the Harbor with Radioactivity signs all around?"

"I have no answer for you. You will see it for yourself..."

"How about the pregnant cat and the kittens?"

"I told you what Bill Scott told me yesterday."

"What do you think happened?" Bill asks Michael.

"Something happened. I am not sure whether it happened before the 'mock' Rescue Operation, during or after. It is puzzling to have a multibillion-dollar nuclear submarine idle in the middle of Pearl Harbor. I guess time will tell."

With that Michael sends Dan back to his seat in Coach and admonishes him not to tell his wife anything about the SARGO Incident.

"Just tell her that we were prepping for the OICC Meeting tomorrow. Tell my wife to come back."

Dan complied immediately as soon as he secured another Drambuie for the road from the First-Class Stewardess and a bowl of nuts.

They arrive in Honolulu at 12:30 PM.

Bill Scott is waiting for them at the Airport. After the introductions, Michael decides that the women should go to the Hilton Hawaiian Village with the rental car, their luggage and check in. Afterwards, hit the beach, shop or go anywhere they wished.

"Rent a full-size car." Michael addresses his wife. "Big enough for four people and our luggage when we go back to the Airport. I think the box will return with us back to Seattle. So count it with the luggage. I predict the As Build Drawings the Engineering Department has prepared will not be returning. The Navy will want a set and the other two sets we will leave at the job site."

The men will go with Bill Scott in his truck to the job site. They will take with them the box and the three sets of As Build Drawings and lock them up at the office trailer. It will be easy to pick them up in the morning. Michael wants the entire staff at the Meeting tomorrow morning at eight o'clock. He tells his wife that they will be back at the hotel this evening between five and six o'clock.

"Are we all on the same page?" Michael addresses the crowd.

They all nod in the affirmative.

They load the cardboard box and the three sets of As Build Drawings in the back seat of Bill Scott's truck. They get in the truck and head for Pearl harbor Naval Shipyard Pass Office.

During the drive the conversation can't get passed the dead cat and the kittens. Dan McCoy is bound and determined to eyewitness them.

"Too late." Bill Scott announces. "They disappeared, sometime last night."

Bill Scott is worried that the site may be hot; but he is unable to prove it.

"Was the cat staying on site at all times?" Michael asks. "It may have roamed around as soon as the crews left for the day and its meal ticket with them. It could have been roaming all over the CIA Area, or for that matter the entire Base and getting into who knows what."

Michael already has his personal Pass from last time. It was issued to him for three years, the duration of the Contract. They stop at the CIA Pass Office to get a Pass for Dan McCoy. Michael gives him a summary of the process, so the pass is issued to Dan in no time.

The SARGO is still in the middle of the Harbor. No one, except Dan McCoy, pays any attention to it anymore.

On the job site, Steve Crane tells Michael that the Big Kahuna accepted their offer and the blessing is all set for 10:00 AM the day after tomorrow. They give Steve the cardboard box and the three sets of As Build Drawings they've been carting since Seattle while Michael explains to Dan McCoy the custom of blessing the project by the Big Kahuna and the subsequent Luau.

They review the contents of the cardboard box. They separate the documents and make separate sets for each equipment chronologically. They are all ready for the Meeting tomorrow morning at 8:00 AM at the OICC Building Main Conference Office.

Michael predicts that it will be a controversial Meeting.

"However, we will kick some Navy butt and get the project moving again, dragging the Navy along." Michael also predicts.

He calls the ROICC Office and informs Commander Walsh that he has arrived in Honolulu. He also tells him that he intends to bring all his staff with him.

"I hope the conference room is big enough." Michael tells Commander Walsh.

"Don't worry it has seating capacity for one hundred." Was Commander Walsh's response.

"The job blessing is scheduled for 10:00 AM the day after tomorrow." Michael informs the ROICC.

"No problem. It will time just right. The day after the Meeting at the OICC."

"Is there an Agenda for the meeting tomorrow?" Michael inquires.

"None that I am aware of." Commander Walsh replies. "The Meeting will be a nice, friendly chat to clear the misunderstandings and get the job going again."

"Maybe the OICC knows of one." Michael probes.

"He is not in his office. He may be off Base." The Commander adds.

Michael is thinking that he got prepared for a battle. Instead, it will turn out to be a cake walk.

"We are all looking forward to the Meeting." Michael says. "And the Project Blessing the next day."

"It will time just right after the Meeting tomorrow." The ROICC confirms. "The job will truly get started then. The Navy will handle all the PR."

"I need a favour Commander. I have brought with me the company Chief Engineer because I did not know what the Meeting was all about. He just got his CIA Pass. We brought along our wives. They will need a Visitor Pass to attend the Blessing and the Luau. I will vouch for both of them…"

The laughter by the ROICC cuts Michael off at mid-sentence.

"No sweat. What's their names, date of birth and Social Security Numbers."

There is a short conference with Dan McCoy, after which Michael gives the requested information over the phone.

"The Passes for the ladies will be waiting for you tomorrow morning at the Nimitz Gate Pass and I.D. Office."

Michael thanks the Commander profusely and hangs up. He has an uneasy feeling about the Meeting tomorrow. He has never attended a meeting in the past without an Agenda. The ROICC was not aware of one. The OICC is unavailable. That sixth sense of his has never let him down, yet. If he was slightly apprehensive before, his telephone conversation with the ROICC got his antenna up and on full alert. Why was there no mention of the two General Accounting Office, GAO, representatives? Overhearing the conversation between Don Davidson and the GAO he was sure that Don specifically requested two representatives for the GAO to attend the meeting.

"I will go to the Meeting tomorrow carrying my briefcase. Danny McCoy will carry the cardboard box and Bill Scott the three sets of Drawings. Roxanne will carry her pad and take meticulous notes of what everyone says at the meeting. By the way where is Roxanne?"

"Probably out to lunch." Bill Scott volunteers.

"Well, let her know, when she comes back and we are not around." He tells Bill Scott. "Tell her to dress conservatively for tomorrow." Michael adds as an afterthought.

"Will do." Bill Scott says.

"If things are as the ROICC says they would be, Bill Scott, Steve Crane and Roxanne may leave and return to the job site. If things are not as we have been told, no one leaves the meeting and I will be the spokesman for the Company. The rest of you, keep your mouth shut unless I specifically ask you to speak and it will be on a specific subject. My attention will be on the Navy personnel, which by the way I was never told how many would be there. I don't want to worry about you and balls coming out of left field."

Bill Scott and Steve Crane think that Michael is paranoid, but it is hard to argue with success. Dan McCoy knows better.

"Steve, you bring with you to the meeting all correspondence and other pertinent documents. I want the exact document in my hand the moment I start describing it to the Navy. Are we clear?"

They all nod in the affirmative. That's the moment Roxanne shows up. Bill Scott lets her know that he will be talking to her as soon as they were done here.

"If everything proves to be 'kosher' at the Meeting tomorrow, nothing is lost except the time and effort spent preparing for the

Meeting. However, if the Navy has set up a trap on us, we will thank our lucky stars for being prepared. I consider every Contract a Chess Tournament. I am prepared to play at level 10 in hopes that the opponent is prepared to play at level 9. I am pleasantly surprised when I actually encounter play at level 5 and below." Michael concludes the meeting.

On that note they adjourn and Michael asks Bill Scott to drive him and Dan McCoy back to their wives at the Hilton Hawaiian Village. He wishes everybody a good night's sleep and be sharp tomorrow.

Chapter 19

The Man In The Arena

Michael and Christina wake up at eight o'clock in the morning...Seattle time, which makes it five o'clock in the morning Honolulu time. They cannot go back to sleep. One thing leads to another and......'Morners' at any rate were Christina's favourite.

Michael, when the subject came up and the question was asked at a party 'What is a morner?', he replied: A 'morner' is a 'nooner' only sooner.

Sex in the morning had a calming effect on Michael. It was part of his training schedule before a golf tournament. He rarely three putted after a 'morner'.

Michael and Christina have breakfast on the Lanai watching the morning activity at the Ala Wai Yacht Harbor. Michael tells his wife that he will be back before noon, so they will have lunch together with the McCoy's, somewhere nice. They might put their bathing suits afterwards and drive around the island of Oahu. Michael always wanted to see the North Shore and Waimea Bay.

Dan and Michael pick up their wives' passes at the Nimitz Gate Pass Office and arrive at the job site by 7:30 AM. Every one of the staff is already there waiting. They go over what each person is supposed to say when asked by Michael. They are not to respond to the Navy directly. Michael will be the spokesman. When Michael is satisfied that the entire team is fired up and ready to kick ass, he loads them into two company vehicles. He drives his car rental with them at the OICC Building. There are three parking spaces reserved, already, by the Navy bearing the name of the company.

They park, walk up on the second deck of the OICC Building and check with the secretary. Captain Reinhardt comes out of his office all smiles. The smile disappears as soon as he sees five people waiting.

'How was your flight over?" He asks Michael, the smile reappearing. "I was under the impression, talking to the ROICC yesterday, that you would be attending the Meeting alone."

Michael's antenna is up. He had said no such thing to the ROICC. Yesterday, he was told by the ROICC that the Captain was off Base and unavailable, now he is told that they had been talking. He looks at his watch. It is almost eight o'clock. He starts for the Captain's office.

"We will be meeting at the main OICC conference room.", Captain Reinhardt says, stopping Michael's progress. "There is more room there." He adds looking all around; implying that the change of venue was as a result of Michael bringing with him four extra people.

A little more room. Michael is thinking. There are only four more people. What do they need with an arena sized room. The room has seating for 100 people. First it was that the OICC was unavailable yesterday, while he was available to talk to the ROICC. Now was the conference room.

Michael introduces Dan McCoy, the Chief Engineer for the company, to the Captain and explains that he will need the Chief Engineer at the meeting as he was the one who handled the submittals. The Navy may ask technical questions that he may be the only one who could answer them. The other three may return to the job site, if the Meeting turns out to be as advertised.

"If not, I will need them." Michael concludes. "Are you sure we will need the big conference room, Captain?"

The captain remains silent. Instead, he takes a hold of both the doorknobs of the door they were standing in front of and swings the door leaves inward with a flourish

There are over fifty people seating around an immense table. There were enough Admirals present to conduct an invasion against an outer Pacific country. He counts seven of them real quickly, with Captains, Commanders, Lieutenants and a few civilians in the mix.

Michael's gaze goes around the table for a familiar face; finally settling on the red face of the ROICC, Commander Walsh, who as of yesterday, wouldn't even be attending the meeting.

All the talking in the room ceases immediately. All eyes riveted on Michael who is framed by the double door casing. Dan McCoy right behind him loaded with the banker's box. Bill Scott with the three sets of rolled up As Built Drawings. Steve Crane is carrying another banker's file box. Roxanne, the only woman in the room, is carrying her note pad and two pencils. Michael turns his head to make sure that all his staff was still with him. He had a nightmare that they had all bolted as soon as they saw the crowd. He turns his head only to face the triumphant gaze of the OICC, Captain Reinhardt bringing up the rear.

Michael felt a weakness in his knees and had to muster every ounce of concentration to take the first step forward. Where is he going to sit down? Where will his staff of four will be able to sit? They needed to sit together. Was the Navy's plan to scatter them all over creation? There was not a single seat unoccupied around the table.

Michael took the initiative and slowly went around the table while white clad uniformed men were tidying up next to each other to make room for him. He stopped in the middle of the table looking towards the double door he came in. He flings his briefcase on the table with a thud, and points at two table settings to his right and left. A Rear Admiral and a Commander scurry down the table counter clockwise. There is a shifting and tightening of the line, but two chairs appear vacant to his right. Michael waves that he needs two more seats. More scurrying produces the additional two chairs.

Michael signals to his staff to proceed forward. He puts Dan with the submittals box to his right. Bill with the three sets of Drawings to his left. Steve next to Bill at the far left. Roxanne next to Dan at the far right. He takes his seat in the middle of his staff and does not take his eyes away from Captain Reinhardt even for a second.

Captain Reinhardt takes charge of the meeting and starts introducing all the participants from the government side. It sounded like Noah's Ark. Every government Agency sent two representatives. Two from NAVFAC, two from the State Department, two from the GAO, WESTDIV, MIDPAC, CINPACFLT, OICC, ROICC, the A/E...the list goes on, including the OICC Attorney by the name of Jeffrey Wayne and two representatives from NIS, but not Dave Brown.

Michael introduces Dan McCoy as the company's Chief Engineer and himself, representing the contractor. He states that the other three were his staff on the job site; all known to the Navy. He states that he did not expect to walk into such a big production. He was led to believe yesterday by the ROICC that it would be a little chat with the OICC alone.

"Now it's half the government here and a few civilians who they were not introduced. Probably more government lawyers. At least I am sure of one Jeffrey Wayne, the OICC Attorney. If the government is allowed to bring in attorneys at the meeting and I was made aware of this, I would have brought our company Attorney with me. If this will turn out to be that king of a meeting, dominated by attorneys, I will feel compelled to walk out. I feel like I was invited to a stick fight, but no one bothered to inform me to bring my own stick."

Admiral Rifey stands up and immediately Michael realizes that he must be 'the Man', the way everyone deferred to him.

"I apologize for the misunderstanding," Admiral Riffey announces, "however, the meeting has to go forward, because more than half the people around the table are from out of town and they have come specifically for this meeting."

He excuses four civilians who had not introduced themselves; probably attorneys. Michael's guess was right on target. The four lawyers open the door leaving the room.

Admiral Rifey goes on to state that the meeting was called because of behind the scenes manoeuvring by the contractor trying to bring political pressure to bear upon the Navy.

"The Navy will have none of that. The issues will be examined on their Merit and the chips will fall where they may. The Navy has a proud History and will not change that honourable tradition by cowering to cigar smoke filled backroom politics and favouritism." Admiral Riffey concluded.

This last was stated staring directly at Michael and specifically at the two cigars he carried in his shirt pocket.

Michael is listening to the Admiral's speech with clenched teeth. After the Admiral finishes his speech and sits down, Michael takes the floor.

He starts by explaining that the project is currently under a Suspension of Work Order issued by the Navy several months ago due to a Differing Site Conditions Change. He pulls a copy of the Navy Suspension of Work letter from his briefcase together with the OICC issued Change Order and sets them on the table.

"Specifically, the uncovering of the underground communication ducts not shown on the Contract Drawings and occupying the same real estate as the Chemical Tanks and the Demineralizing Water System Tanks. I recommended a new location to the Navy, but was told by the ROICC that the Navy will decide the new location and not the contractor. This is the reason we were given the Suspension of Work letter by the OICC.

"I happened to be on the job site at the time and personally warned the Navy that the Change, ordinarily in the neighbourhood of $5,000.00, with the Suspension of Work, Demobilization, Remobilization and assuming a thirty-day delay in the issue of the new NTP, Notice to Proceed; the Direct Costs would be in the neighbourhood of $35,000.00.

"I gave the ROICC revised Drawings on which I had drawn the new equipment location and all the revisions in the piping to make it a functional system. As of the date of this meeting I have received neither the NTP nor the promised revised Contract Drawings indicating the new location of the affected equipment.

"This is the real issue on hand, the 'de facto' suspension of work, which the Navy has obfuscated by moving the spotlight to another, fabricated, issue: The Submittals.

"The Submittals and the serial rejection of which is nothing more than an attempt by the Navy to use them as a negotiating leverage, because they don't want to pay the increased costs of the Change, namely the Demobilization and Remobilization that they have caused by issuing the Suspension of Work. This has escalated the incurred costs of the Change, because, presently, due to the delays, the Indirect Costs outnumber the Direct Costs.

"The equipment submitted, were in compliance with the Contract Documents, only to be rejected repeatedly by the Navy's A/E on bogus and unjust issues for no other apparent reason other than to create the appearance that the contractor was holding up the project, instead of the real reason: The inability of the Navy to administer the Contract in accordance with its Terms; or worse, to use the submittals as a negotiating leverage against the contractor to prevent him collecting just money due, on account of the Change which would prove damaging to the Navy because of the delays."

Michael sits down.

Silence in the room. Admiral Rifey looks around the room for someone from his troops to step in. They are all busy with their pads and pencils writing notes.

He clears his throat.

"These are serious allegations and accusations you are levying against members of the government. Do you have any shred of evidence to support what you are saying? Talk is cheap. Where I come from someone has to bring forth evidence. At this time, as far as the Navy is concerned, the evidence," he points towards the pile of documents in from of the A/E, "are against the contractor."

"Did you review the documents yourself?" Michael asks the Admiral.

"Of course not!" The Admiral says indignantly. "I am busy defending the USA. I delegate that authority, to review the submittals, to the OICC and our A/E Consultants on the project."

"Well." Michael says. "Evidence you want. Evidence you shall see."

He picks a copy of an OICC letter which acknowledges that there is a Change to the Contract due to Differing Site Conditions, and slides it across to the Admiral. The Admiral's Aide scoops it up, examines it and hands it to the Admiral. He is reading it. As he is reading it, a civilian from the State Department goes behind the Admiral. His eyes fall on Roxanne who despite Michael's warning regarding dress code at the meeting, she is wearing a very revealing top. The State Department representative shakes his shoulders, turns his attention to the Admiral and asks to read the document himself. The Admiral hands it over to him immediately. The State Department representative reads it. He asks why was he not told of this before. No one answers. He walks over and shows the Navy letter to the Captain from NAVFAC. The Captain reads it.

He turns to Michael and says, "It appears there are two problems. The apparent faulty Submittals and the Change. How do you propose to resolve the issue of culpability? In essence, is the Change the cause of the delay or the Submittals?"

'If you notice, the date of the letter predates the first returned Submittal." Michael responds. What this means is that the Navy had the Submittals for months. They are required by Contract to return them to the contractor Approved or Disapproved within twenty-one days. The Navy kept them for months with no action taken. That in itself is a breach of Contract at worse. At best, it indicates quiet acquiescence. This means the Submittals were Approved. Doesn't the Captain find it strange that soon after the Change surfaces and the OICC letter is written, all of a sudden, all the Submittals come back Disapproved?"

The NAVFAC representative looks at Admiral Rifey questioningly.

The Admiral clears his throat and says: "All that is smoke and mirrors. The contractor has no evidence that the rejection of the Submittals was not rejected for valid reasons."

All heads turn looking at Michael. This is the moment he was waiting for. He stands up.

"Ordinarily, at this point, had I believed the OICC when he invited me to this meeting, that this was going to be a friendly chat between the two of us, I would have come empty handed. However, as I no longer trust the government, I beg the Navy's forgiveness for using terms of their rival branch, the Army, and accordingly, I will call the cavalry."

Some sporadic chuckles are heard, silenced by the Admiral's angry look.

Michael signals to Dan McCoy who opens the banker's cardboard box.

Michael pulls the Submittal Log from his briefcase and slides it across to the Admiral. This time Admiral Rifey beats his Aide in retrieving the document.

"What you have in your hand Admiral is the Submittal Log of all the documents submitted to the Navy with the dates of their submittal and return. Please select any of the submittals on your list so we may follow through the submittal process."

Admiral Rifey picks the first item which happens to be the Boilers.

Dan McCoy goes through his box and retrieves the Submittal package on the Boilers. Dan sets the documents on the table in accordance with their chronology. Then he goes through reading the comments of each Submittal by the A/E and explains why they were bogus and totally unnecessary because they were not required by the Specifications.

The A/E argues that they are necessary. They go back and forth for a while.

Finally, Michael steps in and asks the A/E representatives to kindly point out to him in the Specifications where does it say that any of their comments was a Contract requirement. The Consultants are busy leafing through the Specifications. The government representatives are watching, hoping for a glimmer of hope. A tiny victory to what so far has been a contractor show, exclusively. Finally, the Consultants look up. One of them stands up.

"We are unable to locate them. However, our intent…"

Michael interrupts him. "Do you expect the contractor to be clairvoyant?"

John Muchmore, who had been quiet up to that point, comes to the A/E Consultants rescue by picking another piece of equipment Submittal.

John Muchmore is in his late fifties, bald, five ten, 165 pounds. A handlebar moustache and long sideburns give him that 'I'm British' look, he so much wants and cultivates. He is a behind the scenes type of person. A survivor of numerous scrapes and ambushes over the years. He is presently a G-14 and desperately wants to please his Masters so he could retire in Hawaii with his recently acquired Philippine Mail Order Bride, eighteen years old.

He is a truly evil person. More so than anyone who Michael had encountered in the past. He firmly believes that the Cause justifies the Means. He has no conscience and he is very vindictive. He is an easy person to hate, so the government has made him many a time the 'scape goat'.

He hates Michael personally, because Michael represents what he views himself to be like. If he was only a little younger and out in the real world, away from the government and their required grovelling and progressing by attrition, seniority and waiting in line for a handout. The government did neither prize nor reward individuality. He had made every effort in his career so far to cover even a wisp of individuality. Michael had immediately and accurately pigeonholed him as 'a Legend in his own Mind', with limited capabilities.

John Muchmore stands up and goes to the A/E side of the table and after a few minutes of paper shuffling, he selects another piece of equipment submittal. Same outcome. He goes back to his seat. The Navy is shut down.

The other NAVFAC representative asks Michael whether he reviewed the Submittals himself.

Michael states that he had reviewed all the submittals with the Chief Engineer.

"Was there one comment by the A/E that he found legitimate?"

"At the end I have not. Let me explain. When the rejected Submittals started arriving, Dan McCoy, our Chief Engineer complained to me. However, like a prudent contractor I directed our Engineering Department, through Dan McCoy the Chief Engineer, to comply with the government's wishes, with no argument. Only when I received the last letter from the OICC blaming the Submittals, I consulted with our company attorney and I review the Submittals in detail. Until then I trusted the Navy was operating in good faith for the good of the project. Evidently, this trust was misplaced."

"Are you telling us that all the comments by the A/E are bogus?" Admiral Rifey almost screamed.

"This is exactly what I am saying and we are prepared to go through every single submittal to prove it. But it gets worse."

"How worse can it get?", Admiral Riffey mumbled.

"Let's pick the Chemical System Submittal.", Michael started. "Where in the Drawings is it shown? Where in the Specifications does it state its requirements?"

The A/E representatives are shuffling through the Drawings and Specifications.

"You will not find them.", Michael admonishes them. "However, it is a requirement on every Power Plant to scavenge the Oxygen from the boiler feed water. Otherwise, the plant will be completely shut from rust..."

"Are there any other equipment required and not shown on the Bid Documents?", Admiral Rifey interrupts Michael.

"Continuous Blowdown Tank, Intermittent Blowdown Tank..."

"Have you submitted on that equipment?"

"Yes, and they were Rejected."

One of the NAVFAC representatives stands up. "I've heard enough. The contractor has superior knowledge on the issues of this case. The government has to look into the competency of the A/E Consultants..."

"Muchmore told us to review the Submittals aggressively and find reasons to reject them." One of the A/E representatives' shouts.

John Muchmore attacks the Consultants calling them incompetent.

The A/E representatives attack the OICC naming him part of the Submittal conspiracy.

Admiral Rifey jumps in to stop the airing of the Navy dirty linen.

"As of this point consider all the Submittals Approved." He announces to Michael.

"I will need this in writing." Michael responds.

"You will have it in writing before the end of the day." The Admiral says signalling his Aide. "When can you get back to work?"

"As soon as the Suspension of Work issued by the Navy is lifted." Michael replies deadpan.

The Admiral looks at the OICC, who looks at MIDPAC, who looks at NAVFAC; one of the representatives stands up.

"Let me get this straight. The reason for the Suspension of Work was the Differing Site Conditions Constructive Change Order Request. Is this correct?"

"You are correct." Replied Michael.

"However, our records indicate that the issues pertaining to the Change Order have been resolved."

"I was not aware of that." Michael said.

"Didn't the OICC provide you with revised Contract Drawings, months ago?"

"No. I have not seen revised Drawings other than the ones I provided to the ROICC on the day the Change was discovered."

"Were those the red line Drawings drawn on top of the blueprints?"

"Correct." Michael exclaimed.

"We received these Drawings from MIDPAC as prepared by the OICC Office. Now we find out that you were the one with the ideas who drew them. We approved these Drawings within thirty days from the day we received them."

"Well, these Approved Drawings did not make it to the contractor. If they did, I would have provided the ROICC with a Cost Estimate Proposal around $35,000.00 and we would have been back to work months ago."

"Is that all that's holding you up?" Admiral Rifey exclaimed. "$35,000.00 and withdraw of the Suspension of Work letter?"

"It was, nine months ago, if the OICC had provided us with the revised Contract Drawings and withdrew the Suspension of Work letter."

"What are you telling me?" Admiral Rifey shouted. "This is no longer the case?"

"The original guesstimate of $35,000.00 I provided the ROICC was mostly Direct Costs associated with the Change. I warned him at the time that time was money. Provided we received direction within thirty days the $35,000.00 in Direct Costs was fairly firm. However, now, almost a year later, I am afraid that the Indirect Costs exceed the Direct Costs."

One of the representatives from the GAO Office who have been quiet all that time stands up and asks Michael.

"Could you give us ballpark figure of the cost of the Change in both Direct and Indirect Costs."

"A million dollars." Michael replies deadpan.

Every side conversation in the room stops. The Navy representatives are speechless. Admiral Rifey looks chocked. His Aide is reaching for the water carafe to pour him a glass of water.

One of the GAO representatives breaks the silence and calmly asks how did Michael arrive at that figure.

"I calculated the Direct Costs associated with Demobilization and Remobilization; the Direct Costs associated with the preparation of the As Built Drawings, because the contract Drawings are deficient and we are unable to construct the project based on them; the Indirect Costs utilizing the Eichleay Formula…"

"What is this Eichleay Formula?" Captain Rifey interrupts.

Michael explains the concept of time delay converted into dollars utilizing the formula used by Eichleay Corporation vs. The U.S. in the early sixties for the first time…

"Did the Navy hire a Contractor or a Lawyer?" Admiral Rifey explodes.

The GAO representative tells the Admiral that the contractor is correct and the Admiral is off base.

"You have no one to blame," the GAO representative continues addressing the Admiral, "but the incompetence of your command. You have managed to make a $5,000.00 Change into a million-dollar Claim. The Navy is wasting taxpayers' money on petty power plays that have backfired and the GAO has to come up with the money. This will be put in a Report to Congress and I am certain that it will be taken into consideration and back charged to the Navy with punitive damages when they appear before Congress to seek Appropriation for next year's Budget."

The meeting breaks up with the Navy representatives fighting among themselves and pointing fingers at each other. John Muchmore appears the obvious scapegoat. He could pass the buck higher up, but like a good civil servant he lets himself become the sacrificial lamb. Everyone from the government side attending the meeting will go home except the GAO representatives who together with NAVFAC, Admiral Rifey, OICC and ROICC will try to settle the Change with Michael tomorrow mid-afternoon, because the morning will be taken with the project blessing ceremony and the Luau.

Michael and his team leave the meeting. They load the company pickup truck with cardboard boxes and the three sets of rolled up As Built Drawings which will end up replacing the Contract Drawings, provided they are accepted by NAVFAC.

Michael ends up in Roxanne's company truck. She is driving. Dan McCoy drives the car rental. Bill Scott drives his truck with Steve Crane in the passenger seat. They start as a convoy back to the job site. Roxanne is delirious. She is about to have an orgasm repeating "a million bucks" over and over.

"If the other truck and the rental were not following us bumper to bumper on our tail," she tells Michael, "I would have kidnapped you by now. Park in a remote, secluded, area of the Base and rape you."

'Money is the biggest aphrodisiac.', Michael is thinking.

Roxanne is regretting teaming with the NIS. Maybe she backed the wrong horse. Everything in the meeting went exactly how Michael said it would. Except for the money. This he kept from them. They were as surprised as the Navy. That damned paper she signed with the NIS. She will have to talk and level with Michael and hope he forgives her. Hopefully, he will come up with something to make her agreement with NIS null and void.

* * * * *

Admiral Rifey, the OICC, ROICC, NIS and Muchmore have a debriefing meeting in the OICC office.

"What a massacre?" The OICC announces. "We have got to discredit Michael now more than ever. He is too smart for his own good. He has to be stopped. What's going to happen the next time, or the time after that? He takes our own Rules that are supposed to be our safeguard and turns them against us. We have to do something, because Michael can bid future work when he feels like it and we cannot stop him. Just to stay even with him, we have to put attorneys on the staff and more people. How are we going to justify the added cost of simply administering his Contracts to the GAO?"

"How can a Change climb from $5,000.00 to a million dollars?" The ROICC says.

"It's all Muchmore's fault." The OICC concludes.

John Muchmore is crying that Michael must be defrauding the government, but he doesn't know how he does it.

"He is like a fucking lawyer bending the Rules to suit him."

The Admiral is trying to keep the Navy team intact and stop the infighting.

"We got to face Michael tomorrow with the damn GAO representatives looking over our shoulders. What is the number Michael will settle for?" The Admiral asks his cohorts. "NIS should try to get a hold of Roxanne and find out whether Michael said anything to her. Maybe we will get lucky and find them together in a compromising position."

* * * * *

At the job site Michael tells his staff that he will go back to his hotel with Dan McCoy. The morning meeting has exhausted him. He thanks them all for their help.

"I couldn't have pulled this off without all of you..."

"Likely story." Dan McCoy interrupts. "I was floundering arguing with the A/E, until you stepped in and with two succinct questions you knocked them out of contention. No one thinks like you. Like a laser you zero in to the heart of the matter and argue the facts based on the Contract Documents..."

"Do you remember, I told you I will collect the costs for the Drawings I made you produce..." Michael changes the subject feeling uncomfortable with all the talk about him.

"I do. I will have for you before tomorrow, a complete cost estimate of the Direct Costs associated with the Drawing preparation..."

"Whatever it may be, if the Navy disagrees, we will argue with them to disclose to us what they have paid their A/E for the defective Contract Documents."

Everyone is excited and wants to do something to celebrate their victory. They need a release of their tension. Roxanne invites Michael to her house for drinks and 'pupu's', hors de vowers, in Hawaiian.

The guys are going out on the town and want Michael to come with them.

Michael is being pulled three different directions at once. Christina, Roxanne and the boys. He finally relents. He will go with the boys to celebrate. He designates Dan McCoy to announce it to their wives.

"However, I want to warn you that it would be an early night out for me. I need some rest for tomorrow's meeting. Don't forget we have a blessing bright and early tomorrow. All of you, your attendance is mandatory. Afterwards I will have to attend the Change negotiating meeting and try to justify the million dollar figure I threw at the meeting."

Roxanne wants to come with them on their night out.

They refuse unanimously.

"It's a 'GOLF' night!" Bill Scott announces. "Gentlemen Only, Ladies Forbidden."

Chapter 20

Bar Hoping In The Red Light District

Roxanne at her beach house is sulking. Drinking and smoking 'weed'. The T.V. is on without the sound. The stereo is playing. Roxanne is getting drunk and stoned and it's not even sunset yet.

Two NIS Agents drive up to Makaha and knock on the door of Roxanne's apartment. They identify themselves and ask to come in to talk to her. Roxanne is in no condition to talk. She's been drinking and smoking 'weed'. Its smell is present in her apartment in quantities that would make everyone high inhaling the second-hand smoke. The two NIS Agents walk quickly inside the apartment and open the Lanai door. They settle in one of the outdoor furniture chairs.

"What do you know and tell us about the negotiations that are to take place tomorrow?" They come right to the point of their visit.

"Michael left the job site early, right after the meeting, he did not say much of anything. Dan McCoy, the Chief Engineer told him that he would have for him before tomorrow a Cost Estimate Proposal for the Drawings the Engineering Department had made to correct the deficiencies in the Contract Documents. Michael left with him. He only took his briefcase. It's one of these Carnegie type and does not hold much..."

"So, everything else was left at the trailer!" They press her and threaten her with the confession she signed.

"I am not afraid of you anymore. I will confess to Michael all that. I am sure he will find a way out of it. Look what he's done this morning to a room full of Admirals!"

She does not make much sense. They decide she will do them no good in her present condition.

They drive back to Pearl Harbor Naval Shipyard to report to the NIS office.

* * * *

Michael, Christina, Dan McCoy and his wife, MaryAnn, are having an early dinner at the Royal Hawaiian Surf Room. They are sitting at a table by the parapet running along the beach. They watch a spectacular sunset. Then the lighting of the tiki torches. They watch the beach combers and late swimmers.

Michael gives Christina and MaryAnn a brief summary of the day's events. Dan McCoy lays out blow by blow the events in detail. He is still stunned how Michael was able to argue effectively with everything thrown at him.

"It was like he had written the scenario and he was just filling the blanks, as the meeting progressed. Absolutely amazing. You cannot do it justice by just retelling it. You had to be there. What can I say? I have heard from others about Michael being quick on his feet…I can now say I witnessed it."

Christina gets caught up in the excitement. Michael orders a bottle of Dom Perignon champagne to celebrate.

Dan McCoy tells the wives that Michael and himself will have to go out at eight tonight but they should be back before midnight.

"A night out with the boys to blow off steam." Dan McCoy states.

"Is Roxanne included as one of the boys?" Was Christina's immediate question.

"I can assure you that Roxanne will not be with us." Dan McCoy hurries to add.

"Where are you going?" Christina insisted, looking at Michael.

"I don't know. I am just going along." Michael replied.

"Probably some Korean bars." Dan supplemented. "They have girl shows. I am guessing. I really don't know and have never been in one. As a matter of fact, his is the first time I've been to Hawaii."

Christina is still treating Michael like a sexual suspect. Michael spends the rest of the evening trying to assure Christina that nothing will happen. He is like a little boy asking his mommy if he can stay up late and play with his friends. Christina relents.

"But I will stay up, waiting." She warns ominously. "I will demand a full report afterwards, complete of what happened. If I find out that Roxanne somehow showed up, you are in deep shit.

* * * *

There is a meeting with Dave Brown and the two Agents who returned after visiting Roxanne at her house in Makaha. The two NIS Agents seem to think that the documents that will give them a hint of Michael's intentions, are either in his briefcase currently inside his hotel room, or inside the office trailer at the job site.

Dave Brown doesn't think he can pull off another break-in at the hotel on such a short notice. He calls in two more NIS Agents. He tells the four of them to go to Building 155 job site office trailer and make a search without disturbing anything.

"They probably have an intrusion alarm. Cut the power to the office trailer before you do anything. The last thing we want is for you to get caught by the SP's patrolling in the area."

* * * *

Michael, Dan, Bill and Steve are bar hopping on Hotel Street. Honolulu's Red-Light District at night. Naked girls are dancing on top of them. The girls can touch the customers. The customers cannot...well the rules vary from bar to bar depending on the tip.

A taxi pours out Michael and Dan in front of the Rainbow Tower of the Hilton Hawaiian Village hotel in the wee hours of the morning. The early morning showers have already started. The deluge sobers up Michael somewhat; at least to pay the taxi, make it through the lobby and catch the elevator unassisted.

Christina is, thank God, asleep with the T.V. on. Michael shuts the T.V. and goes to bed himself.

* * * * *

The NIS Agents have no trouble making it through the CIA Area security Gate. They arrive in Building 155 job site and park their single car outside the chain link fence gate. They do not open the gate. They make it single file through the gap of the two gate panels instead. They make a bee line towards the power pole that feeds the office trailer. One of them pulls the office trailer wire from the power pole panel. It won't give. They have no tools between them. Someone notices a splice on the wire which feeds the office trailer. They make a two-man team of tug of war and separate the two wires. They throw the two ends on the ground. The live wire from the power pole ends next to the ground depression in front of the steps.

The flimsy office trailer locks give them no problem. They open them with a paper clip. They start with the two boxes on the floor and extend their search throughout the office trailer using their flash lights. They pile documents that look relevant on the secretary's desk. They come to realize that they really don't know what they were looking for.

They call Dave Brown at NIS and tell him that they need an expert to go over the documents. Dave Brown tells them to keep looking and gathering evidence. He will have an expert at their trailer within the hour.

The NIS Agents return to their laborious work. John Muchmore shows up at the job site trailer. He starts going over the documents they had gathered. He cannot find anything that will help them tomorrow. The NIS Agents start putting things back where they found them as Muchmore keeps reviewing more documents.

They are all exhausted and irritable. It's well past midnight and they have nothing to show for their efforts. They return everything as they found it and lock up the office trailer. They come down the steps of the stairway from the office door. It's dark. They are afraid to turn on their flash lights because they will be seen by the SP Patrols.

John Muchmore almost trips on a wire at the bottom of the stairway. He kicks it and it lands in the middle of the ground depression. An NIS Agent wants to reconnect the wire splice. John Muchmore discourages him.

"The bastards will be out of power for a while." He tells them cackling. "Let them suffer until they notice that the splice had come off."

They get into their cars to report their failure to Dave Brown at the NIS Building who would be burning the midnight oil.

The car windshield wipers are turned on to wipe off the first drops of rain, the deluge of the early morning showers not far behind.

Chapter 21

The Electrifying Roxanne and the SARGO Disappearance.

Michael wakes up feeling very thirsty. He drinks the warm water from the bathroom cold tap. It's still dark outside. He is not sleepy. The adrenaline of yesterday's snatch of victory from the jaws of defeat, is still running high. The anticipation of the start of today keeps his nerves tense, high and fine-tuned. He has the beginning of a headache though. He gets up and goes to the bathroom. He takes four Aspirin tablets and chases them down with the tepid water from the cold tap. He lays back on his side of the bed carefully so he won't wake up his wife. Twenty minutes later the Aspirin kicks in. The pain dissipates as he starts sweating. He sheds his shorts and tee shirt.

He is fading losing track of time. In his dream he feels hands touching him all over his body. He is in that narrow band between being asleep and awake. He doesn't want the hands in his dream to stop. He feels himself getting hard.

"I am glad you didn't use it all up last night." He hears a voice coming from the end of a tunnel. The sensations are now bringing him fully awake, but he is faking sleep.

Everything stops all of a sudden. His eyelids tremble with the sensations, but he is not cracking them open to spoil the moment. He feels weight on his pelvis as his penis sinks into something viscus and warm. A pair of strong thighs are gripping his waist. Before he has a chance to exhale, he becomes part of a rocking motion, its crescendo building into a trot, leading into a canter, exploding into a full-blown gallop.

He can no longer feign sleep. He squints into the first rays of sun light framing the mane of a Menes on top of him. Chin up, neck extended, eyes closed; a racing Phaethon, crossing the finish line, letting out a victory scream. The gallop turns back into a rocking motion as Christina lays exhausted on his broad barrel chest letting out soft moans and trying to catch her breath.

The breathing returns to normal. The moans turn to sighs of content, followed by an occasional shudder of the muscles. The pivot point holding the rider anchored in position. The wave starts from the head, reaches its zenith at the pivotal point, dropping to its nadir.

The rider becomes the surfer resting on her board, sizing the waves. The ocean has taken over. She rides the waves gripping her board tightly. The apex increases with each successive wave. The surfer dips her nails into the shoulders of her board, hanging on in an exhilarating anticipation of the next ride.

The ocean reaches its apogee and holds still. The surfer grips her board tighter with her thighs, pushes her pelvis downward as much as the pivot point will allow and becomes one with the ocean riding out its fury, manifested in controlled explosions, bobbing the surfer and then collapsing, pulling the surfer, falling, falling, taking her breath away,

The ocean becomes a lagoon. The surfer lays on top of her surfboard, motionless, hardly breathing. The pivot point relaxes. The surfer falls on her back next to the water glistening, dew drops from the exertion, stretching, smiling, content.

Michael and Christina look up at the time simultaneously and leap out of bed. They will be late for the blessing. They start getting ready in a hurry. Michael calls Bill and MaryAnn's room. They are ready and waiting.

The drive to the job site feels wonderfully refreshing. The early morning showers got everything washed and clean smelling. They stop at the Nimitz Gate Pass Office and pick their wives visitors passes. Christina and MaryAnn are excited. They haven't been to the Pearl Harbor Naval Shipyard before. They are a little late arriving at the job site. The only parking space available is right in the puddle, full of water that extends a little in front and behind the stairway to the office trailer.

Michael is driving and has the ladies to consider in the back seat. They will get their shoes muddy and their feet wet. He stops and parks in front of the puddle. The rental car sticks out of the row of parked vehicles by almost a car length. They get out of the car. Michael looks at Bill Scott who is waiting on the porch of the office trailer in front of the main entrance. Michael is grinning in mock anger and points to the rain puddle. Bill Scott smiles and extends his hands outward; 'mañana'.

"This rain puddle has been like this for months now." Michael explains to his passengers. "That darn Bill Scott was supposed to have filled it up and had the ground level, last time I was here, months ago."

They head over to the blessing. Michael behaves like a guest, rather than the Boss. Roxanne has taken over and is running the show. The ROICC and OICC make a fuss as soon as they are introduced to Christina. The tea leaf ceremony and blessing are about to begin. A Navy T.V. crew and a Navy photographer arrive on site and park outside the job site gate. They carry in their gear and set up their equipment.

"Where is your foreman?" Michael asks an employee of Pacific Boiler and Piping, his mechanical and biggest subcontractor on the project.

"Haven't you heard?" The employee responds with a strange kook on his face. "He was diagnosed with leukemia yesterday. He quit the company and is in the Hospital fighting for his life."

"I am sorry. I have not heard." Michael admitted. "Which Hospital?"

"Kaiser Permanente."

Michael makes a mental note to visit Bill Fleming at the Hospital. They had become friends and they even went out to dinner with their wives at Bobby McGee's.

Roxanne checks her make up with a hand-held mirror she retrieves from her purse. Her lipstick has smeared. She takes out a tissue and wipes the lipstick clean off her face. She searches her purse to find her lipstick to put it on. Nothing. It is not in her purse. She looks over at Christina's direction with a frumpy woman at her side talking. They are the only other women on site. No, she would rather go without, than ask Christina. She suddenly remembers putting her spare lipstick in the middle drawer of her desk, after they had come back from the meeting with the Navy.

"Wait. Don't start without me. I will be right back!" She yells at the Big Kahuna and the Navy film crew.

She walks towards the office trailer. Michael's rental car is on the way. The rain puddle extending three feet in front of the first step of the stairway. Michael's rental parked location prevents any head start. To jump or not to jump. To dirt the shoes or not.

Finally, she takes her high heels off and sets them on top of Michael's rental car hood. Thank God for not wearing pantyhose. She has a whole role of paper towels behind her desk at the office trailer. Holding the office trailer keys in one hand, she extends her right foot and toe first and steps in the middle of the puddle.

Zap. Sizzle. She falls in the middle of the puddle, her body convulsing, lifeless, her breasts swelling, her nipples engorge the size of walnuts.

The crew and guests cannot believe what they have seen taking place right in front of their eyes. Steve Crane locates the source of power and pulls the wire out of the puddle. Roxanne's body stops convulsing. The ROICC is busy calling from his walkie talkie for an ambulance.

Michael is wondering how did the wire cable got disconnected and the live wire ended up in the puddle. How long it has been like that? A ticking time bomb.

The OICC assures Michael that the Navy will get to the bottom of this. They will have NIS investigate the accident. He will keep Michael posted of their progress.

The ambulance arrives and takes Roxanne's body away.

A crew of Seabees reconnects the splice in the wire and the office trailer lights come on.

Michael notices that. He noticed the office trailer lights off when he arrived this morning, but he thought nothing of it. The splice on the wire that provided power to the office trailer must have been disconnected sometime last night after they went home. Who would want to do something like that? Deliberately set a death trap. Unless it was done accidentally, in an effort of the intruder(s) to avoid the security intrusion alarm by cutting power to the office trailer. Someone must have searched the office trailer last night. He made a mental note to investigate and confirm his theory by carefully conducting a search of the location of pertinent documents.

The blessing is cancelled. The Luau has turned into a wake for Roxanne. The GAO representatives approach Michael.

"We are sorry for what has happened, but we must proceed with the Change negotiation. We have to return to Washington D.C. with the whole matter wrapped up. We are booked on a red eye flight this evening."

Michael is like a zombie. The accident and the lack of sleep have caught up with him. He wants to get over the negotiating meeting as soon as possible.

He hands Christina a company check for the full $2,000.00 amount and leaves her in charge of the Luau directing the caterers. He tells his wife to give them the full amount. He takes his briefcase out of the trunk of the rental car and tells Bill to take the three rolls of As Built Drawings from the office trailer with them for the meeting. He returns the rental car keys to Christina and tells her not to wait.

"As soon as the Luau is finished, go with MaryAnn back to the hotel. Dan and I will hitch a ride back to the hotel with Bill Scott."

Michael, Dan and Bill and follow the GAO representatives, OICC, ROICC and Muchmore out the job site gate. As soon as they clear the gate, he feels a hand grabbing his shoulder. He stops. It's Bill Scott with a conspiratorial look on his face. Michael lags behind the group Bill Scott remains silent until the others get out of hearing range.

"What's the matter?" Michael asks anticipating a last-minute hot tip of the impending negotiation.

"Did you notice anything?" Bill Scott inquires.

"Like what? In association with Roxanne's accident? What are you talking about?"

Bill Scott nods towards the water.

Michael looks. Nothing registers.

Bill Scott nods again.

Michael turns, scans the Pearl Harbor end to end. Nothing.

"What is it Bill? I don't see anything. Spit it out."

"That's exactly this. There is nothing in the middle of Pearl harbor. Where is the nuclear submarine SARGO that was anchored there as late as noon yesterday?"

"Where do you think they moved it?"

Bill Scott shakes his head and moves his shoulders up indicating ignorance.

Michael notices that John Muchmore at the head of the parade has stopped and is peering around the chain link fence post at the corner to see what was holding up Michael.

Michael disengages from Bill Scott and speeds up his pace to catch up with the procession.

He passes by Dan McCoy who has a funny look on his face.

"What's up Dan?" Michael inquires.

"Someone opened up the roll of the As Built Drawings last night."

"Anything missing? Added to the roll? Altered?"

"Nothing like that. But I am positive someone unrolled all three rolls of Drawings. They were not rolled back the same way I do with the sketches and writing facing outwards. I do that so when I unroll them, they do not curl inwards."

"Dan, this is alarming. I had similar thoughts, that someone paid us a visit last night. They probably wanted to check the accuracy of your As Built Drawings. I doubt the NIS has that expertise. Neither does the ROICC or OICC. I don't think the A/E could be talked into a midnight raid. They are independent Consulting Engineers. That leaves John Muchmore. I believe he was one of the midnight visitors. He also found that I do not bluff. The Contract Drawings are deficient."

* * * * *

The GAO representatives, the NAVFAC representatives, OICC, ROICC and John Muchmore on one side; the trio of Michael, Bill Scott and Dan McCoy on the other side, meet at the OICC office.

Small talk ensues about what just happened on the job site.

Dave Brown is called in. He is already aware of the accident. Roxanne did not make it. She was DOA at Trippler Medical Centre, the Military Hospital on the island of Oahu. Dave Brown assures the meeting participants that he will personally head the NIS team who will conduct a thorough investigation.

Dave Brown leaves the meeting. Michael is tired. He is trying to keep a stone face. His mind is elsewhere. Roxanne, Bill Fleming, SARGO... The Navy is waiting for Michael to take the lead and start. Michael looks like he is waiting for the Navy to take the lead. The GAO representatives have had enough of the eyeball to eyeball starring contest. One of them stands and takes the floor while the other takes out his pad getting ready to take notes.

"Michael, let's cut through the chase. I have been authorized by the head of my organization, the General Accounting Office, to offer you on behalf of the Navy a settlement offer of $825,000.00 for the Change and the delays and $50,000.00 for the As Built Drawings which henceforth will replace the Bid Drawings. The Navy has agreed that as of this day, all Submittals are Approved.

"The Contract Modification reflecting the sum of $875,000.00 will be issued and ready for your signature within thirty (30) calendar days from today at which time the contractor will resume work.

"If you refuse to sign the Contract Modification, the Navy will issue a Unilateral Change Order accompanied with a Notice to Proceed, NTP, and your company will be required to proceed and file a Claim with the ASBCA, Armed Services Board of Contract Appeals. A trial will ensue and you will be required to justify every single cost line item. Of course the Navy will order an Audit by the Defence Contracting Audit Agency, DCAA.

"Bottom line, Michael, it is $875,000.00 now or maybe $1,000,000.00 with interest a year from now?"

"You got yourself a deal!" Michael gets up without hesitation and extends his hand.

The GAO representative grabs it and shakes it vigorously.

"We now have a Gentlemen's Agreement. The Navy will follow up with the details. I would like to have a roll of the New Contract Drawings to take with me. Please give a roll of Drawings with the NAVFAC representatives to take with them and leave the third set with the OICC. I am sure you have the originals in Seattle and you may reproduce them easily for your staff in the field and your subcontractors. Just copy them, provide them to all your subcontractors and label them as the new Contract Drawings. The government will be responsible to reimburse your subcontractors for all their Direct Costs associated with the differences between the new set of Contract Drawings and the Bid set of Drawings. You will be allowed to put your mark-up on top of each subcontractor's and supplier's Change Order amount."

Dan McCoy passes a roll of Drawings he was carrying to each of the appointed parties. They all get ready to leave the OICC office.

John Muchmore stands up and raises his hand wanting to be excused. "I have to go to the Airport to pick up my bride." He offers as an excuse. Leaving the meeting in a hurry. Michael assumes that Muchmore will be picking up his wife on her return from the mainland. He didn't want to shake his hand anyway. He was a dangerous man in his book, worth to keep an eye on.

Michael extends a hand to the OICC and ROICC and tells them to let him know when the paperwork for the Contract Modification will be ready so he can come back to sign it.

The OICC tells Michael that it will be ready for him to sign exactly thirty days from today.

"What's with Muchmore leaving all of a sudden?" Michael threw it in. "He was the one that caused the Submittal controversy. I wanted to ask him about it?"

"His mind is not on any submittals right now." The OICC said maliciously.

"Oh!" Michael said. "He is probably thinking about his wife..."

"What wife?" The OICC chuckled. "You must mean his Mail Order bride..."

"At his age?" Michael wondered. "I mean he must be in his sixties."

"His bride is a third of his age." The OICC chuckled. "He is the talk of the Base. His Mail Order bride from the Philippines I mean."

"I did not know you could order a bride by Mail." Michael said.

"It's a whole industry here in Hawaii." The OICC said. "You pay 'x' amount of money and you get a catalogue with young girls from third world countries. You pick one. You go visit her. And if you like her, you pay another sum for 'her ticket' and there she is."

"A new way to get right down to business without the dating and all the other bull shit." The ROICC summed it up.

"You learn something new every day." Michael concluded.

"It's no different than it was in the old wild West. Only in this case the girls do it for the money and a green card. At his age he will not last very long, she is thinking. I will fuck him to death and then bring the rest of my family to the United States." Commander Walsh added.

Michael thanked them for the information and told them that he was getting ready to join his staff, trying to decide if he was more tired or hungry.

Both Captain Reinhardt and Commander Walsh invited Michael for a late lunch at the Officers Club. They want to talk to him about another matter that had nothing to do with the Contract. They sounded very mysterious. Michael tells them that he will take a rain check on the lunch. After all, he will be back in thirty days.

* * * * *

John Muchmore is thinking, driving towards the Honolulu International Airport. Back at the start of the meeting he was fearful that his midnight ride would be revealed. Too many people were aware of it. Four witnesses saw him doing it. However, as the meeting went on, his fear turned into rage and hate for Michael. Here he walks in and plucks $875,000.00 right out of the government. He didn't even have to put a fight for it. The GAO representative just offered it to him and thanked him when he accepted it. The Navy paid $875,000.00 to Michael and they have nothing to show for it.

"By God I will never forget this and I will make him pay. Not today, or next year, or the year after...but by God as long as I live, I will make him pay, one of those days."

* * * * *

Michael arrives at the job site unobserved. He sits on the top step of the stairway to the office trailer looking down at the where the water puddle had been only a couple of hours ago. Someone must have filled it with dirt; still wet. He must have done it in a hurry. No compaction. Steve Crane will have the puddle back in no time with his driving. He pulls out of his pocket a Romeo y Julieta Churchill cigar, cuts the head with his guillotine cutter and lights it with a wooden match, remembering Roxanne doing that for him at her Lanai that fateful first day, when he almost...

Right where the new dirt met the old pocket of water formed, he aimed and threw the wooden match which went out with a sizzling noise which made his hair stand.

A final tribute to Roxanne.

Chapter 22

The Jungle Fighter And His Mentor

The news of the Change Order negotiations with the Navy and the ultimate results, preceded Michael's arrival at his office. He presumed Dan McCoy was to blame. At any rate, coming up with a Change having $875,000.00 pure Profit was nothing to sneeze at, as Michael discovered in the Partner's Daily short meeting at the conference room, first thing each morning, drinking coffee and eating donuts. An excuse really to discuss the current events and separate the facts from fiction, fuelled by rumour.

"You really came home with $875,000.00?" Was the first question asked by a dozen of the other partners. Rick Black the Manager of the Atlanta, Georgia satellite office being the only one absent.

"I have not signed the official papers, yet. I was promised by the General Accounting Office representative that amount and we had a gentlemen's agreement. We shook on it in front of several witnesses." Michael responded modestly.

"The paperwork will be ready within thirty days from yesterday." Dan McCoy added. "I was there. In other words: It's in the bag."

"I have already scheduled an overnight trip for myself to sign the Change documents." Michael admitted. "Thirty days from yesterday's date. I left an open date return, however, because I want to eyewitness the start of the work. I need to see you Dan, though, immediately after you finish your coffee and eat your donut."

With that, Michael got up and left the conference room to head to his office at the end of the hall, on the second floor of the company building. He hurried his steps because he could hear the phone in his office ringing. He looked at his watch. It was eight fifteen in the morning. Five fifteen in the morning in Hawaii. The phone call could not be from there. Eight fifteen in San Francisco. The call could be from Mare Island Naval Shipyard. The project was approximately ninety percent done. What could go wrong at that point. If it was during start up and commissioning now, a couple of months from now, it would be a different story. He hurried to his office. He picked up the phone buried under mail on his desk.

"How did the trip to Honolulu turned out?" The superintendent, Bill Denton, from the Mare Island Shipyard wanted to know.

"Why the sudden interest Bill?" Michael wanted to know.

"The Architect visited the job earlier and was not happy. He told me that you had him kicked off the Hawaii Project."

"I didn't get him kicked off. His deficient Bid Drawings and his rejection of legitimate Submittals did it. You know how it does. The Navy never loses. It must be the fault of the civilians they hired. The A/E they hired just happened to be the weak link."

"Well, get ready. He is prepared to drill you a new one during start up and testing on this project. At least that is what he promised me this morning."

"Thanks for letting me know Bill. I will assign as start-up Engineer the 'wienie wagger', I mean Wayne Wagner. He has over 40 years boiler start up experience. He forgot what the Architect on the Mare Island Project knows. He has definite superior knowledge and will make mincemeat out of the Architect if he interferes. I wouldn't be surprised if he calls in the Navy Shore Patrol to arrest the Architect."

"That will be fun. Now after talking to you, I can't wait for the start-up."

On that note Michael hangs up the phone and goes back to the conference room to write the name of Wayne Wagner as the start-up engineer on the Mare Island Naval Shipyard Project Construction Schedule Chart. He leaves the conference room heading to his office with his phone ringing welcoming him. Now what?

"What's up FU?" Are the first words out of Michael's mouth. "Are you about done?"

Forrest Upton Wallace, FU for short, was the latest superintendent for the James River Corporation Absorbent Paper Mill project, short for toilet paper, in Berlin, New Hampshire. He was put there because the project completion date was overdue. A problem infested Contract and the reason Michael was put in charge, to make sure it gets finished as soon as possible and it is in working order when it's finished.

To visit the project job site was brutal and it took an entire day. There was no Airport in Berlin, New Hampshire. The closest Airport to the job site was Portland, Maine. two and a half hours drive from there to Berlin, New Hampshire. There were no direct flights from Seattle, Washington, where the company main office was located and where Michael lived, to Portland, Maine. Michael had to catch a flight from Sea-Tac Airport to Boston, Massachusetts. From there catch a commuter flight to Portland, Maine and rent a car there to drive to Berlin, New Hampshire. Fighting the snow and ice in late Fall and Winter, the Frost Heaves in the Spring and Summer.

"I will be done in a couple of weeks." Forrest Wallace exclaims enthusiastically.

"I should call you 'a couple of weeks Wally' form now on. This is exactly what you said two weeks ago, and two weeks before that and so on. Maybe what we need is a set of new eyes to look at where you are and come up with a realistic Construction Schedule to complete the work."

"Is this necessary?"

"It is. Because you are behind schedule and you've been missing consistently all subsequent Contract Completion Dates you've been expounding. I cannot even schedule a start-up under these circumstances. The General Manager of the Mill called me the other day and he wanted to know when the new mill will be completed and operational. I didn't know what to tell him, because I cannot rely on your reports. I was told that they had stockpiled toilet paper for the duration for the project. Well, they are getting down in their stockpile and soon the stores will be experiencing shortages. Wally, you cannot keep the entire New England by the asshole indefinitely!"

"You are the Boss." Was Forrest Wallace response. "You will do what you have to do."

Michael severed the telephone connection with Forest Wallace and dialled Grace's intercom. He wanted to catch a flight tomorrow morning for Boston with a commuter flight to Portland, Maine with an open return.

"Notify Forrest Wallace, the superintendent to be at Portland, Maine Airport to pick up a company employee. Leave it vague. Don't tell him that the person he will be picking up would be me."

Dan McCoy sauntered to Michael's office with a blank writing pad. He sat uninvited into one of the guest chairs.

"What's on your mind victorious Emperor?" Dan said sarcastically.

"Do you want to keep on working on record Profit breaking Projects?" Were Michael's first words in response.

"I am sorry." Dan said. "I was just joking. Irish humour."

"Make two dozen full sets of the As Built Drawings and one dozen of half size sets of the same Drawings and ship them priority mail to Bill Scott in Hawaii. Break up the shipment in sections, so that a human being could easily lift each package.

"Call all the equipment manufactures and inform them that their Submittal has been approved as originally submitted. Send a letter to each by Certified Mail with receipt signature return required to the same equipment manufacturers repeating in writing what you told them over the phone.

"Send a form letter to Bill Scott addressing all the subcontractors and informing them that the Navy Suspension of Work will be lifted on, thirty calendar days from yesterday. Attached herewith please find a Revised set of Contract Drawings. Should the new Contract Commencement Date and/or the Revised Set of Contract Drawings constitute a Change to your subcontract, please inform our main office with a detailed Cost Estimate Proposal within thirty calendar days of your receipt of this writing. If we do not receive a letter from your firm within the specified time, we will be of the understanding that there will be no additional costs for your portion of the work and you will perform your work for the originally agreed to amount and time of performance.

"Write the same letter yourself, under your signature and send it Certified Mail to all the suppliers."

"Did you get all that Dan?"

"Word for word." Dan McCoy continued writing.

"Good. Because I will be out of town starting tomorrow."

"Where are you going?"

"Berlin, New Hampshire."

"Oh! It was about time for someone to straighten out 'a couple of weeks Wally'. I would love to be a fly on the wall to see FU's expression when he sees you coming out of the airplane."

Dan McCoy left Michael's office still laughing. Michael looked at his watch. It was approaching eleven. He started thinking where he wanted to go to lunch and with whom as his telephone wrung.

"Hi Bill! Bright and early at the office. I see."

"What do you want to do with Roxanne's body?" Was Bill Scott's first question.

"Hasn't anyone claimed it?" Was Michael's follow up logical question.

"None so far have come forward."

"Where is the body now?"

"At the Tripler Medical Centre morgue, I would assume."

"Well, she died at Pearl Harbor Naval Shipyard, government property. She was picked up by government ambulance. She died on her way to Tripler Medical Centre, an Army Hospital where she is currently held, another government institution. I would let the matter rest, if I were you. Has anyone from NIS bugged you about it?"

"Why should they? They were the ones who caused the accident. I can't prove it, but they were the ones who raided our office the night before the meeting to settle the Change. They were probably trying to find out what was your bottom line on the Change."

"Did she list the name of a person to contact in case of emergency in her application?"

"Let me see. An aunt in Worcester, Massachusetts. I have her name, phone and address."

"Call her and let her know. If she wants it shipped to Worcester, Massachusetts, she will have to foot the bill, or at the very least the difference between Roxanne's last pay check and the cost of the transfer. Maybe the Navy would volunteer to foot the bill. I believe the NIS severed the wire splice to silence the feed to the intrusion alarm of the office trailer."

"Sounds like we are both thinking the same." Bill Scott said. "The reason though that I called you was to let you know that JG, the Iron Forman of American Welding was just diagnosed this morning with Bone Cancer..."

"Not JG!" Michael uttered disturbed. "The JG who is wider than he is high?"

"The same one."

"He was a monster. The strongest man I've met. I remember when I first arrived at the job site, what was it nine months ago; Steve Crane was fucking around with him and JG picked him up single handedly by the front of his shirt and lifted him off the ground making Steve do push ups in the air just with the strength of his right hand. He then, when he got his message across, set him down standing up on the ground as gently as he could be. An amazing show of upper body strength as I remember it."

"Well, he was going downhill fast. He was losing weight. He was worried about his balance on the job. Ironworkers you know, their sense of balance is outmost. Finally, Francis the President of American Welding had him see a doctor. The doctor ordered some tests at the Hospital. The test results came in this morning. A death sentence. Bone Cancer."

"Do you think it may have something to do with the SARGO Incident?" Michael said cautiously.

"What else?" Bill Scott exclaimed. "First the cat and the kittens, then Bill Fleming the Foreman of Pacific Boiler and Piping came down with Leukemia. Now JG with American Welding came down with Bone Cancer. You don't have to be Einstein to conclude that something is rotten on the job site."

"But...Bill I don't have any solid evidence to contradict what the Navy is saying. The Navy assured us that it was just a rescue exercise simulating as a nuclear accident. I have not been able to find the smoking gun. Do you have any evidence to contradict the Navy?"

"Simulated my foot. Did you see how quickly the Navy painted over the name and number of the submarine and towed it in the middle of Pearl Harbor, fenced around with nuclear magenta signs. All the naval traffic was keeping their distance from it. Now, the last evidence, the sub itself, is gone. I ask around and I am told 'What submarine'? It's like asking Sergeant Schultz of Hogan's Heroes. His answer was always: 'I know nothing'. My wife who is a Junior at the University of Hawaii studying to be a nurse tells me that what's been happening at the job site are symptoms due to radiation exposure. I am worried Mike."

"All I can do Bill is investigate further when I come back to sign the Change; in a month or so." Were Michael's final words before hanging up.

He dialled immediately the company attorney, Don Davidson of Fergusson & Burdell and was put immediately through.

"Hi Don. Do you have plans for lunch today?" Michael asked.

"For you my boy, even if I had plans, unless I was in Court, I will change them. By the way, I did not know you were back from Hawaii. How did the meeting with the Navy go? I can't wait to see you and find out. Hurry up and get here as soon as you can."

"Not an elaborate lunch this time Don. I have to go home and pack. I am catching an early flight tomorrow morning for Berlin, New Hampshire. Another fire to put out."

"You are the regular Captain of the 'SWAT team of one' for your company. I don't know how you do it."

"I am in a mood for a New York style pastrami sandwich, Don."

"I know just the place. Schmoes! Right downtown, almost across the Street from our offices. They deliver. As soon as you get here, I will order you the best pastrami sandwich you tasted in your life. Hurry up!"

Michael hangs up and goes out in the parking lot to his car parked in his designated parking space. 'MAM - VP'. In no time his SAAB EMS Turbo was across the Lake Washington Floating Bridge and into the City of Seattle proper. He parked in the Parking Structure of the only Building, Union Square, which was straddling the I-5 Interstate. He took the elevator for the top floor of the building home of the Fergusson & Burdell Law Offices.

Nora, Don's private secretary immediately led Michael to the familiar corner office whose decor resembled a mechanics shop. Don Davidson was in a meeting with a fellow in his early thirties, same age as Michael. Don waved Nora through, so the meeting must not have been with a client.

"Michael, I want you to meet Tom Wolfendale, our latest acquisition from the Prosecutor's Office. Tom, I want you to meet Michael, the fellow we were talking about. Tom, will be working with me for a while Mike, until he gets the hang of things around here."

"I read your Resume." Tom Wolfendale interjected. "You graduated from Washington State University in 1970. Your major was Chemical Engineering. My wife went to WSU also about the same time you attended. You were Sigma Chi, she was Tri-Delta. I was wondering if you ever met in any of the Greek parties."

At the mention of Tri-Delta Michael became beet red. Tom noticed it immediately.

"What's the matter. Did I open the wrong closet and all the skeletons came tumbling out?"

"Michael, you appear ill at ease, and this is not like you." Don Davidson said enjoying the fact that uncharacteristically Michael appeared ready to throw up.

"Is your wife's name Barbara by any chance?" Michael asked Tom when he got control of what was bothering him.

"Bingo!" Tom responded.

"Is she a natural blonde?" Michael kept up the interrogatory.

"Jackpot!" Tom yelled exuberantly. "What happened with you two. Do I dare to ask?" Tom asked sombrely.

"Your wife was my first date in College." Michael said with a smile. "It was my first day at WSU. January 3, 1966 and your wife volunteered and was assigned to show me around campus. We spent the entire day together."

The food was ordered and Michael spent the rest of the time, until the food arrived talking about what made him come to the USA. Why he selected Washington State University. His first night at the Sigma Alpha Epsilon toga party. His next day meeting with Barbara of Delta, Delta, Delta sorority whose members did not kiss on a first date.

"I can't wait to get home!" Tom Wolfendale exclaimed. "Do I have stories to tell?"

"It was fifteen years ago Tom. She probably would not remember. For me though it was the first girl, by name I met on campus. I don't count the toga clad girls at Sigma Alpha Epsilon. I remember them as a group."

"Don't you worry. I will refresh her memory." Tom replied with a glee.

"Enough of going down memory lane." Don Davidson interrupted. "Back to the present. I want to know how the Navy meeting went."

"And I want to discuss with you some consequential issues that could be resultant of the SARGO Incident." Michael concluded.

He went and explained blow by blow how he prepared for the meeting, how he presented his case and turned the Navy tables around so that their own Rules applied equally to them, resulted in an award of $875,000.00 for damages, based on the Eicleay formula.

"What have I been telling you Tom. He thinks like an attorney." Don Davidson exclaimed. "The Navy did not have a chance."

"The Navy had five attorneys at the meeting. One local and four from Washington D. C. The latter got up and left the meeting when

I asked them to identify themselves. The local attorney had identified himself as the Legal Council of the OICC office. He stayed throughout the meeting; but did not say a single word."

"When are you going back to sign the Contract Modification?" Tom Wolfendale asked.

"Twenty-seven days from today." Michael replied.

"You did well my boy. What are you going to do with all that money?" Don Davidson wanted to know.

"I already bought a sailboat. A brand new 41-foot Newport, I had my eye on at the Seattle Boat Show. I plan to send a picture of it with me at the helm, sailing on the reach, to the A/E, the OICC, John Muchmore and Dave Brown of the NIS with an inscription 'Thank you. Living Well is the Best Revenge'." Michael declared.

Both Don Davidson and Tom Wolfendale were laughing so hard, they were crying.

"You won't do that. It will piss them off to no end. Remember, the government is not smart like you, but it has staying power and unlimited resources." Tom Wolfendale cautioned Michael.

"I can see him doing exactly that." Don Davidson said. "You don't know Michael like I do. He has 'Thrasos', that's Greek for arrogance, to the point of 'Hubris'."

"And that is my downfall. According to my wife." Michael concluded.

"It has served you well so far." Don Davidson disagreed.

"Winning through intimidation is a fable." Michael said. "The reason that I usually prevail is that I outwork the competition. I know when I step into a meeting that I am prepared to play level 10 chess and my competition is prepared for level 2. I can smell their fear and this is pure oxygen for me."

"I sure don't want to be on the wrong side of you." Tom Wolfendale exclaimed.

"If you stick with Fergusson & Burdell you won't. They have been our company attorneys for over ten years."

"What about the other issue you wanted to discuss." Don Davidson deftly changed the subject, in order to convert their lunch into billable hours.

Michael started from the beginning for Tom Wolfendale's benefit. He continued with what he eye witnessed and what he was told by others.

"We have a file in our safe regarding the issues associated with the SARGO Incident from the start." Don Davidson further clarified. "It was a good thing too, because Michael was at risk to joining the ranks of 'desaparasitos', for a while."

Michael went on to explain that he was questioning the Navy's explanation that the SARGO Incident was simply an emergency rescue exercise simulating a nuclear accident.

"If it was an exercise, why didn't the Navy produce the Geiger Counters I requested that first day to test our job site and insure the veracity of their claims?

"Look at the cat, pregnant at the time of 'the rescue exercise', and the monster kittens it berthed a month later. Look how swiftly the cat was poisoned by persons unknown together with the deformed kittens and then mysteriously taken away and disposed.

249

"Four months latter from the date of the SARGO Incident, Bill Fleming, the Foreman of Pacific Boiler and Piping, our mechanical subcontractor on the project, was diagnosed with Leukemia.

"Eight months later from the date of the SARGO Incident, JG, the Foreman of American Welding, our steelwork subcontractor on the project, after continuous weight loss and balance problems on the job is tested at a hospital and the tests come back positive, Bone Cancer.

"Our own superintendent's wife who is a junior in the Nursing School of the University of Hawaii says that the above are symptoms of Radiation Exposure. The problem being that I do not have undisputed evidence of wrong doing by the Navy. The examples I have brought above, could be circumstantial. The whole incident has been covered by the Navy under their 'Code of Silence'. Even the ghost submarine, that for months now has been parked in the middle of Pearl Harbor surrounded by a fence bearing magenta signs indicating the presence of nuclear material, has disappeared. When the Navy is asked for the submarine's whereabouts, their response is: "What submarine. We know nothing of what you are talking about." How do we break this 'Code of Silence' the Navy has adopted?"

"I'll tell you the answer to your question." Don Davidson expounded ex Cathedra. "The Freedom of Information Act. This is a fairly new Law passed by both the Congress and the Senate, recently signed by the President. Under the statures of the Law, any citizen may ask the government to disclose and provide copies of everything under the sun, within thirty calendar days of the Freedom of Information Request. If an attorney inquires, the time element for a response is cut down to ten calendar days. I will write a Freedom of Information Request to the OICC Perl Harbor Naval Shipyard today, on your behalf, requesting copies of everything regarding the nuclear submarine SARGO from the date of the Incident and henceforth. They are required to respond within ten (10) calendar days. In ten calendar days from today, you will have your answer."

"Thank you Don." Michael gets up to leave. "I knew I could depend on you."

Chapter 23

The SWAT Makes a Diversionary Trip to New England.

Early the next morning, before the crack of dawn, Michael with a suitcase full of winter clothes in the trunk of his black SAAB EMS Turbo is making his way South on I-405 to the Sea-Tac Airport to catch his flight to Boston, Massachusetts. In Boston he will catch a commuter puddle jumper which flies every hour on the hour, from sunrise to sunset, to Portland, Maine. It only holds twenty passengers with a pilot and co-pilot aboard and a single stewardess.

Michael recalls that he was asked by James River Corporation at the start of the Project to attend a meeting on a Monday morning. He refused to fly on a Sunday, on account of a family conflict. Specifically, a dance recital that same Sunday by his daughter. The meeting was rescheduled for Tuesday morning. He went to his daughter's recital on Sunday evening and flew out of Seattle on Monday morning. When he arrived in Boston, he found out that the commuter flight he was scheduled to take on Sunday out of Boston, had crush landed in Portland, Maine and all passengers on board together with the two pilots and the stewardess perished. It was a sobering experience. His love for his little girl saved his life.

Michael parked on the fourth floor of the Airport Parking Structure so he could walk towards the causeway on the fourth floor; connecting the Parking Structure with Ticketing, without having to take an elevator. He checked his suitcase all the way to Portland, Maine. He caught the underground train for the South Satellite Terminal. He found his Gate and shortly afterwards he boarded First Class. He had breakfast on board; followed a few hours later by a snack. He landed at the Boston, Massachusetts Logan Airport at 2:00 PM. He caught the 3:00 PM commuter flight to Portland, Maine and landed there forty-five minutes later.

He was the first to exit and spotted Forrest Wallace immediately in the waiting area. Forrest Wallace's face drooped as soon as he spotted Michael.

"That bad, eh!" Forrest uttered in almost a whisper. "You had to come yourself."

Michael was known throughout the company as the 'SWAT'. He appeared only on the jobs that were in the process of 'heading South'. He had an unlimited budget in his hands and authority to fire anyone in the company and hire replacements to bring the Project back into profitability. Michael was the last person you wanted to meet and greet at the Airport.

"They call you a 'couple of weeks Wally', back at the office. No one seems to know what's been happening on this Project. I have not been able to get the straight story from you over the phone and your Daily Construction Reports contradict each other. What would you do in my shoes?"

"It is a big Project scattered over a large area. I have to rely on second hand information provided by my foremen." Forrest Wallace said timidly.

"Well, that's the reason I am here." Michael declared. "Assess the situation and propose possible solutions."

"Are you going to fire me?" Forrest Wallace voiced his immediate concern, born as soon as he laid eyes on Michael getting out of the airplane.

"I don't know. I have not made up my mind. I would like to see the job site first." Michael replied as diplomatically as he could. "We go a long way back, you and I. I always felt we made a good team. Although, at opposite ends of the polarity spectrum. I like you as a friend and I will make every effort to work with you on this project. As long as you do exactly what I tell you."

"You are the Boss!" Forrest Wallace exclaimed. "Of course, I will do what you say."

They picked Michael's suitcase from the carousel. They got into the company pick up and headed West towards Berlin, New Hampshire though scenic back roads.

"I got you checked in already at Gorham Inn." Forrest Wallace said. "So we can go straight to the job site."

Michael was aware that Gorham Inn was six miles South of Berlin. They arrived on the job site right upon quitting time of the construction crew. Michael went to the office trailer to pick up a set of Drawings. He noticed a young woman in the process of putting new lipstick at a nearby desk. He said a hurried hello as he got the roll of Drawings on his way out.

"You hired a secretary?" Michael addressed Forrest Wallace. "I have not seen a female name in the Project payroll?"

"She is the daughter of the Chief Engineer at the Mill. He asked me and I am doing him a favour. I pay her out of the petty cash, under the table. She is a sweet thing and very useful answering the phone and doing the time sheets. It leaves me time to visit the job site."

Michael said nothing. He recalled however, that one of the reasons Forrest Wallace brought up at the Airport for not having a firsthand knowledge of the site conditions was that he relied on second hand information provided by the foremen. He walked the site and made notations on the Drawings he was holding. Several hours later, when the sun started setting and was getting dark, he rolled up the Drawings and headed for the company truck.

"Where to Boss?" Forrest Wallace inquired. "Back at the hotel or dinner first."

"Is the Lobster Trap in Conway open?"

"It is. Dinner fist, then, it is." Forrest replied. "What did you think of the job site?"

"You want the bad news first or the worst?"

"That bad, eh!" Forrest Wallace repeated.

"The bad news is that you are six weeks from being completed, provided you change the method of construction you've been utilizing. The worst news is the method of construction you've been utilizing. Everything got started and nothing has been finished. Your crews want the project to go on indefinitely so they can keep their jobs. You on the other hand have no idea what was accomplished each day, if any. The job looks the same every day, with no way to determine the productive output. This will change. Starting tomorrow."

"Tell me what to do and I will see that it gets done." Forrest Wallace responded, eagerly.

"Stop at that stationary store on the right." Michael pointed. "I need a roll of flimsy paper."

Michael got out and went inside the store. He came out with a big roll of flimsy paper. He got back in the truck.

"From this point on, this will take the place of the Drawings." He said holding the roll of flimsy paper. "I will make sketches of the work missing from each equipment site. You will hand the flimsy paper to a crew of two or three of four workers, according to what I have indicated at the bottom of the flimsy. You will write their names at the bottom of the page. You will hand it to them and tell them that you expect all the work shown on the flimsy to be accomplished at the end of the day. If it is. You hand another flimsy,

I will prepare for you, the next day. If the work is not accomplished you find out why it was not. If all the material was on hand. Fire the crew responsible. If they provide you with a reason and you find that it is valid, correct it immediately, or you will be fired. Are we clear. By the time I leave, you will have a stack of flimsies and a new Construction Schedule I will prepare that ties into the work shown on the flimsies. Keep that to yourself. If you stay on schedule, you will be done in six weeks."

They arrive at the Lobster Trap restaurant. The walls of the restaurant were salt water aquarium tanks filled with lobsters. They sat at a table for four and a waitress immediately wrapped them in a plastic bib. There was no choice. The only thing on the menu was lobster cooked and prepared in a number of ways. They ordered a pitcher of beer and pointed at two enormous lobsters inside the tank closest to them, cooked the traditional way, steamed, with french fries. They each ordered a baby greens salad with blue cheese dressing.

A giant articulated claw retrieved the two lobsters and they were off to the kitchen. Their salads came next accompanied with a steamy loaf of French bread and butter with a steak knife through the bread. Michael had said all that was needed to be said before. Forrest Wallace was reluctant to bring up anything else. They were both busy eating. Michael sliced the bread and took an end slice for himself slathered in butter, which he noted was European butter. His favourite. It was a little saltier than its American variety.

The two lobsters arrived in platters with a side plate of French fries and cole slaw. The appropriate tools were set on the table beside each dinner. A lobster fork and a shell cracker. A cup of melted butter on a stand with a lit candle at the bottom to keep the butter melted and warm. A plate with lemon slices and a spare empty platter for the shell waste.

They started with the lobster legs sucking the meat like a straw. Followed by the legs with the claws. The lobster elbows being the most delicate meat. Finally, they cracked the end fan tail and slipped the lobster tail from the other end. They sat back sated. They ordered ice cream for dessert. They were done for the night. Michael paid and got into the company truck. Gorham Inn here we come.

Michael picked up his key from the reception and bade Forrest Wallace good night. Michael's room came equipped with a desk and immediately started working. He had a photographic memory and put it to use. He overlaid an 8 1/2 x 11 piece of flimsy against the Drawing detail and copied all the missing portion of the work. He kept going completing enough for a week's worth of work and at the back of the last full size Drawing he prepared a bar chart Construction Schedule showing thirty working days on top. He numbered the sketches he had made and tied their number to the Construction Schedule.

He got undressed afterwards and fell asleep.

Bright and early the next morning Forrest Wallace knocked on Michael's door. Michael invited him in and explained his plan of attack. He showed Forrest Wallace the Construction Schedule and handed him the numbered stack of flimsies.

"Call a meeting as soon as we arrive at the job site and start handing the flimsies to the crew teams with the understanding that you would be inspecting the final product at the end of the day. Don't worry. A good crew would be done with the work in half a day. I want to see their productivity that first day and adopt the results to all future work. I will stay in the office trailer and complete the Construction Schedule with the rest of the flimsies."

They get in the company truck and head for a quick breakfast at the Inner Circle restaurant, in Berlin. A hippie joint, was Michael's first impression, left over from the sixties. The breakfast was a health Nut's nirvana. Fruits and nuts with a splendid carrot cake. They had to put with herbal tea, coffee was not on the menu. Michael made a mental note to avoid the joint in the future. He spotted the Mystic Pizza across the street and made a note for lunch there, later today.

Forrest Wallace called for a General Meeting as soon as he parked the truck. Twenty workers showed up. The entire crew, according to Forrest.

"I would like to introduce you to my Boss, all the way from Seattle, Washington. The work progress has not been satisfactory. So, we are going to change our Method of Construction, starting today. Everything got started and nothing has finished. This will change, starting right now."

Forrest Wallace went on to explain that the job assignments will be a daily occurrence.

"You will be handed a flimsy and assigned to a crew. By the end of the day the work assignment shown on the flimsy is to be completed and the flimsy returned to me signed by the entire crew as completed. If the work is not completed by the end of the day, with no explanation as to why, I will personally fire the crew at the end of the day with a negative recommendation to the Union on their behalf."

The crew members gathered around Forrest Wallace and started receiving sketches and assignments. Michael retreated to a spare desk and commenced with his sketches and Construction Schedule completion. The young woman kept her eyes on Michael the whole time. She appeared smart and soon caught on to what was happening. She introduced herself as Jennifer.

Forrest Wallace did not step foot in the office. He spent all his time overseeing the work performed and accomplished, for the first time, by the work crews.

"What's a good place to have lunch around here?" Michael asked Jennifer.

"What would you like?" Smart girl Michael is thinking, answering his question with a question of her own.

"I was thinking Pizza." Michael replied.

"Mystic Pizza." Was Jennifer's reply. "The best in the world…"

"How would you know? Where have you been to compare?"

"I have not been anywhere, besides New Hampshire." Jennifer replied blushing.

"Let's go find out." Michael extricated her of her embarrassment. "You drive. I will pay for lunch."

They got into a new FORD escort. Jennifer's graduation present. She was bound for Dartmouth, Michael found out, in a couple of months.

"I thought Dartmouth was an all men's College." Michael pointed out.

"That was at one time. They allow women now."

"What are you going to study?"

"Law." Jennifer answered laconically.

"That's all we need!" Michael responded smiling. "Another lawyer!"

"Did you know that the majority of the corporations in this country are headed by lawyers?" Jennifer responded deadpan. "And 100% of the corporate boards in this country include an attorney?"

"You have done your homework. That's for sure." Michael acknowledged chastised.

"Currently, women are underrepresented in the Board of Directors. I predict that by the time I graduate, there will be a mad rush to hire women for upper management." Jennifer concluded.

"You are a very smart and astute young lady." Michael concluded.

"Coming from you, it is a great compliment." Jennifer said mischievously.

"What do you mean?" Michael said surprised.

"I made my job to find out from F U Wallace, isn't what you call him, all there is to know about the head of the Project I am working."

Michael looked at her profile, as she was driving, with new admiration. The young getting ready to replace the old guard, he was thinking. With the technology changing by leaps and bounds, the old guard did not have a chance. He suddenly felt old and he was what, fifteen years older than his companion.

They arrived at the Mystic Pizza. Michael pointed out the Inner Circle restaurant as the place he had breakfast.

"The worst breakfast I had. No wonder I am so hungry." Michael admitted.

"I would have thought it would have made you homesick. Didn't you grow in the sixties?"

"I was not involved in the hippy movement in any way. I was a student athlete with a scholarship. I visited other campuses to play, but the hippies there were a mere spectacle. Soon to be forgotten, after I returned to Pullman, Washington. The school, Washington State University, was still anchored in the fifties. Ten years behind the California and Oregon Schools' culture. We were the PAC 8 back then."

They went inside the Mystic Pizza. Jennifer was greeted as one of the crew. She whispered something at a couple of girls and the neutral service protocol was transformed instantly to VIP. Michael ordered a medium pepperoni pizza with mushrooms, green onions and Anaheim peppers.

"I like what you ordered." Jennifer said. "Make that a large one for both of us." She said to the waitress.

Michael ordered a large soda for himself and Jennifer followed suit.

The pizza was the best Michael had tasted in his life, and he considered himself a connoisseur of pizza since his college days on his first date with his present wife Christina at the WSU Rat Haus. Mystic Pizza was far superior than any Pizza he had ever tasted.

"You were right!" He said to Jennifer. "It may be the best pizza in the world."

"It's Sicilian with all the spices from the old world. The owner and his wife are from there."

"A Sicilian decided to immigrate and start a Pizzeria in Berlin, New Hampshire?"

"No stranger than a Greek deciding to immigrate and start building Power Plants all over the United States, and doing classified projects for the Department of Defence." Jennifer replied with a smile.

"Touché!"

They finished the rest of the pizza and returned to the job site. Forrest Wallace greeted them ecstatic holding a bunch of flimsies in his hand.

"Half of the work assignments are finished and signed off."

"Did you check them?"

"That's where I am coming from. You have reduced the job as always to activities with the workers simply being the cogs and sprockets, all running at the speed you have predetermined. Your system is efficient, but it dehumanizes the worker."

"Do you think the assembly line is any different?"

"I am not arguing with you. I just don't have the talent you have to ignore the people. They come to me with all sorts of their family problems. I like that."

"Well, that's where we differ Wally. I would just walk away. Or rather I would send the individual back to work and tell him to quit wasting my time."

"What do you want me to do with the ones that have finished early?" Forrest Wallace inquired.

"Inspect their work and if they are truly done, let them go home early then." Was Michael's reply. "Tomorrow's assignment will be racked up a notch. By the way do you have any equipment or any other material shortages? I mean do you have everything you will need on hand?"

"Everything is here and accounted for, except for the stack."

The stack made of fiberglass and mounted on top of the scrubber was being fabricated in Bellingham, Washington. Michael had not visited the facility there which was fabricating the fiberglass stack. He called them several times and was told that the stack fabrication was on schedule. Bellingham was two and a half hours North of Seattle by car. Located on the coast, very close to the Canadian border.

"I will personally drive to the fabricator in Bellingham as soon as I get back to Seattle and verify the status of the stack. If it is done? I will direct them to ship it to you immediately. I am sure you will have it on hand in a couple of weeks."

Michael went back to his desk and finished the rest of the sketches and completed the Construction Schedule. Michael told Forrest Wallace at the end of the day that he would be leaving tomorrow.

"My job is done here, as long as you remain on schedule and follow the same procedure. You will be done in six weeks. I will schedule a start-up engineer to show up in six weeks. Probably, Jack Bell. Cut down your crew to five on that day. That's all you will need during start up and testing."

"Thank you Michael. You make me look good. I won't forget this."

"Keep your eyes open tomorrow for falling tools around me. I plan to inspect the work, early tomorrow morning." Michael said laughing. "You don't need to drive me to the Portland, Maine Airport. I will rent a car locally and drop it off at the Airport in Maine. I am sure they will be delighted at the arrangement; as rental car traffic usually runs the other way."

Michael called the office in Seattle from the office telephone and talked to Grace. Bill Scott had called from Honolulu and left a message for Michael to call back.

Six hours' time difference he thought. They will be just arriving at Pearl Harbor Naval Shipyard. He dialled the familiar (808) area code number. Bill Scott answered the phone.

"Two more workers were diagnosed with lung cancer." Bill Scott announced without preamble.

"Did they smoke cigarettes?" Michael asked cautiously.

"That they did. Over two packs a day." Bill Scott admitted.

"You cannot blame SARGO conclusively. I cannot bring it up with the Navy. I already know their answer." Michael concluded.

"With that wait and see attitude yours, pretty soon we will all be dead..."

"I had our company lawyer Request pursuant to the Freedom of Information Act everything pertaining to the SARGO nuclear submarine from the day of the Incident forth. The Navy must have received the Request by now and they have less than a week to respond. Have you heard anything?"

"Why would they bother with me?" Bill Scott replied. "It's you they will talk to because they are scared shitless of you. When are you coming over?"

"I will be there in a couple of weeks." Michael said hanging up the phone.

"What was that all about?" Forrest Wallace inquired listening in on the telephone conversation.

Jennifer was still in the office and she was listening too. Michael explained to them the abbreviated version of the SARGO Incident and what was Michael doing about it.

"Was it a nuclear accident?" Jennifer asked breathless.

"I don't know." Michael admitted. "The Navy officially called it an emergency rescue exercise. I eyewitnesses the exercise and it looked real to me. However, I have nothing to compare it with and so far I have found no concrete evidence to argue with the Navy, other than the pregnant cat and a couple of examples of Leukemia and Bone Cancer, I already told you. I have not come down with something, so far.", Michael said smiling. "I am curious though to discover what will be the Navy's response to the Freedom of Information Request."

They locked up and left early. Michael wanted to visit a jewellery shop before it closed. He bought for his daughter's gold bracelet another 14-carat trinket to add to her collection. A miniature replica of the Hotel New Hampshire. His daughter Elli had gotten the gold bracelet from his mother in Greece when she was two years old. He had been adding to its links ever since gold replicas of local monuments from the places he had jobs. A gold streetcar from San

Francisco, a gold pineapple from Honolulu, a gold Space Needle from Seattle, a gold Hobie Cat from Florida, a gold horse from Wyoming, a gold lobster from Maine, Paul Revere riding a horse from Boston, a gold Empire State Building from New York and so on. Pretty soon all the links on the bracelet would be filled up. It was already weighing over a pound. A treasure full of memories. It would be very valuable, when she grew up.

The trip back to Seattle was uneventful. At Logan Airport in Boston, he bought four lobsters and had them packed in dry ice for the trip home. He put them in the overhead compartment of the Airplane.

At home, his daughter Elli was delighted with her gold trinket and immediately secured it on her bracelet. Todd, his son, thinking that the box his dad was carrying and had set on the kitchen counter was his present, opened the box and dumped four frightened lobsters on the kitchen floor. The lobsters started scurrying around trying to escape with the kids chasing them; their mother screaming at them not to touch them or lose finger from their claws which they had positioned up front in a karate posture.

Michael finally retrieved them and dumped them one by one in a pot of boiling water. The kids, particularly Elli was repulsed at the lobsters screaming the moment they were suspended above the boiling pot. As soon as the lobsters turned from green to deep red, Michael retrieved them and demonstrated how to slip the tail on the lobster.

Elli declared that lobster was the ultimate in food and she could eat lobster every day for the rest of her life and never get tired of it.

Chapter 24

Sailing Navigation Comes Handy

"Where are you headed in such a hurry?" Michael screeched to a stop as he was crossing the open door of Bob Westlake's office. The President of the company.

"I am heading North, to Bellingham. I want to check on the status of the fiberglass stack they are fabricating for the James River Corporation Paper Mill in Berlin, New Hampshire."

"How are you getting there?" Bob asked.

"Driving of course. How else?" Michael replied perplexed.

"You know…I got my flying pilot's license last week." Bob Westlake said with pride. "I went ahead and bought an airplane this week, I had my eye on. A brand-new single engine Cherokee Piper. I would like to put some miles on it on company time…" Bob suggested wishfully.

Flying for fun and charging the company on top of it. Michael was thinking. Who was he to complain with a 41-foot Newport sailboat he recently purchased at the Seattle Boat Show. Money was running like a river in the company as a result of the Trident Submarine Base Power Plant. Another of Michael's projects. The partner's bonuses were big enough to make the purchase of all these toys.

"OK." Michael conceded. "Lead the way."

Bob Westlake literally leaped from his desk after Michael's last remark.

Michael picked up the phone from Bob's desk and called the Bellingham fabricator, warning them that he was coming to check the status of the stack they were fabricating.

"It's all done." He was told. "Ready to be shipped."

"We still like to inspect it." Michael insisted.

He really did not. He could just as well release it for shipment to Berlin, New Hampshire over the phone. He trusted the fabricator's Quality Control that the stack was fabricated in accordance with the Drawings and Specifications he personally had written. He looked at Bob. He was crestfallen anticipating that the trip to Bellingham was cancelled.

"We will be at the Bellingham Airport around noon." He said instead. "Please provide a car to drive us to your fabricating facility. There will be two of us." He concluded.

"Thank you. Thank you, Michael." Bob could hardly contain his exuberance.

Michael called Grace McDonald, his secretary and informed her that he was flying to Bellingham with Bob Westlake, the President, to inspect the fiberglass stack being fabricated there and they would be back before quitting time, four o'clock in the afternoon.

They proceeded to the parking lot and boarded Bob's Mercedes 220D. The morning commuter traffic was at the tail end so they made good time to SeaTac Airport. They avoided the commercial Airport and made their way to the private airplane lot which had plenty of car parking with no parking fee or parking meters in sight.

"That's handy." Michael commented carrying his briefcase out of the Mercedes.

"The only way to fly!" Bob commented proudly, bursting at the seams.

They walked inside the unguarded chain link fence, with Bob leading the way to his airplane which was tied down on huge eyebolts embedded onto the pavement. Bob proceeded with his prefight inspection and release of the airplane from its ties to the ground. He produced a detailed list of items to check and was proceeding down the list with gusto, putting a checkmark beside each item he had checked.

Bob headed, followed by Michael, inside a building the size of a large tool shed and filed his flight plan. Afterwards, they headed back towards the Airplane.

Bob indicated, that he was done with the outside of the plane inspection, and they could now board the airplane. Michael stepped on the designated spot on the wing, he couldn't really miss it having the outline of the bottom of his shoe coated in non-skid material, and climbed into the cock pit. Bob continued with his interior pre-flight inspection and proudly at its completion started the engine. The propeller up front started turning. The weather was clear and sunny. Rare for Seattle. Not a cloud in the sky, Michael noted looking up as Bob closed and locked the cockpit overhead cover.

Bob called the control tower, gave the make and serial number of his airplane and requested permission for take-off. He was directed to a specific runway away from commercial airplanes which were taking off and landing nonstop every few minutes. They proceeded at the end of the runway and Bob gunned the engine. They started rolling on the runway at progressively higher speed, until suddenly the airplane lost touch with the runway and soared in the sky, heading North.

Bob kept the airplane altitude at 5,000 feet and basically followed the I-5 freeway North, the same route Michael would have been taking if he had driven. They reached the Bellingham Airport a little before noon. They were the only airplane in sight. Bob called the Bellingham control centre and asked permission to land. They directed him to the designated runway and in no time, they were on the ground.

"Flying looks like a piece of cake Bob." Michael commented with admiration at Bob's flying skills. "Sailing, on the other hand, is a hell of a lot harder."

"I never sailed in my life. Nor have I been on a sailboat in my life." Bob added sadly, angling for an invitation to Michael's 41-foot Newport sailboat moored on Lake Washington in Kirkland, which Michael ignored.

The Bellingham fabricator true to their word had sent a car. A full-size affair driven by the President of the company with his Chief Engineer in the passenger seat. They introduced themselves and stated that they already had made reservations for lunch before heading to their plant. Bob and Michael were being given the VIP treatment.

After a leisurely lunch at a sea food restaurant right on the water, they were driven to the plant. There were given a tour of the facilities ending up at the James River Corporation Paper Mill stack which was being crated to be transported in forty-foot sections. A fiberglass stack was a fiberglass stack. The big question: Whether it was done or not? Was being answered 'de facto' as the stack was being crated. Shipping out of the fabrication facility was scheduled for first thing in the morning, tomorrow. The purpose of the trip North was accomplished.

Michael asked for a ride back to the Bellingham Airport. The same car with the same two people made the return trip.

"All in all, a very enjoyable and productive day." Michael pronounced.

He gave the two in the front seat of the car the telephone number of the Berlin, New Hampshire job site office trailer and asked them to make sure they provided the information to the truck driver who would be transporting the stack, with instructions to stay in touch with Forrest Wallace, the name of the superintendent, on a daily basis and report to him each day the current location of the truck transporting the stack.

The car dropped them off at the Airport; which was nothing more than a glorified prefabricated metal building. Bob filed his flight plan and they both met at the airplane, which had been tied down.

"Shouldn't we refuel?" Michael asked. Basically, ignorant of the procedures.

"They charge here twice what they charge in Seattle." Was Bob's succinct comment. His trademark to walk over a five-dollar bill to pick up a dime.

They went through the pre-flight rigamarole and were airborne a short time later. Bob decided to forego the I-5 route they had followed on the way up and instead followed the Washington State coastline on the way down. Michael noticed clouds and fog forming on the right over the San Juan islands, but thought nothing of it. He started paying closer attention however, a few minutes later when the fog started rolling inland at an amazing speed.

"Check the fog on the right, coming off the San Juan islands." Michael prompted Bob.

"Never mind the fog. We will beat it." Was Bob's casual response.

"I don't think so." Michael commented. "I've been watching the fog since take off. Its progress inland is at an accelerating pace."

"We will head West and fly over the San Juan islands." Bob pronounced. "We will catch the tail end of the fog and get around it."

That's exactly what Bob did. They were now inside the fog heading West. The fog was very thick. It looked like they were flying into the night and it was only 3:00 PM my Michael's Omega Chronograph watch. One of his pride and joy. The first and only watch worn on the moon in 1969. Michael could not even see the airplane propeller a few feet in front of them. Bob turned on the windshield wipers because the fog was condensing on the front window like it was raining. The fog was all around them with no end in sight. The talk through the headphones was alarming with several private airplanes in trouble already. The unknown tower speaking was of little help other than urging the air traffic to head East. The airplane carrying Bob and Michael was heading in the opposite direction, West, out to sea.

"Maybe it is time to consult the airplane flight instruments." Michael suggested politely.

"I am not cleared for instrument flight." Was Bob's response.

"What do you mean?" Michael exploded. "You told me you got your pilot's license last week!"

"I did." Bob confirmed. "But it is for visual flights, and only in daylight hours."

"Like following I-5 freeway on the way going North." Michael concluded.

He picked off the floor of the airplane a map of the area. He positioned it on his lap the same way they were flying, West. He opened his briefcase and extracted his portable tritium compass from his sailboat. He always kept it handy to double check the sailboat's main compass. He positioned it over the map and plotted a diagonal course back to the mainland. He looked at Bob. He was white like a corpse. All the blood had drained from his face.

"Bob turn the airplane at a 270-degree heading." Michael spoke with undisputed authority.

Bob looked at Michael, but he did exactly what was told.

They continued flying blind to the heading Michael had charted using his sailing navigation experience.

"Do you have any idea where we will end up on the mainland?" Bob asked timidly.

"I calculated the wind side slip and adjusted accordingly the compass heading. With any luck, we should hit the mainland somewhere in the vicinity of Everett. There are a lot of factories and stacks all over the place there, so you should maintain your altitude or we may hit something there..."

"Don't worry. I am not allowed to fly lower than 500 feet."

They continued on the course plotted by Michael hopping for the fog to abate so they could have a visual of where they were and where they were heading. Instinctively, Michael was hopping that they were heading in the right direction with his 'seat of the pants' navigation.

Suddenly, silence descended. Michael could not hear the engine noise.

"What happened?" He asked frantically.

"We are out of fuel." Bob replied mechanically.

Michael was getting ready to tear a new one for Bob, for not taking fuel in Bellingham, like he had suggested. But what was the use. He kept quiet watching the airplane on its glide path, hopefully towards the mainland. The silence was deafening. Michael watched the altimeter slowly winding down. The fog steady, all around them. How low was the fog hanging? Probably all the way to the ground, Michael was thinking. At that moment they passed the altitude of 1,000 feet from the ground. They were entering the FAA regulations No! No! Zone. Five hundred feet the FAA limit was staring at them, up ahead.

The moment they passed the 500-foot limit several things happened. For one they broke clear of the fog. They could finally see! And what a sight. Michael thought he was at a video arcade in front of a game screen. In front of them lay a lighted runway like in a video game. Was it a mirage? They had no choice the airplane touched in the centre of the runway, bounced a couple of times and settled. Bob turned down the flaps and applied the brakes so they soon stopped there in the middle of the runway.

"Where are we?" Were Bob's first words.

"Who cares! We Landed! We are on the ground!" Was Michael's exuberant reply.

Soon enough they heard the sound of police sirens, fire engines and other emergency vehicles converging on them.

They found out soon enough where they were.

Evidently, they had landed on the private Boeing Airfield in Everett where Boeing was manufacturing and testing their 747 airplanes.

* * * * *

A COUPLE OF HOURS EARLIER

The telephone rings at Michael's house. His wife, Christina answers the phone.

"Do you know where your husband is? This very minute?"

"He is at work mother!" Christina exclaims.

"No. He is not." Christina's mother insisted. "He is in great danger. We should pray for him."

"Stop that nonsense!" Christina concludes. "I will hang up the phone with you and I will call him at work."

Christina hangs up and dials Michael's work. Laura the receptionist answers.

"Hi Laura. This is Christina. May I speak to Michael?"

"He is not here at the moment." Laura states cautiously.

"Where is he?" Christina persists.

"Hm...I am not allowed to say." Laura replied painfully.

"That's nonsense." Christina responds. "Let me talk to Grace!"

Laura transfers Christina's call to Grace McDonald who Christina knows is Michael's private secretary.

"Hi Grace. This is Christina. I just talked to the receptionist and was told some very disturbing revelations. I just want to speak to my husband. What's the mystery? I understand he is out of the office. Where is he? When is he coming back? Could I get a straight answer from you?"

"He went to Bellingham to check on the fabrication status of some fiberglass stack. He was going to drive there and drive back. Bob Westlake talked him into flying him there on his new airplane..."

"Well! When are they due back?"

"That's exactly the point. They are overdue. We just got a call from SeaTac Airport that they have not landed. They are overdue."

"What's exactly the definition of overdue." Christina asked cautiously.

"They have not landed and the fuel quantity they had on board has expired. In other words, they have run out of fuel. The whole company is up at arms and rumours are flourishing. A directive has been issued to all employees to not say a word to anyone about the matter. It is so serious for two key people to vanish that the rumours may take the company down. Everyone here is terrified. I shouldn't have spoken to you. I violated the Directive. But then again Michael is...Michael."

"Could they have landed somewhere?"

"There is heavy fog between here and Bellingham. There is no record that they have landed anywhere. The FAA presumes they crash landed somewhere. They were getting ready to send search parties to find the crash site. As soon as the fog lifted."

The telephone call is interrupted by Christina's crying.

"I am sorry." Grace wants to end the call as soon as possible. "I told you all I know. Don't despair. Everything will turn out just fine..."

A click on the line indicates that Christina has hung up.

Christina calls her mother back and relays to her the information she was told by Grace McDonald, her husband's secretary. They both start crying on the phone.

"How did you know?" Christina inquired. "I heard of premonitions…but this is uncanny. You knew that he was in trouble and fighting for his life. How could you know?"

"Well, it is something I felt. Not the specifics you told me. Just that your husband was in danger and fighting to survive and that I should pray."

That was the moment that Christina heard the garage door opening.

"Just a second Mom. Someone is at the garage. I just heard the door opening. Without Michael here, I am scared out of my wits."

Christina sets the telephone receiver on the kitchen counter and opens the door from the family room to the garage. Her husband's black SAAB EMS is parked right where it's supposed to be. Panic seizes Christina. The driver's door opens up and Michael steps out. Is he a ghost? It's Christina's first reaction. Followed by:

"Hi honey. I am home." From the ghost.

Christina hurries into the garage and jumps on Michael hugging and kissing him at the same time to make sure he is flesh and bone.

"How was your day?" Christina asks when she catches her breath, although she already knows the answer.

"Boeing Field for 747's to the rescue!" Michael goes on to explain blow by blow the sequence of events with Christina's mother waiting in vain on the other end of the telephone line.

Chapter 25

Abuse of Power Under Colour of Law.

The new Directive has been decided among the partners, by acclamation: 'Henceforth, no two or more partners and/or officers of the company are to be traveling together on the same mode of transportation'. That's what has come out as a result of Bob's and Michael's excellent Bellingham adventure.

Michael went to his office after the Board meeting and called Forest Wallace at the job site in Berlin New Hampshire.

"What's up FU?" Michael inquired." Keeping up with the Construction Schedule?"

"It was touch and go for a while; just after you left..."

"What happened?"

"The usual shit. He is gone. Now we can relax. You know."

"How did you get around this attitude?"

"As soon as I realized that they would not meet the day's target of work completion, I called for a general meeting. I levelled with them and told them..., basically the truth. That I was required to file with the home office a Daily Construction Report. If at any Report the work assignments for the Day as set by Michael were not met, Michael would be on the next plane from Seattle and fire every single one of them and most likely me too. Michael has planted the fear of God in your Business Agent at the Union and he will get his pick from the Union. If not, he will import non-Union workers from Georgia and they would stay in New Hampshire at the end of the job giving you a run for your money for all future work."

"What did they do?"

"What could they do? They worked overtime with no pay to finish up the tasks you've assigned. Since then, everything has been running like a Swiss clock. All your cogs and gears are running with the speed you have predetermined. I just hand the sketches you made each morning and collect the signed copies in the afternoon. In between, I walk around making sure everyone is working. I feel like another cog in the machine you've assembled." Forrest Wallace said ruefully.

"I visited the Bellingham fabricator yesterday and saw the stack." Michael changed the subject trying to get Forrest Wallace out of his funk. "It is completed. They were crating it for shipment today. I gave them your name and telephone number to give to the truck driver who was picking up the crated stack to provide you with updates. He should be on site with the stack in less than a week from yesterday."

"Another cog for your machine, just fell into place." Forrest Wallace would not let go of his funk.

"Goodbye FU Wallace." Michael responded giving up his efforts to cheer up the superintendent. He will thank me at the end of the Project, Michael was thinking.

His upcoming trip to Pearl Harbor Naval Shipyard, the Change Order and the SARGO Incident escalating collateral damage was on Michael's 'front burner'. How was the Freedom of Information request faring? His trip, less than two weeks away was fast approaching.

Michael picked up his telephone receiver from his desk and dialled the Pearl Harbor Naval Shipyard job site number. The telephone rang and rang util it went to messages.

"This is Michael. Please call me." He left a message. With Roxanne gone, henceforth he might as well resign himself to leaving messages.

Surprise! Surprise! Michael's telephone rang less than five minutes later.

"Bill Scott on line 5." Laura, the receptionist announced as soon as Michael picked up the receiver.

"I was on the phone when you called." Bill Scott apologized. "As a matter of fact, I was just getting ready to call you when the Navy beat me to it."

"What did they want?" Michael asked curious.

"To tell me that they were taking care of the transport and handling of Roxanne at no cost to us. They are treating her like she was their employee…"

"She probably was." Michael said quickly playing back the sequence of events like a film reel.

"Do you know? Or just guessing?"

"I am just guessing." Michael admitted.

"Anyway, one issue out of my plate." Bill Scott said. "Do you think we should go to her funeral in Lynn, Massachusetts?"

"I am not going." Michael pronounced. "Neither should you." Michael said with authority.

"I was not planning to. I just said it to pull your chain. We were all wondering how close you really got with the broad."

"I had just met her on site." Michael replied laconically, eliminating any further discussion on the matter.

"The reason I was going to call you was that I delivered to all the subcontractors and suppliers the letter you wrote and I signed, together with the revised, I will call them, As Build Drawings."

"What was the recipients reaction?"

"They can easily compare them with the Bid Drawings and extrapolate the differences as they translate in direct costs. The rumours, however, of you getting a million bucks from the Navy for Indirect Costs are flying around. They all sense that there is a shitload of money to be made, but they don't know how to go about it and put their request in writing. They keep asking me, but I have no idea as to how you made it happen. They keep asking me for your number in Seattle. I did not give it to them. I understand they called the office in Seattle, but every time they were told that you were out of the office. They all want to meet with you as soon as you arrive here."

"I cannot help them Bill. Although, I would be making 25% mark up on their Change Order Requests. However, I am sure the Navy NIS would be opening a file on me for profiteering, as soon as they were submitted."

"What do I tell them? They coral me every day with questions. You could explain the mechanics of how to calculate Indirect Costs to me. That way you would stay out of it."

"What would happen if the Navy calls each one of them in, separately, and asks them to explain how they came up with the costs. What would they say? I will tell you what they will say: Bill Scott wrote them for us. Just keep doing what you've been doing. Make sure you emphasize to them that if we do not receive their response within thirty days from the date of your letter, we will be of the understanding that there'll be no additional costs involved on their Purchase Order and/or Subcontract Agreement as a result of the revised, As Build Drawings, which they now constitute the Contract Drawings."

"It's shameful for all that money to go to waste." Bill Scott said ruefully.

"I will sleep a lot better knowing that I went strictly by Contract." Michael added. "Be aware Bill that Navy NIS is listening to everything you say or do and act accordingly. You will be better off in the long run. I will see you sooner than you think." Michael hangs up before Bill Scott could answer.

* * * * *

A meeting is taking place at the OICC Office. In attendance are the OICC, ROICC, Dave Brown of the NIS and Jefrey Wayne, legal council of the OICC Office. Absent is John Muchmore who has been labelled 'Persona Non Grata'.

"The paperwork for Contract Modification No. P001 have been completed and they are ready for signature." The ROICC announces. "Should we notify Michael?"

"No." The OICC responds. "Let Michael come here on the originally scheduled date and time."

Dave Brown hands the OICC a copy of the letter given to the Project subcontractors and suppliers bearing Bill Scott's signature. The OICC reads it and hands it over to Jeffrey Wayne.

"Do you think Bill Scott wrote it?" Dave Brown asks ironically.

"What do you think?" The OICC asks equally ironically.

"It looks like a letter an attorney would have written." Jeffrey Wayne states. "It is in strict compliance with the Contract Terms and Conditions."

"What is happening behind the scenes?" The OICC inquires.

"Nothing so far." Dave Brown admits disappointed. "The recipients keep asking for help from the superintendent, Bill Scott, on a daily basis. Unfortunately, Bill Scott does not know how to help them. It appears that Michael has kept the Change Order Request matter close to his vest."

"Michael did nothing wrong; as far as I can tell." Jefrey Wayne added.

"So far." Dave Brown said. "We are waiting to open a file on him as soon as he sidesteps."

"From the little time I've able to observe and what have read, I believe we are dealing with a straight shooter, rare as that may be in our experience." The OICC legal counsel said.

"When did that stopped us in the past from cutting, anyone we have painted a target on his back, to size?" The OICC commented.

"I don't want to hear you talking like this!" Jefrey Wayne admonished. "It is illegal and not the Navy Way as far as I am concerned. In legal terms it is called: Abuse of Power Under Colour of Law."

"Jefrey is right." The ROICC said emphatically "Particularly after the recent meeting we had, the OICC and I with Admiral…"

"Stop right there!" The OICC interrupted. "Our meeting with the Admiral is not a topic for discussing in this meeting."

"I was only going to say that here we are getting ready to ask for Michael's help…"

"Stop right there!" The OICC insisted. "Stay after the meeting and we will discuss how to handle the matter you are so anxious to discuss."

On that note. The meeting ended and the participants, sans Commander Walsh, left the OICC office.

"I will leave it up to you." The OICC addressed the ROICC after they were left alone in his office. "Invite Michael to lunch at the Officer's Club as soon as he signs the Contract Modification. I will invite the Admiral to the same lunch. Let him do all the talking and trying to convince Michael."

On that succinct note by the OICC, the second meeting ended.

* * * * *

Monday morning. Michael parked his SAAB EMS Turbo on the short-term section parking on the fourth floor of the Sea-Tac parking structure. He had an open return, but he anticipated a short stay in Hawaii that was the reason he was flying alone. He had a limited amount of clothing in his suitcase. He figured that if he was forced to extend his stay, a pair of underwear, a couple of Aloha shirts and a pair of chinos could always be purchased at the Ala Moana Shopping Centre, would take him to Friday and his return home. His travel humidor in his suitcase always carried a month's supply of cigars, which were hard to find in Hawaii, although the whole island was nothing but one gigantic humidor.

He took the overpass, located on the fourth floor, from the parking structure to ticketing. He always flew First Class due to the accumulated milage that would have been impossible to use all up. Every Monday morning he would fly to a trouble spot in the country and would always make sure he flew back home on Friday. If he would be forced to stay there over the weekend, he took his family with him. He considered the travel experience to be a good antidote for taking his children out of school. Their four-grade point average was a sure tell-tale sign and proof of his theory.

As always, he looked up the Starbucks corner counter at the South Airport Satellite. One person on duty and no customers. He thanked his lucky stars for declining the offer.

A year ago, the then President of the company and mentor, Don Combs, retired. Or was forced to retire. Anyway, he was retirement age. Don Combs, another Cougar Alum, had hired Michael six years ago as Project Engineer. He strived on the first floor designing and building Power Plants all over the country. Don Combs called him in his office, on the second floor of the building, a year later and offered him the job of Project Manager for a newly acquired Project: The Trident Submarine Base in Bangor, Washington, literally across the Bay from Seattle. It was the first project the company was involved working for the government. The Department of Defence, and everyone was nervous.

"If you take the job and succeed, I will quadruple your salary and will make you the Head of the company Division that does all the work with the government. You will be a separate company within the company with absolute authority. You will be given stock options and you will become a partner. If you fail, I will fire you. If you refuse my offer, I will be disappointed, but you will stay as Project Engineer on the first floor, doing what you've been doing at your present salary. What do you say?"

"When do I start!" Were Michael's first and only words.

"GO COUGS! That's the spirit!" Don Combs exclaimed. "I knew you wouldn't disappoint me. First thing, move your stuff to an office of your choice on the second floor and take charge. I will be watching."

The Trident submarine Base, a multiyear Contract, ended up being the most profitable project the Company had undertaken and completed. Michael was being groomed by Don Combs to take over as President of the Company. The rest of the older Partners were fuming, but they were reluctant to mess around with success. Then suddenly over a behind doors trivial argument, Don Combs resigned. Michael immediately hired a 'head hunter' outfit seeking a new job.

He was directed to an address at the Seattle Public Market. He went for an interview to a hole on the wall outfit selling coffee for years to the Seattle Public Market customers. He was met there by Mr. Starbuck himself, the owner and only employee.

"I heard great things about you." Were the first words out of the old man's mouth. "The man you hired to find you a job is a dear and old friend of mine. I trust his judgment implicitly. If he thinks you are the one! That's good enough for me."

Michael remained silent, but apprehensive.

"I've been in this business for a long time. I have accumulated a significant amount of money doing what I've been doing here. I believe we are ready for the next step. You will be my first employee."

Michael apprehension just grew some more, in leaps and bounds. What was the old man thinking? Michael will start selling coffee in the Seattle Public Market? He hated coffee. He avoided drinking it. Michael was a Twinning Earl Grey tea aficionado since his French convent days.

"I will hire you with the title of the Starbucks Coffee Construction Manager. Your first job will be at the SeaTac Airport. I want you to design and build a coffee shop counter at the South Satellite Terminal. We will serve coffee there and pastries for the passengers. As soon as this is done you will start designing a coffee counter for the Portland, Airport. Then the San Francisco Airport, the LA Airport and the San Diego Airport. Once we get the West Coast taken care of, we will stop for a breather. You will scout other Airports in the country."

Michael stopped himself for a breather also.

"Your concept is based on supply and demand." Michael started in a measured tone of voice. "As soon as the passengers board the Airplanes, the first thing the stewardesses offer them is coffee, among other things. Why would they bother to buy your coffee if they are to have the same thing for free, a few minutes later..."

"You call the swill offered by the Airlines coffee!" The old man exclaimed, interrupting Michael in mid-sentence and almost rising from his seat. "Have you ever tasted my coffee? There is no comparison. I select my beans by visiting the source. I roasted them myself. I grind them to the optimum size. I bring my water from Olympia..."

"I am sorry." Michael interrupted the coffee making tirade. "I don't mean to disparage your coffee, although I am not a coffee drinker myself. I drink Twinning Earl Grey tea..."

"I won't hold that against you. Design a section for dilettanti like yourself. How much are you making on your present job?"

"My salary is $60,000.00 a year plus a yearly bonus based on the profitability of my Projects. I am one of the 14 partners, owning the company. I also have Medical and Dental for me and my dependents."

"You have a family. That's a plus in my book. Do you have kids?"

"Yes. A boy and a girl."

"Perfect. The benefits are fine, but I cannot meet your salary level, to start with. I can only offer $45,000.00 to start. But I will make you a partner, however, right from the start. I will give you 25% of the Company."

"The immediate question is: What is the company worth?"

"Whatever I have in my savings account. Enough to build five Starbucks outlets throughout the West Coast without having to borrow money. Plus, a year's plus worth of waiting until the coffee brand catches on."

"You are leasing 1,000 or so square feet from the Airport. You probably know from your friend, the head-hunter, that I build Power Plants all over the country. I just finished the Trident Submarine Base across the Puget Sound from Seattle that is millions of square feet..."

"You have to stop thinking in grandiose terms and think Mc Donald's type structures in both size and complexity. That's your future. You are staring at a career change if you please, not a continuation of your present career."

"I don't think so sir..."

"I will raise your salary in less than a year to more than what you are making now and I will give you off the bat 33% of the company. That's the best I can do and only because I think you are the person I want. But this is my final offer."

Michael stood up and offered his hand. "Thank you for the offer and your consideration in hiring me. But I will not be happy designing and building coffee houses for a living."

"Do you want to take a time out and think about it for a couple of days?"

"I don't think so. I have made up my mind and I am declining your offer."

On that note Michael left the coffee shop and decided to work out his problems within the company. He was an undisputed money maker. He was the rainmaker. Everyone in the company wanted to work for him on his Projects.

The word was out that if you worked for Michael for a year and did not get fired, it was equivalent experience as if you worked for ten years anywhere else. Michael was a little apprehensive at his decision to turn down Starbucks and stick with what he knew best, as he drove away from the Seattle Public Market. Only time would tell.

He had made his point, however, henceforth to check the Starbucks foot traffic every time he went through any of the West Coast Airports. His eyewitness experience that first year told him that their chance for success was slim to none. Michael was hopping the old man had a hefty savings account.

Michael boarded the airplane with the first group, since he was flying First Class. He accepted the pineapple juice and macadamia nuts offered by one of the First-Class stewardesses as soon as he sat down. He glanced at the inflight magazine and already started inputting on his calculator the Differential Equation and Formula to calculate the mid distance point; the challenge of which invariably would be announced by the Captain as soon as they achieved cruising altitude and the Seat Belt signs were turned off. He hadn't missed yet. It was not really a challenge for him. But the prize of a bottle of Dom champagne was always welcome and expected by his wife.

Michael had the prime rib for lunch. Won the mid distance challenge. Secured the champagne in Styrofoam and placed it in his carry on. He arrived in Honolulu mid-afternoon. Rented a VW Rabbit convertible and was checking in at the Hilton Hawaiian Village before the commuter traffic even started. He called the job site field office to check in.

"Are you ready for the big day tomorrow, Boss?" Bill Scott greeted Michael. "Did you bring everything you would need with you?"

"I brought my Mont Blanc fountain pen. Other than that, the heavy lifting was done the last time I was here."

"I heard through the 'grape vine', that the NIS and particularly Dave Brown is gunning for you."

"I hope you are speaking metaphorically." Michael said laughing.

"This is not a laughing matter. I found out that Roxanne was a Confidential Witness signed up and being paid by the NIS."

"How sure are you of your source, Bill?"

"Is the ROICC good enough for you?"

"I am flabbergasted. How did you manage this?"

"The ROICC is a good guy. He does not approve of the OICC shenanigans. But he outranks him; so he kept his mouth shut. He is glad that you turned the tables on them. He is a fan of yours now. He also told something else in confidence."

"What is that Bill."

"I will tell you, but if word comes back to me that I told you, I will deny it."

"The plot thickens. I will keep your confidence, Bill. Out with it."

"You remember the time you were led away from the job site by the NIS with the excuse: 'to see the Man'?"

"I do." Michael said thinking back.

"You were being monitored all that time by the Navy…"

"I guessed as much."

"Did you know that if the Navy did not fall for your bluff that you had sent your Diary out of Oahu to the company attorney, they were getting ready to kill you…"

"No shit! How?"

"An induced heart attack. Off to Tripler by ambulance. DOA. I don't think the NIS and particularly Dave Brown have given up on that score."

Michael felt a chill in the air even at an 80 plus degree sunny day. He did not wish to know details. That was beyond the scope of the Contract. The Navy, provided Bill Scott was correct, were flirting with Abuse of Power Under Colour of Law. A criminal offense. He said a hurried goodbye and hung up the phone. He looked outside his Lanai. He was on the 17th floor. Halfway between a climb by the NIS and rappelling from the roof. However, there was nothing to steal this time other than his Mont Blanc pen.

Chapter 26

The Request Under Freedom of Information Act.

Michael had a room service steak dinner with a full bottle of Chateau St. Michelle Cabernet Sauvignon. He smoked a cigar in the hotel Lanai overlooking Diamond Head and the Waikiki Beach. He read in bed afterwards and drifted into an early sleep because his clock was 3 hours ahead, Seattle time.

He woke up early as a result. He took a shower. Shaved. Got dressed and took the elevator down to the Rainbow Tower Lobby. He had called the valet from his room, so his car was there and waiting. He drove to the Original Pancake House on Waikamilo for breakfast of Portuguese sausage and eggs, together with a side order of macadamia nut pancakes. He did not know how long the Contract Modification 'signing ceremony' will last and what other side issues would arise. A good breakfast was a must.

Michael arrived at the job site office trailer exactly at 8:00 AM. Bill Scott and Steve Crane were already there.

"Any messages?" Michael inquired.

"The ROICC." Bill Scott announced. "He wanted to know as soon as you came on site."

Michael picked up the field office phone and dialled the ROICC.

"I am here!" Michael announced as soon as Commander Walsh answered the phone.

"The paperwork is all here in my office." Commander Walsh confirmed with a pleasant voice. "Come on over, read them at your convenience and sign the Contract Modification P001, so we can put the show on the road."

Michael left his car rental parked at the job site and leisurely made his way to the ROICC Building. Commander Walsh ushered Michael to his office which had a small conference area on the side, a round table with four chairs, their final destination. Michael sat down on the chair against the wall so he could monitor the traffic out of the open door. Commander Walsh sat on the chair opposite Michael with his back to the open door.

Commander Walsh gave Michael the first set of documents to read. At a glance they appeared to be consistent with the Agreement they had reached with the General Accounting Office, GAO, a month ago. Regardless, Michael read the entire stack of documents he was given, taking his sweet time. He was handed another inch thick set of documents to read and he repeated the process.

It was approaching noon and Commander Walsh was repeatedly stealing glances at his watch. He must have a lunch appointment, Michael was thinking. Commander Walsh finally handed Michael Contract Modification P001. Michael was impressed by the language of the Change. No one was at fault. No effort to justify the amount. Shit Happens! Was what the reader concluded. Differing Site Conditions. Deficient Contract Documents provided the partial explanation and justification for a new set of Contract Drawings. The Contract Modification left the door open for a two-part Change Order depending on the Changes and Additions shown on the New Contract Drawings from the subcontractors and suppliers effected. No explanation as to who prepared them and why. They just appeared as that of the Holy Ghost, conveniently.

The money, $875,000.00 was correct and payable within thirty days of invoice. Michael signed the Contract Modification and handed Commander Walsh a sealed envelope.

"What's that?" The ROICC inquired.

"The invoice for Mobilization and the Contract Modification, minus ten percent Retention pursuant to the Contract General Requirements." Michael replied. "Payable within thirty days from today."

"I am not surprised." Commander Walsh admitted. "You have not even got started incurring costs on site and we have to pay you close to a million dollars for the privilege of doing the work you originally Bid to do, anyway."

"I am not going debate you Commander. The decision has already been made by others, way above your pay grade."

"You are right of course. We had meeting after meeting, here on Base, to determine how we ended up at this point and no one can provide a reasonable explanation."

"Maybe you should have followed the OICC's direction as to how to deal with me." Michael suggested cryptically.

Commander Walsh changed several colours of red to purple and remained with his head down. Bill Scotts rumour just became fact.

"I had nothing to do with that." Commander Walsh admitted. "I was and still am on your side. I believe, with the exception of Jefrey Wayne, I am your staunchest supporter."

"That's good to know. The Project will proceed smoothly with minimum interference by yours truly." Michael concluded. "As long as no more Changes end up in Dispute." He added.

Commander Walsh looked at his watch one more time.

"Are you free for lunch?" Commander Walsh inquired. "Let's go to the Officers Club. The Navy is buying."

"I don't know Commander. I still need copies of all these documents on your desk and the Contract Modification itself." Michael was dragging his feet to make a decision.

"Shirley!" Commander Walsh yelled near the top of his voice. An oriental civilian lady showed up in a hurry, presumably the ROICC secretary.

"This is Michael. The Principal of the company engaged on our largest construction Project on Base. We are going to lunch. Please copy all the documents here," he pointed at the conference table, "and prepare two copies for Michael in a binder, attaching all documents in chronological order. We will be back after lunch, for Michael to collect his copies."

Michael felt outmanoeuvred. The decision to go to lunch at the Officer's Club had already been made on his behalf. He suddenly became a package to be transported. He wanted to ask whether they will be just the two of them alone or should he anticipate a crowd? He recalled the OICC meeting a month ago. He expected to meet with the OICC alone only to walk into a room with over forty Navy personnel waiting for him.

Commander Walsh ushered Michael out of the ROICC Building and into an open Jeep painted grey, the Naval Shipyard colour. Michael climbed into the passenger seat. Commander Walsh started the Jeep and it charged forward with a squeal of the tires. It must have had a V8 engine. There were no seat belts. Michael got a hold of a bar across the open glove box with his left hand and a grab handle attached to the roll bar above the window with his right hand. Not that Commander Walsh was driving like a maniac. Michael had experienced worse. The driving by the ROICC was merely, aggressive.

"Have you eaten at the Officer's Club before?" Commander Walsh asked Michael.

"Not for free." Was Michael's response which puzzled the ROICC because that was not what he was after.

The ROICC kept thinking and thinking for a clever repartee to Michael's response, and he was still thinking about it when they arrived at the Officer's Club. Michael looked at the facility and his first thought was that he was part of the cast From Here to Eternity. The movie must have been filmed right here on location. He followed Commander Walsh who had taken his role as the Host seriously and was ushering Michael forward with determination. They bypassed the other dinners. All in their whites. All keeping their eyes on Michael, like they knew something he didn't. All the way back where a uniformed Stewart opened a private dining room door.

The first person Michael noticed upon entering the room was the OICC with a smile on his face similar to a cat that ate the canary. The other person in the room was a four-star Admiral in is sixties looking like a carbon copy of Jaques Cousteau. Michael knew by reputation and had previously met Admiral Hyman Rickover, who was the father of the nuclear submarine program for the Navy. Now he was fighting to stay on top of the infighting in the Navy. He was the noble hero who must admit that his design of the Polaris type nuclear submarine had deficiencies. The system that helped him achieve his status, was now fighting him with disinformation and cover up.

"The ten days were up yesterday, Captain." Were Michael's first words still at the door of the private room to wipe the smirk off the Captain's face. "What is your response to the Request for Production of Documents under the Freedom of Information Act?"

Captain Reinhardt's smile truly got wiped off his face. "I sent a response to your attorney already. We would be unable to comply with your Request because the matter is under Litigation.

Accordingly, until the Litigation is over, the matter is exempt from the Freedom of Information Act Request."

After this brief exchange, The ROICC Commander Walsh introduced Michael to the four-star Admiral, Hyman Rickover.

"I've heard a lot about you, young man." The Admiral said with a smile. "Glad to finally meet you."

"With all due respect Admiral, this is actually the second time we've met."

"When was the first?" The Admiral asked genuinely surprised.

"Five years ago in Groton, Connecticut at the General Dynamics facility there. They were building the TRIDENT submarine. I was the contractor building the Base which would house the submarines in Bangor, Washington."

"Don't remind me of that scoundrel. He was Greek also. As I recall." The Admiral's face clouded over.

"What are you guys talking about?" The OICC exclaimed looking at Michael.

"The TRIDENT submarine was running 3.2 billion over budget. The Base itself approaching a Billion. So the Admiral called a 'come to Jesus' meeting of all the parties in Groton, Connecticut. My company was involved in building the Power Plant and the Coal Storage Yard with the railroad spur in between plus 100 feet of a 10 feet x 10 feet x 10 feet high concrete utilidor with walls 1 foot thick. There were 84 contractors involved at the time building the Base with the Navy coordinating. After an accident in the utilidor which ran for miles underground the Base and the Base building overruns approaching a Billion, the Navy paid my company a monthly fee of

$40,000.00 for me to oversee and assist the Navy in resolving the Change Orders with the contractors. At the time of the meeting the bleeding of money at the Base had stopped. The OICC and the Naval Headquarters at Bremerton, Washington asked me to come along at the meeting Admiral Rickover had asked for, in Groton, Connecticut."

"I didn't know all that." The Admiral admitted. "Your Navy cohorts were getting all the credit during the meeting. Why didn't you say something to me during the meeting?"

"Admiral, my role in that meeting was that of Cyrano De Bergerac, if you understand my meaning. As long as my company was receiving $40,000.00 a month, I was not about to bite the hand that fed me."

"I understand and commend you on your shrewd thinking. What did you think of your Greek cohort at General Dynamics?"

"Arrogant to the point of Hubris." Michael responded.

"Well, we fixed his wagon at the end." The Admiral acknowledged.

"What happened, in English this time?" Commander Walsh wanted to know.

"The President of General Dynamics refused to justify the cost overruns to the Admiral. Instead, he told him to have the TRIDENT submarine built in Russia instead; knowing that there was not a shipyard in the free world big enough to accommodate the TRIDENT."

"That's right!" The Admiral reminisced. "He said that to my face. He said the same thing to 60 Minutes in an interview on the air a week later."

"What did the Navy do about that?" The OICC asked.

"The government indicted him. He found out about it as soon as the indictment was issued. Wrote himself a fat check at his company's expense and escaped to Greece. We couldn't do anything about it because there was no extradition treaty at the time with Greece. The fellow did his homework. I'd give him that much. Anyway, enough about that scoundrel. Let's go back to the business in hand. I understand Michael, reading the FBI Report associated with your Security Clearance that you belong to the SOG. I would like to approach you in that capacity to investigate and propose possible solutions to the problem we are experiencing with the Polaris - type nuclear submarines."

"It is my understanding, Admiral that you were the original designer of the nuclear Polaris submarine."

"You are correct. What is that got to do with what we are discussing?" The Admiral said irritated.

"I know nothing about building nuclear submarines. However, by education as a Chemical Engineer and by experience for the past 20 years building Power Plants all over the United States, I may be willing to undertake the study you propose as long as we clear a few things."

"Fire away, me boy!" The Admiral exclaimed, revealing in the process Irish roots.

"My Report may reveal inherent deficiencies in the original design..."

"If you are worried about repercussions? I am a big boy. I realize this. The recent Incident with SARGO is enough to tell me to keep my mouth shut and let a different set of eyes look at the issues from a fresh perspective."

"The second issue that I would insist is to conduct my study on the SARGO."

A collective intake of breath was heard in the private dining room.

"What's the matter?" Michael followed. "Is it FUBAR, as we used to say in the Army?" Fucked Up Beyond All Repair.

"No. No." The Admiral interjected. "I am told that the submarine contamination was minor. It is currently deployed in the North Slope of Alaska. Is your company prepared to have you away for a couple of weeks?"

"I was not planning on vacation in the ice caps, Admiral. Two weeks is excessive."

"That's what I thought. We have SWORDFISH here at Pearl Harbor. It is the sister-ship to SARGO. How about you conduct your study on that vessel?"

"I am pressed for time. How about I conduct the study tomorrow. I don't believe it would take more than a day. Anyway, if it requires a second day, I have an open return ticket. Have available a couple of Seabees to assist if any dismantling is required."

"Will do." The OICC said. "The Seabees will be at your service for the day. More will be made available, if it becomes necessary."

"Your time from this point on and expenses will be on the Navy's dime at $10,000.00 per day until the Report is signed. Is this acceptable?" The Admiral asked.

"It is." Michael acknowledged. "I wish I knew of this earlier. I would have brought over my wife and Kids.". Michael added laughing.

"Enough talk. Let's order lunch!" The Admiral exclaimed.

The Navy orderly who was guarding the door came over to the table with a pad and a pencil on hand. Michael ordered a garden salad with blue cheese dressing, a pastrami sandwich with french fries and a Heineken beer. The others ordered steak and lobster. Michael after hearing their order changed his own order to 'surf and turf', the Officer's Club special, also.

They continued discussing the logistics for tomorrow while they waited for their meal.

"The sub interior, particularly in the engine room, is very confined. It cannot accommodate more than 5 people." The Admiral pronounced with finality.

A discussion ensued among the three Navy representatives, which Michael tuned out, watching instead to the blue outside the windows and the activity at the mouth of the Pearl Harbor Port. He came out of his revere when he was addressed by name.

"8:00 AM at your job site." The OICC was saying. "I will pick you up and ferry you to the SWORDFISH submarine. It is tied up close by the Dry Docks."

"Fine with me." Michael responded.

The Naval orderly opened the private dining room door to admit a waiter with a tray loaded with salads and beer. They proceeded to eat in silence. When they were done, the same waiter brought their main meal. Each, a platter with a medium rare filet minion and an

Australian lobster tail of noble proportions, a cup with melted butter and a slice of lemon. A plate of French fries on the side completed the order. Silence and the sound of utensils was the only sound emanating from their table. A second Heineken beer bottle with a frozen glass appeared on Michaels side as soon as he last filled his first glass. The spent bottle of beer was taken way. The Naval orderly single function was to monitor their table and relay information via his walkie talkie anticipating all their desires. Michael was thinking that it was not a bad thing dining with a four-star Admiral.

After lunch, the ROICC drove Michael back to the ROICC office to pick up his two copies of the Contract Modification and all the attachments bound into two books like folder by the ROICC's secretary. He then drove Michael back to the job site and dropped him off at the entrance Gate.

Michael walked to the office trailer. Bill Scott and Steve Crane were waiting for him there. Michael showed them the signed Contract Modification.

"We got our money!" Michael exclaimed waiving in the air the two book folders of the Contract Modification. "Now it is the subcontractors and suppliers turn. Their response and cost estimate proposal is due by the close of business, the day after tomorrow. Hopefully, I will be on my way back to the mainland by then, so tell them all to mail them directly to me in Seattle. The name and address is shown on the left-hand side of their Purchase Order or Subcontract Agreement. It is now 2:30 PM, I will hang around the job site today for a couple of hours, until quitting time and be available if they have any questions. There shouldn't be any."

He gave Bill Scott one copy of the Contract Modification with all the attachments.

"This is a Public Record now. As such it is available for inspection by all the subcontractors and suppliers. Please let them know of this fact. If they possess the smarts and know-how, they may pattern their Change Order Request after my own. However, without any editorializing from you, because it will come back to and bite you. If the NIS gets involved, you will be the fall guy. Am I clear on this score?"

"Perfectly clear." Was Bill Scott's response.

"The letter you gave them and the As Build, now the new Contract Drawings are self-explanatory." Michael said addressing Bill Scott.

No mention of his activities tomorrow. He offered to take both Bill and Steve and their wives and/or companions to dinner tonight at Bobby McGee's. They settled at 7:00 PM and Michael called the restaurant for reservations for five from the office telephone.

* * * * *

A meeting is taking place at the OICC Office. Admiral Rifey and the NIS Agent Dave Brown are present.

"How did the meeting with the old man go?" Admiral Rifey is asking.

"Well." The OICC responded. "I will be picking up Michael at 0800 tomorrow morning to do his inspection on SWORDFISH."

"Any problems there? Was Michael cooperative?" The Admiral inquired.

"No problem, the way the Admiral approached him. He is SOG for life after all. He could have made the Admiral jump through hoops going to SOG headquarters, if they even exist after the government cut them off in 1973. But he chose to comply with the Admiral's wishes. No way I would refuse a four-star Admiral's request. But then again, Michael is a Civilian and he listens to his own drummer. It got a little tricky, however, when the issue of the SWORDFISH came up. Michael insisted that he wanted to inspect SARGO. Thank God you anticipated that and Admiral Rickover did the manoeuvring."

"I hated to lie to the old man." Admiral Rifey contemplated.

"It was for the Good of the Navy, Admiral." The OICC replied. "This was nothing more than a little 'white lie'. Those are allowed in my book and in the book of everyone wearing the uniform.

"So...Michael is golden as far as the old man is concerned..."

"You could say that again!" The OICC exclaimed.

"Not in my book!" The NIS Agent Dave Brown spoke for the first time. I am still gunning for him."

"Don't do anything rush." The OICC said. "Wait until after he signs his Report, its implementation and the follow up testing. Check with me first. I will be the one who gives the all clear."

"I wouldn't think of doing anything else Captain." Dave Brown said with sincerity written all over his face.

On that note the meeting ended.

* * * *

At the end of the day, Michael gave Steve Crane the other of the copies of the Contract Modification book folder and told him to mail it from the Airport Post Office to the office in Seattle to his attention. He had given the other copy to Bill Scott.

"As I said before, this is now part of the Contract. As such, you are allowed to show it to the subcontractors and suppliers. Show it only and allow them to review it in your presence. They may copy portions of it in a separate note pad or for that matter you may make copies of any portion they desire and charge them a copying fee. Do not take it apart for any reason what-so-ever. Do not say anything, other than presenting the book file. Do not answer any of their questions. The file alone is speaking for itself. The Navy in their 'wisdom' saw fit to include my own original calculations to demonstrate what a good job they've done talking me down to $875,000.00. An average intelligence individual would be able to extrapolate my calculations and apply them in their own case. Don't tell them that though, let them figure it out for themselves. Am I making myself clear, Bill."

"Perfectly clear, Boss." Bill said as he grabbed the Contract Modification book file and headed out the door.

Michael picked his briefcase and headed out the door also to return to the hotel and catch a late afternoon swim before dinner.

* * * * *

"How did it go?" Michael asked Bill Scott sitting at a five person circular dining table at Bobby McGee's restaurant.

"Like a charm. Most of them understood exactly what was going on. They took copies for the powers to be at their companies. They may hire a consultant to decipher the Contract Modification and prepare their own Change Order Request. Others, I don't know, they may stick to the Direct Costs approach that they understood."

"Good enough. It's now out of our hands until we receive their response." Michael said closing the subject.

The rest of the evening was just small talk and team building by Michael.

"Have you found anything on the SARGO?" Maria, Bill Scott's wife, asked Michael point blank.

"We filed a Request Pursuant to the Freedom of Information Act, on which the Navy stone walled us claiming privileged information on account of an ongoing Class Action Law Suit by the crew of SARGO." Michael said.

He had talked to Don Davidson over the phone earlier in the day, who had received the Navy's Formal Response.

"I hope the little people take the government to the cleaners." Maria said. No love lost for the government, Michael was thinking. A revolutionary is born every day.

"What happened to the SARGO after it disappeared?" Bill Scott asked.

"According to a four-star Admiral, the SARGO is currently deployed on the North Slope of Alaska. Playing hide and seek underneath the Polar Caps. I was invited as a matter of fact to visit it."

"Of course you declined." Bill Scott added. "I would have too. What sane person wants to go to the North Slope of Alaska. I bet the Navy is getting even with the crew for filing a Class Action Law Suit against them."

"You may be right!" Michael exclaimed. "I had not thought of it that way. However, the orders for the SARGO nuclear submarine deployment 'exude an odor piscatorial'."

Chapter 27

Experimenting Aboard the SWORDFISH

The next day Michael made a point to be at the Pearl Harbor Naval Shipyard job site at 8:00 AM on the dot. The OICC, Captain Reinhardt was waiting for him outside the fence in a Navy Jeep. Bill Scott and Steve Crane were sitting on the steps of the field office. Michael parked his rental at the job site, waived at them and headed for the OICC Jeep.

"Your guys will be wondering where you are headed." The OICC commented. "Or have you told them already?"

"No. I have not." Michael said emphatically. "It has nothing to do with the Contract and frankly it's none of their business.

The OICC gunned the Jeep along Bayshore Drive towards the Shipyard Dry Docks. The SWORDFISH became visible tied up at the wharf as soon as they came around the bend. They parked next to it blocking part of the road. A couple of fellows dressed in Navy uniforms were putting traffic cones in the middle of Bayshore Drive the length of the submarine. Another crew was putting up signs along each end warning the sparse traffic that Bayshore Drive became one lane road along the submarine.

On the other side of the road there was a refreshment shack door with half a dozen tables along the sidewalk. All currently occupied with Naval personnel drinking coffee, sodas and smoking. All curious as to what was happening across the street. Michael was the only one in civilian clothes, so naturally every eye was on him. "What's happening?" and "Who is he?" Could be heard occasionally from the snack shack.

Admiral Rickover's car flying two four-star flags on each side and four stars up front where the license plate should be, pulled over and parked in front of the OICC Jeep. Everyone including the Navy personnel across the street rose as one and saluted the four-star Admiral. Michael shook the Admiral's hand. He could only guess the rumour mill across the street witnessing the drama.

"I will take you below and give you a firsthand presentation of how this sardine can works." The Admiral said to Michael pointing at the SWORDFISH submarine.

Two Navy four door pickups loaded with Seabees and tool boxes in the bed of the trucks pulled into the cordoned parking spaces towards the far end away from the Admiral's car. Michael and the Admiral boarded the sub using the temporary make shift plank entrance with railings set up for the Admiral. They walked along the deck of the submarine towards the manhole type hatch with a cover set on its side that provided access below. A ladder with extended handle bars was protruding from the manhole. The Admiral grabbed one end of it and swung his body around placing a foot on the ladder rung followed by the other foot on the next rung below and so forth until he reached the floor below.

Michael waited until the Admiral disengaged himself from the ladder and stepped away before attempting to repeat what he had just witnessed.

"Not bad for an Army 'REMF', REAR E-SCELON MOTHER FUCKER!" The Admiral exclaimed slapping Michael on his back as soon as he touched the floor.

The submarine felt like Michael was just transported in an RV without slides out. He turned and noticed an Ensign saluting the Admiral.

"This is Ensign Paul Chamberlin." The Admiral made the introductions. "He is the Chief of the SWORDFISH engine room. He will come along and assist me while I explain the Polaris nuclear submarine operation."

Ensign Paul Chamberlin led the way, occasionally stepping over vertical metal plates embedded through the floor that formed the airlocks which served as doors in the submarine. The engine room was basically a 10 feet x 10 feet x 9 feet high metal box. It housed a horizontal condensate tank suspended on the ceiling. A bunch of piping underneath with an array of valves leading to the suction side of two feed water pumps mounted on the floor with more piping and valves in the pumps discharge side. There were three half inch pipes tapped on the suction side pipes to the pumps, connected to three open top vertical tanks with agitators sticking out the top. A heat exchanger was taking half the room space.

Ensign Paul Chamberlin led them out of the engine room to the control room next door. Basically, a glorified closet. The wall across the door was dominated by an Annunciator comprised with a multitude of lighted panels labelled with capital letters and informing the operator of the malfunction that triggered the Alarm. The Alarm was two red lights which blinked and announced the danger loudly with two fog horns built in. The Annunciator panel responsible for the Alarm would start flashing informing the operator of the malfunction. In the case of the feed water pumps it was written on the glass with capital letters "NO FEED WATER"; which meant that there was no feed water flow detected.

Michael was listening, without interrupting, the narrative of Admiral Rickover interchanged with the narrative of Ensign Paul Chamberlin, taking turns and relieving each other as if they had rehearsed. Michael let out a silent scream as something soft and bouncy touched his back. He turned and was face to face with an Angel in white. She had hazel eyes and the look of Bambi. The front buttons of her white shirt were straining ready to pop with the Angel's every breath. Two exquisite breasts surrounded by a lacy bra, Michael was able to verify through the shirt gap of the first two buttons. White skirt and black pumps completed the uniform. The blond hair style was out of the sixties with a modest bee hive and the Navy hat pinned on top.

"Gentlemen, I apologize for being late but I got lost on my way here. The National Anthem added to the delay. But finally here I am." The Angel spoke.

"Let me introduce you." Admiral Rickover said to Michael smiling at his discomfort. "This is Lieutenant Michelle Patterson. She is here to take down every word that comes out of your mouth. The narrative will be edited, typed and will constitute the Formal Report of this encounter. You will be asked to read it, verify its accuracy and sign it. It will become the blue print which the Navy will follow to cure the deficiencies you find. After the material, controls and other appurtenances are on hand, you will be notified to return here under the same arrangements we spoke during our meeting yesterday to supervise, approve and test the results. Lieutenant Patterson, you do not need to know who this gentleman is for security reasons other than he is on loan to the Navy from the SOG, Studies and Observations Group. An organization you are not cleared to even know of its existence. His name and any specific reference to him in the typed Report will be redacted. The Report will be Classified."

The tour continued with the addition of Lieutenant Patterson who had taken out a steno pad and a pen from her purse and hang a portable mini tape recorder from her neck, but had not activated it. Michael kept an eye on her, but true to what her function was in this proceeding, she had not written one word on her pad yet.

After a three-hour tour, both the Admiral and the Ensign appeared exhausted. It was now 11:30 AM by Michael's watch.

"Any questions?" The Admiral inquired of Michael.

Michael remained silent, digesting all the information he had acquired.

"Any ideas?" The Admiral persisted.

"You don't need to take this down." Michael started addressing Lieutenant Michelle Patterson. "I have understood the operating function as explained to me. I have isolated the deficiencies and am prepared to provide a possible solution. Could we go somewhere and sit down. Additionally, I am awfully thirsty. The closed in space of the submarine compartments has dehydrated me."

Without delay the Admiral led the way to the manhole with the ladder. He climbed out first, followed by the Ensign. Michael and the Lieutenant were left alone on the floor underneath the manhole. Michael wished the Lieutenant will be next, leaving him to admire her posterior and whatever other goodies were beneath her skirt. No luck.

"After you, sir." Lieutenant Patterson said in a commanding voice.

Michael started climbing the ladder. He joined the two others on the deck towards the walkway to the wharf.

"No fringe benefits for you, me boy." The Admiral whispered to Michael as soon as he joined them.

The Ensign had a blank look on his face. Michael was beet red. The Admiral was chuckling at Michael's discomfort. The Admiral and Michael turned as one toward the manhole as the blond bee hive of Lieutenant Patterson was emerging.

The Seabees were not needed after all. They were loading up into their pickup trucks and were on their way. The snack shack across the road was empty. Six Shore Patrol sailors with side arms and clubs must have seen to the evacuation and were standing guard around the sidewalk tables. The OICC was sitting in the Jeep fiddling with his walkie talkie. He jumped down and joined the group emerging from the submarine, on the double.

"I took the liberty of ordering lunch from the Officer's Club." He said to the Admiral. "I am afraid it is just sandwiches." He added in a resigned voice. "I also took the liberty of securing the area." He pointed over the snack shack.

Without a word the group headed over to the snack shack. The OICC was busy putting two tables together making room for five people. The Admiral took the head of the table looking at the submarine SWORDFISH. He pointed to Michael to the seat on his right. The Lieutenant next to Michael. He pointed to the Ensign to sit on his left and the OICC next to the Ensign.

"Here we all are and we are all ears." The Admiral said to Michael. "You have the floor."

"The problem appears to be centred around the feed water pumps and their inability out of the blue to pump any more water. This forces the operator to shut the reactor immediately, otherwise, even if he delays to shut the reactor a nuclear accident occurs of unpredictable severity."

"You have hit the nail on the head." The Admiral said. "Have you determined what causes this?"

Lieutenant Michelle Patterson was furiously scribbling on her pad her recorder placed in front of Michael.

"The simple answer is that feed water turns into steam as it reaches the pumps and cavitates the impeller of the pumps. The steam droplets are of such intensity, compared with their size, which is hardly visible with the naked eye and they deliver quite a punch, eating over time the steel of the pump impeller to nothing. This is called cavitation. The pump loses the ability to pump water anymore because there is no impeller left. The force of the steam droplet, taking into account its relative size, is equivalent to the force of the atomic bomb dropped on Hiroshima and Nagasaki during the second world war.

"As soon as there is no water flowing, a signal is sent to the Annunciator and the Alarm sounds: NO FEED WATER. At that point the operator has no alternative but to shut down the reactor immediately.

"This is the result. The question is: What is causing the water to turn into steam?

"The answer lies in the NPSH, for short. It means the Net Positive Suction Head; which is a characteristic of the feed water pump. It is measured in feet. Every pump is designed with an NPSH which the factory labels as Required. What is the Required NPSH of the SWORDFISH pumps for example?" Michael asks Ensign Paul Chamberlin.

"I don't know." The Ensign admits after a while.

"It's in your O & M manuals." Michael prompts him.

"On the double!" The Admiral dispatches the Ensign to retrieve the O & M Manuals from the submarine.

Ensign Paul Chamberlin jumps from his seat and trots towards the SWORDFISH submarine, across the street from where they were sitting.

"I bet the Required NPSH looking at the engine room set up is around 7 feet." Michael pronounces.

The lunch wagon from the Officers Club arrives with their lunch sandwiches. The Admiral takes the roast beef hoagie. Michael the pastrami sandwich. Michelle the BLT. The OICC takes the ham and cheese from the tray placing it in front of him. The tuna sandwich is the one left to the Ensign by default. The OICC goes inside the shack and comes out with five large glasses full of ice. He takes soda orders and returns with five cans. He places the regular coke can in front of the Ensign's place on the table. They unwrap their sandwiches and pour their sodas in the glass. They all proceed eating while waiting for the Ensign to return.

The Ensign returns loaded with several books totalling a couple of feet high, staked one on top of the other. They are water logged and appeared that they were never opened. He sets them on the table in front of the place he is seating. He starts shuffling through them. Michael finishes his sandwich, balls the paper wrapping and tosses it on the tray holding the lone tuna fish sandwich. He takes pity on the poor Ensign and drags the pile of O & M Manuals to his side of the table. By consulting the INDEX of each volume, he quickly discards the rest in favour of one volume. He leaves through it and points the relative line to the Admiral.

"Seven feet. Like you guessed." The Admiral announces impressed.

"The Required NPSH of the feed water pumps on the SWORDFISH is 7 feet."

The lieutenant Michelle Patterson sets her half-eaten BLT side and grabs her pad and pen. Pushing the Record button of the mini recorder in front of Michael.

"The NPSH Available, is measured from the centreline of the pump inlet to the water line of the condensate receiver above minus the friction loss on the pipes in between. The NPSH Available must always be more than the Required NPSH of the pump. Otherwise, the water turns into steam. I eye balled the distance in the engine room this morning and it is 8 feet. Minus the friction loss, I guesstimate at half a foot; this makes the NPSH Available 7 1/2 feet. This is too close for comfort to start with.

"I also noted the introduction of three lines in the pump suction. These are for the Oxygen scavenging chemical Sulphite which turns the water into acid as soon as it adds the Oxygen to its root and becomes Sulphate. The neutralizing chemical, some type of Caustic, a base to turn the water into a neutral pH 7. The third line must be some type of Amine to fight all anaerobic organic growth in the feed water. The mixing of Sulphate and Caustic is an exothermic reaction; which means it generates heat, further raising the water temperature. Playing havoc in the balance between the NPSH Available with the one Required by the pump manufacturer.

"This in a nut cell is your problem, Ladies and Gentlemen."

"Where did you go to school?" The Ensign asked Michael. Evidently he did not have access to the FBI Security Clearance Report on Michael.

"Washington State University, Class of 1970."

"GO COUGS!", The Ensign exclaimed.

"GO COUGS!", Michael responded. "And on that note, here are my recommendations of how to rectify the problem:

"Take out the condensate tank receiver. It is approximately a three-foot diameter horizontal tank. Replace it with a Deaerator. This is a specialty tank manufactured by Permutit, LA and a number of other manufacturers, you can find in the Thomas Register if you look under Deaerator Manufacturers. I am afraid it will be a custom job identical in size to the condensate receiver you are using now. The advantage of the Deaerator is that it is a device that mechanically removes 95% of the oxygen from the water. They probably were not invented when the Polaris submarine was first conceived and designed. Additionally, it is a pressurized vessel with the injection of steam at 5 psig. You take a steam line, I am guessing the submarine uses steam for general use at around 100 psig..."

"It is actually 125 psig." The Ensign corrected.

"125 psig. You use a pressure reducing valve station; that is a pressure reducing valve with a strainer in front and two gate valves on each side surrounded by a by-pass with a globe valve in the middle. You need the bypass because you will occasionally need to open and clean the stainer from impurities. The Deaerator will greatly reduce the use of the Oxygen scavenging chemical and the Caustic used for neutralizing the water. You will need a third of the size tanks you are currently using. That's good because you will need the created space. Simplify the piping between the Deaerator and the feed water pumps by a simple tee arrangement feeding the pipes. I would add a third pump in reserve on standby in case something happens to the other two. Finally, I would switch the point of injection of chemicals from the pump suction to the pump discharge.

"By doing all of the above you have safeguarded from any rise in temperature. Making the system pressurized to 5 psig you elevated the boiling temperature of water from 212 degrees Fahrenheit to 227 degrees Fahrenheit. A fifteen-degree leeway, in other words a safety zone.

"Now for the most important issue of the system improvement. You need to come up with a devise, I will call it a Heat Sensor which will monitor the water temperature at the feed water pump discharge. As soon as the water temperature begins to rise above the level set by the operator, it will send a signal to the Annunciator of HIGH FEED WATER TEMPERATURE and the Alarm will sound.

The operator now has been warned in advance and has a number of options other than shutting the reactor down. I have noticed this morning that the Annunciator has several spare panels that are currently not in use.

"You need to add a blowdown tank in the space made available by the smaller chemical tanks. It will be a vertical tank, say 3 feet in diameter. Six feet high which will be connected to the bottom of the heat exchanger. The reaction between the chemicals Sulphate and Caustic form a precipitate similar to powder which ends op at the bottom of the heat exchanger. The precipitate is a mixture of salt and Calcium Carbonate, commonly called gypsum. You drill a hole at the bottom of the heat exchanger and pipe it to the blowdown tank Use a solenoid valve programmed to open every ten minutes or so. The precipitate from the chemical reaction and all other solids will end up in the blowdown tank instead of clogging the heat exchanger."

"We have to clean the bottom of the heat exchanger every three months of so now." The Ensign volunteered. "Because we lose cooling efficiency. We have to shovel the accumulated sludge."

"Well, you won't have to do that with the addition of the blowdown tank. You will need to clean it out once every couple of years if that, with the reduced amount of chemicals you will be using. Make sure the blowdown tank has a manhole at the bottom to allow access. Run a 5-psig steam line to the blowdown tank with isolating globe valves at each end. The steam pressure would force the precipitate out of the tank through a rubber garden variety hose out of the tank bottom out to the sea. That's all Ladies and Gentlemen. I will provide to attach to the Report a set of specifications for the equipment and material. Sketches for the installation and Details for each component."

Michael's audience was visibly impressed.

"Outstanding! The Admiral pronounced. Let's retire to the officer's Club to give time to the Lieutenant to type her notes. You will find us at the back of the Club. Ask the Stewart to show you to the private dining room."

The convoy consisting with the Admiral's car and the OICC Jeep with Michael on board following started towards the Officers Club at the other end of the Base.

"You are an amazing Engineer." The OICC pronounced as soon as they boarded the Jeep. "Why are you wasting your time in General Contracting and Administration? Here, with a morning visit you solved all the issues plaguing the Navy on the Polaris nuclear submarine, for decades."

"I was a Project Engineer in the beginning. I moved up to Project Management because that's where the money was. Are you forgetting the $875,000.00 you paid me yesterday, for basically doing nothing other than interpreting the Contract correctly?"

"How could I forget. During the meeting you were acting like a Lawyer not an Engineer."

"For your information, I am an Arbitrator with the American Arbitration Association. I have developed an acute sense of right and wrong. Your behaviour of rejecting the submittals in order to use them as a leverage to bring me to the negotiation table, hat in hand, was simply wrong. The subsequent sequence of events proves that exact point."

"You are right. Of course." The OICC admitted. "How is someone to deal with you? You are smart and have superior knowledge."

"Listen to me. If I insist on something, agree with me and move on. If I propose a possible solution with a cost estimate proposal, grab it. If you don't, you will regret it down the road."

"But that is not how the government operates. We are the government; hence we are always right."

"This way of thinking will inevitably lead to confrontations. I view a Project as a chess game and I consider myself a superior player. Not by the Grace of God. But by working harder than the competition and due to my experience as an Arbitrator, I am able to see the issue from all facets, including those viewed by my opponent. And most importantly: I don't tilt at windmills."

On this unresolved method of Contract Administration, they arrived at the Officer's Club and proceeded to the private dining room reserved for the Admiral. They ordered beers and pup-us all around. The Admiral predicted six months until the materials and the controls were on hand. In the middle of their second beer, the Lieutenant showed up with the typed Report. Michael read it. It was word for word perfect.

"It says exactly what I said." Michael said addressing the Admiral.

"Write your name underneath in capital letters and sign it. This will become the official Report for the remediation of the deficiencies pertaining to the Polaris - class submarine. How confident are you that the issues have been resolved?"

"Admiral, the redesigned system will be the type that has its belt and suspenders too. For example: A stand-by pump. A 15-degree Fahrenheit safety zone. No additional heat input on the water by switching the chemical injection point from the pump suction to the pump discharge. Finally, the introduction of the heat sensor which will give the operators advance warning not in seconds but hours, even days. None of these modifications, with safety in mind, exist now."

"You are absolutely right and I take my hat off to you. You are simply amazing, Michael. In all my career I have not met a person with a mind as sharp as yours. You ought to belong not just SOG, but an organization named National Treasures; if we had such a category and organization. You are worth your weight in Gold."

"At least I weigh $10,000.00 for today…"

"That's correct. And a bargain at that. Captain, please write Michael a check in his company's name for $10,000.00."

"I will have that ready for you, as soon as we go to the OICC Office from here."

A few minutes later Michael was placing the $10,000.00 Navy check in his briefcase, Payable to the Company for: Classified Services Rendered to the U. S. Navy.

Michael avoided the job site. He couldn't tell his staff where he was and what he had been doing all day. He was not sure if he was even allowed to in the first place. Although he had not signed any Secrecy Papers for today's work, he was not sure what the papers stipulated, the ones he signed in 1970, when he joined the Studies and Observations Group, or whether they were even applicable after the government disinherited the SOG in 1973.

Chapter 28

VIP Treatment at the Arizona Memorial.

SIX MONTHS LATER:

Laura the receptionist buzzed Michael with the intercom.

"An Admiral, I did not get his name, is on line two for you." Laura announced.

"Good morning, Admiral." Michael immediately picked up the phone and punched the line two button.

"Michael me boy. Are you ready to come on over to Paradise. Everything in your Report is on hand."

"Same remuneration per diem as last time?" Michael inquired.

"Same as before. Cash on hand as soon as the testing and sea trial is completed."

"I will catch the morning flight Seattle - Honolulu tomorrow." Michael committed. "I will be on Base at 8:00 AM the day after tomorrow."

"Same place you conducted the inspection. SWORDFISH will be tied up with a team of Seabees on call to assist you." The Admiral ended the telephone call.

Michael punched another line on his phone and called home. His wife answered the phone on the second ring.

"Hi honey..."

"What's wrong?" Was Christina's immediate response as soon as she recognized her husband's voice.

"Nothing's wrong. I am just calling to tell you that the Navy just called. They want me back to Hawaii to implement my Report on remediation of the Polaris - type nuclear submarines. I am catching a morning flight tomorrow Seattle - Honolulu. The Navy is paying the company $10,000.00 a day per diem. Since I don't know how long the renovations and afterwards the Testing and Sea Trials would take, I thought I would take you and the kids along. First Class open return tickets. You can keep the rental car after you drop me off on Base each morning. I will figure a way for someone from the Navy to give me a ride back and forth to the Hotel. The whole trip won't cost us a dime. What do you say?"

"My middle name is GO! GO!" Was Christina's response. "I will start packing and will tell the kids as soon as they come home from school. They will be so excited."

Michael hangs up the phone and calls Bill Scott, the job superintendent at the Pearl harbor Naval Shipyard project to build a Power Plant and a Demineralizing Water facility.

"I am catching a flight tomorrow morning and will be over at the Base day after tomorrow. Anything you need from here? Anything I should know before I leave Seattle?" Michael could sense the panic in Bill's voice.

"Why are you coming over? The job is running like a Swiss clock, below budget and it is ahead of schedule." Bill Scott said apprehensively.

"The Navy called me and asked me to come. It is the other Navy. The Classified Navy; regarding a Classified Project I am doing for them. As a result, I would probably have very little time to visit the job site while I am involved with that Project. Just be aware that I will be less than half a mile away from the job site. If something develops as an emergency in the meantime, I will make time to attend. After I am done with the Project, however, I am at your disposal."

"I hear you loud and clear." Was Bill's response before hanging up with an audible relief in his voice.

Michael was not given a copy of his own Report. Consequently, he had nothing in writing to review. He will extemporize when he got there. He put in his briefcase a pad of engineering graph paper with 1/4 of an inch squares. A number five Kohinoor Rapidomatic mechanical drafting pencil with HB lead. A sleeve of replacement lead. A right angle and forty-five-degree triangles. A template with an array of circles. Finally, a soft eraser. He felt ready for whatever the Navy threw his way.

He called Grace, his secretary, and told her to arrange for four First Class tickets, Seattle to Honolulu, for him and his family for tomorrow morning with an open return. Plus, a car rental in Honolulu.

"On second thought, make the rental a Jeep with an automatic transmission." He remembered the OICC Navy Jeep he was riding around and it brought him memories from his Army days. "Don't worry, the Navy will reimburse the company for my time and expenses at the tune of $10,000.00 per day."

"Can you take me along as your secretary?" Was Grace's wishful thinking.

He waited until Grace came to his office.

"What's happening? Something wrong on the Job site?" She asked, her concern visible on her face.

"There is nothing wrong with the job site. The Project is moving along, fine. It's the other Navy. The one that has nothing to do with the Project. I was dragged in to assist the Navy on a Classified Project. That's why they are paying the Company $10,000.00 a day like last time..."

"How long will you be gone?"

"I don't know. That's the reason for the open return tickets. However, I doubt if it will be longer than a week, provided the Navy has the material on hand, as they claim, and provide me with adequate manpower."

"Good luck with the Project." Grace said. "Here is the rental car voucher with the reservation number. Your tickets will be with the First-Class Ticketing. Here is the confirmation."

Michael put everything in his briefcase. He also put in his briefcase the Details; a three-ring binder showing on 8 1/2 x 11 pages the PRV, Pressure Reducing Valve Station assembly, the steam trap assembly and all other appurtenances that were part of the Power Plant Construction. He picked up his loaded briefcase, bade Grace goodbye and headed for his SAAB EMS Turbo in the parking lot.

He came home after the kids had returned from school, because he could hear the yelling and screaming of joy clear before he reached the quarter mile long driveway to his home. He had bought a family size pizza on his way home from work. One less thing for his wife to worry about.

His children raised the level of their exuberance, if that was even possible, as soon as he stepped inside the house. They were now experienced travellers to the tropics and able to decide for themselves what clothing and shoes to bring along.

"We are not going to bring our boogie boards." His son and daughter announced. "Since you will win for us new ones on the plane." Meaning that their Dad will guess correctly the halfway point of the course to their destination. A game that the pilot always offered to the Seattle to Honolulu passengers and Michael had, so far, a 100% batting average. More pressure that Michael did not need at the moment.

Christina grabbed the pizza and thanked her husband for his thoughtfulness. She started pre-heating the oven.

Michael went upstairs and started packing himself. Only this time his attire selection was predominately blue jeans, old tee shirts, a pair of steel toe boots and his hard hat. He made up the rest of the available space in his suitcase with chinos, Aloha shirts, a pair of new deck shoes and flip flops for the beach. He decided to wear on his first morning to the Pearl Harbor Naval Shipyard his normal Hawaii uniform consisting of blue jeans and Aloha shirt. Only this time he would be wearing his work boots. He also added to his suitcase a new pair of deck shoes, and several pairs of athletic tube socks for his work boots. He threw in his suitcase on top of everything his WSU varsity soccer shirt and a WSU maroon hat with the school logo in front.

The next day ride to the Airport in his wife's Ford Bronco was uneventful. They parked where they always parked on the fourth floor of the Airport Parking Structure. Michael made a note in his address booklet he always carried in his back pocket, of the parking stall number. They wheeled their suitcases to ticketing. Their tickets were waiting for them in the First-Class Section. They checked in their suitcases to Honolulu. They kept their carry ons and Michael his briefcase. They made their way to their Gate taking the underground train to the South Satellite Terminal.

The Starbucks booth was still in the corner, empty sans the sole attendant, standing idle. Michael was thinking: How long will the cash reserves of the old man last before he is forced to take apart the coffee booth contraption. Will he ever make it? Michael was not sure if he would bet on the business enterprise success.

They were the first to board their flight, flying First Class. The First-Class compartment stewardesses made a fuss when they appeared. After all, First Class was almost empty; while the 'cattle class' was bursting at the seams.

After take-off and leveling out to the assigned altitude, the Captain presented to the passengers through the loud speaker the halfway point problem. Michael did a quick check on his calculator, by inputting the information provided by the pilot and the calculator automatically solved the differential equation and provided the answer. Todd and Elli wrote the answer on the form provided by the stewardess and handed their forms back to her.

"Already!" The stewardess exclaimed. "You must be two smart kids." She added winking at Michael.

"We have two winners!" The pilot came on the loudspeaker a little while later. "Seats 4A and 4B. The amazing thing is that both have the same answer and it is right on the button. All I can say is that we must have an Engineer on board or two extremely gifted or lucky passengers."

The stewardess appeared a few minutes later with two brand new wave ridding boogie boards, still wrapped in cellophane. She presented them to Michael's kids with a lot of fuss and they accepted them like they were due to them from the start. Michael had a brief flight of thought comparing his kid's childhood with his own when he was in Greece, long, long time ago. He looked at his wife. She shook her shoulders indicating what can you do?

"In their mind it was a foregone occlusion that they would win." Christina added.

They landed in Honolulu right on schedule. They deplaned and were immediately assaulted by the heat, humidity and the smell of Plumeria flowers which were growing in tree form throughout the Airport and the City of Honolulu. Their Jeep was waiting for them, big enough to accommodate all their luggage and their children in the back seat. It was an automatic and Christina decided that she was the designated driver. She loved it.

"What prompted you to rent this beast?" Christina inquired of her husband.

"I was riding in a Navy Jeep last time I was involved with the Classified Project which I have now returned to finish. They have sure improved them over the ones I've been ridding. Bench seats with minimum padding. An accident ready to happen on sharp turns. Nowadays they have bucket seats up front, widened the body for stability and with the addition of the anti-sway bars, the oversize tires and the heavy-duty suspension, the Jeep has become the safest vehicle on the road."

"It's like I am driving a tank!" Christina exclaimed "And it sits high so even I can see over the other cars. Do I get to keep it?"

"That's the idea. You can go anywhere on the island, including dirt roads if you so desire." Michael added.

"Oh boy! Will we have fun in this!" She said looking at the kids in the back seat.

They arrived at the Hilton Hawaiian Village. They checked in a suit with two smaller bedrooms with separate bathrooms on their own.

"Can we afford it?" Christina asked her husband with a worried look on her face.

"The company is being paid $10,000.00 a day per diem by the Navy." Michael assured his wife. "The suite is nothing but a drop in the ocean."

"Whom do you have to kill for that kind of money?" Christina asked her husband laughing.

"It's actually the opposite. I cannot tell you details, but my work here will end up saving lives."

"Let's enjoy our stay then!" Christina said decisively.

The bell hop followed them with a loaded luggage cart to their suit. The kids had a short fight as to who will get which bedroom, until Christina intervened and made the assignment. The bell hop showed them where everything was and how it operated. He opened the curtains and the glass doors to their Lanai overlooking the Ala Wai Yacht Harbor. The Lanai was of grand proportions as it continued from the living room to the master bedroom.

"How come our bedrooms don't have a Lanai?" Elli protested.

"Because it will be one less thing to worry about." Christina pronounced with finality leaving no room for further discussion.

Michael gave the bell hop a five-dollar bill as a tip and they were finally left alone.

"Tomorrow morning you need to drive me to work at Pearl Harbor Naval Shipyard." Michael announced addressing his wife. "It will be the only time you will need to get up early though to drive me. I will request that the Navy provide me with transportation. You may use the opportunity to take the Pearl Harbor Arizona Memorial tour. It will be educational for the kids to see the actual footage of the attack they are showing at the Theatre afterwards."

The kids picked up on their father's words and started pestering their mother to visit the Arizona Memorial. Finally, Christina assured them that, that was exactly what they would be doing.

"After the tour, go to the Pearl Harbor Shipyard Officers Club. Tell the Stewart who is standing at the front desk, that you are the wife of the SOG Engineer working with Admiral Rickover. I am sure the Navy will comp the lunch for you and the kids."

Christina took down in her tattered notebook she extracted from her purse, the names and the particulars her husband had just spelled out. They proceeded to change in their bathing suits and make their way to the Hilton Hawaiian Village beach and lagoon for an afternoon swim. They came back, took a shower and Michael took them to the Chart House Restaurant which was within walking distance from their hotel in the midst of the Ala Wai Yacht Harbor they have been looking from their hotel Lanai.

Before going to bed Michael ordered a breakfast for four delivered to their suite at 7:00 AM sharp.

After breakfast the next day they loaded in the Jeep and Christina dropped her husband off outside the Pearl Harbor Naval Shipyard job site gate where a brand-new Navy Jeep hardtop was waiting along the chain link fence. Michael approached it and found out that the Jeep driver was none other than the ROICC, Commander Walsh. Michael asked him after they exchanged pleasantries for directions to the Arizona Memorial tour starting point. The Commander walked over to the other Jeep introduced himself to Christina and produced three complimentary passes to the tour, theatre admission and a Base map circling the location of the embarking for the tour, the movie theatre showing the attack and the Officers Club.

"I will be needing transportation." Michael said when the Commander returned.

"As long as you are working on the 'Project' the Navy will be providing you with a vehicle. As a matter of fact, you are sitting in it. The paperwork and a letter authorizing you to drive it signed by the Admiral himself is in the glove compartment." Commander Walsh pronounced.

"How are you getting back to the ROICC Building?" Michael asked.

"Either someone from your staff will give me a ride or I will walk." The Commander said. "I don't know what you are doing for the Navy. Something very hush hush, with a Clearance label all the way to God and I don't want to know. I am just the delivery boy for your Jeep. I am sure you know where you are going." The Commander said exiting the Jeep and handing Michael its keys.

Michael, wearing jeans, an old Aloha shirt, his construction steel toe shoes and wearing his WSU baseball hat jumps into the driver's seat. The Jeep was a stick shift. No problem. Michael's first car was a Triumph Spitfire with a manual transmission. He actually prefers the stick shift to the automatic unless he was caught in stop and go traffic. His hard hat was laying on the floor by the passenger seat. He will play it by ear. If the Navy demanded it, he would put it on.

The SWORDFISH was tied up where it was before, along the Bayshore Drive. There were numerous vehicles and flatbeds parked on the water side of the Drive. The centreline along the length of the submarine was blocked by traffic cones and flashing lights warning the drivers that the road narrowed to a single lane at that point. Michael parked the Navy Jeep at the end of the line and got out of the Jeep.

He started inspecting the equipment tied up on the flatbeds. Everything appeared to be as he proposed. He was unable to see some of the piping and controls; but he assumed there must be there, stored in one of the vans.

"GO COUGS!" The WSU, Michael's Alma Matter slogan reverberated in the morning calmness.

Michael turned the salute: 'GO COOUGS" and looked forward towards the bow of the submarine and noticed half a dozen Navy personnel, all dressed in work clothes milling around and smiling at him. He spotted their ring leader, no other than Ensign Paul Chamberlin, now sporting Lieutenant JG bars.

They shook hands and the Lieutenant JG introduced Michael to his troops as Michael the SOG Engineer appointed by the Admiral's direction in charge of the SWORDFISH submarine refitting. The two dozen sailors were Seabees assigned to the 'Project'.

Lieutenant Chamberlin produced a copy of the Report Michael had Authored, heavily redacted with Michael's name and signature obliterated.

Michael started talking with the Seabees as a group trying to estimate their level of knowledge and experience. This was difficult because the Seabees were so pumped up for being selected for a Top-Secret Project and so overconfident that they thought they could leap tall buildings in a single bounce.

Michael separated them in groups of four and started taking every group on a tour inside SWORDFISH explaining what needs to be demolished and taken out. The ones that they were muscle bound he separated to assist the other groups in taking out of the submarine piece by piece the obsolescent equipment. The condensate receiver for example took half of the available manpower to wrestle it through the submarine corridors and lift it out of the circular opening entrance on deck. With a twenty-four-man crew detail the work was progressing at an extraordinary speed. Michael watched the men working and within an hour he was able to determine the skill and experience level of each sailor and he mentally pigeonholed them in specific tasks when it came time for the installation of the new equipment.

Michael started drawing and collecting from the Details three ring binder Details to incorporate into the new equipment assembly. He broke down the sailors into three-man crews and giver each group an 8 1/2 x 11 sketch to pre-fabricate and assemble. Just when he gave the last assignment, the Admiral's car pulled over and asked Michael how the work was progressing. Michael explained to him that he had broken the crew in groups of three and were given the assignment to pre-fabricate the Detail which Michael had given them.

"No one knows how the new system will look and how will be put together but me and maybe Lieutenant Chamberlin. If he paid attention and understood the Report. He had a copy. So I must assume that he had read it several times. I believe with him as a foreman, the 'Project' has an excellent chance of getting done in two to three days. By this coming weekend, I believe the new system will be ready for testing and a sea trial."

"Very good!" The four-star Admiral pronounced. "Are you ready to go to lunch. I stopped by to pick you up."

"What about the rest of the crew?" Michael pointed to the sailors.

"They are not officers. We cannot take them with us to the Officers Club. Don't worry though. I ordered lunch for them from the Officers Club. The chow wagon will be here shortly."

"I will eat with the men. If you don't mind Admiral." Michael announced.

"Suit yourself." The Admiral said ordering his driver to move on.

The Seabees had stopped work. Saluted and were watching the exchange between the Admiral and Michael. As soon as they heard Michael refusing to go with the Admiral to the Officers Club, and instead he chose to eat with them, they all simultaneously broke out into a heartfelt repeated yell:

"GO COUGS! GO COUGS! GO COUGS!"

Tears started forming in Michael's eyes and he started swallowing fast to keep them secure in place. He was not about to start bawling in front of the Seabees. The Admiral smiled and saluted Michael, as his car drove away.

The lunch wagon came by less than a minute later. The Seabees stood at attention allowing Michael the first sandwich selection. He repeated himself by selecting a pastrami sandwich. Drinks arrived from the snack sack across the street as if by magic. Michael retired to his Navy Issued Jeep. Opened all the windows and started eating his lunch. He noticed that most of the Seabees went to the snack sack and sat around the tables there. There were no other customers around. Either the word had gotten out that the area was off limits to unauthorized personnel or the Shore Patrol was lurking invisible, keeping all unauthorized personnel off the snack sack. The traffic was also none existent, it finally dawned on Michael. Not a single car used the single lane on the Bayshore Drive Road since he arrived this morning.

The work resumed before 1:00 PM. Michael was walking around the fabricating crews mostly not interfering with the work unless he noticed that the assembly would end up heading South upon completion. In those cases, he interrupted the work, followed by constructive criticism and referral to the sketch they were given.

By five o' clock, an hour overtime at no pay, the assemblies were completed and the crews were beyond exhaustion. Michael was worried at all the piping assemblies laying all along the sidewalk the length of the SWORDFISH submarine. He asked that all piping assemblies be tied together with a chain and a padlock at the end to make it that much more difficult to steal overnight.

He need not have been worried. As soon as the Seabees started for their cars, a three-member team of Shore Patrol arrived armed with hand guns and clubs. The assembled piping systems were going nowhere.

Michael shouted to the leaving Seabee crews that he will see them tomorrow at 8:00 AM. He opened the door to his loaner Jeep and started the ignition. He checked the gas level and was glad to see that it showed Full. He made his way out the Base and headed to his hotel using the Nimitz Highway.

He handed the Jeep and the keys to the Hilton valet and told him to have it up front at exactly the same place tomorrow morning at 7:00 AM.

He picked up his briefcase and took the elevator to his suite on the top floor. Christina and the kids had just come back from the hotel beach and were drying up after a shower. They started talking to him, all three at once about their day at Pearl Harbor Naval Shipyard. Michael raised his hands signalling time out and asking them to talk one at the time.

"Mom first!" He emphasized.

"As soon as I handed my Passes to the Navy sailor at the dock. His demeanour immediately changed. He called on another sailor and we were escorted to the VIP lounge. We were the only ones there. We had our pick of snacks, junk food and drinks. They would accept no money. The tour to the Arizona Memorial was very moving..."

"Yeah, and the boat was full of Japanese tourists, smirking." Todd interrupted his mother.

"No they were not. They were sombre as the rest of us." Christina interjected.

"Did you go to the movie theatre, afterwards?"

"Pictures! Pictures!" Elli started chanting with Christina and Todd laughing.

"What is that all about?" Michael inquired.

"The movie documentary was very graphic." Christina commented. "The bombs and bullets from the Japanese zeroes were coming right at us. The explosions were right next to us. It must have been filmed from the ground and the viewer was right in the thick of things. Elli closed her eyes..."

"Pictures! Pictures!" Elli started chanting.

"She does that every time she gets scared watching something scary or unpleasant. It is not real, she tells herself repeatedly. It is only make believe, like pictures." Christina tossed Elli's hair affectionately.

"I loved it." Todd commented. "As soon as I realized I was not in danger to be hit, I watched the whole thing with my eyes wide open. What an adventure. I didn't want it to end."

"Did you make it to the Officers Club..."

"That was the best part." Christina interrupted. "I went to the Navy Stewart as you told me. I could not remember the Admiral's name because I could not find my address book in that mess of a purse. He, however, immediately knew all about you. It appears that you are infamous at the Officers Club. He led us through the dining room. Every conversation stopped and all eyes were on us. The kids were oblivious. But I was so embarrassed. I was sure I must have been beet red. After like forever, we reached the back of the Club and the Stewart who was escorting us knocked on a door. It opened from the inside and another Stewart appeared. He took our fellow inside and closed the door. Not before, however, I had a chance to notice a single long dining room table in the middle of the room with several white clad Navy Officers sitting around the table talking.

"We waited behind the closed door like forever when it opened and a horde of white clad officers came through the door all smiling at us and trying to engage me in small talk. Finally, our Navy Stewart came out and he handed us to the other Navy Stewart. A sole white dressed officer was sitting at the table. He got up and introduced himself as Admiral Rickover. He told us that he would be honoured to have lunch with us.

"We sat at one end of the long table and the Admiral started telling me how great you were. I am not going to repeat what he told me. You have a sufficiently big head as it is. However, everything he said, was all news to me. And I told him so; i.e., you don't talk to me about your work. The Navy Stewart approached our table and the Admiral ordered lunch for everyone without asking us what we may want..."

"I bet it was 'Surf and Turf'." Michael interrupted his wife. "It is the Officers Club Special and the Admiral's favourite."

"How did you know?" Christina exclaimed.

"I went through the same experience a few months ago." Michael admitted.

"Did the Navy Stewart cut your steak and lobster bite sizes?" Elli asked out of the blue.

Christina and Todd started laughing.

"This was the highlight of her day." Christina admitted. "She was doing goo goo eyes at the poor fellow who was merely doing what the Admiral ordered him to do."

"Tell me the sequence of events in order please." Michael asked. "Remember I was not there."

"We were asked by the Stewart how we wanted our steak cooked. We all said medium. He did not ask the Admiral. He left the dining room and immediately came back with the salad cart. The Stewart asked what kind of dressing we preferred and set out to prepare individual plates of baby Spring Greens of a salad. As soon as we finished, he asked all around whether we might like some more. When we refused, he took way the salad as two other Stewarts arrived carrying trays with our lunch."

"Let me tell you!" Todd interjected. "This was the best steak I had in my life. The lobster was enormous. I ate every last bite dipped in garlic butter."

"I know." Michael admitted. "They import Australian lobsters. They have tails, three times the size of the Maine lobsters, I brought you from Boston. Nothing but the best for the Navy Officers."

"Well, in a roundabout way you got the gist of our lunch experience at the Pearl Harbor Naval Shipyard Officers Club. We were treated like never before in our lives..."

"Can we stay here, like forever." Todd and Elli exclaimed simultaneously.

"Elli was particularly impressed when the Admiral ordered one of the Stewarts, he did not look over eighteen, to prep and help the young lady with her lunch. Well, short of feeding her, he did everything else. We had a leisurely lunch and we are still stuffed. At least I am not going to have dinner any time soon."

"I am stuffed too." Elli admitted.

"Not me!" Todd exclaimed. "Let's go out to dinner just the two of us." Todd proposed.

"I am beat." Michael admitted. "First thing, I will take a shower, order room service and go to bed. I have a long day tomorrow and I will get up early."

"I will take the kids for stroll around Waikiki so they can unwind." Christina proposed. "We may have a late gyro dinner at 'It's Greek to Me' restaurant at the Royal Hawaiian Shopping Centre. We will come back quietly so we do not wake you up."

Michael ordered a hamburger with French fries and an extra-large Kirin beer from room service. Took a quick shower. Ate at the Lanai overlooking the Ala Wai Yacht Harbor. Enjoyed a spectacular sunset. Watched a little TV and went to bed. He fell asleep before his head hit the pillow.

Chapter 29

Putting the Written Report to Practice

The next day, right at 7:00 AM the Navy Jeep was there and waiting at the Hilton Hawaiian Village circular drive as promised. Michael picked up the keys from the valet and roared out to join the commuter traffic to Pearl Harbor Naval Shipyard with a brief stop for breakfast at the Original Pancake House on Waikamilo Road. Fuelled with Portuguese sausage and eggs including a side of macadamia nut pancakes, Michael heads with renewed vigour to the Pearl Harbor Shipyard CIA Area.

Michael arrived at the SWORDFISH nuclear submarine tied up in the same location as yesterday, with the Bayshore Drive Lane blocked in the 'makai' side of the road, towards the water, and the entire contingent of Seabees, all two dozen of them and Lieutenant JG Chamberlin with them already on site. He looked at his watch. 7:45 PM. He hoped to beat them there for a quick look and assessment of the scope of work today. He proceeded nonetheless with his inspection, after a quick good morning, he continued as if no one was there. After he established in his head the sequence of events, he approached the crews.

"The first order of business is the Deaerator," he pointed at the horizontal tank tied up on the bed of a trailer, "the second, the blowdown tank," he pointed at the vertical tank with legs laying down on the bed of another trailer, "these are the hard activities which will require the muscle of nearly all of you to manoeuvre inside the engine room."

"GO COUGS!" Was the battle cry of the Seabees following Michael's instructions.

"GO COUGS!" Michael replied in response. "The sequence of events will continue with the Chemical Tanks installation followed by all their appurtenances, pumps and mixing agitators. The next order of business is the three nuclear reactor cooling water pumps. All these activities should be completed by mid-morning, if we are to have installed the piping assemblies by day's end."

The Seabees dispersed in the same groups Michael had assigned them yesterday only this time merging together and forming larger groups for the task ahead. Lieutenant Chamberlin was Michael's eyes and ears on the ground supervising the activities. Michael stayed out of the way across the street at the snack bar; the sole occupant other than a couple of Shore Patrol clad sailors keeping it that way. Michael sat at the table and proceeded in preparing sketches of the piping assemblies as they are supposed to be installed to the equipment currently jostled around to unload from the flatbeds.

At 10:30 AM Lieutenant Paul Chamberlin approached Michael to announce that all the equipment were installed and anchored in place as shown on the sketches. Michael got up from the table and proceeded to conduct an eyewitness inspection. The work was First Class using the best of supplemental material to complete the work. The only thing he wanted to correct was the pump bases. They were installed as they were originally. He wanted to make an improvement.

"I would like you to install isolating spring mounts between the water circulating pumps and their bases. This way the pump vibration would not transfer to the submarine structure. The other day, while I was making the initial inspection, I thought my feet would go to sleep standing in the engine room. I want to eliminate this problem in the revised design."

"I agree with you whole heartedly." Lieutenant Chamberlin announced. Michael suspected that he was first hand recipient of what he was talking about.

A couple of Seabees were dispatched to retrieve the isolation springs from their vast warehouse. Michael started handing out sketches with the piping assemblies, laying all along the sidewalk, mounted on the newly installed equipment.

The Admiral stopped by just before lunch in his car to check up on the progress. Michael explained to him how he had prefabricated the piping to minimize the work inside the submarine.

"They are installing the piping assemblies onto the new equipment already installed inside the submarine. Everything fits in place as drawn. They should be done with this portion of the work by the end of the day. Tomorrow I will schedule the instrument installation and perform last minute in the field improvements, if any. By the end of the day tomorrow, the submarine would be ready for testing and Sea Trial."

"Excellent!" The Admiral announced. "I will schedule a skeleton crew for Sea Trials the day after tomorrow. I will be onboard for the sea trials and so will you as my guest. By the way, I had lunch with your wife and family yesterday. You are lucky. You have a rock of a wife. She will be with you forever, through thick and thin. Your children also will be very successful in whatever they undertake. I envy you. I lost my son to cancer last year. I hope you never have to go through such an ordeal. It was devastating."

The lunch wagon showed up and this prompted the Admiral to signal his driver to depart. Michael picked up his sandwich, a roast beef this time, with a bag of potato chips and joined the crews at one of the snack bar tables. The two Seabees arrived with the isolation spring pump pedestals, just in time before the lunch wagon departed.

Michael was ever present throughout the afternoon to eye witness the piping installation. He added pressure gauges at each water feed water pump suction and discharge. He explained to Lieutenant Paul Chamberlin who was following him around like a puppy dog.

"The operator should make a note of what the pressure gauges were indicating at the start and monitor the pressure differential to make sure it remains constant at all times. Another set of suspenders to announce trouble at its inception."

Michael made another field change. He run a 3/4-inch 5-psig steam line to the blowdown tank with isolating globe valves at each end. On the blowdown tank side of the steam line, he had them install an inverted bucket steam trap assembly to take the excess water out and avoid a water hammer when steam mixed up with water. He had a ball valve installed at the centre of the lower blowdown tank opening with a coupling at the end forming the male end at its base. Lieutenant Chamberlin was watching wide eyed all these last-minute field changes trying to figure out their significance.

"I just made your life a lot easier when it came time to clean up the precipitate of the chemical reactions which will ultimately collect at the bottom of the blowdown tank. Instead of the dirty manual labour of hand cleaning, all you have to do is pressurize the blowdown tank with the 5-psig steam line. Attach a hose at the bottom of the blowdown tank. Open the ball valve and all the precipitate in the form of sludge will come out. Hang the end of the hose overboard and dump the sludge to the sea. It is a mixture of NaCl which is nothing but salt and Calcium Carbonate which is gypsum. Completely safe and inert. The salt will be diluted into the sea water and the gypsum will eventually settle at the bottom of the sea. Make sure you clean the blowdown tank someplace away from prying eyes because in their eyes it will look like you are dumping milk into the sea."

Lieutenant Chamberlin was amazed and thankful for Michael's ingenuity to make the operating crew's life that much easier.

"The steam inside the line after you close the two globe valves will eventually condense. The steam trap will get rid of the water to the drain so next time you open the globe valve to clean up the tank, you will not encounter a water hammer when the steam meets the water. The pipe would have been cleaned up of the water via the inverted bucket steam trap."

"You are amazing!" Lieutenant Paul Chamberlin exclaimed. "You think of everything."

"Well, we will find out during the Sea Trial the day after tomorrow if you are right or not." Michael said.

The piping assemblies were all installed as scheduled by quitting time. The trailers and excess vehicles departed. The traffic cones and the blinking lights were removed. The Bayshore Drive opened to traffic in both directions. The SWORDFISH submarine sat there tied up as if on a routine sail. The entrance was closed and locked by Lieutenant Paul Chamberlin. Still the three members of the Shore Patrol showed up as scheduled to guard the locked up nuclear submarine all night.

* * * * *

The next day only half of the Seabees showed up. Absent were the muscle-bound strong backs who virtually carried the equipment yesterday on board the submarine. Half of the Seabees were different faces.

"They are electricians." Lieutenant Chamberlin clarified reading Michael's face.

Boxes and boxes were carried and delivered on board. Michael was handed a one foot by two feet box encased in Styrofoam. Michael guessed that it must be the famous Heat Sensor he had spelled out in his report newly arrived from Minneapolis,

Minnesota. The name of the sender was redacted with heavy black markings over the name making it unreadable. Michael opened it with reverence. Inside was a 6 inch by 16-inch plastic panel with three long wires spooled at one end and another long wire at the other end with a metal probe the size of one of his cigars. It looked crude for such a specialty instrument. But then again it was a prototype, Michael was guessing. If it worked, refined duplicates would follow.

"Who made this?" He asked Lieutenant Paul Chamberlin.

"I don't know firsthand." The Lieutenant admitted picking up the box it came in and trying to get a clue. "All I know it was delivered to MIDPAC by currier from NAVFAC. It looks like it must have been made in one of the Navy laboratories."

"In Minneapolis, Minnesota?" Michael inquired.

"The Navy has hundreds of laboratories all over the world. I wouldn't be surprised if we had one in Minneapolis, Minnesota." Lieutenant Chamberlin pronounced with confidence.

"Who cares." Michael concluded. "As long as it works."

He asked for a Philips screw driver and unscrewed the back panel. As indicated in his Report there were temperature settings starting at 212 degrees Fahrenheit, the boiling point of water and going up to 230 degrees Fahrenheit as he had specified. He unscrewed to loosen the indicator and slip it to 217 degrees Fahrenheit before he tightened the indicator screw. This will give them ten degrees leeway from the time the alarm would have sounded, Michael was thinking while screwing the back on the control panel.

He instructed one of the Seabees that were standing around to install a three inch by a one-inch wye to the pumps water discharge line after the three-pump discharge line came together. Install a coupling on the 1-inch wye and socket weld a length of pipe a little longer than the probe. Insert the Heat Sensor probe in the pipe and cap the other end with the probe wire running intact. He ordered to clamp the heat sensor panel to a pipe stance secured with sheet metal screws to the engine room floor. Run the tree wires to the Annunciator panel in the next room and secure them to a spare Annunciator panel which they are to label CIRCULATING WATER PUPMPS in one line and HIGH-WATER TEMPERATURE underneath in capital letters.

He had a 0 to 20 psig gauge added after the pressure reducing valve station to the Deaerator. He replaced the gate bypass valve with a globe valve. He explained to the Lieutenant who was following him around that he would thank him if they ever got a High-Water Temperature Alarm.

"Your first reaction if this happens is to shut down the gate valves on each side of the pressure reducing valve. Then start cranking the globe valve slowly in the open position. Watch the pressure gauge we just installed. As soon as it reads 5 psig slow down and bring it slowly up. As soon as the gauge reads a little above 5 psig the High Temperature Alarm should shut down. Do you know why?"

Silence on the part of Lieutenant Paul Chamberlin.

"Because you have raised the boiling point of the water. Ordinarily, the boiling point of water at ambient pressure is 212 degrees Fahrenheit. We raised the ambient pressure to 5 psig with the pressure reducing valve. At 5 psig the boiling temperature of the water is 227 degrees. By raising the pressure, you just raised the water boiling temperature some more."

"Why did you replace the bypass valve?" The Lieutenant asked timidly.

"The internals of the gate valve is a disc which moves up and down. It's best used either wide open or completely shut. If you try to use it to control the flow; and in this particular case steam, the steam will cut the edge of the valve disc and the valve will start leaking in the closed position. The globe valve internals by comparison is a plunger which forces the steam to go around the bottom. It gives you better flow control and it will not leak afterwards."

"I wish you could write a Manual for the Navy to pass on your knowledge." Lieutenant Chamberlin murmured wistfully.

"The way technology is going forward by leaps and bounds, pretty soon a computer will be operating the submarine and making all decisions for you. Look at the calculator. We did not have calculators when I started. We did everything the hard way by hand using a Slide Rule, but we knew every step of the way why we were doing what we were doing. With the calculator, you input the information and it spits out the answer. The kids nowadays learning math with a calculator, in my opinion are at a disadvantage. Forever slaves to the calculator. What happens if we lose electricity? I will tell you what will happen; either go back to the basics and re-learn math or back to the stone age."

The installation of the new system was completed and inspected by mid-afternoon. The Admiral was told by Michael, during his lunch drive by, that the installation was complete pending the Final Inspection and clean up.

"I will schedule the Sea Trial for tomorrow." Admiral Rickover announced. "I want you present, on board, as my guest, tomorrow."

"I will be there." Michael conceded. "Where and what time."

"Same place...Let's make it nine hundred hours." The Admiral pronounced with finality.

The Seabees started collecting their tools at mid-afternoon and cleaning up. The place looked after a while like no work was ever performed in the engine room and control room. Quite a difference from the start of the day when it looked like it had been attacked with hand grenades.

Michael, still wearing his WSU baseball hat, thanked the Seabees and Lieutenant Paul Chamberlin for a job well done.

The chant: "GO COUGS! GO COOGS! GO COUGS!" By the Seabee chorus followed him to his car.

Michael took off his baseball hat with the WSU logo and swung it over his head in acknowledgment. He made it back to the Hotel in no time, ahead of the afternoon commuter traffic. He dropped the Navy Jeep with the hotel valet. He went up to the suit to change to his bathing suit and surprise his family on the beach.

The surprise was all his. No matter how hard he looked, his family was not on the beach in front of the Hotel. He started walking towards Waikiki Beach. He passed Hale Koa where Admiral Hyman Rickover was staying, all the way to the Shore Bird restaurant. Nothing. He reversed and started the long way along the beach back to the Hilton Hawaiian Village. When he reached his destination, his wife and children were setting up their towels.

"Short day today!" Christina exclaimed.

"Where have you been?" Was Michael's response and the start once again of everyone talking at once.

He gathered that they were on an excursion on the North Shore.

"You should see the Golf Course we discovered." Todd raised his voice to be heard. "Right on the water. It reminded me of Pebble Beach. It's called Kahuku. They only allow hand carts. $2 dollars a round on weekdays and $3 dollars on weekends. I dare you to find a better deal."

"The shrimp was wonderful." Elli added. "It tasted like the ones in Greece. Same as the ones you fry for us."

"She is right!" Christina added. "There is an old sugar mill just before the Golf Course. It has been shut down and converted to outdoor restaurants and souvenir shops. One of the restaurants is shrimp only. That's where we ate lunch and had the fried shrimp still in their shell, spiced like in Greece. I asked to see the Owner. He was Greek, married to a Japanese woman. I told him that I was not surprised tasting the shrimp he cooked. They reminded me of Greece."

"We ordered a whole plater." Todd added. "And another one when we literally inhaled the first. Greek salad with authentic feta cheese and French Fries fried in olive oil."

"He is right." Christina added. "What a surprise to find a little of Greece on the North Shore of Oahu of all places. The Owner sat at our table as soon as he found I was married to a Greek. He wanted to know where you were. I told him that if I told him, I would have to kill him. He understood immediately. Pearl Harbor. He answered his own question. Anyway, he was from the island of Andros. He knew all about Hydra. He gave us a lesson of the Greek Revolution. He told us that one of your ancestors was a famous 'bourlotieris'. He went on and on explaining how the 'bourlotieri', ended up blowing up the entire Turkish fleet by the end of the war."

"It sounds like you guys had a lot of fun. Good, because we are leaving the day after tomorrow." Michael added sadly.

Groans and moans followed Michael's announcement.

"Why are we leaving?" Christina exclaimed. "Are you done with what you've been doing?"

"I will be done with the $10,000.00 a day gravy train by the end of business tomorrow. To answer your question. We have been living on that while we have been here. No thought of what we were spending. Our per diem after tomorrow, comes out of our own pocket. However, I intend to live it up till then. Tonight, we are going to Kobe for dinner."

"What kind of name is that?" Todd inquired immediately "What kind of food do they serve?"

"Kobe is the finest beef. Flown all the way from Japan When the calf is born, they restrict its movements by tying it in four stakes. They feed it grain, barley, milk and a little beer. They massage it every day to make its meat tender. When they slaughter it, its meat is so tender you can cut it with your fork…"

"Dad this is sad." Elli chimed in. "All that so we can eat tender beef. The poor animal is tortured, being held virtually immobile so it would not develop muscles."

"How different than the rest of the cattle born and bred for food. At least the Kobe enjoys better food while it is alive." Michael rationalized to appease his daughter.

They swam and sunbathed the rest of the afternoon. They went back to their suite to take a shower and change. Michael had made a dinner reservation for six thirty. They walked along the landscaped grounds of the Hilton. They arrived at the hotel entrance. They took a left and here they were in front of the Kobe restaurant.

They were seated in a horse shoe shape table for eight. The other four were a couple from the Mid-West on vacation with their two kids, a boy and a girl, similar age as Todd and Elli. Only the reverse. The girl was older and the boy the youngest. There was a hot plate table in the open end of the horse shoe where the chef would be cooking in front of them.

Michael ordered Kobe beef steaks all around. The other family, when they saw the price of Kobe beef, opted for chicken. They were immediately served a soup of clear both with two or three vegetables swimming in the broth.

"Prisoner of war soup." Michael whispered to his wife seated next to him overheard by both their children who broke out in an uncontrollable laugh.

Christina glared at her husband who shut up and started spooning his soup. The soup half eaten, was whisked away by their Japanese waitress dressed in Kimono, only to be replaced by a salad with greens resembling flowers and a strange sweet and sour dressing. There were no forks to eat the salad. Only chop sticks. Michael ordered three rubber bands and a Kirin beer for him, a glass of the house Pinot Noir for his wife and two sodas for his children. The waitress pulled three rubber bands from her pocket and handed them to Michael. The whole table was in rapt attention of what Michael intended to do with the rubber bands.

He took the paper cover of the chop sticks. Rolled it into a tight tube and placed it on the top edge of the chop sticks. He wrapped the rubber band around the paper tube and tested the chop sticks. They were instantly converted from chop sticks into tweezers. He handed it to his wife and did the same for his two kids. They all started picking and eating their salads. Michael was an expert at handling the chop sticks. The Mid-Western family tried to emulate him. Their efforts fell short until the waitress took pity on them and brought them forks.

Their salad was whisked away as soon as they were done and the chef appeared pulling a cart with the fare they had ordered. After he determined who ordered what, he set himself to work by turning on the hot plate and pouring some sort of oil and butter to heat up. He set large plates in front of everyone and two small dishes for each. He started pouring with a ladle a sauce identified as ginger sauce for the shrimp and vegetables. Another sauce from a different bucket in his cart identified as mustard sauce for the meat or chicken.

The hot plate had reached its optimum temperature and the chef commenced to dazzle the dinners with his acrobatic skills and dexterity at handling an array of knives to peel and chop the shrimp into bite size pieces, cooking them in soy sauce and tossing them with accuracy into Michael's and his family's plates. The Mid-Western family were not merited this delicacy with their order. They started eating immediately dipping the shrimp morsels into the ginger sauce. The chef was busy preparing and cooking the vegetables. They all looked exotic sans the Maui onion whose slices he stacked into a pyramid, soaked it with Saki and set it ablaze. He then proceeded to slice it among the volcano like effect into bite size pieces which he tossed, this time to all the plates, followed by sprouts and numerous other vegetables.

He brought out the four Kobe steaks and asked each how they would prefer to be cooked. They all decided medium. The chef proceeded into slicing, dicing and chopping each steak into bite size pieces adding liquids and spices in the process. He tossed a piece of meat into each plate of Michael's family and urged them to try it out. Todd devoured his piece with hardly chewing. The rest of the family were chewing and moaning because of the exquisite taste and texture.

"I will have your steak also." Todd declared looking at his sister. "You wouldn't want to eat the poor defenceless and tortured animal." He repeated his sister's words earlier on the beach.

"No!" Was Elli's war cry. "I will eat my own steak. I did not know it tasted so good."

The chef distributed the remaining pieces in equal portions among the four plates and brought out the chicken. No one said a word for the next twenty minutes, busy eating every morsel on their plate. The dinner was followed by tea ice cream desert.

They all wanted to go for a walk into Waikiki to digest. Michael insisted that they all return back to their hotel first, immediately. He was anyway, and he warned that if the rest did not follow suit, they would regret it. He started on a fast walk back to the hotel his family on his wake trying to keep up.

It hit them as soon as they crossed the threshold of their suite.

"It's the ginger sauce." Michael explained. "If you are not used to it, it turns whatever was in your stomach to liquid."

Thank God they had three bathrooms in their suit. For the next half hour, they were taking turns moving their bowls and emptying themselves.

"I like it." Todd announced. "I now know what to eat if I am constipated."

"Enough!" Christina exclaimed. "Too much information!"

After they were done, they left their hotel suite and resumed their intended walk along Waikiki, the kids visiting every tourist trap with their newly acquired allowance from Daddy War-bucks.

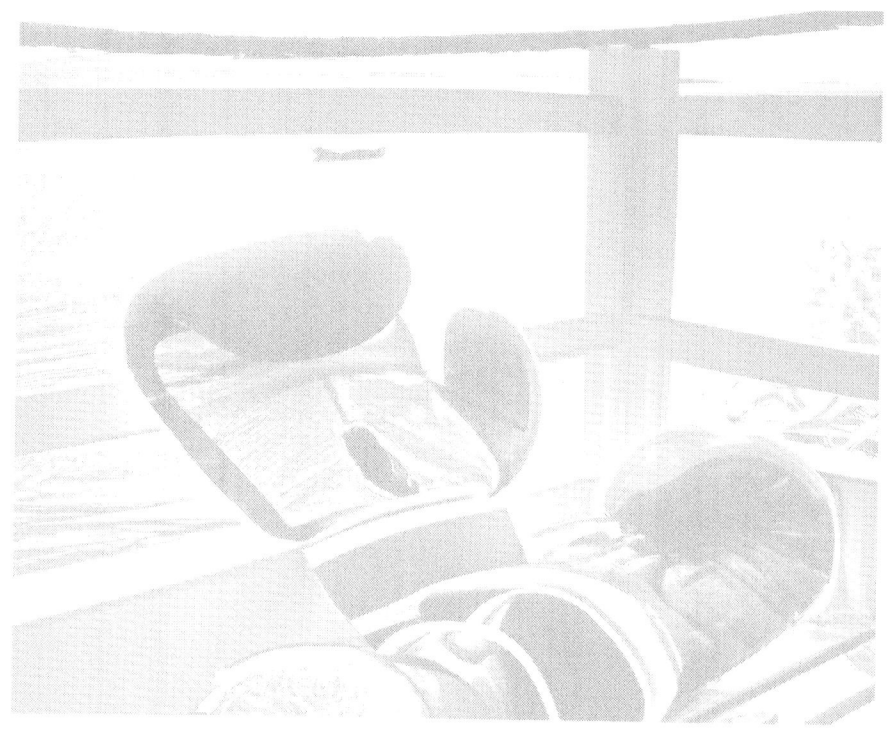

Chapter 30

Sea Trials Aboard The Swordfish

The next morning Michael had breakfast with his family at their Lanai overlooking the Ala Wai Yacht Harbor. He ordered a Portuguese sausage omelette for himself from room service. He did not know how long he would be out to sea or what accommodations the Navy had made for sustenance. He was sure they would provide something to drink, being in Hawaii and the heat. He did not know whether they would stay on the surface or submerge to make the Sea Trial more realistic. He ordered a large fresh squeezed orange juice to go along with his omelette which he doused in Tabasco sauce.

The rest of the family had Papaya, fresh Pineapple, a basket of croissants and other cake type delicacies. They were still full from last night. In spite of the trips to the bathroom immediately after dinner. Ever since: 'I have a Ginger attack', became the battle cry in the family of having to go, urgently.

He got caught by the National Anthem playing through the loudspeakers at Pearl Harbor Naval Shipyard. He had to stop the car wherever he happened to be at the time, get out of his car and stand at attention. Starting with the US National Anthem meant that no ships from other countries were visiting. Otherwise, their National Anthems would be playing first. Hence the salute to the flag was short-lived.

Michael made it to the CIA Area with plenty of time to spare and parked in the snack shack parking lot across the street from the nuclear submarine SWORDFISH tied up at the wharf. He wore jeans and his old WSU soccer varsity shirt. He still was wearing the same crimson hat he was wearing all along the submarine renovations with the WSU logo up front.

He greeted the Shore Patrol sailors guarding the submarine and made his way down the ladder of the submarine open hatch on its deck. The interior of the submarine seemed crowded, making it more claustrophobic than usual. Admiral Rickover was there already with a number of Captains all around him, so Michael was not able to tell who was the actual submarine Captain and who were the Admiral's assistants, or guests since the grovelling was universal.

Finally, Michael was spotted by the Admiral who literally dragged him to his crowd of Captains. Evidently, everyone knew of

Michael's role in the whole affair. Additionally, they already knew his name and bio. Michael was definitely at a disadvantage which he covered up with his usual look of aloofness, who adopted whenever he felt uncomfortable among strangers, as if greeting inferiors who would never see again.

"These are Captains of other Polaris - type nuclear submarines that happened to be berthed here at Pearl Harbor at this time." Admiral Rickover announced to Michael. "They were busy earlier taking pictures of the renovations." A good way of rationalizing by calling the correction of deficiencies 'renovations'; Michael was thinking.

"Could you summarize for these good men the renovations." The Admiral asked of Michael.

"Replaced the condensate receiver with a Deaerator. The reason for that is to remove 95% of the oxygen from the water, by mechanical means so the system uses less Oxygen scavenging chemicals.

"Pressurized the Deaerator to 5 psig so the boiling temperature of the water was raised from 212 degrees Fahrenheit to 227 degrees.

"The Available NPSH of the submarine is 8 feet. The previous two water circulating pumps had a Required NPSH of 7 feet. They were replaced. The new three water circulating pumps, one of them as spare, have a Required NPSH of 5 feet. The Available NPSH has to be more than the Required otherwise the water flashes into steam and eats up the pump impeller.

"The Oxygen scavenging chemical, Sulphite, should be in pounds per hour instead of gallons per hour like it was originally. The Caustic to neutralize the acid which would form as the Sulphite trapping oxygen becomes Sulphate. The chemicals injection point in the system was changed from the pump suction to the pump discharge. The reason for this is that the neutralizing chemical reaction is exothermic Which means it releases heat which would raise the water temperature.

"The neutralizing reaction produces a precipitate. A solid powder. A mixture of salt and gypsum. This used to clog the heat exchanger tubes reducing its efficiency. The precipitate is now a small fraction of the original amount since the system now uses a twentieth of the original amount of oxygen scavenging chemicals. The precipitate is blown down cleaning the heat exchanged tubes constantly and it ends up in a newly installed blowdown tank. The tank occasionally, say once a year, is pressurized and the precipitate collected at the bottom of the tank is blown out to sea.

"Finally, 'Le piece de resistance', the Heat Sensor. Originally, the operator was notified by the Annunciator Alarm of a problem when the light was flashing that there was no cooling water circulating. This meant that the pump impeller had seized to exist, eaten away by the water turning into steam. The steam bubbles exploding against the pump impeller with the force of an Atomic Bomb of the size dropped in Hiroshima. That is the power of the steam bubble not visible by the naked eye, viewed in its relative size to the size of the Atomic Bomb. The Heat Sensor monitors the water temperature and if it increases towards the boiling point, it sends a signal to the Annunciator.

"We simulated yesterday with Lieutenant Paul Chamberlin, who is in charge of the SWORDFISH nuclear submarine engine room, exactly such an emergency and what to do to remediate it. We simply, manually, shut off the gate valves on each side of the automatic Pressure Reducing Valve which maintained a 5-psig pressure to the system which translates to a 227 degrees water boiling temperature and manually opened the globe bypass valve and increased the pressure to the system by a couple of psig's resulting in increase of the water boiling temperature and the Annunciator Alarm stopped. There was no damage to the pump impeller since no steam was formed because the Alarm point had been pre-set at 217 degrees Fahrenheit.

"This is the summary of the improvements performed on this submarine. As you can see a lot of redundant measures were implemented for all conceivable potential problems encountered It has become a situation of wearing a belt and suspenders." Michael concluded.

"Did you play soccer in College?" One of the Captains said after Michael stopped talking.

"Yes. I did." Michael responded.

"What position?" Another Captain asked.

I guess they were paying attention on my shirt instead of what I was saying, Michael thought. Typical government brass. They get promoted until they rise to their point of incompetence. The Peter Principle.

"In College I played Centre Half. In High School, however, I played all positions including goalkeeper."

"He was also in the US Olympic Team in boxing during 1967. He was a shoe in for the 1968 Olympics. He had the best record in the Welterweight Division; 23 - 0 -1, before he quit." Admiral Rickover said, having read the FBI Report on Michael.

"What happened? Why did you quit?" There was a cacophony of excited voices.

"I'd like to find that out myself." Admiral Rickover admitted.

The Sea Trial was all but forgotten. Michael's boxing career has moved up in the front burner.

"I had never boxed in my life, until College." Michael launched. "I was just starting College and taking PE because it was mandatory. The class I was in was gymnastics. I saw an old man sitting against the wall watching the class. He stood up and approached the PE teacher. After a brief conversation the old man went back and sat in the same place against the wall. The PE teacher called me over and instructed me to go see Ike Deter, pointing at the old man sitting against the wall. I went over."

"Young man what's your name?" Were Ike's first words.

"I told him."

"Come closer." Ike Deter said. "I want to feel your thighs."

'Oh Shit! I thought. What am I getting myself into.'

"Have you ever boxed?" Ike Deter asked me. "You have the most powerful thighs I have encountered in my career as a boxing coach. They will generate unbelievable power in close ups. I bet you would win by Technical Knockout most of your fights. No one will be able to continue with cracked ribs. How much do you weigh?"

"165 pounds."

"That's too much for your height. But this will not be a problem. We will put you on a high protein diet. You will be eating 4,000 calories just to maintain 147 pounds. That's right, then you will have the ideal built for a Welterweight."

"So, the training started. Three hours a day. Seven days a week. By the end of the training session, I was dripping wet from the effort like I had come out of a swimming pool. Ike was right I was 23 and 0 and had won most fights on a Technical Knockout I was devastating in the clinches. But so far, I was fighting other Colleges. Student athletes as myself. I was selected to be part of the Golden Gloves who made up the US Olympic Team. I was the only one selected from my school.

"My first Golden Gloves match was in Pullman, Washington right at the Bohler Gym Basketball Court, which was converted with a boxing ring in the middle of the basketball court. My opponent was a black from the Tacoma Boys Club. I had never fought a black before. Nor a Southpaw, a boxer who leads with the right hand. In other words, a lefty. It was like I was boxing in front of a mirror in reverse. Very confusing. Additionally, my opponent was immune to pain. He was in fact seeking to get hit, enjoying it, fuelling a devastating attack. He was fast. Beating me to the punch and scoring. I tried to get him against the ropes to break a rib and thus end the match, but he must have studied me in films and would always find a way to escape or hold on to me until the referee would come over and pull us apart.

"I was left-handed by birth and when I started attending grade school, they viewed being left-handed as a handicap. They tied my left hand against my belt during classes, making me at the end ambidextrous. Accordingly, on round two I switched leading with my right hand. He was taken by surprise and was beaten up bleeding all over the place. If the round was thirty seconds longer, I am certain the referee would have stopped the contest in my favour.

"During the break his coach must have whispered to him some of my weaknesses because the third round was basically equally divided in punches. The decision was unanimous. My opponent won the first round. I won the second round. The third round was even. Final result: A tie. I had to fight him in Tacoma for a rematch. I refused. This fellow was uneducated; looking into boxing as his ticket out of the poverty and ignorance. I was studying Chemical Engineering. What was I doing lowering myself to his level. That's how I viewed the matter. So I quit the Golden Gloves. My opponent from the Tacoma Boys Club ended by default representing the United States in the 1968 Olympics and he won the Gold Medal."

Michael's tale ended up with applause by his audience and a scattered 'GO COUGS!'. The Captain of the SWORDFISH gave the order and the submarine was on its way sailing on the surface and reaching the Pearl Harbor Exit to the open ocean in no time. The submarine increased its speed and settled at a cruising speed of 21 knots. They went through all the simulated exercises the Admiral and/or each of the Captains could dream, always coming through with flying colours. The Sea Trial became anticlimactic. The highlight of the Sea Trial was the balancing of the new oxygen scavenging chemical and then the balancing of the caustic to neutralize the acid. A sample of the water was taken. A probe was immersed into the sample and a pH readout was obtained instantly.

"In my day we would have had to perform a full-scale Titration procedure." Michael commented shaking his head at the technology advances.

"What is a Titration?" Lieutenant JG Chamberlin inquired.

"Collect the sample. Put it under a gradated glass column full of a chemical of known pH with a cock at the bottom of the glass column. Add a drop of indicator to the collected water solution; usually the indicator was a chemical called Phenophthalein. Then open the cock slowly and adding the known pH liquid into the collected water sample. When it was neutralized, it turned purple. At that point we read the millilitres expended of the liquid with the known pH and measuring the millilitres of the water solution we collected, we ran calculations to determine the pH of the water sample. It was a process of determining the water sample pH by trial and error by many samples, collected over a period of time..."

"What a hassle!" The Lieutenant exclaimed. "I bet you did not even have calculators. All the calculations were done by hand and a Slide Rule."

"Don't forget that with a Slide Rule we put a man on the moon!" Michael exclaimed followed by the combined applause of the Captains and the Admiral.

The Admiral notified the submarine SWORDFISH Captain that he had seen enough and the Captain ordered the submarine to head back home.

Lieutenant Paul Chamberlin was called in for a short conference after they docked at Pearl Harbor and he came with all the sketches Michael had done. Copies were made and distributed among the Captains of the other nuclear submarines currently berthed at Pearl Harbor along with copies of the original Report, Specifications, sketches and Details.

"The SWORDFISH would be berthed, tied up at Pearl Harbor Naval Shipyard to serve as the model for the refitting of the entire fleet which should take less than a year to complete." The Admiral announced addressing two of the Captains who were part of his entourage. "You are in charge of the logistics. Schedule the refitting of the submarines. It will all take place at Pearl Harbor Naval Shipyard."

"When will the SARGO show up?" Michael inquired after the Captains were dispersed and he remained alone with the Admiral.

"I am afraid we have seen the last of SARGO." The Admiral admitted sadly. "We lost her this past week somewhere under the ice caps of the North Pole. Aren't you glad you did not elect to implement the changes on board the SARGO. Your Sea Trial may have ended in tragedy..."

"What happened? What went wrong?" Michael asked with alarm in his voice.

"No one knows. Lost to the bottom of the sea with all 99 on board lost. It is a tragedy for the Navy which is kept under wraps on need-to-know basis. So keep this to yourself. We only announced it to the select Congress Intelligence Committee. The reason we gave was a repeat of what probably plagued the SARGO more than a year ago at Pearl Harbor Naval Shipyard."

"It is a tragedy. Thank you for telling me." Michael concluded.

"I informed however, the Congress Intelligence Committee that the problems with the Polaris - Class Nuclear Submarines will soon be cared for thanks to a smart member of SOG. They did not know what SOG was and for what it stood for. Sad really for all you had to go through during the Viet Nam war. Well, in my book you are a Hero."

They shook hands and Michael headed for the OICC office to settle the remuneration issue. He was surprised that a $50,000.00 check was waiting for him for a five days' worth of work, when in fact he was through with his work and Sea Trial within less than four days.

Michael picked up the check and put it in his briefcase. It was 1:30 PM. He was surprised he was not invited to a fare well lunch at the Officers Club. I guess my usefulness has come to an end he thought. Like yesterday's Holiday leftovers. 'Veni Vidi Vici', I came,

I saw, I won, Michael was thinking visualizing Cesar's succinct explanation to the Senate after his Greek campaign.

He wished he had an advisor handy repeating in his ear during his glory and triumph: 'Fame and Fortune are Ephemeral and it's Fleeting'.

Chapter 31

The Top Dog of The Navy Archives

FIVE YEARS LATER, December 12, 1985.

Five years have gone by since the disappearance of SARGO. The mystery, however, did not last long. Evidently the Navy had succeeded to decontaminate the SARGO submarine and it sailed off in the night, because a year later it was reported lost underneath the North Polar caps with all hands-on board. Did the Navy conduct all the modifications listed in Michael's Studies and Observations Group Report on all the remaining Polaris - Class attack submarines? Whom to ask? How to go about verifying it?

What was the cause of the SARGO accident underneath the polar caps? Did the Navy manage to retrieve the submarine? Was it at the bottom of the sea leaking radioactivity? All these questions and no reliable answers, were bugging Michael's thoughts.

Michael and his partners sold the Seattle company with all its affiliates to a Publicly Owned Corporation and got their money out, tenfold.

Steve Crane left the company and moved to Hanford, Washington where he died a year later from Leukemia. He was a young man. Barely thirty. A lot of nuclear plants however, at Hanford. Additionally, the area had been utilized by the Atomic Energy Commission for years as a nuclear waste storage facility. It was after all the Eastern Washington desert. Michael was surprised by Steve's death. However, he did not connect it to the SARGO Incident of two years ago.

Michael was saddened to find though that Bill Scott also died from Leukemia, leaving behind a very young wife, Maria, who fortunately managed to finish the University of Hawaii School of Nursing while her husband was still alive. Bill Scott was in his late fifties when he died. Not very old. He opted to stay in Hawaii, after the completion of the Power Plant and the Demineralizing Facility at Pearl Harbor Naval Shipyard. He started working for the Sheraton Corporation as a maintenance superintendent at one of their Hotels on Oahu.

Was Bill's death connected to the SARGO Incident five years ago, Michael is thinking while attending Sunday Service at the St. Constantine and Helen Greek Orthodox Church in Honolulu. His wife, Christina, is nudging him on the ribs with a curt command to pay attention and quit daydreaming. It always amazed Michael how she could always tell.

Their two children at their side. Todd, their son, 14 years old checking out the young females, his age attending Liturgy with their families, and the not so young. Elizabeth, their daughter, 11 years old with long dark curly hair and a budding figure, is paying attention and follows the Service via the book she is holding.

Throughout his career, Michael had to go wherever his job took him. After the sale of the Company in Seattle, he no longer had to do that. They sat down and had a family meeting to decide where did they really want to live, now that they had money. They all decided Hawaii. So, they moved to Honolulu, on the island of Oahu. Last year Michael started a company, Akamai Engineering & Construction, Ltd., doing defence work and getting richer.

The Service ends and they go up to the priest to receive 'Antidoro', the blessed bread during Liturgy. They go outside to meet all the other families for the social part of the Service. Michael and the kids would rather skip that part. They were hungry and could not wait to hit the brunch buffet at the Waikiki Yacht club. Christina, however, felt compelled to meet and greet all the guests and newcomers. She wanted them to feel welcome. If they were in a new community, that's how she would like to be treated. She is doing no more for the newcomers.

It's hard to argue with 'Mother Christina' or 'Saint Christina', as Michael and the kids call her. Todd once voiced the opinion: "Mom wants to get her two dollars' worth." Referring to dollars' worth the money she once deposited in a special tray for the earthquake victims of Peloponnese, Greece.

All is not lost, Michael is thinking as he lights his first cigar of the day, a Romeo y Julieta Churchill series. The same kind his father got hooked on during World War II during the German occupation of Greece. He strolls over and joins the other cigar smokers in the church garden. Good opportunity to practice his Greek, although the glossary of his cronies is limited and out of date.

Christina and the kids are a few steps to the right, talking to a couple; the husband is dressed in a Commander's Naval Uniform and their two daughters. One, Elli's age and the other that Todd seems to have taken a particular interest, a little older. Michael is mentally counting how long it would be before Christina dragged him from his cigar smoking buddies to meet "this nice couple" ...

On cue, Christina comes over and apologizes to the group for taking her husband away for a few minutes.

She walks over to where she's been with Michael in tow. She introduces him to Julie and Greg Saddler and their daughters Marianna and Catherine.

"I understand that you do work for the Navy." Greg Saddler says to Michael as soon as the introductions are over.

The two men step aside leaving the women and kids by themselves.

"The company I work for does primarily defence work for the Army, Navy, Air Force, Marines and Coast Guard." Michael responds.

"Well, from what I hear your modesty proceeds you, because in fact you are 'Mr. Akamai'." A play in words because Akamai is the first word in Michael's company and at the same time 'Akamai' in Hawaiian means Smart.

Michael feels blushing. With a red face he admits that the company is really owned 100% by his wife.

"I am just an employee there." Michael admits.

"Why is that?" Greg asks.

"It started as a joke more or less. After I sold my company in Seattle, I put $25,000.00 of my money into starting a Consulting Engineering Firm. Nothing big. Just enough to do a little defence work consulting to keep me busy. My wife went to my attorney and started the paperwork for the corporation. He issued all the stock in her name. I didn't say anything because I had all the Engineering and Construction Licenses in my name. I figured anytime I wanted, I would hand Christina a twenty-five-thousand-dollar check and buy the company back.

"The company grew and grew and grew. It was no longer just me and my wife. We now had employees. As soon as I saw it snowballing, I offered Christina $25,000.00 to buy it back. She refused my offer of equity, which after all was the sum total of her initial investment, and instead presented me with the last Audited Financial Statement showing a net company worth in excess of two million dollars. "In case," She said, "I found someone else to be tempted with. You have to consider: Is the bimbo worth 2 million bucks?"

Greg breaks up laughing when he hears the story.

"It's the funniest Insurance Policy story I've heard." Greg admits. "But very effective. And I bet the price tag keeps going up and up with time."

"Where are you folks coming from?" Michael asks to change the subject in a hurry.

"We just came from San Diego, last week as a matter of fact. First time in Hawaii."

"What do you do for the Navy?"

"I am in charge of the Archives for the Pacific Fleet. Stationed at Pearl Harbor Naval Shipyard. By the way, everyone there is afraid of you, but they admire you at the same time. I am dying to find out why, but I am reluctant to ask, being the new kid on the block."

The two women and four kids join them.

"We got to get going!" Christina announces. "Our kids are hungry."

"We are hungry too!" The two girls announced in unison.

Michael offers to take them all to the Waikiki Yacht Club for brunch. Christina is a little surprised, because she knows her husband does not extend invitations on such a short notice. She looks at Michael with an arched eyebrow, pretending she did not hear him well. Michael repeats his offer. Christina is trying to guess her husband's ulterior motives.

The Saddlers accept gladly. The kids have become buzzum buddies already. Greg and Julie are not familiar with the Waikiki Area. They live in Ewa Beach on the other side, the Leeward side of the island of Oahu.

"We will try to follow your car." Greg says "But what happens if we get separated coming down the Pali?"

"Why don't you ride with Greg!" Christina proposes addressing her husband. "We came to church in my car, which is big enough to accommodate all four kids in the back seat."

They all head towards the parking lot. The Saddlers car is a little yellow FORD Fiesta. Christina's car is an '85 Mercedes SDL Turbodiesel, gleaming white with a cellular phone antenna. Only the seventh vehicle in the State of Hawaii to have one. Christina calls from her car phone the Waikiki Yacht Club, gives them her name and tells them that there would be eight coming to brunch. Julie is teasing Michael that he was giving up the lap of luxury and has to follow in their little car.

Michael and Greg have hit it off right away. They both like golf and Greg promises to get Michael in as his guest to play for free at all the military golf courses on the island. Michael in turn will take them all out sailing on his 41-foot sailboat, tied up at the Waikiki Yacht Club.

They follow Christina's Mercedes, which is not a very hard thing to do, according to Greg.

"It's like following a Navy carrier." Greg adds.

Greg is complaining to Michael that he would have preferred a Command at Sea assignment, rather than being tied up to an office job shuffling paper.

"Your job in charge of the Archives is very important. More than you realize." Michael says speaking ex cathedra. "You have a chance to find out all the skeletons in the Navy's closet. This type of knowledge is Power."

Michael gets Greg to start talking about his job.

"I bet I can put my hand on a letter you wrote to the Navy, say five years ago on such and such Project." Greg brags to Michael.

Michael teases him and tells Greg that he accepts the challenge.

"I wrote a speed letter to the Navy on December 12, 1979. See if you could find a copy and correspondence regarding all the events associated with that letter from beginning to end."

"You are on, buddy. I will have the entire copy of the package in your hands next week Sunday at Church."

They arrive in front of the Waikiki Yacht Club Gate to the parking lot. Christina opens the gate with her Members Card. The Gate slides open. The Mercedes goes in as well as the Fiesta on its tail. They park side by side and Michael leaves on the Fiesta dash board a piece of paper explaining that the car is a guest of his with his name and membership number.

They have a wonderful table by the water. City view from the water side. Boats tied up within spitting distance from their table and bobbing. A swimming pool in the background. A wonderful feast of food and drink. Michael gives Todd the sailboat keys.

"You can open it and let all your friends climb around. However, under no circumstances are you to take the boat out by yourself."

The kids all leave like a shot. Julie is really scared for all the kids unsupervised messing around on the sailboat.

"What if my daughters pressure your son to take the boat out by himself, in spite of your warning and he disobeys you to show off?"

"Todd has been sailing since he was three years old. He is a member of the Waikiki Yacht Club Racing Team. They even race the Navy." Michael says addressing his last remark at Greg. "Even if he disobeys me, they will not founder. Todd knows what he is doing. If it would make you feel better, go check on them. Dock 'G', stall 28."

Julie leaves the table. Christina, Michael and Greg stay behind.

"I will need another piece of information from you." Greg tells Michael. "What was the topic of the speed letter?"

"SARGO." Michael replies laconically. "In capital letters. It's the name of a POLARIS - type nuclear attack submarine."

Christina looks at Michael in disbelief. He is still thinking about that? She has forgotten all about it.

Julie comes back to their table.

"I can relax now. Todd seems like a responsible young man." Julie states.

"I know my son better." Christina adds. "I wouldn't leave the kids alone for too long. Todd might get ideas about locking himself with your oldest daughter in the forward state room..."

The Saddlers start laughing.

"Marianna would hardly need encouragement." Julie says. "She may attack Todd, the way she's been looking at him all afternoon."

After a while the women decide to go check on the kids together.

Michael offers Greg one of his cigars. They light up.

The cigars are almost smoked to the bitter end and their wives are not back. Michael signs the Club receipt and leaves a generous tip. Greg offers to pay his share, but Michael tells him that the Club will not accept money and non-members cannot sign.

"After all. I was the one who invited you. You are my guests." Michael states leaving no room for further argument.

Greg is very thankful. He admits to Michael that this kind of living is unknown to them on his government salary.

They both leave the table in search of their wives and kids. They find them on the boat; all wearing bathing suits. Their wives sunning themselves content on the sailboat bow deck after a good meal and a full tummy. Evidently, Christina must have scoured the boat and gone through all the closets and found bathing suits for everyone.

"We were wondering." Christina said. "What took you so long to come along."

The women and kids start pestering Michael to take them out on the boat. Finally, Michael goes below to change. The girls are squealing with joy. Michael and Todd take the boat out and they all enjoy an afternoon sail on a beam reach along the Coast Line between the Waikiki Yacht Club, by the Waikiki Beach, all the way to the Diamond Head Light House and back. They all wished they had a camera to take pictures of Honolulu from the water.

Chapter 32

How to Unearth a 5-Year-Old Letter from the Navy Archives.

Greg Saddler loved a challenge. His job was to track down documents and dig up paper trails. However, this project he volunteered to undertake pertaining to Michael's Speed memo, got him stumped. There is no reference about the project on the computer. But there should have been. The Power Plant and the Demineralizing Facility are all built. You can see the 300-foot-high concrete stack with the red and white checkerboard pattern on top from every place on Base.

He is sitting in his office in Pearl harbor Naval Shipyard at the basement of Building 159 and furiously working the computer keys scanning the Contracts for the past five years. Maybe the Contract when it started was over five years ago, he is thinking. But it should have been listed, if it was ongoing.

He decides to go to his other office at the Mid Pacific Division (MIDPAC). He drives over and parks in the Underwater Warfare Museum parking lot next door to the MIDPAC Archives. He parks his car and goes to his other office there. He uses his clearance to get access and finally locates the Contract.

He goes over to the shelves and pulls down the box marked with the Contract Number he had found. The box feels light. He opens it and finds inside three checkout cards. The original document file was at CINPACFLT, one copy was with the NIS and the other with the Judge Advocate's Office, JAG on behalf of the General Accounting Office, GAO.

The suspense is killing Greg. What took place to make this Contract such a Hot Item. He puts the box back and returns to his office. How can he get his hands on the Contract Documents? Forget NIS, JAG and GAO. He has no access there. CINPACFLT now is a different story. He goes there almost every other day to chase down overdue files requested and on the desk of some Admiral there, who believes the Rules and Regulations were made for the rest of the Navy, but certainly not for him.

Commander Saddler looks at his watch. Approaching lunchtime. He shuts off his computer and goes out to his car. He heads out of the Base at the Makalapa Gate and runs on Kam (King Kamehameha) Highway. He turns at first opportunity inside the CINPACFLT Complex. The Compound has turned into a fortress, he is thinking, after the attack on the Marines barracks in Lebanon by terrorists.

They installed three concentric sets of barricades, so, now the cars going through the Gate, had to do three tacking manoeuvres, same as if they were sailboats and the wind direction was blowing straight from the gate. He negotiates his way through and parks in Building 250 parking lot, the upper level. He goes inside the building and asks the Lieutenant on duty, a female, where could he find Contract N-1155.

"It has been checked out of the Central Files at MIDPAC and never returned." Commander Saddler informs the Lieutenant.

"We show no such Contract in our possession." The Lieutenant replies after she checks with her computer. "Do you have a Code entry that may go with the missing Contract?"

Greg Saddler remembers asking Michael the same question at the Waikiki yacht Club. What did he say? Finally, he remembers.

"SARGO." He tells the Lieutenant.

The Lieutenant types the entry 'SARGO' next to the Contract number Commander Saddler had given her previously. The computer gains access. At the same time, it triggers a silent alarm somewhere.

"The Contract is in the vault on the second deck." The Lieutenant informs Commander Saddler. "It is being held there by Admiral Rifey. It's eyes only Permit to remove. Unfortunately, Admiral Rifey is on leave. Accordingly, documents could not be removed from the Vault."

"May I go in the Vault and see what this is all about?"

"You are free to go inside the Vault and inspect the contract File. Only you cannot remove it from the Vault for any reason. For that, you need specific authorization by Admiral Rifey."

Commander Saddler thanks her and takes the stairway up to the second deck. About the middle of the building on his right-hand side he sees a six-inch-thick Vault steel door open against the hallway wall. Inside the Dutch style Vault door an Ensign was sitting down with a log book recording the traffic in and out the Vault. Commander Saddler signs the log book and enters the vault.

* * * * *

At Pearl harbor Naval Shipyard, inside the NIS Building, two Agents are watching television screens and various control panels that are lining up the room walls. A red light comes on and starts flashing on the number five Annunciator, followed by an intermittent beeping sound.

One of the Agents shuts the beeping sound and checks the recorder.

"Number 8072 - 04." Announces to his partner.

"We better notify Agent Number 4." His partner says looking up from the Code Book he was consulting. "It's his case."

The first NIS Agent walks from the recorder and calls through the intercom requesting to speak to Agent Dave Brown. He finds from Agent Brown's secretary that he has gone out to lunch.

"He will be back at thirteen hundred. He is always prompt." Dave Brown's secretary informs them.

"Please leave a note on his desk that case Number 8072 was activated on 12:05 PM by computer terminal Number 47 in the MIDPAC Administration Building."

The red light on Annunciator No. 5 quit flashing after a while. The NIS Agents return to their monitoring activity. Their conscience is clear. They've done their job.

* * * * *

Commander Saddler is amazed at the volume of files in the Vault. This is his first time inside. Normally he would have ordered the Lieutenant from downstairs to go up and retrieve the files. The Vault itself was a masterpiece of engineering. The second floor was shored. Someone formed a box 16 feet x 32 feet x 10 feet high with a foot thick cast-in-place concrete wall. The vault was ventilated, heated and/or air conditioned. The temperature inside the vault was a constant 70 degrees Fahrenheit. It would have made a great cigar humidor, if the humidity inside the vault was also maintained at 70%. However, the humidity inside the Vault was a constant 10%. Commander Saddler feels a downward draft. It looked like someone went to a lot of trouble to make this room impregnable.

He goes to the back of the vault and turns right. The Contract File consists of three standard metal file cabinet size drawer boxes. He goes right into the Correspondence File to find the December 12, 1980 Speed Letter, Michael had written. He leafs through the documents scanning for the correct date. Once in a while he glances at a document text. He starts paying more attention and pretty soon he is totally absorbed in reading. He shakes his head once in a while in disbelief.

* * * * *

Dave Brown is eating lunch at the Pearl Harbor Naval Shipyard Officers' Club, where he goes every day for lunch. He eats alone out in the Lanai overlooking the entrance to Pearl Harbor, watching the noon traffic A paddle wheeler is going out to sea, loaded with organic garbage. He watches it rounding the far point of the entrance, drifting with the leeward current out to sea, while a school of sharks is swimming tight on its wake, their fins visible, getting ready for the feast to follow.

Twelve miles out to sea, the boat's live bottom discharger will come on. It will start pushing the trash towards the paddle wheel, which in turn will disperse it out to sea. The sharks having the right of first refusal on the choicest pieces.

Dave Brown tries to change his thought pattern as the garbage scow veers to port on a North-western course, away from his field of vision. He wants to enjoy his meal without negative thoughts.

The water is now calm at the entrance to Pearl Harbor. The surface suddenly breaks as a dark sleek profile object emerges from the deep, with less splash than a humpback whale. It is a POLARIS - type nuclear attack submarine coming into Pearl Harbor Naval Shipyard. Refitting? A little R & R for its crew? Who cares, he is thinking.

The vision brings back memories of SARGO, five years ago. He pushes the plate of his half-eaten lunch away. He lost his appetite. Anyway, it's time to head back to the office. He goes to his car and drives along the Bayshore Drive following the nuclear submarine's progress until he reaches the NIS Building.

He parks, gets out of his car and goes inside the NIS Building to his office. He finds the note left on his desk by his secretary. He calls the NIS Monitoring Room. The people on duty have changed. The new crew knows nothing regarding the alarm at 12:05 PM. He goes back to his car and starts heading towards the MIDPAC

Building. He wished he had a cellular phone in his car to call ahead. The government, with their restricted budget and the new policy of austerity, put in place by President Jimmy Carter, will be the last to start buying them.

* * * *

Commander Greg Saddler finished reading the files. He has a blank expression on his face as he mechanically starts putting things back where he found them, in a daze. He signs out at the Vault entrance. The Ensign indicates next to his signature that nothing was brought in or taken out. He goes to the first empty cubicle and calls information for the phone number of Akamai Engineering & Construction, Ltd. He dials the number and asks to speak to Michael.

He is put through immediately and Michael comes on the line. They exchange pleasantries. Michael has just finished a Bid which goes out for a 1:30 PM Bid Opening.

"You are lucky catching me in the office. I was just getting ready to go out to lunch." Michael tells Greg Saddler.

"I did not have lunch either." Greg Saddler admits. "Where are you going to lunch? I want to talk to you immediately, face to face, because I have for you important news that cannot be discussed over the phone regarding the matter we discussed last Sunday."

"I was going out to the Outrigger Canoe Club." Michael told Greg. "Take Kalakaua Avenue all the way to the end of Waikiki. Stay straight on the road that is running along the beach. Do not turn left on Kapahulu. The Outrigger Canoe Club is after the Aquarium 'makai', on the water, to your right."

"I will be there as soon as I can." Greg Saddler assures Michael as he hangs up.

Michael calls the receptionist and informs her that he will be out of the office, possibly the rest of the day. He can be reached, however, in an emergency on his mobile phone.

"Otherwise, just take a message."

* * * * *

Greg Saddler calls his secretary and tells her that he will not be in the rest of the day. He calls his wife and tells her that he is having lunch with Michael from the church at the Outrigger Canoe Club past Waikiki Beach towards the Diamond Head.

"It may be a long lunch." He adds. "I may be late coming home."

* * * * *

Dave Brown of the NIS finds out that the person who triggered the Alarm was the new Archives Director, Commander Greg Saddler. He calls from the MIDPAC Building the Commander's Office at Pearl Harbor Naval Shipyard. He finds out that the Commander was out for the afternoon and will not be back until tomorrow morning. NIS Agent Brown calls the home phone number of Commander Saddler. Julie Saddler answers the phone. Dave Brown identifies himself and asks to speak to Commander Greg Saddler.

"He is out for a late lunch with a family friend from Church at the Outrigger Canoe Club."

Dave Brown hangs up immediately and calls the NIS Building at Pearl Harbor Naval Shipyard. He dispatches two NIS Agents to the Outrigger Canoe Club and informs them that Commander Greg Saddler driving a yellow FORD Escort was having lunch there with an unknown person.

"Observe only. Do not interfere. You should have no trouble spotting Commander Saddler as he would probably be the only person there in a Navy uniform. Try to identify the person he is having lunch with and report back to me from a pay phone."

Dave Brown goes to the CINPACFLT Building to determine the damage.

Chapter 33

What Happened With The Sargo

Michael is getting into his car at the Gold - Bond Building Parking Structure where his office is. He starts the car, a black SAAB EMS Turbo convertible and takes the top down. He gets out of the building and turns left on Coral Street. He stops at the light and turns right on Ala Moana Boulevard going towards Waikiki.

He is intrigued by Greg's telephone call. What did the fellow want to see him about? It couldn't have anything to do with SARGO. They only talked about it yesterday.

Ala Moana Park stretches out to his right all the way to the beach. 85 degrees Fahrenheit and not a cloud in the sky, glancing up. If nothing else, they will have a good lunch and enjoy the ambiance from the Outrigger Canoe Club Lanai.

Before he knows it, Ala Moana Boulevard merges into Kalakaua Avenue. He slows down watching all the tourists walking and browsing at the displays of the tourist shops along the way, looking red like lobsters from too much sun. Others, wearing matching Aloha shirts and muumuus of the loudest colours are strolling hand in hand. Are they going to wear the same clothes back home? He wonders, smiling. He went through the same exercise with his wife back when they were tourists themselves. They were now 'kamaaina', locals in Hawaiian. Hard to believe what the future holds in such a short time, he is thinking.

The black SAAB stops in front of the Moana Hotel stop light which turned red. The tourists stream across the pedestrian walk on their way to Kuhio Beach Park and the Waikiki Beach stretching all the way to Kahala. A few tourists stop and look at Michael. It's obvious he lives on the island where they can only visit for a week at most, after they have worked all year in a miserable job, in a cold place. Michael feels lucky and fortunate to be blessed that way.

He guns the SAAB across to the ironwood lined Seaside Avenue, passed the Aquarium and pulls into the Outrigger Canoe Club Parking Structure. Nothing yellow catches his eye. Greg has not shown up yet. Although late for lunch, the place is pretty full. He asks for a table by the water and immediately has his choice. It helps to be well known. The Head Waiter adjusts the umbrella to shade the table and welcomes Michael by name to the Club. He has not seen him for a while.

"I was out of town." Michael admits. "I have another guest coming, momentarily. He will probably be in a Navy uniform and looking a little lost."

"I understand, sir." The Head Waiter acknowledges. "I will keep an eye for him."

Michael orders a Beck's Beer checking and nodding to acquaintances. The beach is full of hard bodies and beautiful people. The various Club catamarans with colourful sails fill the horizon.

The Head Waiter brings Greg to the table who looks flustered and absent minded. He doesn't seem to be aware of the place or notice the fantastic view. A waitress appears at their table with Michael's beer. Greg orders the same for him. More to get rid of the waitress hovering at their table than anything else.

Greg Saddler starts right away on what transpired. Blow by blow, what he had to go through to find Michael's Speed Memo. Michael lets him talk without interrupting him. Is this why Greg wanted to see him right away? Michael is thinking and pondering. Big deal. But Michael likes Greg and lets him talk.

"The Navy lied to you when they told you that the Incident was nothing more than an exercise in emergency evacuation procedures. They had a nuclear accident aboard the submarine. The mobile hospital was treating real victims. To make matters worse, the submarine was dumping contaminated, nuclear water, in the Pearl Harbor Bay. The submarine and the immediate area were hot, emitting radioactivity. The Navy knew it and did nothing to warn or protect the people working in the vicinity. All your workers were being exposed to radiation."

Michael took a sip from his beer digesting what he was hearing.

"The NIS were after you. They were considering getting rid of you any way they saw fit. One of the ways was induced heart attack. There are minutes of meetings between the Navy Brass outlining the ways to do away with you. They were considering their options and the risks involved."

"I was told by the ROICC in passing something like that. But I was not aware that they had put it in writing." Michael admitted.

"The nuclear submarine SARGO was towed over and anchored in the middle of the Bay. Months went by and the Navy Brass were trying to decide what to do with it. The entire submarine was contaminated. They could no longer use it."

"I was told by Admiral Hyman Rickover, five years ago that they managed to decontaminate it." Michael said.

"You met the four-star Admiral?" Greg said in amazement. "The man is a legend in the Navy. Only a handful of people have met him."

"Not only I met him, But I worked for him directly after he approached me to work on a solution to the problem plaguing the POLARIS - class nuclear submarines..."

"So, you are the SOG character referred to in the Archives. You are not mentioned by name, by the way, in the Archives. You are referred to as the Studies and Observations Group subcontractor the Navy hired to offer an opinion on some issues and they refer to in a Classified Report that is not included in the files."

"I was the one who wrote the Report." Michael exclaimed with passion. "Let me correct myself there. I did not write the Report with my own hand. I was talking and explaining the issues to Admiral Rickover aboard the nuclear submarine SWORDFISH, a sister ship to SARGO and a Navy stenographer was taking down in shorthand and recording at the same time everything I was saying. She then typed everything and the Navy made me sign at the bottom, after I had read it. I thought what I was signing pertained to the accuracy of the six pages I was presented with. It had everything I had said. Then, I found out that what I had signed, became the Report and blue print which the Navy used to address the deficiencies."

"I am worried about you Michael." Greg Saddler said after the while. "You are the man who knows too much. People like you have the tendency to disappear."

"I solved the problems that were plaguing the Navy for decades. Afterwards, Admiral Rickover told me that I am a National Treasure, worth my weight in gold..."

Greg motioned with his hand indicating talk, talk, talk...

"Why did the Navy select the nuclear submarine SWORDFISH?" Greg asked, changing the topic.

"Because, I was told that the SARGO was deployed at the time on the North Slope of Alaska, according to Admiral Rickover. It was decontaminated and exploring underneath the ice caps. It was either me going to Alaska and missing two weeks of work or examining SWORDFISH which was right there at Pearl Harbor Naval Shipyard. I couldn't afford losing two weeks' worth of work, even at ten grand a day the Navy was paying my company for compensation."

The waitress comes over to take their order. Michael orders the mixed greens salad with blue cheese dressing and the lunch steak. Greg tells the waitress to make that ditto. Michael tells Greg that the chef slices the garlic in thin slivers and embeds it into the steak so it disappears when he char broils it. Afterwards at the end before he puts it on a plate, he puts a dab of herb butter melting on top mixing with the meat juices. They char the steak on the outside and it is medium rare inside. Chicago style. It's their specialty. Greg will have his done the same way. The waitress leaves with their orders.

Michael asks Greg as soon as the waitress left their table.

"How did the Navy decontaminate SARGO?" Michael asks Greg. "I was not aware of an existing method to do so."

"That's it." Greg responds. The Navy never did..."

"Hold on a minute Greg." Michael interrupts him. "If the Navy did not, how did they lose it a year later in the polar ice caps?"

Greg smiles wryly. Michael takes a long pull of beer from his glass. The beer is half gone. He signals the waitress for another round. Greg drinks half of his down in one pull. He is thirsty with all the talk. The waitress comes over and sets two bottles of Beck's Beer on their table and picks up the two empty bottles. She leaves and comes right back with their salad order. Commander Greg Saddler notices for the first time the beauty of the place. The mosaics. The Koa wood. The beach stretching at their feet. All the beautiful women in revealing bikini's frolicking by the water. The catamarans and the sailboats on a beam reach following the same course they did last Sunday.

"Julie and the kids had a wonderful time, yesterday." Greg Saddler tells Michael. "They have not stopped talking about it. Marianna is in love with Todd. All they talk is when will they go out sailing again."

"Any time." Michael tells Greg.

"Well, next weekend is boys out. If Christina can give Julie and the kids a ride back from the church. I will take you out on Kaneohe Marine Golf Course. Right on the water. Make sure you put your golf clubs in the trunk your wife's 'aircraft carrier' of a car. After church, we will go to the Kaneohe Marine Base Officers Club for lunch, followed by a round of golf. Our tee time is 2:30 PM."

Michael thanks Greg from the bottom of his heart for the outing. They are done with their salad and the waitress appears with the main course. They dive into their steaks and continue sporadically the small talk while they eat.

After they are done eating, Michael lights a cigar and offers Greg one and asks for the rest of the story. What happened to SARGO?

"The Navy just towed it out to sea. They flooded it and sunk it."

"Where did they sink it?"

"In a reef, just outside the 12-mile limit of Japan, by Hiroshima. They decided on that location because it is deep and was contaminated anyway from the atomic bomb we dumped during the second World War. That whole area is still saturated with radiation. It would be hard to detect and isolate the radiation source coming from SARGO. Bottom line is they figured one more source of radiation won't make that much difference."

"What about the story of losing the sub a year later under the North Pole ice caps?"

Greg smiled. "Call it an Accounting Journal Entry. How else are they going to account for the missing submarine to Congress and GAO?"

"What happened to the crew?"

"Mostly died in the hospital. A few died a few months afterwards from exposure to radiation. Some survived. I am sure some money changed hands towards the survivors to shut them up. This lasted a while. Some more died. The survivors filed a Class Action Law Suit against the Navy. The government shut these few up by putting them in jail so they could keep an eye on them. The Class Action Law Suit is being Continued indefinitely."

"On what charge did the government put the few survivors in jail?"

"Michael, in your position you should know that the government could indict and incarcerate a 'Ham Sandwich'. At least that's what the U.S. Attorney is bragging about. My guess is banking fraud. Remember, the government gave them a little money, enough for a down payment on a car or a house. They applied for a loan for the difference. They probably overstated their net worth or some other chicken shit reason on their loan application. Guilty for Bank Fraud or Mail Fraud or Conspiracy to Commit Fraud or some other reason applicable only in the United States Justice System. I correct myself. It equally applies to Russia, China, North Korea or other such enlightened forms of government."

"What happened to the Class Action Law Suit?"

"It remains on hold. I am sure the lawyer representing the survivors has been paid by the government under the table to monitor the Class Action Law Suit indefinitely. Time cures all."

"That's the reason the government refused to honour our Request for Discovery, Pursuant to the Freedom of Information Act. They claimed the matter was under Litigation and the Requested Files were an integral part of a Law Suit. They implied that a number of the crew were injured during the Rescue Exercise and brought a Class Action Suit against the Navy."

"Typical government 'modus operandi'. Stick to the basic truth and build a lie around it. Repeat it enough times and it becomes the Truth."

"I will put all that information in writing in my office." Michael tells Greg. "I will mail it this afternoon to the same lawyer I had used five years ago. He is a good friend of mine and he is keeping a File on SARGO in his Law Office safe. I believe that's what has kept me alive all these years."

"So, you know!" Greg continued. "The SARGO is not the first POLARIS -Class submarine the Navy has lost. They lost SCORPION in 1968. However, with the Viet Nam Tet Offensive at the time taking over the headlines to all the media, the SCORPION was just a blip in the news radar. The files I have read cover the loss of SCORPION. They also include the miraculous solution to the POLARIS - Class attack submarines problems which were plaguing them for decades. All is well that ends well was the Closing Report of the SARGO File."

Except for the poor yellow devils in Hiroshima, Michael is thinking, getting dumped for a second time by the Americans, this time without really knowing.

The waitress comes over to their table to tempt them with desert. Michael's stomach is in a knot. Greg is on a diet trying to lose weight. He has put on a bunch ever since he arrived in Hawaii. Michael signs the bill and they both walk out to the parking structure. Greg admires Michael's car as he unlocks his own FORD Fiesta. Michael puts the top of his car down and shows Greg the inside of his car. Michael pops the hood up and they both look at the powerful engine like a couple of teenagers.

Greg is a car nut and really appreciates a good car when he sees it. Michael on the other hand looks at cars as something to reliably get him from point 'A' to point 'B'. He likes SAABs because that's what he drove after College when he was participating in Rally Races. He tells Greg of one incident when he rolled his SAAB down an embankment, taking a turn too fast. The car ended up on its side. He got out of the car and with his navigator, they pushed the car back on its wheels. They got back in the car and finished the race.

Greg gets in his own car and reminds Michael of their Golf game next Sunday.

"Looser pays for the drinks on the 19th Hole." Commander Sadler mentions.

Michael agrees.

"You are on!"

Greg starts his yellow FORD Fiesta and pulls out of the Parking Stall. Michael follows him out of the Parking Structure right on his tail.

* * * *

The NIS car is waiting with the two Agents inside, by the curb among all the other parked cars under the ironwood trees. They knew that Commander Saddler was driving a yellow FORD Fiesta. One of them went so far as to enter the Outrigger Canoe Club Parking Structure on foot to verify that it was parked there. However, he was discouraged to investigate further because it was a private Club. He could not get in unless he was a Member or a

Guest of a Member. The private guard walking around at the Parking Structure, a huge Samoan, was looking at him suspiciously.

He went back to his car parked on the street, under the sun. He told his partner that he saw the Commander's car parked. He was unable to see him eating. He was almost intercepted by an NFL size Samoan guard. The Commander was probably having lunch with a Member of the Outrigger Canoe Club. The afternoon heat and the sun beading on the car roof was making them sleepy. They shed their sleep as they saw the yellow FORD Fiesta nosing out of the Parking Structure, followed by a black SAAB convertible with Michael at the wheel; their old Nemesis. Any doubt that the Commander and Michael were together, was dispelled when the two cars honked at each other in greeting and the two drivers waived at each other.

Chapter 34

Friends Come and Go; Enemies Accumulate

Early morning meeting at the NIS Building between the two NIS Agents who were following Commander Saddler and Dave Brown, at the latter's office.

"We followed Commander Greg Saddler to the Outrigger Canoe Club." The spokesman of the two NIS Agents started. "He went inside the Club's Parking Structure. He must have been a Guest of a Member there, we thought. We parked in the street and waited. I went on foot and reckoned the Parking Structure. The

Commander's vehicle; i.e., a yellow FORD Fiesta was the only such vehicle parked. I returned to the NIS vehicle and waited with my partner. Two hours later we observed the yellow FORD Fiesta coming out of the Parking Structure followed by a black SAAB convertible. The Commander apparently had lunch with the driver of the SAAB. The black SAAB is a company car registered to Akamai Engineering & Construction, Ltd. Driven by their President, Michael."

Dave Brown's face drained as soon as he heard the company name. He knew who the driver of the black SAAB was without hearing it from his two subordinates.

"Go to the Pearl Harbor Naval Shipyard Archives Building and pick up Commander Greg Saddler." He orders the two NIS Agents. "Bring him here to the NIS Building for questioning. Follow the usual routine."

Dave Brown is visibly upset and tells the NIS Agents on their way out of his office that they should have reported to him yesterday.

"We followed the Commander. He went straight home from the Outrigger Canoe Club. However, due to the traffic from Waikiki all the way to Ewa Beach, where the Commander lived, we did not get there until half hour past our quitting time. Sir, surely you must remember the government Memorandum we all received last week: No overtime will be allowed and paid until prior written approval. Since you did not authorize overtime in writing, you must have thought that the case was not important enough to merit it."

Dave Brown dismisses the two NIS Agents, seething. If he knew about all that yesterday afternoon, he could have done something about it. He didn't know exactly what he would have done, but at least he would have had options.

Knowing Michael, by now he has sent everything to his lawyer. He better find out exactly what the Commander passed on to Michael.

* * * *

The two NIS Agents enter Building 159 and go directly to the basement where all the Archive Offices for the Command are located. They stop by Commander Saddler's office and request to see him. They identify themselves and order him to follow them.

"If you refuse to follow us voluntarily, we are prepared to arrest you on a Federal Warrant." The spokesman of the two NIS Agents informs a shaking Commander Saddler.

Commander Sadler followed them in his car to the NIS Building where he goes through their standard procedure and is locked up in a dark padded cell with a single metal bench. Dave Brown walks in, after an hour's worth of waiting by the Commander, carrying his briefcase and the familiar folding student chair.

Dave Brown extracts a single page document from his briefcase, glances at it and hands over to Commander Saddler with a ball point pen to sign. In its Commander Saddler is being informed that he is being held under a Federal Writ as a potential witness. He is informed that the government has a right to hold him under this status for a year, unless he is willing to cooperate with the NIS investigation and forego his rights to have an attorney present during questioning.

"If you are unwilling and/or unable to cooperate, the government is prepared place you under protective custody, starting immediately. The NIS will turn you over to the U.S. Marshall and start you immediately on a diesel therapy ride to see all the federal prisons in the country. Your records will follow you, but by the time they arrive at the place the record shows that you are being held, you will be long gone...and so on."

Commander Dave Saddler signs the Disclaimer immediately. He is absolutely terrified. Dave Brown puts the document the Commander signed, back in his briefcase. He can now start the interrogation without consequences.

He reads Commander Saddler his Miranda Rights and emphasizes for the record that the Commander had signed these rights away. He warns him about false statements and the consequences. He informs him that the information gained from this interview may be used against him and he has no recourse since he signed his rights away. If he refuses to answer any question posed to him, he will be turned over to the U.S. Marshall. If he lies, he will be turned over to the U.S. Attorney's office to be prosecuted for perjury.

"Yesterday, at approximately 1:30 PM you were observed eating lunch at the Outrigger Canoe Club with Michael, the President of Akamai Engineering & Construction, Ltd. Michael is the target of an ongoing criminal investigation. How did you come about knowing Michael, the subject of the NIS investigation?"

"I met Michael last Sunday through the Greek Orthodox Church on the island of Oahu; to which both our families are members."

"Why were you having lunch with Michael, on a Monday?"

"We see each other socially. As a matter of fact, our families had Brunch together this past Sunday."

"What was the subject discussed during lunch yesterday?"

"We were setting up a Golf game next Sunday at the Kaneohe Marine Base Golf Course. You could check. Only this morning I made the tee time for 2:30 PM next Sunday for two."

Dave Brown is busy writing things down on a tablet.

"What were your whereabouts yesterday, prior to your lunch?" Dave Brown asks. "Time, place and what were you doing there."

"I was searching for a missing Contract..."

"How did you get interested in that particular Contract?"

"I stumbled across a box in the Archives. It felt very light. I opened it and instead of seeing the Contract documents that should have been there, instead all it had inside were three cards informing me who had checked out the originals and three copies of the documents. One of them was CINPACFLT. I went there to retrieve the Contract documents. But I was unsuccessful because an Admiral Rifey, who had the File, was out of the office. You could check with the Archives Clerk at the CINPACFLT Building."

"How did you know that the Contract File was kept at MIDPAC?"

"Because, I first searched for it in the Main Archives Room at Pearl Harbor and the Contract File was not there. So I went to MIDPAC to look for it."

"How did you know that the Contract File was kept at MIDPAC? The Contract was not listed in their log book. I looked it up in their computer." Dave Brown said anxiously waiting for Commander Saddler's answer. "How did you know the password to enter?" Dave Brown asked sitting at the edge of his seat.

This is what has been bothering him all along. How did the Commander know the password "SARGO"? The only people who knew the password were himself, Admiral Rifey and the OICC Captain Reinhardt. Admiral Rifey was away on an interview with an international lobbying firm in Washington D.C. He was scheduled to retire from the Navy and he wanted to arrange for a smooth landing in a plush lily pad. The lobbying firm was owned by Koreans who wanted to do business in Hawaii and open an office right here in Honolulu. Who told Commander Saddler the password? He is afraid to ask him straight out. He knows it was not him? There must be a leak in the chain of command, Dave Brown is thinking.

Commander Greg Saddler is sitting silent, contemplating. What to say? Where did he hear the word 'SARGO'? If he tells the NIS Agent the truth, he will implicate Michael. God knows he is already in a heap of trouble being the target of a criminal investigation. Who knows what they are after him for? One thing for sure. Michael is not taking him down in whatever he is involved. He will come clean to the NIS.

"Michael told me the word 'SARGO' in passing, last Sunday while we were driving to Brunch.", Commander Saddler admits. "Michael did not know it was a password. I tried it out accidentally."

That Michael, Dave Brown is thinking. He is either clairvoyant, smarter than we thought, very lucky or all of the above. In any case we have to take him out. His name is popping entirely too much.

"Did you read the Contract File at CINPACFLT?" Dave Brown returns to interrogating Commander Saddler ignoring his previous answer for the time being.

Greg Saddler is thinking hard before he answers. If he lies, NIS could find the truth soon enough by asking the Ensign in front of the Vault door. All they have to look is the Vault log. They will have in writing that he was for over an hour inside the Vault. What was he doing?

"I just went into the Vault to make sure the Contract Files were there. However, as soon as I saw that they were all accounted for, I left. I did not read the file. I decided to wait until Admiral Rifey had returned to ask for them and place them in the MIDPAC File box."

Dave Brown is staring at Commander Saddler sternly and tells him:

"Your actions warrant that I turn you in for Court-martial. You have breached the Secrecies Act you swore to uphold. However, at this time I have decided not to press charges. Provided you follow my instructions to the letter:

"You are in no way to contact Michael again or allow to be contacted by him. If you receive anything in writing from him, you are to turn it over to the nearest NIS Office, unread. Michael is the target of a criminal investigation by the government with far reaching implications. You are to disclose this to no one. You and your family should abstain from attending the same functions Michael and his family do, including the Greek Orthodox Church. Finally, you are to put in for early retirement. You will be compensated as if you have served for the full duration, 20 years. You are to move immediately to a City of your choice in the mainland. The government will find you suitable employment in the Law Enforcement Field."

Dave Brown gives Greg Saddler an Agreement to sign, which he signs gladly without reading it.

* * * *

Meeting a couple of weeks later between Admiral Rifey, OICC Captain Reinhardt and Dave Brown of the NIS Office at the CINPACFLT Building 250.

"Michael knows everything. The whole story. I am convinced of that." Dave Brown starts the meeting. "He is a civilian with a permanent association with the Studies and Observations Group, SOG, which the government has formally disbanded in 1973. Accordingly, if he signed something pertaining to the Secrecies Act, it is null and void. Even his involvement with Admiral Rickover in solving the issues with the POLARIS - Class submarines is wide open to disclosure.

"The Navy has limited that ability by not naming him by name in the Archives, only that he is a contractor associated with the SOG. Every copy of his Report has been redacted, his name and signature obliterated.

"He got his story stashed with a powerful and influential Law Firm in Seattle, Washington. This means that bumping him off would open a can of worms of unprecedented proportions. His death will be counterproductive as far as I am concerned.

"He cannot be bought off. He has that Greek 'PHILOTIMO' in capital letters. I don't know how this Greek 'Philotimo' would be applicable if he was poor. It is easy to wave the banner of 'Philotimo', if you are rich. Even if we pay him a king's ransom, there is no guarantee that his silence is assured. It all depends on his mood at the time. He won't sign anything. We tried. And we cannot make him sign, because he writes on the document "I am signing under Duress".

"The only way we can be assured of Michael's silence is to destroy his reputation and discredit him as soon as he comes out with the story. A felony conviction may do the trick. It is going to be however, a lengthy and difficult task. Michael knows how the system works in Government Contracting.

"The government opposed him 183 times and the government lost 183 times in the Armed Services Board of Contract Appeals, ASBCA. We cannot take him on, on a Civil Case like we've been trying for years. He knows more that our attorneys representing us. More than the Judge, himself. He can get any Contract he wants and make as much money as he feels like. Government Contracting Officers who got in his way, had their careers suffer, they quit or they got indicted."

"I hear what you say." Admiral Rifey weighted in. Take a break. Forget about Michael. I will put John Muchmore in Charge of this matter right away. His mission will be to find a way to take Michael out. Discredit him in a way that his spirit is broken, so he appoints an Attorney to represent him. This will limit his involvement on the case. No attorney is as good as Michael. We know that. We will make sure that he stays dispirited and unable to come after us. Because of what he knows about SARGO and his ability to Administer Contracts, he presents a Clear and Present Danger to the U.S. Government."

* * * * *

Next Sunday at church, the Saddlers are a no show. The priest approaches Michael after the Service and confides in him that he received a call from Greg Saddler and was told by him to relay this to Michael.

"He decided to take early retirement from the Navy with all benefits as if he had worked 20 years. He will get a full pension. He is still young so he landed a good high paying job with the San Diego Police Department. They are in the process of moving from

Honolulu to San Diego. The Navy is paying for his move. He apologizes about the Golf game."

Michael thinks nothing of what he just heard. He wishes in his mind good luck to Greg Saddler and his family. He is grateful of all he found out about the fate of the SARGO nuclear submarine from him. What is he going to do with all that knowledge? Knowledge is power he is thinking. One of these days it may prove useful.

Michael and Christina decide to go to Brunch at the Waikiki Yacht Club with the kids, anyway. Michael feels fortunate. Reality has surpassed his dreams. The kids are doing well in private schools, on their way to a College of their choice. No student loans for them. Michael is the deep pocket who will pay for everything plus a Bonus upon graduation. In the meantime, the kids have everything, before they realize they want it. Michael is having entirely too much fun and making a shit load of money in the process. He is getting paid to do what he loves doing.

"It feels like I am dreaming." He admits to his wife. "One of these days someone will slap me with a rude awakening and tell me: Kid you are having too much fun. Life is not supposed to be that much fun. You have not suffered."

"What are you going to tell him?" Christina gives her husband a sidelong look as she drives her Mercedes down the Pali Highway.

"I don't know." Michael replies. "Something like: Happiness is a State of Mind."

THE END

Epilogue

In the POLARIS – type attack nuclear submarines the coolant was circulated by pumps.

After the SARGO Incident the U.S. Navy developed natural circulation nuclear reactors.

U.S. Navy attack submarines of the OHIO – class developed in the late 1980's were powered by natural circulation reactors. These were safer and inherently quieter than the pressurized water units because they required no pumps.

The reactors were arranged so that the differences in temperature, for example, between the portion of the reactor containing the reacting fuel and the rest of the reactor, force the water to circulate naturally.

Typically, in these natural circulation reactors, cooled water from the heat exchanger is fed to the bottom of the reactor, and it rises through the fuel elements as they heat it.

Authors Note

Moira in Ancient Greece was the Goddess of Destiny, Fate and Serendipity.

Moira is the single word that defines and has become the driving force in this book.

What are the odds of the Source to eyewitness the SARGO Incident as it was happening and unfolding at Pearl Harbor Naval Shipyard?

What are the odds of the Source to be involved as Project Manager with the construction of a multiyear Project to build a Power Plant and Demineralizing Facility in the CIA Area of the Pearl Harbor Naval Shipyard, less than forty yards away from the SARGO nuclear submarine and witness firsthand the nuclear accident, the attempted rescue and all the subsequent events of cover up?

What are the odds of the Source meeting fifteen years later and interviewing the sole survivor, at the time, of the nuclear accident aboard SARGO, part of the Navy crew, who was working at the time in the engine room?

What are the odds of the Source meeting five years later, the newly appointed and transferred from the mainland, to Head the Navy Archives at Pearl Harbor Naval Shipyard and the individual being a Greek Orthodox same as the Source, attending the same church in Honolulu, Hawaii and finding out from him, after he had read, at the Source's prompting, classified and sealed archives, describing the nuclear accident, the Navy cover-up and the ultimate fate and disposal of the nuclear submarine SARGO, five years after the Incident?

What are the odds of the Source to be part of the Studies and Observations Group, SOG, and be approached by the Navy to help resolve the problems and issues facing the Polaris Class Nuclear Submarines?

The Source, as a result wrote a Report with recommendations, which the Navy followed and the problems plaguing the Polaris Nuclear Submarine program went away. The Source wanted to elaborate on this last issue, because in his opinion, it is the greatest manifestation of Moira at work.

You remember that one of the main issues addressed in the Source's Report to the Navy was that of the need for a Heat Sensor to sense any temperature change in the nuclear reactor cooling feed water at the pump discharge, and if any was detected, to send a signal to the Annunciator the moment there was a change in the water temperature. It did no good for the Annunciator to receive a signal, as originally designed, when the reactor cooling feed water pump could no longer pump water and only then sound the Alarm. At that point the operator had no other option but to shut down the nuclear reactor immediately. The more he delayed in doing so, the higher the risk for a nuclear accident.

The Source relayed to you how the Navy presented him with such a Heat Sensor devise, months after the Report, manufactured in accordance with the requirements laid out in his Report to the Navy, setting forth the issues and their possible solution.

The Source had assumed all along that the Navy fabricated the device. At least that's what he was told and led to believe by the Navy. Let me now tell you 'The Rest of the Story', like Paul Harvey used to say in his Radio Program.

Every summer, for the last fourteen years, the Source has gone fly fishing in the White Mountains of Arizona, and specifically staying with his RV at the Waltner's Resort by the Show Low Lake.

The Source was sitting one night in front of his RV enjoying a cigar. A gentleman, by the name of Duane K, was walking his dog and stopped by to say hello. The Author had met that particular gentleman before, during his fourteen years staying during the summer at the Resort. He knew his name but he did not know any details about him, other than that he was a widower and retired from the Air Force. The gentleman, Duane K, knew even less about the Source other than what he had learned of the Source's biography written in his first book which he had purchased and was currently reading. He also may have known that the Author had signed government papers in 1970 which made him a member of the Studies and Observations Group, SOG, for life. They exchanged pleasantries and small talk and they appeared to have exhausted the subjects they were talking about. At that point, Duane was getting ready to leave, when he stopped, looked the Source in the eye and said:

"I will tell you something that I have not said to another living soul before in my life. The greatest achievement in my life. A top-secret project I worked on. I was told to fabricate a device, a Heat Sensor, while I was with MINCO Products, hired by the Air Force, in Minneapolis, Minnesota. With no blue prints to go by, other than a darn Report, heavily redacted, written by an Engineer, his name and signature blacked out. The whole Report was over my head. I read it many times, something about NPSH or something..."

"Net Positive Suction Head. That's one of the nuclear reactor cooling water feed pump characteristics..."

"How do you know? Did you read the Report? It was Top Secret."

"Most likely, I wrote the Report. I was asked by the Navy, under my SOG clearance, to write the Report for the Polaris Class Nuclear Submarines; outlining the problems they were experiencing and offering possible solutions."

"I thought it was for the Navy! I was working in an environment where they operated on the 'Need to know basis'; however, an Air Force sergeant, a real hard ass, let it slip one time that the devise I was making, was for the Navy."

The Source went on to describe the pump feed water issues with the Polaris Nuclear Submarine and that he just happened to be writing about the nuclear accident he witnessed, that same summer. A book describing The SARGO Incident and what he just heard from Duane K was another piece of the puzzle falling into place.

"I was handed the Heat Sensor devise by the Navy at the Pearl Harbor Naval Shipyard. I was given the impression by them that the Navy had made it. A panel 6 inches wide by 16 inches long with a wire at one end connected to a probe to sense the reactor cooling feed water temperature changes and if changes were detected, send an alarm signal to the Annunciator..."

"That's the device I made with my own two hands. The Seabees couldn't find their ass from a hole on the ground, using both hands." Duane said full of indignation.

"Anyway, I tested the Heat Sensing devise you made on the nuclear submarine, SWORDFISH, and it worked like a charm. I made some more changes on some other aspects of the nuclear submarine design, mentioned in my Report and the problem the Navy had of the nuclear reactor cooling feed water turning into steam and destroying the reactor cooling feed water pump impeller went away. Copies of your Heat Sensing devise were made and installed on all the Polaris Class Nuclear Submarines the Navy had at the time. No nuclear accidents have occurred, to my knowledge, since the installation of your device on the nuclear submarines. Your Heat Sensor saved numerous lives."

"We were working together on the same Project, not knowing each other, 6,000 miles apart!" Duane K exclaimed. "What are the odds? And meeting you here in this out the beaten path place, in Northern Arizona forty years later?"

What are the odds, indeed, that the Source and Duane K would be staying in the same Resort and meet over forty years later to discuss The SARGO Incident during the time that the Source was working with Me, The Anonymous Author Kanenas, the book you are holding in your hands?

It could only be the work of Moira. AAK

INTERVIEW WITH ANONYMOUS AUTHOR KENANAS ABOUT

***

THE SARGO INCIDENT

So right off the bat the question for all Anonymous is Authors is, why be Anonymous?

Well as you can tell from the content of The Sargo Incident, this is very sensitive information that I am writing about, even though this incident happened almost 40 years ago, the US Navy still has denied it ever happened and all documents relating to the USSS Sargo are still classified to this day. When you read the book and see what happened to Michael at the hands of the NCIS, it should then become clear why I needed an organisation like Anonymous Publishing to help me get this story out there. In a small way for my own protection, but mostly to protect the source of the story. The character Michael in the book.

This story has been on my desk for about 8 years, and I was at the Post at the time. My editor didn't want to go anywhere near it, considered it too dangerous which was when I realised it was time to start investigating more. The more I found out, the more I understood his reluctance to chase it down any further. Now I' retired and able to take this risk and coming back to your question, through APH, I am able to write about this, and other stories I've been around through the years in a safe way, without personal risk.

Is Everything in The Sargo Incident True then?

I loved it when the Publisher came up with the phrase 'True Fiction,' because it truly sums up this book. I have spent the last 8 years building a very concise picture of what happened at Pearl Harbour in 1980 from a mixture of sources. My primary source is the character Michael, whom kept diaries of everything documented. This was supported by other primary sources, there, on board on that day and since.

Piecing all of that together in a way that was informative but also interesting was a challenge and with that came some poetic license to build the whole story, even the pieces we couldn't see. So 'True Fiction' was a perfect way to describe what we had achieved in putting this book together and getting this story out.

What was it about The Sargo Incident that you couldn't let go of?

I got into journalism during a time when the truth mattered, and we fought hard to ensure we uncovered the truth. This seemed to end around the time of the Iraq war and journalism stopped being about the news and speaking truth to power. It shifted and most of my colleagues were acting as voices for the power. When I came across blatant violations of simple human decency during my time, these were the stories I couldn't let go of. I met one of the men that died from Leukemia in my early investigations and frankly, it pissed me off that his suffering would never be recognised by those that caused it.

It's a pretty cagey book, it has the feel of a Spy thriller, is this something you were aiming for?

No, truthfully, I was just trying to tell the story as best I imagined it happened, scene by scene. The facts of the incident and the way the Navy behaved are all told as they occurred, which when you piece it all together does read like a spy novel. Sometimes truth is stranger than fiction, but in this case, it has blended with fiction to become a spy novel. The artwork by Anonymous Jase also followed that theme and I think captured the time and feel of the book perfectly.

What would you like the reader to take away from The Sargo Incident?

Firstly, I want to make sure the reader understands what happened and how the government is capable of keeping things from us when they feel it is in our best interests. To ensure they ask relevant questions all the time, of everything, because you never know when your being lied to.

Secondly, I want the journey to keep them guessing and to enjoy the ride with Michael and the team as they take on the might of the Naval Intelligence Service. It's a battle all the way through the book and having spoken to Michael many times personally, one false move during any of this and he wouldn't be here today for sure.

Lastly, I do want them to have fun. That's why we are all here after all.

What's Next for The Anonymous Author Kanenas?

I have 3 other novels already written that I am working with APH on and we are hoping to have them all ready for release during 2023. It does mean that I am spending a lot of time in rewrites and edits rather than creating, but it is a good time and good opportunity to work with APH to build the brand as a whole. There were rumours of a Netflix screen play being written, which is exciting, but first we need to see how the wider public react to the book. This is why I wrote it as a novel rather than a historical expose so that we can try and get this story to a wider audience, rather than the history buffs and Naval boys.

Any last words to the readers?

Only that I hope with your help, that this book can help expose and deliver the truth to the many thousands of men and women of the US Navy that pay so much for you and I. The requests for further investigations are routinely denied and hopefully with enough exposure and pressure we can finally get them to admit the truth and take care of the survivors and their families. Help apply that pressure simply by having a critical mind and by not being afraid to ask questions.

OTHER BOOKS BY
ANONYMOUS PUBLISHING HOUSE

THE NIBIRU CHRONICLES – PART 1 – Nibiru Rising

In the heart of New York, the explosion of a young Muslim student on a packed commuter train, sets in motion a series of events that leads a simple call centre manager on a journey to unlock the truth about Jesus, about Religion, about Hitler, about The Legacy Families and most shockingly, about the plans of the American President, Joe Biden.

Join Theo Miller on his epic adventure as he follows an unexpected path to the Vatican's secrets, buried deep under St Paul's Basilica. Ultimately leading him to the site of the Crucifixion of Christ in the heart of the nuclear wasteland that Baghdad has become. His greatest wish is to save us all.

But be careful what you wish for, it may come true.

Open your eyes to the battle between the Catholic controlled Western Civilisations and the Muslim dominated Middle Eastern Societies.

Then Spare a thought for the Human's, stuck in the middle as the battle for control of Earth heats up in this fast paced, controversial, epic novel from.

OTHER BOOKS BY ANONYMOUS PUBLISHING HOUSE

CAR DEALERS & OTHER PROFESSIONS

The 1960s to the 2000s were when Car Dealers sold cars, drugs, and sex. Government authorities never questioned the practice of bribery and corruption. It was an accepted way of doing business.

I was shot, stabbed, bashed, glassed, and car firebombed.

"I'm still breathing."

I smuggled US dollars out of Korea and Gold out of The Philippines.

"I'm still free."

In 2009 I was diagnosed with a crippling muscle disease.

"I'm still standing."

I apologise for my errant ways, it's not who I am; it's what I did. Nobody can change the past. We learn from mistakes and become better people. We are products of our times.

MEMOIRS...
MULLANE

CAR DEALERS & OTHER PROFESSIONS

A CONTROVERSIAL NEW MEMOIR FROM
THE ANONYMOUS PUBLISHING HOUSE
1ST EDITION

ANONYMOUS PUBLISHING HOUSE CONTACT

www.anonymouspublishinghouse.com

info@anonymouspublishinghouse.com

theanonymouspublishinghouse@gmail.com

www.facebook.com/anonymouspublishinghouse

www.tiktok.com/@anonymouspublishinghouse

SYDNEY
LONDON
NEW YORK

Made in the USA
Monee, IL
31 July 2023